Edie's Sinner

by

Lynn Shurr

A Sinner's Legacy, Book 9

Edie's Sinner

Cover Art by *Diana Carlile*

The Wild Rose Press, Inc.
PO Box 708
Adams Basin, NY 14410-0708
Visit us at www.thewildrosepress.com

Publishing History
First Edition, 2023
Trade Paperback ISBN 978-1-5092-4726-4
Digital ISBN 978-1-5092-4727-1

A Sinner's Legacy, Book 9
Published in the United States of America

Ty dismounted, knowing that his horse wouldn't go anywhere as long as the eats held out. Edie patted a place beside her. When he arrived, she leaned back on the blanket. One of those straining buttons popped at the top of her shirt. She didn't appear to notice.

"Isn't it great in here? So quiet and private."

"A little spooky, too."

"City boy," she said as he sat next to her.

"What's beyond the woods—an enchanted castle with a moat full of alligators?"

"Sadly, no. Just more of my dad's cane fields behind a tall fence with a motion sensor on top in case anyone tries to get in—or out as my brothers sometimes attempted in their teens. Once upon a time, Tom's kidnapper came in that way before all the security."

Seeking any cameras hidden in the foliage, Ty eyed the branches of the trees ringing the glade

"I know what you're thinking, but the grove isn't bugged, I believe because my parents liked to come here sometimes and, um, enjoy themselves. Probably still do. I suspect my brothers made use of this spot, too, with their high school girlfriends. Nothing to worry about. Lie down and enjoy it."

He tried, but Edie's hand reached out to stroke his arm and run over his bicep, giving it a squeeze.

Praise for Lynn Shurr

"Shurr is a wonderful storyteller."

~The Romance Studio

"Lynn Shurr's delightful New Orleans Sinners series is sure to please both non-sports fans and sports fans alike. Do yourself a favor and dive into the world of the Sinners."

~ Farrah Rochon, USA Today best-selling author of the New York Sabers football series

"The author has created a family full of surprises with the Billodeaux bunch. After reading just one book, I am eager to read more about this colorful family."

~Rachel's Willful Thoughts, The Romance Reviews

"Very easy reads, well written, combined with conflict, believable plots and secondary characters that make the plot come alive."

~Jane Lange, Romances, Reads and Reviews

Dedication

To Farrah Rochon-Wonderful Author, Kind,
Supportive, and Generous.

A SINNER'S LEGACY

The Children of Joe and Nell Billodeaux who fulfilled the prophecy that they would have twelve offspring, this way, that way, all ways.

1. Dean Joseph Billodeaux - Joe's illegitimate son by a one-night stand with a woman who planned to shake him down for money. He is adopted by Nell who believes she cannot have children of her own. Current Sinners quarterback. (Wish for a Sinner, Son of a Sinner)

2. Thomas Cassidy Billodeaux - a redheaded son who enters the family through an open adoption with a teenage mother. His birth father is Joe's no-good cousin. He is a kicker for the Sinners. (Wish for a Sinner, Kicks for a Sinner, She's a Sinner)

3. Jude Emily Billodeaux - twin of Ann, conceived by in vitro fertilization using eggs purchased from Nell's sister, Emily. (Wish for a Sinner, Edie's Sinner)

4. Ann Marie Billodeaux (Annie) - Jude's quiet twin. (Wish for a Sinner, The Heart of a Sinner)

5. Lorena Renee Billodeaux (Lori) - First of Nell's little frozen babies to be born, one of the triplets. (Kicks for a Sinner, The Aussie Sinner)

6. Mack Coy Christopher Billodeaux - Second of the triplets to be born. (Kicks for a Sinner, The Bad Boy Sinner)

7. Trinity Billodeaux - Youngest of the triplets and named for the Father, Son, and Holy Ghost, smallest of the three and in need of a powerful saintly help to survive. (Kicks for a Sinner, Dream for a Sinner)

8. Xochi Maria Billodeaux - child of Joe's no-good cousin by a young Mexican woman. She is Tom's half-

sister and is adopted into the family after the terrifying deaths of her parents. Her name means "blossom" in Aztec. (Kicks for a Sinner, Sister of a Sinner)

9. Teddy Wilkes Billodeaux - a child with spina bifida abandoned by his mother at Nell's health care center and adopted by the family. He believed himself to be Joe's natural son. (Paradise for a Sinner, Never A Sinner)

10. Anastasia Marya Polasky (Stacy) - daughter of Nell's sister, Emily, and a bogus Polish prince. She becomes a ward of the Billodeauxs upon her parents' deaths but is never adopted by her own wish. She arrives on their doorstep the same day as Teddy (Paradise for a Sinner, Son of a Sinner)

11. Edith Patricia Billodeaux (Edie) - a normally conceived child, twin of Rex. (Love Letter for a Sinner, Edie's Sinner)

12. Rex Worthy Billodeaux (T-Rex) - Edie's twin brother and future Sinner's quarterback, maybe. (Love Letter for a Sinner)

Chapter One

Edie Billodeaux set her phone on record and placed pen and notebook on the functional, sturdy table belonging to the LSU library. She'd reserved a group study room for the interview, better than meeting in the student union, so noisy, and where they were sure to be interrupted by high-fiving fans and flirtatious sorority girls. Certainly not in his athletic dorm room or her small campus apartment. She wanted to keep this strictly professional even if the article would run only in the weekly student newspaper, *The Reveille*.

As it was, she sat in a glass-walled space, open near the top, where anyone could observe and might hear them speaking. For the moment, she had only her reflection for company, large dark eyes staring back at her out of a small heart-shaped face, curly black hair tangled by the wind. She ran her fingers through it hoping for a better look, but that didn't happen. She considered grabbing a thick library book from the stacks to put on the chair and give herself more height and authority, though as football players went, he wasn't all that large, five-ten, one-ninety according to his stats.

Checking her watch again, she noted the big man on campus, the hero of the day, now ran fifteen minutes late. Tyson Ramsey, the Golden Ram as the fans called him, did plenty of media events. Perhaps, he considered an article in the school newspaper to be too piddling. Or perhaps he'd forgotten the time and was tooling around on his sleek, black motorcycle with its gold detailing, always a leggy blonde or a built redhead on the rear pressing their breasts against his back. The thrum of that machine went right to the heart. She'd never seen him give a ride to a short brunette like her.

She should leave and try to reschedule instead of sitting here tapping her pen against the table top. No, there he was appearing lost like a guy who spent little time in libraries. She waved to get his attention. He homed in on the gesture, found his way to the glass door in the box, and took the seat across from her, slouching down to get comfortable, while she drew herself up as far as she could go. Good, they were nearly eye-to-eye now.

Tyson offered an unapologetic grin that exposed perfect white teeth, a sign of good orthodontia she recognized, having gone through the same painful process of wearing braces because her mouth was too small to contain her teeth without overcrowding. One thing they might have in common, good smiles, otherwise, not so much.

Her skin tone, Cajun, tending toward olive. His had the color of dark honey. He did have tight curls, but light brown, shaved up the sides and topped by a mat of bleached blond hair in honor of his nickname, a Golden Ram indeed. Okay, the man was handsome with his high cheekbones, straight nose, and unusual hazel eyes that seemed mostly green ringed with brown under the fluorescent lights. She'd overheard some starstruck coeds saying that in the sunlight they could turn as golden as the rest of him. She snapped her own eyes away from studying them when he spoke.

"I know I'm late. Fans stop to talk to me, and then I had to ask directions to the study room. I mean, I'm never late for team practice. I try to get there early." That smile said he usually received forgiveness for everything outside of football, team practice being more important than anything else on his schedule.

Casually, she wrote that down for something to do with her hands. "Sounds like you have a good work ethic."

"Hard work pays off."

"So does natural talent. As a free safety, you need speed and the ability to tackle, but also must be able to diagnose the plays as they unfold and get where you are needed most. I'm not sure that last can be learned."

He gave an almost modest shrug. "Whatever, winning the Chuck Bednarik Award for best defensive player says I can do all of that well."

"Impressive stats, sixty tackles, fifteen assists, and six fumbles—but you failed to win the Heisman. Did it bother you that our quarterback, Rex Billodeaux, won instead?"

"Nope. I'm defense. He's offense. A team needs the best of both to win. And as they say, there's always next year. My mother won't let me enter the NFL draft this year. She wants me to finish college because she didn't."

"So does Rex's mother, but she just believes in education because she has an advanced degree in psychology. You'll both be back in the fall and maybe take another national championship."

"That's the plan. Say, are you some kind of relative to the Billodeauxs?" He peered hard at her face.

She looked down, reluctant to be dominated by those eyes again, but came back with a sassy reply.

"You've just figured that out?" she said, as if now doubting his intelligence.

"Same last name, and how else would you know what Rex's mother believes? Now I get why they sent a girl to interview me. Not just any girl."

"I'm Rex's sister. His twin sister. I do know football. I grew up with football players." There, she was becoming defensive again just as she had when pitching the idea to the sports editor.

Well, that had punctured his self-assured attitude or simply aroused his curiosity. "You surely don't resemble each other. Besides, Rex has tons of brothers and sisters. How would I know?"

"You don't believe me because I'm short, not six-three like he is?" No, no, no, she mustn't make this interview about her.

"That and you look like a freshman."

"In fact, I'm five minutes older than Rex. I'm twenty-one, you're twenty-one, all of us are twenty-one. Size does not determine capability. Let's get back to the interview."

"I know. I'm considered small and light for a free safety, but I get the job done."

Good answer. He did have attitude. She'd throw him a curve. "Why did your mother quit college?"

"I think you know she's a single parent. I'm what made her one when she was nineteen. Kind of obvious, isn't it?" She could envision the chip forming on his shoulder, the one that helped make him a ferocious fighter on the field.

"You also have a younger sister, Olivia, eight-years-old."

"Yeah, what of it. I'm going to do all I can for her

4

and my mama when I make the big time."

"Yet, you didn't grow up in poverty. You went to St. Augustine, an expensive traditionally black Catholic prep school in New Orleans. Did you have a football or academic scholarship?"

"Not at first. I was starting to give my mother some trouble, so she and my granny found the money to send me there. My grandmother has a dress shop in the French Quarter that does pretty well. My mom helps her out. They both thought I needed a place like that. One thing the Josephite Brothers believe in is discipline. They used to whack boys with a board if they got out of line, but that ended long before I got there. Instead, they routed me into sports, football, basketball, baseball. I was good at all of them but excelled in football. Nothing is as satisfying as tackling."

"Did your mother name you Tyson because she wanted you to be a fighter?"

"No, she always said she just liked the name."

"What kind of trouble did you get into before going to St. Augustine?" This could be interesting.

He shrugged again, but this time his shoulders raised as if lifting a weight. "Just adolescent stuff. Kid without a daddy crap. Are we about through here?"

She'd majored in communications, but taken a minor in psychology thinking it would improve her interview skills. This guy had both mommy and daddy issues, but if she kept pressing, he'd up and leave her twiddling her pen. Time to change tactics again.

"Your grandmother must be quite a woman to make a success of her business in the French Quarter where it's very competitive."

"She is. Florinda Ramsey found her niche when she

opened Flo's Fabulous Fashions for Larger Ladies. Lots of big women in Louisiana. She says it's the cooking, and she's always telling my mother to put some meat on her bones because a puny size eight is bad for business." Edie heard the fondness in his words. She offered her own smile in return.

He leaned across the table, and she got lost in his gaze again, found herself bending toward him. "You're pretty cute when you aren't so serious. Want to go out some time?"

Edie stiffened her spine. "Uh, no."

"You don't date black guys?" he challenged.

She cocked her head and did a bit of self-examination, then shook her head. "I don't think I'm prejudiced. I love my brother-in-law, Junior Polk. He's black. And my dear little niece, Lizzy, is part Melungeon. That's a mix of black, white, and Cherokee. She's so much fun. I admire Gayle King and Oprah Winfrey and hope to be able to do interviews with their compassion and yet firmness. Frankly, I've never been asked out by a black guy before—though you are hardly black."

"High yellow they used to call people like me. Octoroon is another old name for what I am. My granny told me I should marry lighter than myself. It was a way to get ahead in the old days. I guess my mom believed her because my daddy was probably white, and I know granny's husband was. He didn't stick around long, but at least we have a picture." He stopped talking as if realizing he'd revealed way too much. "How about football players, you date any of those?"

"No, Rex warned me away from all athletes, and my twin sisters told me not to date frat boys either. That narrows the field. I don't go out a lot."

"Do you always do what Rex says?"

"Hardly, just ask him. But you see, it wouldn't be professional for me to date an interviewee. That could slant my opinion."

Tyson checked an expensive watch on his wrist. "No, this wasn't a bribe to attend LSU. It's my high school graduation gift. No story there. I have a class. Don't want to be late." He left with the same grin on his face that he'd worn when he arrived.

Edie pounded her fist against the table. He *was* smart and had turned the ball over on her again and again. She hadn't gotten to the tougher questions like were the rumors true that he took drugs to enhance his performance or to relax. Well, he'd just deny it. So far, all his drug tests had come back clean, but the guys he hung with were questionable to say the least, according to Rex.

She needed something different, fresher. An idea occurred. This Friday, she'd get in her little hybrid car and make a trip to New Orleans. Inspiration waited only an hour and a half away.

Chapter Two

Edie started her research by seeking out Tyson Ramsey's home address on Esplanade Avenue, wide and leafy with a bush-covered neutral ground in this old section. The single-story shotgun house sat discreetly behind a wrought iron fence. A very short walkway bordered by two large azalea bushes now past their prime bloom led to a shallow raised porch upheld by slender columns. The blinds on two tall windows were drawn down to the sills, perhaps because the fame of the Golden Ram attracted the nosey.

She glanced around at the neighboring houses, some painted in brilliant colors, others two stories, and one or two that might be considered mansions. The Ramsey home remained painted traditional white. Though it looked small and narrow, she knew the house made up for that in length. Not wanting to be caught loitering, she returned to her car and went around the nearest block to discover the house did indeed span through to the other road, but any view of it was blocked by a far more modern, windowless two-car garage.

Sometimes being little could have advantages. She managed to squeeze through the small space between the garage and the neighbor's ligustrum hedge to get a view of the backyard, also tiny, but with a screened porch holding two hospitable rocking chairs overlooking a plot of grass with an ornate bird bath ringed by red begonias.

Other than that, only a concrete path leading toward the garage. A small dog began yapping behind a fence on the other side of the yard. She fought back through the ligustrum and drove into the French Quarter. All in all, Tyson Ramsey's family lived in a place that seemed to say "nothing special here"—though she knew with all the renovations going on in the area, a seemingly modest home here could sell for $500,000. She'd checked the real estate ads.

Parking at the big pay lot by the Jax Brewery building, she cut through the ground floor and stopped in a candy shop for a pound of deep, dark chocolate fudge and a dozen pecan pralines, two bagged separately. The May weather was winding up for the heat clobber of summer, but not too bad yet for a brisk pace. Bearing gifts, she walked along the cross street by Jackson Square alive with tourists, panhandlers, and artists displaying their works until she intercepted Royal Street noted for its galleries and antique stores, the complete opposite of Bourbon Street. A little early, she window shopped until reaching the cross street where Flo's Fabulous Fashions for Larger Ladies occupied a bright nook easily seen from Royal.

Two display windows exuded color on either side of a plain brown door. The crumbling bricks with ferns growing in the cracks typical of the oldest area of the city covered the front of the second floor. A hardy vine crept over the edge of the roof. Not that anyone would notice with eyes drawn to two plus-sized mannequins, one lounging in a beach chair and clad in a tropical print bathing suit while the other stood in a brilliantly striped coverup, a large straw hat upon its head and oversized sunglasses shading its eyes. Enormous totes in turquoise and yellow spilled towels around their feet.

The other window was just as arresting. Hefty black mannequins showed off summer fashions in flashy florals, bold pinks and purples. These ladies were not ashamed to show their upper arms or meaty thighs. Edie rather loved them. "You go, girls," she murmured, as she opened the wooden door and entered a room devoid of black garments. An overhead brass bell alerted those inside to her presence.

A woman more rotund than the mannequins and with a friendly face the color of gingerbread sized her up. "Oh, honey lamb, we have nothing in your size, baby. Plenty of that in the Riverwalk Mall. Y'all go on back down Royal to Canal and left to get there."

"Oh, I'm here for our three-o'clock appointment concerning your grandson, Mrs. Ramsey. Edith Billodeaux from the LSU *Reveille*." She noticed Flo practiced what she preached, wearing a vibrant lime green shift with diagonal gold stripes. A short black wig nicely styled most likely covered gray hair, but the proprietor had nary a wrinkle despite a broad smile.

"Then, you must call me Flo. I have coffee on. Let's step in the back. It's our break time. Portia, who we got in the dressing room?"

"Miss Tassy. She's trying to make up her mind about a couple of bathing suits," answered a gorgeous, light-skinned lady far less substantial than Flo, but still curvaceous. Straightened black hair parted in the middle flowed long about her shoulders and curled on the ends. Her dark eyes tilted upwards slightly in the corners giving her an exotic look. She had Tyson's straight nose, his mother, Edie presumed.

"Hey, Tassy, you buy one, I'll give you the other

half off." Flo directed a bonus-sized voice toward one of two dressing rooms, spacious with wide doors painted red. "After she decides, come on back and join us, my darlin' child."

They stepped behind a curtain into another section of the shop dedicated to alterations judging by a sewing machine and a rack of clothes awaiting adjustments. Along the wall by another door sat a coffee station with a large pot fresh-brewed and a row of mugs in various colors, none of them dull. Flo poured two cups and brought them to a table already set with a pitcher of milk and a basket of sugar and Sweet 'n Low packets. Edie took a seat in a substantial wooden chair, one of three, large enough to make her feel like Baby Bear, and doctored her somewhat bitter chicory-laced brew with milk. She offered her gifts to go with it.

"Now, that's sweet of you. Let me put this out on a plate for all to share." Flo returned with the block of fudge speared by the white plastic knife that it came with in the middle of a platter arrayed like a cheese board with the pralines forming a ring around the outer edges. She carved off a small piece of fudge, put it in her mouth, and savored it with her eyes closed.

"Been a while since I had fudge. We usually have a plate of goodies for the clients out front, but we were real busy this mornin', and they cleaned us out. I had no time to go and get refills."

"I have to say your shop truly is fabulous. Tyson is very proud of your business."

"That so? Not much when he was younger. We all lived in my apartment upstairs when he was small." Flo nodded toward a staircase at one end of the room. "But he started getting teased about living over a dress shop so we found a house for him and Portia."

As if on cue, a little voice issued from the stairwell. "May I come down if you aren't busy, Granny?"

"Sure, honey. We have a special guest who is writing an article about your brother for the school paper."

That prompted Edie to put her phone on record and take out a list of topics from her crossbody bag. No thief was going to take advantage of her small size to steal this purse.

The child emerged, head peeking out first with two light brown fuzzy pompoms on top and those extraordinary eyes like Ty's set in the same honey-colored skin. The nose was different, broader, but this was undoubtedly his sister, Livy.

"Come on out, Olivia. Meet Miss Billodeaux."

"Edie, you should all call me Edie. Would you like some fudge or a praline? I brought plenty." Same father, she concluded, even though the siblings were thirteen years apart in age.

As more of the child emerged, she could see Livy wore the white blouse and blue plaid skirt of a parochial school and held a fist full of papers clutched in her thin hands, no weight problem here as her body was downright skinny. "May I see your drawings? Do you want to be an artist when you grow up?"

"No, a fashion designer. See." Livy held out her pictures of round figures decked out in clothes colored by every crayon in the box and definitely better than most eight-year-olds could do.

"I think you are very talented. Keep designing. So, praline or fudge or both?" Edie offered the plate.

Her granny got up again. "Coffee milk, baby?"

"Yes, ma'am. Thank you," the child said as she carefully selected a praline.

"You also have very good manners," Edie complimented. "I'll have a praline, too."

"She ought to. She goes to St. Mary's Academy, and those nuns teach 'em young. I think I'll have just one praline." Flo presented her granddaughter with a mug containing a dollop of coffee, the rest filled with milk.

"Tell me how Fabulous Flo's got started. It must have taken a lot of effort?" Edie dunked an edge of her praline into her coffee and sucked on the softened brown sugar patty. Livy did the same in imitation.

"Right time, right place, good idea, but it all started with him." Flo took a photo from a pocket in her dress. "This here was my husband, Tex Ramsey. We married in the late Sixties." She let Edie examine the picture. "White musician who liked black women and a nice big booty."

Tex had a bony frame and a greasy black ducktail, dark eyes, and an arm around a much smaller but still bodacious young Florinda. One tattooed arm held her waist and the other a trumpet almost as tenderly.

"I got pregnant in no time being Catholic. He had a fine gig in the Quarter. For a while, things went good. I never did lose my baby weight. Said he didn't care, but he started tomcatting around. I kicked his skinny ass out the door. I thought he'd come crawling back. No way. Next thing I know, he's signed on with a band on one of those tourist steamboats. I'd get a check now and then for the baby, he always said. They stopped coming when he decided to stay in Chicago. He died up there of a heroin overdose. There I was with a toddler and a job waiting tables, but I wrote up my idea for this shop and got a minority business loan for rent and stock and advertising. We saved money by living upstairs. When the time came, I made sure my beautiful and smart baby girl was awarded a scholarship to St. Mary's, same place Livy attends."

Flo paused to pick up a second praline. "The business grew and grew exactly like me. Now we have some famous clients. When Lizzo is in town, she always stops by to see what's new. You know Mariah Coy who has the nightclub where all the Sinners football players hang out? She's not fat but has that huge bust. We tailor whatever she wants for her and lots of other plus-sized celebrities like our own Caressa here in the Quarter, and Precious Armitage whose husband used to play for the Sinners. That woman loves purple. I call her whenever her favorite color arrives."

"Impressive, really impressive. I've seen Caressa perform. She always dresses with flair. Mariah is sort of a relative of mine since my brother Tom's birth mother is married to Howdy McCoy, Mariah's son. She claims us all as her grandkids."

Portia Ramsey pushed back the curtain. "Mama, she came here to talk about Tyson, not hear your life story. I can't believe you dragged out that old picture and talked about Tex in front of Livy. I could hear every word you said out there. I'm just glad Miss Tassy is somewhat hard of hearing."

The bright-eyed child piped up, "Don't do drugs or you'll be dead. May I have some fudge now?"

"How many sweets have you had already? Is that coffee milk?" Portia fussed. "And you, Mama, you're diabetic and should know better."

"The pecans in the praline offset the sugar I do

believe. This child could use some building up, and it wouldn't hurt you none either, Miss Size Eight." Still, Flo put the brown sugar patty back on the plate.

"I'm so sorry. I didn't know. Next time, I'll bring fruit," Edie apologized.

"Don't you dare. Here, Livy, take the platter out front for our customers." The child obediently obeyed her granny. "Cut off a piece of fudge for yourself before you come back or Tassy gonna eat it all."

"Miss Tassy is gone. She bought both swimsuits, a tote, and a coverup. She said she saved enough on the second suit to treat herself."

"That's how you get more sales. Anything else you want to know about me before we move on to Ty?" Flo eased her chair back and went for a coffee refill and a mug for her daughter who used the artificial sweetener, only half a packet.

"Actually, your grandson told me about this picture. I'm so glad to have seen it and gotten to know your family story." How badly she wanted to ask about the Golden Ram's daddy, but figured that question was off limits and might get her escorted out by Portia. "I asked if you named him Tyson so he'd be a fighter, but he said you only liked the name."

"That's right," Portia replied, cool and comfortable, looking Edie in her eyes as if daring her to ask more. Flo helped her out.

"He did turn out to be a scrappy kid. He used to do our deliveries in town on his bicycle. One day some thug kids waylaid him. He came back with a broken bike, a black eye, and lots of scratches. I guess he was about thirteen. While we were fussing over him, he said we should see the other guys—and then tried to parlay that into getting a motorcycle. But he was too young for it."

Again, that small voice came from a crack in the curtain. "Uncle T says if anyone hits you, you should hit them back hard as you can, and they'll let you alone. Ty says the same."

"Uncle T isn't always right," Portia said. "Neither is your brother."

"Uncle T?" Edie queried.

"Friend of the family," Portia answered promptly.

"He gave Ty a motorcycle when he got old enough," Livy supplied through chocolate smeared lips.

"Olivia, go upstairs and wash your face. You may have an hour of TV time."

The bribe worked. The child dashed up the stairs.

"There, now we can talk about Ty without the childish commentary." Their mother took a serene sip of coffee.

"Your son did tell me he got into some trouble, and you sent him off to St. Augustine's to straighten him out."

"Fighting mostly, sometimes for money, because he usually won. There was no need for that. He had everything he needed. I suppose he wanted to prove himself. Gangs tried to recruit him, get him hooked on drugs so he'd agree to sell drugs. He settled down when he discovered he had a talent for sports at St. Aug's."

"Yes, I already did a phone interview with his high school coach. He said some boys need to channel their adolescent anger in a productive way, and a good coach can act as a father figure, too. He knew Tyson would do well the first day of football practice. The other sports kept him in good condition for football in the fall. He was a trifle short for basketball but played like a demon to get that ball. Baseball was a little too tame for him even though he could whack a ball way into the outfield when he got a piece of it. Best all-around athlete he'd had in his career."

"That's our boy," Flo beamed.

"Yes, we're very proud of him, but I do worry all this success will go to his head. Lots of people hang around him to bask in his glory, and some of them won't be good for him. Plus, football is such an uncertain profession. One bad injury, and you're out of the game. That's why I want him to finish college as a backup even if his degree is in physical education. At least, he could coach in high school, but I had hoped for something better, my boy is so bright." Portia sipped her coffee to cover the concern on her face.

Edie studied her for a moment. A woman of forty, she could pass for much younger, no gray in that hair, no cracks in that smooth complexion, voluptuous lips, those exotic eyes. At around five-eight, Ty's mom stood as tall as she'd like to be and had curves to go with it. No one would mistake her for a child.

"He did say you hadn't had the chance to finish, and he was the reason why."

"I've never regretted having him."

"Ty is a blessing in our lives as is Livy. I wanted Portia to be a lawyer or a nurse, but sometimes the Lord has other plans. As my business partner, my daughter does all the alterations and designs some original creations for our clients. She's a marvel with a sewing machine."

"Mama, I'm nothing more than a seamstress."

"Don't put yourself down that way, my baby. It's a God-given talent to make beautiful clothes, especially for big people. I wish you'd take more credit for it."

"Thank you, Mama. I prefer to keep a low profile. I don't want to be overwhelmed by custom orders." Portia turned to Edie. "One advantage of working here besides being available to my children is that I can cut down any dress I like and have enough left over for a jacket or a wrap." Portia smiled, the first time she'd done so.

"I'd let you pick out something for Portia to alter for you, Edie, but you'd just wind up with three dresses you're so petite." Flo let loose with a boisterous laugh.

"Mama, you've made her blush. You don't like when people make fun of your size and shouldn't remark on hers."

Edie shook her head. "It's fine. I'm used to being called short stuff and peanut by my brothers. I'm the same height as my mom. She's says it's a problem when a woman is young and no one takes you seriously."

"We do, absolutely we do," Flo assured her. "You write a great article about our boy."

"I'll do my best."

The brass bell chimed. Portia immediately rose to answer its call. "That's all the time we can spare you."

Edie also stood. "Just one more thing, could I take a photo of all of you in front of the store? Livy, too."

"Why not?" Flo shouted upstairs. "Liv, come get your picture taken. Make certain that face is clean."

"Oh, Mama, no. You know I like to stay out of the spotlight. Just you."

"Please, the whole family. I'll see Ty gets a copy of it." Edie shifted her phone from record to camera.

They pushed through the curtain where the next customer, a hefty white lady clad in stretch jeans and a far too tight tee with sweat stains in the armpits, helped herself to the fudge. Difficult to tell if she only wanted out of the heat and a snack or had a real interest in shopping, but she had tourist written all over her. "Nice place you got here. I can't believe it's so hot in May."

"You should be here in August. Actually, no one should. People from up north drop like dead flies. Look around. We'll only be a minute," Flo said.

They trooped out the door and let Edie pose them between the two colorful windows. She backed up enough to get the shop sign in the view even though it meant crossing the narrow street and waiting for traffic to pass. Flo to the left, Portia to the right, and Livy situated in front of them. Snap. Snap. One in color, one in black and white. She returned to the store only long enough to thank them for the interview.

As she started back to her car, she heard Flo's boisterous voice say, "I'll just bet you want something really nice to take back home from New Orleans," before the shop door closed.

She'd wager the tourist would drop over a hundred dollars before leaving. If she'd been a way larger size, she probably would, too.

Chapter Three

Edie found a parking place she could squeeze into in front of her brother Dean's house in the lush garden district. Rex would have gone directly back to his life and his football buddies at LSU, but family mattered to her. She'd phoned ahead asking if she could stay the night, catch up with her niece and nephew, and indulge in a pizza Dean baked in his own backyard oven. With both their children still in school for a few more weeks, she knew they wouldn't have gone away on an offseason trip like most of the others. Happy to have her of course.

Before she could get out of the car, her phone rang. She wasn't surprised to hear Portia Ramsey speak, could even guess what she wanted.

"My mother was very open with you as she is with everybody, but I'd like to ask that you not mention my father's death by overdose. I know there are rumors about my son using drugs. He's told me so and doesn't want me to worry."

"I guess I can downplay that." So much for her professional ethics. She changed the subject before Ty's mother could ask for more deletions. "Say, how did you do with the tourist?"

"We put her in a lovely, airy dress. She bought a matching handbag and a statement necklace to go with it. Come in feeling frumpy and leave feeling fabulous, my mother's motto."

"I just love Flo. She's an original."

From the doorway of the white, two-story home, her sister-in-law, Stacy, beckoned. "Are you going to sit in your car all day?" Wynn and DJ, her children, squeezed by her and raced toward the gate. They stopped there like eager, fenced-in puppies trained not to go outside the yard, which was entirely true. Within seconds, they were joined by their white, poufy dog, Mati, who started barking in greeting and excitement.

"I have to go. Don't worry about the article. It will be positive. Bye."

She eased out of the driver's seat and carefully opened the gate because the dog was more likely to escape than the children. They followed her up the walk, straight into the house, and down the hall which took them outside again, across a porch, and into a courtyard centered around a fountain burbling merrily. The dog stood up on the rim and took a drink.

Her eldest brother, Dean, franchise quarterback for the Sinners, rose from a picnic table in the shade. "Hey, peanut, you want something to drink, too? I have beer and uh…" He eyed a pitcher on the table. "Purple Kool-Aid."

The first offer marked her as an adult, the second as a child. Then, Stacy intervened. "How old are you now?"

"Twenty-one. I could have a beer if I wanted. I just don't care for it much."

Dean grinned in that heart-stopping way he'd inherited from their father. "What, you were drinking beer before you turned twenty-one? Tsk, tsk, the baby of the family sneaked a few brews before she was legal."

"Yes, I'm not that goody-goody, and I'm not the baby of the family. Rex is five minutes younger. He's the last born. You know that."

Stacy went to her husband and linked an arm around his waist. "Stop teasing her. You did worse things."

"True, so true. It's hard to imagine Rex as a baby when he's the same height I am. My guess is Stace has some diet drinks in the fridge for ladies watching their weight."

"I do. What would you like?"

"Coke Zero if you have it."

"I'll bring it out with the relish tray. The kids won't eat any veggies once there is pizza on the table. Hey, my big lout, when will it be ready?" Stacy hugged her husband closer.

"Half an hour. My dough is resting. You have to wait for perfection, princess."

Perfection, that's what Edie saw when she studied the couple, she so tall, blonde, and gorgeous, he so muscular, dark, and handsome, both so fond of each other they still used pet names, princess and big lout. Heck, Dean had gone for a vasectomy because Stacy had so much trouble with her pregnancies. Now that was love. Would she ever find the same?

"Aunt Edie, what did you bring us?" DJ asked, tall for a kindergartner, he came almost up to her waist.

"Hmm, let's see." She took the two pralines out of her purse and handed one to each child. "For after dinner."

"Thank you, Aunt Edie," blonde Wynn said with perfect manners while her brother seemed a little pouty. Well, she was a girl and older.

"What were you hoping for DJ?"

"An LSU tiger." He thought big.

"It wouldn't fit in my car. I can't get you a real one,

but the next time you visit to see Uncle Rex play football, we'll go visit the mascot."

"Okay." He began to nibble his praline.

"Mom, DJ is eating his treat before dinner." Wynn was also a big sister and a snitch.

Returning, Stacy handed Edie an ice-cold Coke Zero and placed the relish tray on the table. "DJ, put the praline on a napkin and snack on some carrots or celery until the pizza is ready."

Reluctantly, the boy submitted. He dunked a baby carrot up to his fingertips in the large bowl of dip, sure to be made of yogurt and not sour cream, and ate half in one bite. Wynn daintily held a cherry tomato between her finger tips and immersed just the tip before eating it. Edie went for the broccoli florets and washed them down with her drink.

"Any others coming?" she asked.

"No, Tom and Alix are at Howdy's ranch. Matt and Annie took Dre and the boys to the theme parks of Orlando, though I think they are still a trifle young to appreciate it. Xochi and Junior are back in Chapelle. You know what homebodies they are. As long as he has his restaurant and she has her herbs to keep her busy, they're happy. Oh, I think Xo is planning baby number four, but she isn't telling." Stacy filled her in on the city dweller side of the family.

"No! Every time she conceives, I keep hoping none of them are as big as KC at birth. Thank God the girls take after Xo." Edie took a large bite out of a celery stick to prevent herself from saying anything critical about a sister she dearly loved.

"Let's see. Jock and Lori are in Australia. Josee and Trin went vacationing in the Bahamas. Sarge and Mack are back at the ranch with the rest of the family and staking out their new house next to Teddy and Jessie's place. I guess that's everyone."

"Jude?" Edie asked out of fairness about everyone's least favorite sister. Becoming a doctor and surviving the Covid virus hadn't made her any more kind or social.

"We didn't bother. She usually says no, too tired or busy since she became a gastroenterologist."

Dean presented that dashing grin again. "I think Jude loves giving colonoscopies, especially to men. Well, more pizza for us. Let me show you my new skill." He advanced to his prep table next to the oven, kneaded his dough, split it in half, and started spinning a hand-tossed crust. His audience applauded. Once he placed the dough into the pans, he took requests for toppings: one with pepperoni and cheese, the other half veggie, half meat loaded. Into the furnace they went. "Won't be long."

"What about you? Why are you in the Big Easy when you should be studying for finals or partying with friends before the semester ends?" Stacy concentrated on filling up on crudités before the main dish arrived. Another of her tricks for staying slim, Edie knew.

"I came to interview Tyson Ramsey's family for a *Reveille* article, my last piece of the year. I wanted a different slant. You know, what made him into the Golden Ram?"

Cautioning the children not to touch the hot trays, Dean brought his masterpieces to the table. "Did you interview the Ram himself? What's your take on him?"

"Yes, more briefly than I wanted. He's good at escaping both on and off the field." She felt honored that her big brother and winner of three Super Bowl wins would ask her opinion when her editor had doubted her ability to do a sports story. Dean had come close to ring number four with Jock Brown and his brother Mack added to the team but lost in overtime.

"We need more defensive players. He looks great on the field, but what about attitude?"

"Arrogant, touchy about his family."

"Football has a way of taking care of arrogance. Why is he touchy about his family?"

"Raised by a single mother and his grandmother, but that isn't so unusual anymore. He has a younger sister he wants to protect. Very chippy about her. They were born twelve years apart but obviously to the same father no one will name. They live in a modest house on Esplanade, and real estate is high there. Something is going on, but I don't need to know for my story. I want to be positive."

"A chip on the shoulder can work well for a player, but he can't believe he is better than the team as a whole. The Sinners are looking at him for the next draft. He'll probably go in the top three if he has a senior season as good as his last. We'd have to trade a lot to get him. I'll ask Rex how he works with the team. Thanks for your insight."

She didn't mention that he'd hit on her. That had nothing to do with his football career or his family, and she believed she'd handled him well. Leave it to Stacy to say, "Are his eyes as spectacular in person as on TV?"

"Oh, yes, but I wasn't tempted." Only a small lie.

"Tempted to do what?" Stacy was on to her.

"Go out with him."

"He asked?" Dean questioned.

"It was nothing. I'm sure I'm not his type. He

wanted to needle me. I told him it wouldn't be professional."

Stacy cocked her beautiful head. "Why wouldn't you be his type? You're as cute as can be."

"Guys like him date cheerleaders and sorority sisters because they can, though he seems to play the field, not staying with any one of them long. I'll rather not be one of his groupies."

"Daddy, can we eat now?" DJ's hand hovered over the pepperoni pie ready to dig into dinner.

Dean tested the heat with a finger. "Ready, get set, go!"

The melee began, a slice of the simpler pizza for each of the kids. Dean took one veggie, one meat, as did Edie because they both knew Stacy would eat only one veggie. Once the kids finished, the rest of the second pie came up for grabs, mostly to Dean who polished it off.

The children ate their pralines and begged to be excused for playtime. The adults enjoyed their beverages and the cooling of the day into a balmy evening. When the offspring went in for baths, Edie went with them. Her fingers itched to start on her article.

In the privacy of her assigned room, she sat at a handy desk, opened her laptop and began.

Tyson's Women

Most know Tyson Ramsey's amazing statistics achieved as a free safety on the football field, the sixty tackles, fifteen assists, and six fumbles that led to the Bednarik Award for best college defensive player and a nomination for the Heisman Trophy. Who are the people that made him the phenomenon he is today?

She began with his grandmother whose story tried to take over much as the real woman did. Though reluctant, she had to reduce Flo to a paragraph when she deserved a story of her own. Left with a small child when her husband, Tex Ramsey, a French Quarter musician, died young, she'd started her own business based on a unique idea, fabulous clothes for larger ladies. Edie made sure to give her a plug for the shop by name. When Flo's daughter found herself in a similar situation, the ladies joined forces to raise Portia's son in an apartment over the store

Teased and bullied for living in a dress shop and attacked when delivering purchases for his grandmother, Ty fought back hard and discovered his feisty attitude and fast-moving fists quickly improved his reputation as a kid to be left alone. Unfortunately, it also attracted the attention of local gangs who tried to recruit him into a violent drug selling and using culture.

The women in Ty's life took action and found the means to send him to St. Augustine Academy, a traditionally black prep school for boys located between Law and Hope Streets which spells out their purpose. Under the strict discipline of the Josephite Brothers who address their students as sir and require them to wear white shirts with a dark tie and keep their hair trimmed close, Tyson flourished. His aggression was channeled into sports, football, basketball, and baseball, but he excelled in the first.

Edie added in the long quote from his high school coach and went on to Ty being highly recruited by a number of top universities but choosing LSU. At his mother's insistence, he would complete college there and go into the draft after his senior year. She didn't want to overlook the importance of the third lady in his life.

Tyson Ramsey has another influential woman in his

life, his eight-year-old sister, Olivia. Livy wants to be a fashion designer. He means to succeed in his football career to make all things possible for her, a very sweet incentive and one he is sure to earn.

There, along with the picture she thought she'd done her job well. Still, Flo did deserve a story of her own, not for *The Reveille,* but for one of the magazines that specialized in New Orleans life. She started her freelance piece entitled *Flo's Fabulous Fashions for Larger Ladies*, centering the address under it, and envisioning the photo beneath it captioned with names. She began with the motto: Come in feeling frumpy, Leave feeling fabulous, and went on from there.

She wanted more details and pictures inside the shop. Flo's opened on Sundays from noon to five. No sense in unlocking the doors earlier as the tourists were still sleeping off a night on Bourbon Street and the good people of the city went to church, Flo had stated. Eight o'clock, not too, too late for a brief phone call asking permission to stop by tomorrow. Her call went to voice mail but was returned immediately.

"Sure, you come on by in the afternoon. Livy and me are watching Disney Channel and having us some popcorn. I'm not out carousing because she's staying over."

Edie had no doubt that Flo could still carouse with the best of them. She laid out the story and left Flo well-pleased with the idea.

Chapter Four

Edie slept late. People with young children don't. She found the family gathered in the sunny breakfast nook they used far more often than the formal dining room. DJ had a pancake with a smiley face picked out in blueberries on his plate. His sister's flapjack bore a figure something like a unicorn.

"I wanted a t-rex but mom said she didn't have enough berries. She used them all up on Dad's," DJ complained. He drowned his in syrup and got to work stuffing his face.

"More like I wasn't sure how to make a t-rex," Stacy admitted.

"What does mine have on it?" Edie poured herself a glass of orange juice.

"Sorry, I threw what berries were left into the batter. Next time I'll take requests the night before."

"Want to see mine?" Dean asked, slanting his plate to show the design on top of a stack. There it was, a Sinners devil-tailed heart like the one rumor said he had on his butt with Stacy's name in the center. Again, Edie sighed for a love like that.

She took her seat and settled for two regular blueberry pancakes with much less syrup than DJ had poured on his. The small sausages on a platter did not last long. She got her own coffee when Stacy sat down to eat.

"Growing girls should drink milk. That stuff will stunt your growth," Dean teased.

"It didn't hurt you any, you big lout," she retorted, borrowing Stacy nickname for her brother. "Say, Stace, I'm going back to Flo's shop today to get more info and some pictures. Want to come along if Dean will watch the kids?"

"Go if you want, princess. Matt left a key so we could use his new pool while they're gone. That's where we'll be when you get back."

"Might be fun. I know where the shop is, but I've never been inside," said the woman with a model's figure and a degree in several foreign languages who wore a bathrobe as if it were a ballgown. "Let me clean up and get dressed."

"By then, we'll be right on time. I'll take care of the dishes," Edie offered, knowing Stacy would not set foot outside the door without makeup or a stylish outfit. By the time her sister-in-law appeared dressed in fashionably ripped jeans worn with high heels and a snug melon-colored tee that showed off her perfect breasts, Edie waited jingling her car keys, her overnight bag already stowed in her car. If she'd dressed like Stacy, she'd resemble a ragamuffin child, so she'd gone for a sundress in perky pink and put on white sandals instead of her usual sneakers.

"I'll drive. My car is easier to park. Afterwards, I'll drop you off and head back to LSU."

"Fine with me. I hate French Quarter traffic." Stacy slid into the little hybrid, angling her long legs and swinging them in together like a move star getting into a limo. She made a quick move to shove the seat backward for more room. "It's cramped in here."

"Even the tall and beautiful must suffer some time," Edie replied blithely. She maneuvered her Honda Insight deftly through the mass of cars going their way once they crossed Canal Street and parked again on the Jax lot.

"I need to stop in at Walgreen's first. It might take a while. Could you pick up a deluxe selection of nuts in the candy shop and meet me in the square?" She rooted out two twenties from her small purse and handed them over.

"I'd be happy to treat if you have a yen for nuts," Stacy said waving the bills away.

"They're for Flo. She diabetic. Last time I took fudge and did not endear myself to her daughter, everyone else, yes, but not Portia."

"Done. See you soon." Stacy moved away, her high blonde ponytail bobbing. Male eyes turned in her direction missing Edie entirely. Not that she cared.

The photo section in Walgreen's wasn't too busy. She printed out three eight by ten glossies of the Ramsey women and purchased an inexpensive frame for one of them in short order. Fending off offers for carriage rides and the insistent beggars with her usual cool aplomb, Stacy awaited her by the gate to Jackson Square. They covered the distance to Flo's in no time with Edie jogging alongside Stacy who could cover ground even in heels. She arrived grateful for the blast of cold air when they entered the dress store. A couple of queen-sized shoppers browsed the goods, but the place sat otherwise quiet.

She offered the nuts to a delighted Flo. "There are some chocolate-covered almonds in the center, but the rest are just lightly salted." Portia gave her a nod of approval and set the tray on the refreshment table alongside a plate of jumbo chocolate chip cookies. One of the browsers scooped up a few almonds as she passed. Livy, who must have been hiding among the racks, popped up to take some, too.

"I also have this. I thought you'd like it—the photo I took outside the store." She offered the framed version. "I'll use it for the story and for the other piece about the shop if it sells."

"Oh, I surely do," Flo assured her. She set it by the register for all to see. "Now what more did you want to know about the business?"

"I forgot to introduce you to my sister-in-law, Stacy Billodeaux, Dean's wife."

"As if all of New Orleans doesn't know that. It's an honor." Flo shrewdly measured Stacy with a glance. "Our sizes are too large for you, honey, but tall as you are if you see anything you like, my daughter will alter it to fit. She does custom work, too." The sales pitch over, she turned her bulk to Edie again.

"The shop seems small. I wondered how you kept all the sizes in stock and have such variety?"

"Let me show you." Flo led the way through the break room and out the back door to a metal building filling the space where a yard used to be. Entering in a code, she revealed a climate-controlled space brimming with dresses on hangers and handbags and accessories stacked on shelves.

"When we need another size, we come back here, scan the code on the tag and take it out front. We have an inventory system that relocates the item or tells us we are out of stock. Ty designed it for us as a project he needed for school. He can do that what cha call it—coding. Makes it easy to reorder, too. Now way in the back are my favorites, ballgowns with lots of bling."

They walked the length of the building to the area where special occasion dresses hung covered in zippered bags. Flo opened several and exposed the glitter. "We don't have them out front this time of year when it's more beachwear and such, but come Mardi Gras we can't keep enough in stock. Portia gets slammed with alterations and requests for originals. Customers need to order early. We love putting glam into every woman's life no matter what size."

Very quotable, Edie wrote that down. Stacy, who had been trailing behind pulling out dresses and carefully putting them back again, caught up. Flo anticipated her arrival, already holding up a stunning full-length gown that could wrap around Stace twice.

"We call this color midnight blue with silver accents, no sequins, you aren't the type." Flo held it up against Edie's elegant sister-in-law and turned her toward a convenient mirror mounted on the back wall. She bunched up the extra cloth behind Stacy's back. "It's one of Portia's originals. When Mardi Gras approaches it will be gone in a snap." Flo dropped the cloth and snapped her fingers for emphasis. "We could use the extra material to make a wrap for you."

"Stunning, simply stunning. Let's do that." Obviously, Stacy had fallen under Flo's spell. Still, she and Dean went to many formal occasions, charity balls and such. He had his own custom tux. Edie saw no reason why Stacy shouldn't get the dress despite a price tag that made her gulp. She almost wished Flo had something for her though she had no use for anything so fancy. What did any non-sorority girl need but a good supply of jeans, tops, and comfortable shoes for walking the large campus?

Flo showed off a few more gowns thick with sequins, Mariah Coy's favorite style, and the bright colors favored by Caressa. Edie snapped a few pictures of Flo holding the dresses, and they were on their way back to the shop where Portia wrapped a purchase for one of the browsers.

"I got one more thing I want to show you upstairs. Portia, get Mrs. Billodeaux's measurements. She's buying your midnight blue creation." They left Stacy examining oversized leather totes. They trudged up a narrow staircase, Flo's wide body scraping the sides while Edie bobbed along behind like a tug boat assisting a cargo carrier.

"Here's where we raised Ty in his early years. People asked me why I don't move in with my daughter in that fancy house she has, but I like to be near my store, and she needs to be on her own."

The furnishings were large and comfortable. A wide-screen TV filled part of a wall in front of a well-used recliner.

"That's where I watch my Sinners and LSU games," Flo said. "But look at this, Ty in his St. Aug's uniform. Ain't he handsome? We cried when we had to have his head of curls shaved off. I'm not so sure I approve of that bleached blond look he has going now. The Augustine Brothers sure wouldn't approve, no, they would not."

"I'd love to see those curls," Edie suggested, not really meaning it, but out came a photo album from a cabinet drawer. She found herself turning over page after page on the coffee table, Ty's life from babyhood to his early teens. At one point, he did have a head of adorable curls.

"He stopped letting us take his picture around twelve. What a shame," Flo bemoaned.

"Guys are like that. My brothers were the same but as part of a celebrity family, they didn't have much choice. We were always being lined up for photo shoots. As the shortest kid, I was always front row center. I didn't like it very much either." She had no intention of revealing to Ty how much of his life had been revealed to her.

The rest of the apartment consisted of a kitchen, two bedrooms and a bath, and a rear door that led to a fire escape style metal stairs because, Flo said, she'd never make it down the interior stairs in a hurry. The room once shared by Ty with his mother retained not a whiff of his presence. It had been redone girly for Livy's frequent stays with her grandmother.

They made their way downstairs again and encountered Stacy up on a short pedestal having her measurements taken for the gown reduction. Portia ran a measuring tape from her waist to her ankles to get the length, circled her chest for the bust line, and moved to her waist.

Livy observed, "You're a beautiful lady."

"Thank you, dear. You're very cute yourself and bound to be as pretty as your mother when you grow up," Stacy answered, making both mother and grandmother beam.

A card with Stacy's information was duly filled in and filed. Flo would call when the dress was ready.

"Now you, Edie, step on up and let Portia do yours," Flo ordered. "If I see something right for you, we'll be ready, a gift for all you are doing for us."

Edie waved her hand. "Whoa, I can't take anything

for my work. I do get paid for my job."

"Oh, come on," Stacy urged. "Get up there. If they find something for you, I'll pay for it. After this year, you'll be going out into the professional world and will need more than jeans."

She endured the measuring, not tall, not busty, more childlike though she did have breasts appropriate for her size, her mom often said in consolation. "We'd better be going. I need to get back to campus and finish my articles. I'll let you know if the commercial one sells."

As they left, Stacy picked up the big tote she'd purchased in a color that matched her melon top. She popped the purse she'd brought along inside it.

"You have the height for a large bag," Flo assured her. "Take some cookies with you. Here." She'd already wrapped two in a paper napkin.

Stacy added them to her new tote. They left with a friendly wave.

"If you get tired, I can put you in this with the cookies and carry you back to the car," Stacy joked.

"Thanks, now you sound like Dean."

"Yeah, I guess so. Sorry. Flo has her style and so does Portia though it is more subdued. When you get out of college, you'll find yours, and no one will notice how short you are. Thanks for inviting me along. I'd never have gone in there otherwise. I'll tell all my friends about it."

"You don't have any fat friends."

"Some of the Sinners' wives are pretty hefty, but if Portia does custom work or can resize a dress, what does it matter? This has been fun. Why don't we do more together?"

They passed the snake handler waiting for someone

who wanted a picture with his boa just outside the Cabildo. Edie dropped a dollar in his hat. Snakes have to eat, too.

"Because I'm the youngest girl. The rest of you think of me as a child that needs protection. You left me out entirely when y'all trooped up to Lorena's room and voted on whether she should give Jock Brown second chance."

"The conversation did get a little intimate."

"I know all that stuff. If I didn't then, I do now."

"Point taken. But you are our baby sis. I sort of hate thinking of you with any man, and your brothers are probably worse. I guess since you're heading into senior year, there have been a few."

Edie knew she blushed and hoped the warm afternoon covered her embarrassment. "I've been busy and haven't gotten around to—uh."

"Really, don't be in any hurry. Wait for the right man."

"Yes, Mom."

"Not quite old enough to be yours. If you ever want to talk to someone other than our mother, call.

The enticing aroma of chicory coffee and fried beignets heaped with powdered sugar drifted their way as they passed Café Du Monde. "Want to stop and have a snack? This time, I'll pay," Edie said to assert her adulthood.

"I really should join Dean and the kids at the pool, get some exercise, and let the children have the cookies, or I will fit in Flo's clothes soon enough. Drop me off before I give way to temptation."

Edie squeezed her little car in and out of traffic like a pro, and dropped Stacy at her house. She made her way back to I-10 and Baton Rouge writing her stories in her head all the way.

Chapter Five

Edie stayed up late adding some details to the article on Tyson and completing her piece on Flo's Fabulous Fashions. Before she closed her laptop for the night, she'd sent the sports article to her editor and a query to the magazine she'd targeted for the business profile. The next day being Sunday, she slept in until noon when she went out to find some lunch. Finals started on Monday. She prudently started studying, but her fingers kept straying to her e-mail and messages in hope of positive responses way too soon.

Restless all night, she stoked herself with caffeine in the form of coffee the next morning and made her way to the Manship School of Mass Communications for a critical early exam. On the way back, she hit the student union for more coffee and a quick trip to the book store for another frame, thinking Ty might like to have the picture of his family, not that she'd get anywhere near the athletic dorms, but just in case she ran into him.

And so back to her on-campus apartment because her family could afford it, and she liked being in the heart of things. Though it gave her privacy and a quiet place to study, she sometimes felt a little lonely, having always been one of many at home. It didn't seem fair that her older twin sisters had roomed together and Xochi and Stacy, while Lorena had lived with the rest of the athletes on her volleyball scholarship. Of course, Rex stayed in the same dorm as Ty.

Her freshman year, she let the university assign her a roommate, figuring she got along with everyone, and ended up with a snobbish girl, a blonde hair flipper named Brooklyn, not from New York but from Dallas, who asked if she could get her a date with Rex. Ah, nope, her brother picked his own women. Brooklyn immediately entered the sorority rush, dragging her along to various tea parties where they were eyed like show poodles who might or might not win a prize ribbon. One glance at a list of the wardrobe she'd be expected to have—x pieces of formal wear, blazers, heels, etc.—and she'd tossed it out with her paper cup of punch and the napkin that had held cookies. Brooklyn already owned the wardrobe stuffed into the small residence hall closet.

"I don't see why you don't want to join. As one of *those* Billodeauxs and not just any old Cajun, why you'd be a shoo in. I'm a legacy pledging my mother's sorority. My mother says you make friends for life and some of them can help you move up in the world. She married one of her sorority sister's brother."

It wasn't in Edie to outright say she didn't want to be told how to dress or who to date by an exclusive club that ignored others. She been raised to be independent and accept all kinds that found their way to the ranch, especially in the summer when her family ran Camp Love Letter for children with serious illnesses. She'd met interesting and courageous people and would be willing to bet none had been a sorority member. However, not wanting to argue or destroy someone else's bliss, she simply said, "I don't want to wear that dumb bow and go through hazing."

Brooklyn's hand patted her head where a huge white

hair ribbon sat atop her sleek, blonde hair, something a small child's mother would force her daughter to wear. "It's not so bad. The hazing rituals are what make you a member of the group."

"We will agree to disagree, but do what makes you happy."

They struggled along together until the end of the semester when Brooklyn moved into the sorority house and Edie volunteered to room with a student from India named Amoli Bhat. She'd been in the States long enough for that to be transformed into Molly Bat. Edie had no objections to the little statue of elephant-headed Ganesha Molly placed on her dresser or to the beautiful saris she wore on dressy occasions. She took her home for the Christmas break right after they'd been introduced and planned to bring her back to the ranch for Easter and Spring Break. A studious, bespectacled girl studying biochemistry, Amoli did not attempt to drag her out to wild parties or take her on shopping sprees. Edie intended to ask her to room with her again sophomore year. Then, the world fell apart.

The first inkling came when Molly was summoned home before spring break as her mother and grandmother were terribly ill. That quickly, Edie was without a roommate again, but not for long as students began coming down with the Covid-19 virus. By March all students were sent home, dorms sanitized, and classes held online. Rex fretted over whether football would be played in the fall as he'd been designated as the new starting quarterback.

Their Mama Nell gathered as many of her offspring as she could behind the gates of Lorena Ranch, but some had been trapped abroad like Lorena and Jock staying at their house outside of Melbourne, Australia, where her sister trained for Olympic volleyball, and Trinity with Josee in London on a business trip when lockdowns were declared and flights canceled. Nell had her youngest home at least and managed to convince Xochi and Junior with their brood to move in for the duration. Teddy and his family already lived there.

What to do about the four living in New Orleans, a Covid hotspot? Mack and Sarge agreed to leave their French Quarter apartment and moved into Teddy's old room next to the handicap bath that would accommodate Sarge's missing foot. They intended to build on ranch property someday and could spend their time planning. Dean and Stacy, Annie and Matt tried to hold out in their Garden District homes, but Mama Nell begged in the name of their children and soon wore them down. As for Jude, now Dr. Billodeaux, she said she could not leave her patients, period, and stayed in the city. The only other Nell could not reach was Ilsa, the German mother of Dean's illegitimate son who'd been taken to Europe for his spring vacation. They were confined with his overseas grandparents and well-taken care of if Dean's frequent Zoom calls rang true.

Edie had to admit she could be secluded on worse places. Most folks wouldn't have a pool and a gym, horses to ride, and a built-in movie theater. Instead of helping with the now canceled Camp Love Letter, she assisted with entertaining ten young nieces and nephews. With the camp newsletter out of commission, she set herself to working up chore lists since the maid service quit early on and it seemed with so many in the house, the washer and dryer ran incessantly. Thank heaven, the gym had the same appliances as did Teddy and his wife in their home.

She assigned laundry days, and help with the cooking and cleanup days, days taking care of the children to help frazzled parents get a break. Everyone was expected to keep their rooms tidy and their baths clean, not so different from when all twelve children had lived there year-round. Since her dad and Knox Polk, the ranch manager, were getting up in years, though neither would admit it, she also devised a barn chore list. Their own elderly Nurse Shammy did not hesitate to volunteer for taking temperatures every day and with the assistance of Brinsley the butler, her husband, doing nose swabs once a week. Edie envisioned how she would explain this strange summer on her resume someday—acquired organizational skills.

She thanked heaven for the world wide web keeping her in touch with Amoli and other foreign friends she'd made, not to mention the family members abroad. Both Amoli's mother and grandmother had passed. Covid cases were dire in India, bodies dumped in the rivers without the customary immolation, not enough medical supplies in one of the world's most populous countries. She prayed for their safety.

To lift moods, she started blogging about the amusing incidents of a large family in quarantine such as her dad buying a forklift in order to haul the mounds of groceries delivered on a palette outside the gate to the house. She suspected he just wanted a forklift for the fun of it. Knox Polk distributed fair amounts of non-necessities like cookies, chips, and cheese curls to each family as if he doled out military rations. Her mom had relaxed the healthy eating rules for the duration. Frankly, Facebook kept her sane.

She also drew up a schedule of fun family activities: movie nights, line dancing sessions led by Mack, yoga classes and workouts run by Stacy, supervised pony riding for the little ones, and as the weather warmed, pool parties with shared lifeguard duties. If anyone had a special skill or hobby to share, they did.

Their housekeeper and Junior's mother, Corazon, taught all who wanted to knit, crochet, or sew simple patterns on a machine. Junior shared his culinary skills in cooking classes and his wife, Xochi, taught herbal remedies which often included short hikes to gather wild plants and flowers. Xo, Stacy, and Corazon also held classes for those with a desire to polish their Spanish since most of them spoke it a little. Knox Polk set up a shooting range for target practice, a skill several members in the family had found handy in the past. She needed a refresher course in both.

In the camp class rooms, she put out tables with jigsaw puzzles of various difficulty and board games even small children could play. While their mothers exercised in the next room, the clatter of Hungry, Hungry Hippos filled the air as well as accusations of cheating at Candy Land or Chutes and Ladders. Whoever had nursery duty was expected to resolve these issues, sometimes by folding the game and directing the children to the piles of picture books by the beanbag chairs. Higher shelves held novels and nonfiction for adults.

Time passed but too slowly when the governor, unhappy with the still high Covid rates, extended the lockdown into June because too many failed to use their face masks. He kept the bars closed, and disgruntled drinkers of which there were many tried to have him recalled. Pictures of a deserted Bourbon Street illustrated the dilemma. Such was life in Louisiana.

One thing that did go on and would always go on was football, both college and pro. Dean, Junior, Tom, Alix, Matt, and Mack were recalled to New Orleans for training camp, leaving their families behind. Jock Brown and Lorena, her Olympic dreams put on hold, left Australia with the understanding they could not come back until the crisis had ended and had to go into quarantine for two weeks upon arrival. Only half the preseason games were played, and teams started the season a little rusty. Other games folded when some teams had cases and also had to go into quarantine. Piped into the Super Dome, fake crowd noises attempted to make the situation seem normal.

Rex received a summons to report to LSU in August. Supposedly, he would be staying in an athletic dorm bubble under strict supervision. Who broke that rule? Tyson Ramsey and his cronies who went to a party the second they got back to Baton Rouge and caught Covid. All recovered well, but really, no excuse for such behavior in Edie's viewpoint. What if he had infected her twin brother?

As for her education, it got relegated to distance learning for the first semester. Amoli in far off India did the same, but worried about not having the labs so vital to her chosen career. Not a normal college experience at all.

Her phone rang breaking her reverie about the past two years. "Hey, Edie, it's Sterling Thomas."

The sports editor, a grad student, who had reluctantly given her the assignment for *The Reveille,* the call she had been waiting for all day. "Yes, hi. How did you like my story?"

"Ah, well-written and certainly interesting, but…"

That's when she knew he'd started with the good news first. "But?"

"I showed it around to some of the other editors. We all agree it isn't a sports story, more, um, feature writing. It's warm and fuzzy and fails to answer any hard questions, though you did ferret out the trouble he got into as a teen."

Warm and fuzzy, the kiss of death for a journalist. Were they going to kill her baby? "Will it run?"

"Oh, sure. In the human-interest section of the last issue for the term this week. Like I said, well-written, but not a sports story. Really that's what you should stick to. It's your strength. You have the ability to observe and draw people out, never saying a bad word about anyone."

"Okay, thanks for finding a place for it." She strove to keep the disappointment from her voice and the tears from her eyes.

"Women will love it," he added as an extra sop.

"Sure, I'll want to send it to Tyson's mom and grandmother."

"We hope to have you back on the staff in the fall. Have a good summer."

"Sure, you too." They always needed puff pieces for filler.

She'd taken extra classes to make up for time lost to the Covid years and learned for one thing that her voice was too light and girlish for radio. She lacked the smooth and mellow voice of her brother Teddy whose slight twang only added interest. When interviewing before a camera, she stood so short that she had to raise the mic into the air for the person to answer. Basically, she looked ridiculous standing on her tiptoes. Understanding people and writing about them, that was her strength. Now, she was no longer sure about that.

Chapter Six

Just her luck that her finals stretched out the entire week, but having one a day was better than two or three. Now finished with tests, Edie had only to go back to her place, pack, and begin the drive home. She stopped by the Union to pick up copies of *The Reveille* to send Flo. Still no word on the business feature which she'd shopped to another magazine. Oh well, she'd get plenty of practice doing the Camp Love Letter news and helping with the activities this summer.

She shoved the copies into her backpack. Her fingers grazed the framed photo she'd been hauling around. As if that touch summoned him, there sat Tyson Ramsey with two of his entourage lolling on a low wall outside the bottom level of the building. She might as well get rid of it now. Taking a deep breath, she feigned self-confidence, reinforced it with a smile, and walked right up to him.

"Hi, I have something for you."

"Oooh, she has something for you, Ty. Wonder what it is?" said one of guys with him.

They didn't look like they belonged on campus, no backpacks, no expressions wrinkled with worries about finals. They wore LSU gear, go Purple and Gold, and very expensive athletic shoes out of reach or scorned by most students. She ignored them. Time to take charge.

"Would you mind stepping over here?" She moved

away and balanced her backpack on a railing.

He answered her with that annoying shrug of his. "Be back in a minute."

Ty sauntered over and accepted the picture and the copies of the paper. "What's all this?"

"Your interview and a photo of your family I thought you might like. I already gave one to your grandmother."

Now he frowned, and it wasn't about his grades. "I can't put this up in the athletic dorm. The team will think I'm a wuss." Still, he pushed it into his backpack.

"Then shove it under your bed." She would have liked to tell him to shove it somewhere else but restrained herself. "The article is in the middle if you want to read it. I was going to mail it to Flo, but if you are going home…"

"I'm hanging around here for a while, but I'll get it to them." His eyes flashing gold in the sunlight, he scanned the story.

"Do you like it?"

"Hell, no! Who gave you permission to interview my granny and mom?"

"They did. I think they'll be happy with it."

"Probably. It's more about them than me or football."

"Sorry about that." No, she wasn't, not one bit. "They are the people who have shaped your life."

"True enough. I guess I should thank you. Here, give me your phone."

"Huh? Do you need to call someone?" It rode in an outer pocket of her backpack so she plucked it out and opened it for him.

He put his cheek, rather scratchy as if he hadn't

shaved today, against hers and snapped a selfie of the two of them, showed it to her briefly. He appeared smug, she wide-eyed and confused. Before handing it back, he inserted his phone number in her contacts list. "If you change your mind about that date now that you've done the article, call me." Tucking the phone back into its pocket, he walked away toward his friends.

"Whadda she give you? A nudie pic?" the guy in the LSU tee said. His skinny brown arms, heavily tattooed, hung out of it like limp ropes, no football player he.

His buddy, a university ball cap pulled low over his eyes, guffawed. "I bet she got no hair on her c…"

"Shut up. She's a nice kid." Ty approached with his muscles bunched as if he'd take them both down in a single tackle. Most likely could.

Kid? They were exactly the same age. Yes, she'd heard that vulgar remark and didn't need him to defend her. She came up behind Tyson, catching him off guard. "Any man who makes a remark like that about a woman has no balls, or I'd hit you in them right now."

"Oh, I'm so scared," jerk number two said and put a hand on her forehead as if fending her off.

"Don't touch me, you creep." She bunched her hand into a fist and drew it back. Ty shoved it down and slapped away the hand clutching her hair.

"You should be scared. Her brother is Rex Billodeaux. You'll have the whole football team out to get you if you touch her again, me included. Go over to Chimes, get a table, and some brews." His questionable companions stood and slouched toward the university gates.

"I don't know why you'd hang out with pricks like that."

The skinny one turned back. "Because we got the best weed, right, Ram?"

"I told you what to do. Now do it." That honey complexion darkened, and his eyes burned gold. Edie suspected he wore his game face, fierce, very fierce.

"Sorry about this. My mama raised me better." All the smug had left his handsome visage.

"Theirs didn't. They could get you into trouble. Find better friends. I have to get on the road. Maybe I'll see you at our Fourth of July bash. All of Rex's friends are invited. If not, then next semester."

"Who knows?" That teasing glint in his eyes had returned. He made the Call Me sign with his hand. Why did he enjoy messing with her so much?

"Don't hold your breath waiting." She shouldered her backpack and marched back to her apartment.

Chapter Seven

Independence Day burst forth at Lorena Ranch like the sky rockets they'd set off later in the evening, full of heat and color. The event drew about the same number of people as the fireworks held downtown: Sinners players, retired and new plus their families; a vast amount of Billodeaux relatives; and college friends of Rex, mostly. Edie reflected that she'd spent so much time catching up on her course work she hadn't really socialized or bothered with the hassle of dating while Rex had a built-in group with his football team buddies and a girl on his arm whenever he held it out.

She noticed Tyson Ramsey among her brother's guests, not that she'd been looking for him. He wore jeans cut off at the knees, pricey athletic shoes, and an old jersey with his number on it, the sleeves ripped off to show his guns tattooed with an LSU Tiger on one bicep and a ram with actual golden horns on the other. No, she would not approach him to get a better look. Plenty of Sinners' female offspring were already doing that along with some of her cousins.

A small commotion in the parking area drew her attention away from the picnic table where Ty held court. Someone parked a silver Mercedes sedan a distance away from the huge SUVs and double cab pickups. Dr. Connor Bullock slid out of the driver's side and went around to the passenger door, but it had already been flung open by her sister Jude. Mama Nell had crossed half the space already and arrived to wrap her daughter in a hug that she then turned on Connor, squeezing his waist with abandon since he'd inherited some height but not the massive bulk of his father, Revelation Bullock, a legendary Sinners cornerback. He'd been like family since his birth.

Edie went to join the greeting party. While Jude had put in a brief appearance at Christmas, almost mandatory in the Billodeaux family, she'd skipped Easter, and hemmed and hawed about coming for the Fourth.

Nell finally released her grip. "Thank you so much for bringing her, Connor. I know you are both very busy, but we never see enough of the two of you. I haven't really been able to tell you how much I appreciate the way you took care of Jude when she caught Covid and I wasn't allowed to go to her."

Her mom got a little teary-eyed, but Jude answered with her usual brusqueness. "Except for the splitting headache and fatigue, it wasn't a big deal. Yet he insisted on leaving me meals and groceries at the bottom of my steps and checking on me when he went off duty. I don't know what he would have done if I hadn't answered when he shouted what he'd brought. I told him I was entirely capable of ordering takeout by myself."

Connor switched his wire-rimmed glasses for prescription sunglasses and covered those green eyes he'd gotten from his light-skinned mother's side of the family. They weren't as gorgeous as Ty's, but then whose were? He'd taken to shaving his black hair, less trouble, more hygienic, he claimed, and now had a shiny light brown dome that added to his gravitas as a sought-after orthopedic surgeon.

53

"I would have run up those stairs, ascertained your condition, and admitted you to the hospital. We lost two valued medical colleagues to Covid. Granted they were older than us, but I was not going to lose another. Then, I'd have quarantined myself for two weeks."

"Depriving your patients of care," Jude shot back.

They'd gone ring-around-the-rosy about this before. Edie interrupted to change the subject. "Nice ride, Connor. New?"

"Yes, its first outing. No sense in both Jude and I driving here alone and wasting gas."

"It is more comfortable than mine, I will admit," said Jude who rarely admitted anything and still drove her subcompact from her college years. "Don't make anything out of it."

"Well, your parents are already here. I think your father is helping Joe supervise the pig pit and your mother is in the pavilion getting things set up there. They will be so happy to see you." Nell led the way to the shade under the live oaks. "Cold drinks anyone?"

Brinsley the butler appeared as if by magic with a selection of brews on his tray. He wore Bermuda shorts and sandals with white socks, but he had such formidable dignity no one mocked him—ever. Jude and Connor made their choice while Edie went to one of the many coolers and fished out an icy Coke Zero. They settled at a table near the barbecue pavilion, Jude and Connor side by side, Edie peering at them from across the way.

She studied her sister and their long-time family friend. They sat not touching but closer than mere friends. Let's see. To leave groceries for Jude, Connor had to have a key and the entry code to her apartment over the Korean electronics store. Her dad had turned the place into a fortress for his girls, complete with hidden security cameras. Not unusual to give a friend a house key, but still.

Unlike her sister, Xochi, she didn't see or read auras, but was picking up a vibe here. Xo once said Jude and Connor both had flaming orange auras full of ambition, pride, and self-sufficiency. Nothing wrong with that but one reason Xo had settled on gentle Junior for a husband rather than Connor who had seriously dated her with marriage in mind. He would not have accepted her work as a *traiteur*, a Cajun herbal healer, and had in fact told her auras might be cured with drugs or surgery. Some said Xo had the gift of healing with the laying on of hands. She denied this. Couldn't cure cancer or mend broken bones, but she could lend the ill the strength to overcome their challenges, sort of an immune system boost, she said. She and Connor were so wrong for each other, but he hadn't chosen another. Until—maybe Jude.

With her face cupped by her hands, elbows resting on the table top, she blurted it out. "You two have so much in common you should get married. You aren't getting any younger."

The targets of her comment did not protest as much as she thought they might. Ah-ha!

"We're not old, Edie, it's just that you are still a kid.

That always riled her, and Jude knew it. "I'm twenty-one, Jude."

Connor didn't play the distraction game as well as her sister. "I've asked her to move in with me, tried proposing, offered to get her the ring of her choice, but it's always she's happy with things the way they are. I keep reminding her that a woman in her thirties doesn't have many reproductive years left."

"And I told you I don't care because I don't want children." Jude rapped her beer bottle so hard on the table, Edie half-feared her sister might break the glass and use it as a weapon against Connor for having the nerve to say such a thing.

"We have great genes and owe it to society to have a least one child. Besides, my mother wants more grandkids."

"Let your sister have them. One of these days Li'l Joe will settle down and get married. She'll get her wish, but not from me. No children, do you hear?"

"Um, it's good you two have discussed this issue beforehand," Edie said, trying her best to clean up the mess she'd made, though her instincts had been spot on. Despite her psychology minor, she didn't see a future for herself as marriage counselor.

A sweeter voice intervened. Annie sat down next to her twin sister and put an arm around her shoulder. "Does he know everything?"

"Yes, so he should understand."

"What happened to you years ago has no bearing on the here and now. Don't deprive yourself because of it."

Edie's glance swiveled from one face to another, all in possession of a secret she didn't comprehend. Annie's three little boys, the one she'd adopted, the one she'd given birth to, and the one belonging to her husband's former sister-in-law, clambered up on the bench beside her. They followed Annie around like goslings did a mother goose. Not the oldest, but the biggest and boldest, Gabe, attained the table top and shinnied toward his mother's lap. Annie plucked him up and offered her boy to Jude.

"Here, hold one," Annie said as if offering her sister

a puppy.

"They're always sticky or wet." Jude folded her arms tight.

"All of them are housebroken now." She nuzzled Gabe. "Are you sticky?"

"Nope, not now. Mama Nell washed us after we had red Popsicles." The child held out his hands for inspection, but his lips were still rosy from the treat.

"I'll take him," Connor said. "Hand him across to me, Jude."

Jude refused to comply, so Annie set Gabe up on the picnic table and let him walk into Connor's arms. "Hiya, Uncle Con."

"He isn't your Uncle Con, yet," Jude snapped.

Although not entirely comfortable, Connor settled the dark-haired, sturdy Gabe on his knees. "Tell me, little man, do you want to be a doctor when you grow up?"

"No, a football player like Dad."

"You do know you can get serious concussions playing football?"

"What is…"

"Um, a brain owwie."

Even Jude laughed and let down her guard. Annie reached over the table and moved the smaller blue-eyed, blond Drew into her lap. "Here, this one is really tame and might end up going into medicine. He's very bright, and he loves to cuddle." Not to leave Daniel out, the once premature baby she'd cared for in the NICU, Annie lifted him to her lap where he stared up at her with happy dark blue eyes almost covered by a shock of black hair.

"Oh, I have to get a picture of this," Edie exclaimed and pulled out her phone. She leaned way over to get them all in the shot, too far back, and just as she clicked the shutter, she found herself toppling toward the ground. Two strong arms caught her and set her upright again. Probably Rex, but no, not Rex's arms. These were dark honey furred with gold.

"Does she get herself in trouble a lot?" Tyson Ramsey asked.

"Not really, but sometimes curiosity and gravity get the better of her," Annie answered. "Did you take the picture, Edie? They're starting to squirm to get down."

"I'm not sure." She handed her phone over, all too aware that Ty still stood behind her.

"Oh, yes, you did. It's so adorable. Look at Drew all snuggled into Jude." Annie reversed the phone and snapped another shot. "Here, one of you and the man who saved you from a brain owwie. Tyson Ramsey, I presume."

"I'm surprised you recognize me."

"Oh, we all follow LSU football as if it were a religion."

False modesty, Eddie thought, but she had to make introductions. "My twin sisters, Annie and Jude, Dr. Connor Bullock on the end, and the boys are mostly my nephews, Gabe, Drew, and Danny."

"That's a lot of family."

"You don't know the half of it."

"Hey," another voice intruded. Now, Rex showed up of course. "My dad is signing up the teams for the dragon boat races, Ty. If you want to be in my crew we have to hurry. Edie, you're my drummer, right?"

"Anything I can do for my dear brother."

"We have to claim the small, light ones to keep the beat or else we'll have a heavier load, which we don't want. Come on."

"See you later," Ty said in general to everyone, Edie was certain.

Rex moved off with his cohorts toward the man with the clipboard, his dad saying, "Last time for crew members" in his audible calling voice.

Dre, Drew's mom, a slim young woman, her blonde hair cut pixie style, approached their table. Her haircut made her blue eyes seem bigger. "Your turn for a break, Annie. Enjoy some time with your sisters. Boys, how about pony rides?" Now the children wriggled in earnest to be set free. As soon as their small sneakers hit the ground, they raced off toward the corral with Dre one step behind.

Edie watched Tyson turn his head as Dre jogged by the clot of men signing up for the boat races, checking out the blue-eyed blonde. She was about the same age as herself but far more mature looking. He'd probably lose interest if he learned she'd had a son at the age of seventeen and wasn't simply an au pair. Though Dre had a good arrangement with Matt and Annie, Edie often pitied her with a future much more limited than she and Rex had by having a baby so young.

"We'd hire a nanny of course so the child wouldn't interfere with your practice," Connor said as his gaze also followed Dre and the herd of children.

"Will you leave it alone," Jude demanded.

"Okay, enjoy your day off," Edie piped up. She'd started the discussion but didn't want to finish it. Off she went to offer help with the pony rides as she and Rex usually did, but not her brother, not this Fourth. None of his friends turned her way.

****

Daddy Joe supervised the raising of the roasted pigs

from the earthen umu oven. They emerged from their wrappings of banana leaves dripping luscious juices and sending the aroma of well-cooked pork into the air. One pig earned a spot on a slab of wood to be hoisted onto the shoulders of six young men and carried throughout the campground as a message that dinner was soon to be served. The other earned a placed on the buffet table where big Rev Bullock began carving. An occasional piece of the crispy skin found its way into his mouth. Simply watching the gesture made Edie's mouth water.

The custom started when Adam Malala, a football player from American Samoa, had stayed with the Billodeauxs the summer Teddy and Stacy joined the family, long before Edie and Rex came into the world. It continued on despite the Malalas not being present this year. Having holed up in their home in Florida during the Covid epidemic, they'd gone for an extended stay in Samoa to aid the villages there. Edie had heard the story that Teddy helped bring Adam and his wife together in the palm grove, also laid out by Adam, so why was her suggestion to Connor and Jude terrible?

Her dad raked foil-wrapped yams, plantains, and potatoes from the pit to add to the table already crowded with side dishes brought by the guests. Some were labeled with a skull-and-crossbones, indicating they contained Joe's lethal hot sauce. That task finished, he beat on a large, wrought iron triangle to summon those not on the route of the pig which was returning from the palm grove and sand volleyball court followed by her sister Lorena wearing her Olympic gold medal for the sport—earned with her partner Maisie Morton for Australia which some people would never forgive. She handled it well by saying that with Maisie now retired, the next one would be for the USA. She'd had to delay her victory when the Olympics were canceled for a year, Covid of course. Now, she wore the medal not out of vanity but because so many asked to see it having it around her neck only made it easier.

Those flushed from the shade of the palms or the heat of the court ran at her heels as if she carried the Olympic torch—which she might in a few more years. Her brothers may have Heismans and Super Bowl rings, but only Lori had gone to the Olympics and triumphed. Edie admired her so much and tried not to be jealous of those long, tanned legs, lengthy straight black hair pulled back into a French braid, and well, nicer boobs than she had. She didn't have an athletic bone in her body unless you counted drumming on a dragon boat once a year.

Lori had married the Aussie, Jock Brown, three years ago at this same gathering. In their honor, a three-tiered wedding cake formed the centerpiece of the dessert table. He pounded along beside his wife, all six-feet-six of him, making even the six-foot Lori appear small. Edie admitted to herself that she'd crushed a little on Jock all the while encouraging Lorena to accept his ring. Heck, she'd eaten Vegemite to impress that man. But she was way over that now, much more mature and grown up.

Done with the summoning, Daddy Joe acted as gatekeeper to the barbecue pavilion. He announced that families with young children went first. Edie noticed that meant with two little girls Teddy and Jessie in their wheelchairs entered before any others, and he hadn't called attention to their handicap at all. How she loved her dad, and there weren't many like him—if you didn't count her brothers.

She fell in with Lori's group almost lost in that forest of long limbs, but that made no difference once she sat down with a full plate at one of the extra tables set up for the occasion and listened to Jock tell tales of Australia, his brothers, one now an EMT and the other interning to be a doctor. During the lockdown, they'd housed Maisie's family which included a crying baby girl, two small boys, and two recently acquired Australian shepherd dogs he'd bought for their Covid anniversary. Setting up a sand volleyball court at his winery, the women continued to practice throughout the crisis giving them an edge when the Olympics came around again the following year.

"There we were surrounded by enough wine to knock us all on our arses, but I'm the one changing the nappies on Lori Junior, and mucking out the stalls for the quarter horses, which amounts to the same thing, because Maisie's husband is working from home, our home, and the ladies are staying in shape."

"Good practice for later," Edie quipped and started to devour a dab of Mawmaw Nadine's famous bread pudding, the last thing she could cram into her stomach.

Lori nearly choked on a bite of wedding cake. "How did you know we were trying? We didn't tell anyone."

She shrugged. "Because it's a few years before the next Olympics and now is a good time. Logical."

"She hears too much, she sees too much," her sister claimed. "Always nosy."

"Because no one will tell me anything." Edie guessed she'd have to find another crowd to join before the boat races. Time to push back from the table and snooze in the shade before the big event. She did exactly that, lying down on a blanket spread by Jessie for her girls to nap.

****

With Lizzy and May glued to her body by sweat, Edie awoke to the sound of her dad's bellowing voice and the clang of the triangle. "Teams for the dragon boat races assemble along the bayou. Get your life vests on early."

His announcement set an exodus toward the water in motion. Guests folded their chairs and grabbed their beach towels to relocate for the best view. Edie rubbed the sand from her eyes and felt the welt left on her face by a fold in the blanket. Running her hands through her hair confirmed that the humidity had done its work on making her curls go out of control, not much different from Lizzy.

Rex bore down on her. "Wake up. We're in the first heat." He gazed around. "Where's Ramsey? I gave him a center oar. Look around for him, Edie. I need to get my team lined up." Off he went full of urgency as if this were an Olympic event.

She stood and stretched. Knowing she'd be someone's drummer, she'd prudently dressed in khaki shorts, a sleeveless top, athletic shoes, and sunscreen. No feminine sundress and sandals for her today. Glancing around, she saw no sign of the bleached blond topknot that stood out in a crowd. The camp cabins were kept locked and the house declared off limits for the Fourth party. Only those overcome by heat or alcohol would be given sanctuary, but no way did Mama Nell want to encourage the many teens and college students in any sexual hanky-panky.

But the barn doors stood open to accommodate the tired ponies with water, shade, and what breeze existed.

She moved against the rip tide of humanity and angled toward its wide entry. Walking the length of the building, her eyes adjusting to the dim light, she stroked a velvety nose here and scratched some ears there as horses hopeful for a carrot or apple slice nickered for her attention. "Sorry, guys and girls, only passing through."

She checked empty stalls along the way and considered climbing up into the hay loft when she spotted that blond crown of hair illuminated by a beam of sun at the far door. Ty Ramsey lounged against a bale of straw. He drew in a deep breath and exhaled a cloud of smoke from the joint in his hand. Her nose wrinkled and took in the distinctive aroma of marijuana. She didn't use, but had scented it often enough leaking from behind closed doors in campus housing. What he smoked wasn't the worst of it.

She charged the remaining distance and snatched the doobie from his fingers. He offered her a lazy smile. "If you want a toke, just say so."

"I wouldn't pollute my mind or body with that stuff, but that's up to you. I know you're a city boy, but no one smokes anything in the barn with all the straw and hay around the place. Start a fire and some of these animals don't get out alive." She ground the joint out under her heel, then picked it up and doused it in the water barrel kept for the horses. After that, she shredded it to bits and scattered it outside the rear door.

"Overkill, don't you think? I needed some space away from all this, your perfect family, your perfect life." He waved a hand slowly as if clearing cobwebs.

"Hardly perfect if you know us. I don't want anyone to find evidence of that stuff around here. My folks don't allow drugs on the ranch. A person that uses here is not invited back."

"Aw, so sweet. You don't want me to be thrown out of the party."

"Not right now. Rex is waiting for you to row. It's his first year as a captain, and he's eager to win. You are in no condition to help him."

"It's just a silly game, Edie." The same laconic smile stayed in place.

"So is football. You could be thrown off the team for this."

"Medical marijuana is completely legal here and soon recreational will be."

"Right, I suppose you have a prescription."

"Hey, I've got my aches and pains from playing."

"Even if I bought that excuse, you're breaking team rules. You couldn't pass the drug test right now. If my dad finds out, he'll report you."

"You gonna rat me out to him, little Edie?"

He stood up, so much stronger than she. He could easily upend her into the water barrel and hold her down, a writer's imagination kicking its way to the front of her mind. Ridiculous. He swayed and still had that stupefied expression on his face, his golden eyes gone hazy. In his current state, she might be able to do the same to him.

"No, I'm giving you a second chance. I'll go ahead and tell Rex you aren't feeling well and can't row. No team is allowed have more than four football players in the boat. One of his other friends can be drafted."

"Don't you do that. I'll be fine in a few minutes. I'll be clean by summer training. Run along, baby, and get your life vest."

"Suit yourself, but expect consequences if anyone else figures this out." Infuriated, she stomped from the barn and made for the river. She wished she had time to take a dunk in the pool and cool off, but Rex counted on her.

She said nothing as she stood in line for her vest, putting on one of the smallest kept for children and skinny adolescents. In order for the races to remain competitive, they'd made new rules, only four professional athletes could row. The rest of the crew had to be filled out by women and eager teens. Of course, Lorena and Alix, who kicked for the Sinners, were counted as pro athletes, not women. She noticed Annie climbing aboard a boat to drum for Rex's competition, her brother Dean whose crew leaned toward the female. He'd placed his brother, Mack, and Mack's wife, Sarge, behind Lori and Alix. Sarge might have only one foot, but the rest of her was trim, fit, and highly competitive. He'd also drafted his wife and Trinity's for a slot, tall blondes, one a fashion model and stronger than most knew.

Rex began to seat his crew, the gap left by Ty's absence obvious. "Edie, did you find Ramsey?"

"No," she lied. "I think you should choose someone else. He's bailed on you."

"I'll give him a few more minutes. He might be in one of the Porta Potties with all he chowed down for lunch. Or maybe he tried to be a macho man and ate some of Dad's hot sauce dishes. You gotta build up a tolerance for that. Oh well, let's get you into place." He picked her up and lifted her onto her seat behind the drum.

Inside, she fumed. Ty had called her little and baby, not in a sexual way either. Now her twin brother manhandled her into place as if she couldn't get there by herself. But she did want him to win his first race and tried again. "Just get another of your teammates to row."

"Here he comes. Ramsey, get your ass over here before we have to forfeit," Rex shouted.

Ty didn't amble along in a stupor. He appeared full of energy. "Yeah, let's get this boat out in the bayou." He pumped the air with a fist. What went on behind the dark sunshades he wore, she had no idea, but this wasn't the stoner she'd left behind in the barn.

He grabbed a flotation device and shot his arms thorough the holes, but didn't bother to buckle it. Rex did that for him. "Won't do you any good if you float out of it, and it's points off if anyone doesn't wear it right. We've had some collisions in the past that put the rowers in the water."

"I gotcha." Ty gave him an exuberant thumbs up and clambered into the only vacant seat, making the long, narrow boat wobble. The dragon head on the prow bobbed and seemed to flick its red tongue in anticipation. He high-fived his partner. "Let's win this bitch of a game."

Much as she wanted to hit him over the head with one of her mallets, she held her temper and took three deep breaths as Rex directed his awkward boat to the starting line. When both vessels were aligned, Teddy ashore, gave the signal for Joe start the race. This year DJ had the honor of setting the competition into motion by pulling the string of the miniature cannon. With a boom that sent a flock of redwing blackbirds into the air, they were off side by side along a straight stretch of bayou, each racer determined to reach the first bend in the river and win.

Edie started pounding the drum to give the rowers a rhythm, slow at first, then faster and faster until her arms burned. For all her efforts, some didn't listen to the beat. Ty's strokes went deep, then shallow, just missing entanglements with the oars in front and behind him.

"Hey, man, watch out." someone complained.

Edie noticed her brother's jaw knot before he said, "Get your act together, Ramsey. Listen to the beat."

In the end, Ty's erratic motions cost the team. Dean's experienced and more mature crew kept up a smooth rhythm and soon pulled ahead first by a tongue, then a dragon's head, then by a boat length, leaving a clean slipstream behind. Rex's vessel created its own chop turning the brown bayou water to chocolate. Dean won by a length and a half.

His crew cheered as they went across the finish line, and Dean shouted, "Age before youth!" as he slowed the boat and steered it toward the muddy bank where planks had been laid down to aid in debarking. Edie wondered if that remark referred to the fact that Rex, sure to go first in the draft, would be his competition in pro football next autumn.

"Damn, I thought we had 'em," Ty announced to one and all as he pushed a few others aside to get ashore.

Rex, frowning and not happy with Ty in the least, said, "We weren't coordinated enough. Anyhow, thanks for participating. Edie, you need help getting out?"

"No, Rex, I might be short, but I can manage." She brushed past Tyson without a word. He shouted after her. "Told you I'd be here ready to win."

She backpedaled for a moment. "Well, you didn't."

She kept right on walking, back to the starting line, back toward the barn while the rest of the crowd leaned forward to watch the next heat, taking a short detour through the barbecue pavilion for a handful of baby carrots from the nearly depleted relish tray as an excuse for going there. As she entered the shady interior scented with hay, a touch of manure, and by now, a mere whiff of pot, the horses and ponies again moved to the stall doors to greet her. She fed each one a carrot as she made her way down the row in no hurry to discover what she thought she might. But there it was, white residue on the edge of the final unoccupied stall and shallow grooves where someone had cut into it. She washed it away with water from the barrel.

Fine if Tyson Ramsey wanted to trash his life. Not her business, but she wouldn't leave any trace of his shit at the ranch.

Chapter Eight

Halfway through July, Edie finally heard from the two magazines she'd queried about the Flo's Fabulous Fashions article. The first to arrive offered the usual "not right for us" kiss off letter with no mention as to why. That sent her into a slump deep enough for family members to remark she wasn't her usual buoyant self. She blamed being out in the heat all day doing lifeguard duty or supervising outdoor Camp Love Letter activities which resumed after the Fourth. Then, she confessed she'd failed to sell an article dear to her heart while having coffee with her mother one morning.

Mama Nell consoled as usual. "We've all faced rejections in our lives. Let it strengthen you. Who knows, it might lead to better things."

Mentally, Edie surveyed her highly successful siblings, happy with their spouses and careers, not a failure among them. Even Mack, the family screw up, had matured and settled down thanks to Sarge. Her own twin stood poised for success as another great Billodeaux quarterback. She said as much.

Her mom laughed. "You were too young to know if they did or not."

"Well, there is Beck, but we all love him."

"That's right. A good thing that came from bad. Stop worrying about it."

She tried. It wasn't simply not having the article

published that ate at her. While Tyson Ramsey was not her problem, it wasn't in her nature to let another human being make a big mistake without saying something to someone. She'd thought she might use good news about her story as an excuse to call Flo and hint that her grandson faced trouble again. She'd have to work up the courage to do the right thing and get his family to set him on the straight and narrow path again.

Her dad, busy downstream, hadn't noticed Ty's erratic behavior. Rex certainly had, but as far as she knew kept it to himself. Though he wasn't pleased with losing his first race as a captain, he'd shrugged it off. Dean won often and had taken first place again along with the leis for the team Adam sent as well as a carved coconut trophy. She had to say her twin wasn't a vindictive guy.

She gave herself a few more days to mope, then set her emotions aside to make the call. But the mail arrived first—with an acceptance letter for her article, a check, and a cordial invitation that she apply for a paid internship after graduation to work at glossy *New Orleans Lifestyle*. They planned to run the story in an autumn edition and send two-plus-sized models and a photographer to hype the clothes. Picking up the phone became much easier.

"Hello, honey lamb. Nice to hear from you again."

"Flo, I have the best news. *New Orleans Lifestyle* is going to put your business in their magazine. They want to send a photographer and two models to show off your fall fashion line. Portia should have some of her custom-made items ready to go. They'll call to set up a date."

"That's as fabulous as my business. Now, little girl, are they paying you for this? Don't give nothin' away."

"I already have a check in hand. Even better, I might be able to work for them once I graduate. Everything did work out like my mother said." She took a deep breath. "One other thing I want to tell you. Ty came to our Fourth of July party at the ranch."

"That's wonderful. Are you and he…"

"No, I think he regards me as a pest, but…"

"I thought that boy had better sense than to pass on a girl like you."

"He did ask me out, but I couldn't because it wouldn't have been professional at the time since I was interviewing him." No sense in adding how obnoxious he'd been.

"Next time I see him, I'll give him a nudge in your direction."

"No, no, don't do that. Flo, I think Ty is mixed up in drugs again. He, ah, didn't seem himself at the party. Have you seen him lately?"

"We haven't, no. He's staying with friends in Baton Rouge for the summer. Says he can work out there using the LSU facilities."

More likely staying close to his dealer and away from those who might suspect what he's doing. She couldn't say that. "Maybe ask him to come home for a week or two before training starts and see if you notice any difference in his behavior."

"We'll do that. Maybe get Uncle T to talk to him man to man."

"Good. I hope my article brings you lots of business."

"Take care of yo'self, sweetie. Visit when you come to town, you hear?"

"I do. Can't wait to see y'all again. Bye." Whew,

she'd done it, and perhaps saved Tyson Ramsey's career.

****

Edie stayed on at the ranch until the last of the Camp Love Letter kids left to get ready for the start of school in mid-August. Rex had been gone weeks before for summer conditioning and practice before the new football season started the first week in September. In a further return to normal, she received the good news that Amoli would return to be her roommate again. Nice to have the company of someone serious about education who would not pressure her to party hearty and do all sorts of stunts as she'd heard her twin sisters had done many years ago. Nope, all she wanted was to work at the university newspaper and rack up as many by-lines as possible to put on her resume.

Returning to campus a little early, she lurked at the paper's headquarters hoping to get a wider range of assignments this year, and that is where she first heard the sad news as she eavesdropped on an editor's meeting. Tyson Ramsey would not be playing football for LSU in the fall.

At a very brief press conference that she begged to attend the coach stated their star free safety had failed his drug test not once but twice. The only distasteful choice for flaunting team rules was to remove him from the team. Coach wished him good luck with his future. Hands went up. What kind of drugs? He didn't answer, just shook his head in a sad way and left the podium. Edie could have answered that, one to help a person relax and another to rev his engine. She returned to the newsroom knowing more than she could say.

"Well, what did you learn since you were jonesing to attend the presser?" the news editor, another self-assured male, asked.

"Poor choice of words, Claude," the feature editor chided. Edie received most of her assignments from Natalie Gibbons, a little on the chubby side but she revised with a light hand and a kind heart. "This is a serious subject."

"Well, it isn't for the sports page anymore," Sterling Thomas said as he pushed his black-rimmed glasses back into place. "He's old news already."

"Why not let Edie nose around and see what else she can find from her, um, special contacts," Natalie suggested as she drew a pencil from a messy bun on top of her head and wrote down the assignment.

What special contacts did she have? Edie couldn't think of a one.

"She wrote that fine article about him and his family and has another one coming out in *New Orleans Lifestyle* next issue. Plus, I suspect she knows guys on the football team," Nat prompted her.

"Oh, those contacts. Sure, I'll get right on it." She left the building before making the call to Rex. The team should be off the field by now as heat grew more extreme by mid-afternoon. Her brother answered but not on the first ring. Irritation tinged his voice.

"What in hell do you want, Edie? The guys got me out of the showers for this. It's your baby sis calling, T-Rex. Must be important."

"How did they know it was me?" She thought about that for a second. "Do you have special ringtone to avoid my calls?"

"What if I do?"

"Tell me what it is, or I'll tell them you are the baby of the family not me, and weighed less at birth."

"By a few minutes and a few ounces. It's the theme from *Jaws*, okay. Look, I'm standing here dripping wet in nothing but a towel." He paused. "Did something bad happen to anyone in the family?"

While many a female would have loved to imagine that image, she'd seen plenty of her brother growing up not to care, but she did relieve his mind immediately. "No, not our family. I heard Tyson Ramsey was kicked off the team for failing his drug tests."

"Yeah, he wasn't performing well since he reported for training. Plenty of rumors about what he liked to do for relaxation, but it couldn't be ignored anymore. He let us down. I mean our team is deep, someone always waiting in the wings for a chance, but he'll still be hard to replace. We were hoping to take the national championship again which will be harder without him."

"I'm sure you'll manage, but what about him? Will he have any chance of a pro career now?"

"Maybe, but he'll be way down in the rankings, and he'd have to keep in shape on his own until spring to enter the draft. Somebody will probably take a chance on him, but he'll go cheap, and they can always cut him if he can't stay clean."

"Good. Thanks for you input. May I quote you?"

"Absolutely not."

It had been worth a try. "Do you know where he is now?"

"No idea. His room in the athlete's dorm was cleaned out this morning. He lost his scholarship and all the perks that went with it. Dumbass, him, not you."

"Thanks for taking my call. But why *Jaws*?"

"Because you are relentless when you get involved with people and have a big mouth."

"A better nickname for a journalist than *Kitten on the Keys,* I guess. Go get dressed, brother."

Despite the humidity that coiled her curls and glued the phone to her ear, she'd made her way across campus and took a break on a bench in the shade by the lake behind the girls' dorms. A few hopeful ducks swam her way but reversed course when they saw she had no bread to feed them. The turtles on a log didn't give a glance her way.

Time to think this through. Did she want to be the kind of journalist who ambushed people in a time of crisis or someone who told a story with compassion? The latter of course. It's what Oprah or Gayle would do. She'd wait the few days until her article on the dress shop appeared, then call and work up to Tyson's problem.

Trudging on, trying to stay in the shade of the massive live oaks, she took a detour to the Union in order to pick up a life-saving Coke Zero and a bag of Zapp's chips. Caffeine and salt, just what she needed for restoration. She left the building at the same place where she'd spotted Tyson with his druggie friends, even looked around for them because they might know where he'd gone. No luck there. She doubted if they would have helped her unless she offered the last twenty-dollar bill in her purse.

Now, sipping and crunching, she hiked to the far side of the campus where her apartment sat. Unsettling that she found her door cracked open. Could Ty have sought her out?

No, someone who knew the key lay under the doormat, not that it was hard to figure out. Dark eyes shining from behind her glasses, Amoli stood amid her baggage. Her wide smile shone white against her darker skin and a red bindi mark rested between her brows. A modest gold ring pierced one nostril. She'd traveled in a sari, not a bad idea to cope with the heat in Louisiana but wrinkled from the trip.

Slightly impeded by the Coke and chips, Edie raced to embrace her. "So glad you're here. So sorry about your mother and grandmother. Happy about your brothers and father surviving." Both burst into tears.

When the weeping stopped, she helped Amoli carry her things to the second bedroom left exactly as before her hurried trip to India. "Good to be here. We did lose more family members. One of my aunties lost her husband. She has moved in to care for my father and brothers and made it possible for me to return. I am behind in my studies and will not graduate with you, I am afraid. I see Ganesha is still facing north as he should be."

"I kept him dusted for you," Edie remarked. Ganesha, she'd been told, was the elephant-headed god of intellectuals, authors, scribes, and oddly, bankers who made much more money than any of the others. "Modak sweets are hard to come by here so all four of his hands are empty."

"But you left him a banana which he also loves. We are sure to have good fortune this year."

Edie didn't contradict her. She often figured out of many gods, one, who had numerous saints to divvy the work among them. Perhaps, Ganesha was simply a kind, benevolent, if unusual saint. She'd put the banana at his feet yesterday anticipating her roommate's arrival.

"Why don't you unpack, and then, we'll go find some dinner. Indian food?"

Amoli laughed in that rich way of hers. "I have been

eating Indian food for many years. What I would like is Raising Cane's Chicken Fingers with fresh lemonade. Is their restaurant still open?"

"Just outside the gate as always."

"Good. Are there any changes I should know about?"

"Tyson Ramsey was kicked off the football team for using drugs."

"No! Tell me all about it."

Relieved to have a confidant she could trust who was not family or into football, she told as much as she knew, then let the topic rest until she could find out more.

Chapter Nine

As it turned out, she didn't have to call Flo. When the feature article came out in *New Orleans Lifestyle*, Flo called her.

"I tell you, baby girl, since your story hit the streets, this place has been jumpin'. Keeps up, I'll have to hire me another seamstress and a part-time clerk so I get off my feet in the afternoons."

Somehow, when Flo called her baby girl, she felt loved and not belittled. That made her all the more determined to help the Ramseys if she could, but how to tell them that?

Flo took a deep breath. Edie could imagine her great chest heaving beneath some bright cloth. "I guess you heard about my grandson being let go from the football team and why. I couldn't believe it, didn't want to even after you warned us."

"Has he come home?"

"No, and that got me worried. He did call before the news broke. I told him he better get his butt in motion and return here for a talkin' to, but, no, he hasn't showed up yet. Oh, that was hard to see, the coach on my big screen talking about him that way. So, he isn't around the campus?"

"I haven't seen him."

"If you do, you tell him Uncle T is covering his tuition for this semester since he don't have a free ride no more. He better register for classes. His mama wants him to finish and get a degree despite everything. He needs to earn a living somehow."

Edie racked her brain for something positive to say. "My brother, Rex, believes someone will take Ty if he enters the NFL draft in the spring. His football career doesn't need to be over if he stays clean and in good shape."

"Thanks for telling me that. You take care, honey lamb. Stay away from those frat boys, and come visit when you can. We might have to take this shop to a bigger location thanks to you."

She'd done a good deed with her article, but hadn't been able to stop Ty's fall to the bottom. She'd keep an eye out for him and maybe finish that story with a happy ending, too.

****

Classes began, but the heat didn't let up a bit. Coming out of the Union with an iced coffee in her hand, wondering if she had a caffeine addiction, Edie spied Tyson Ramsey moving off to the left. He'd changed so much she wondered that she'd recognized him at all. No entourage of admirers in sight, and his golden topknot gone, shaved down to a mere glint in his light brown hair. He wore a black tee free of logos or slogans with sleeves long enough to cover his tats, dark jeans and shoes as if he'd gone into mourning for himself. Though he still had an athletic stride, he walked hunched over giving the impression that his backpack contained rocks, not textbooks. The same shades that he'd worn for the boat race covered his fascinating eyes.

She almost lost him when he ducked under a limb of a live oak, discarded his backpack, and slid to the ground to rest against its trunk, making himself barely noticeable to anyone passing. Edie picked up her pace in case he changed his mind and darted out of hiding. No problem for her to follow him below the arm of the tree and take a seat on the leaf-covered earth next to him. He jerked his head in her direction.

"You again. Why don't you leave me alone like everyone else?"

"I'd like to say because I care about you, but the truth is I care more about your family. You promised me you'd be clean by the time summer training started."

"That was a statement, not a promise to you or anyone else. Did you squeal to your dad and Rex after you caught me in the barn and set me up to be caught?"

"No, I thought your word might be good. Besides, you failed yourself and your team with no help from me."

"True enough. The stress got to me. Could I perform as well as last year? Would I be dealt a career-ending injury? I needed something to take my troubles away, and then something else to pick me up to perform. I got caught. Bye-bye fame and fortune." He lowered his head, not looking her way.

He seemed to assume she'd accept his answer, but not Edie. "I'm trying to feel sorry for you but I don't. What about your plans to help your sister? Didn't that matter?"

"Big fat chance of doing that anymore. I took the easiest classes I could find to concentrate on football. My mama is insisting that I finish this year and get a diploma for all the good it will do. I don't want to be a fuckin' phys ed teacher in some random high school even if anyone would hire me with my…drug problem." He put the last words into air quotes with his fingers.

"You think you don't have one. I can smell marijuana on your clothes." In his hair, too, she sat that close to him. "Where have you been staying? I know it's late to find housing for this semester. Your grandmother is worried about you."

"With friends."

"If you mean those douche bags I saw you with, they aren't friends, they're dealers. You can do better than this. Maybe change your major. Flo said you are great with computers."

"I can't do that, stay here catching up for years. Everyone knows what I've done. I wouldn't be here at all, but good ole Uncle T said it's this or go into rehab."

"Then do rehab. Get clean. Rex says if you do that and stay in shape someone will pick you up in the draft this spring because you are that good." Not exactly what Rex had said, but a trifle of extra encouragement couldn't hurt the guy now.

"Gee, I didn't know the high and mighty King Rex cared." The sarcasm dripped like venom from his tongue. "I was his main competition for the Heisman, but now I'm out of the way. Maybe he'll win twice."

"He did say no matter what the depth of the team, they'd feel your loss. So, how about it, rehab and a second chance?"

"Uncle T is going to be pissed that he paid for this semester and I wasted his dough, but he'll still cough up the cash to put me away for a while. You're a smart girl, I guess you've figured out who he is by now."

"I'm an intelligent woman, and yes, I have. He's your daddy, your rich white daddy. He and your mother have had a long-term affair and never married because he already is. I'd bet he has another family, maybe a high-profile job. Your mother was raised Catholic and so were you with the best parochial school education. Maybe, he's Catholic, too, and his wife won't let him go. It's sad, but he appears to have looked out for you at least financially."

"Bingo. Give the little lady a stuffed tiger. You ever study black history, baby?"

"As a matter of fact, I have, boy. I took it as an elective to better understand people I might interview someday." Now she'd done it, used the boy word to retaliate against his baby. Asshole might have been a better choice. His golden skin darkened and his hands clenched.

"Do you know about *placage* in New Orleans where rich white planters came to the city and picked out black mistresses at the octoroon balls? They set them up in nice houses and had second families. Educated their offspring. It's a dirty secret. I'm a dirty secret."

She kept her cool. "That part of black history wasn't mentioned in class though I have heard of it. It's in the past. That doesn't make you dirty."

He still spoke with anger in each word. "When I was in my early teens, I thought maybe Granny had set them up that way, but no, they met right here on this campus when he came to talk to mama's poli-sci class. Granny is a good business woman and held him to his obligations. She's not afraid to ask my *uncle* for anything she feels we need. Livy's tuition at St. Mary's. Mine at St. Aug's. Our house on Esplanade is built over the area where the slaves' pens of New Orleans existed. You're the writer. Isn't that called irony? He got himself appointed to the board at St. Aug's so he'd have an excuse to come to my football games because that made him proud. Yea!"

He picked up a pinch of dirt and brown oak leaves and tossed it into the air. Some landed in his hair. Edie resisted the temptation to brush it away.

"Sounds as if he does watch over you. Is he still on the board?"

"No, you won't find out who he is that way. He does give hefty donations to the school for taking me in hand after I acted out. He'll pay for rehab if I call him."

"Call, right away while I'm sitting here."

"What, you don't trust me?"

"I do not. I'm waiting. I dare you. Prove it to me."

The Westminster chimes in the Memorial Tower rang the quarter hour. She'd be late for class if she didn't leave now, but what did punctuality matter when this man's life had reached a turning point. Sipping her now lukewarm coffee, she waited as if rooted to the ground like the live oak tree.

Ty took out his phone, punched in a speed dial number. It rang three times and was picked up by a male voice, not a secretary or a wife. No hello, no greeting. "I can't pretend I'm a student anymore. Sign me up for rehab. Yeah, I'll be home tonight." No good-bye, only a disconnect. "There, are you satisfied?"

"I'm not the one you have to satisfy, but I will check to make sure you went back to New Orleans for your own good."

"Dammit, what do you want—a pinky swear, baby?"

"If that will make it a promise." She held out her little finger.

He linked it with hers. "I swear I'll go home and get into rehab. Let me have your phone number."

"Huh? Why?" She removed her finger from his because such a small touch shouldn't be giving her inexplicable vibes.

"I gave you mine. You didn't call. Maybe I wouldn't be such a mess if you'd called."

"Again, I am not to blame for your problems." Perhaps, she should give up on being a tough journalist and get a master's in psychology.

"I'd like someone to talk to who isn't family."

"You'll get plenty of that in rehab, but fine." She took the phone still warm from his hands, entered her number into his contacts, and offered it back to him.

He didn't release her hand, but pulled her in for a kiss. The man had had a lot of practice compared to her. He knew how begin softly, prolong it with a little tongue, and end it abruptly leaving her wanting more. "Thanks, Edie." And he was gone, leaving his hiding place, striding away to an unknown destination, his backpack appearing much lighter on his shoulders.

Shaken, she decided she didn't need caffeine and poured out her coffee to water the oak. No way could she concentrate on classwork now. She'd take a cut, go back to her apartment, and write her story on the fate of Tyson Ramsey while it still burned hot in on her lips.

****

"Good job, Edie." Claude DuVal acknowledged. "*The Reveille* scooped major network news in announcing that Ramsey chose to go into drug rehab, kick his habit, and train for the NFL draft in the spring. It took you long enough, but nice."

She'd fleshed out the article with Rex's words, paraphrased and assigned to no one about how the team had depth, but would still miss Ramsey's fierce defensive skills. Ended with a prediction that he would find a pro team in the spring if he kept clean and practiced hard, still a credit to LSU where he'd gotten his start. Claude though he might have to take that last part out, but he'd run it by the coach. He might be able to use her for more assignments in the future. To be honest, she'd lost her taste for news. She'd be better off in feature writing where being positive counted.

She'd also made good on her threat to call and make sure Ty went home. Flo answered, not him. "Honey lamb, he's back with us and ready to try rehab. Thank you for that."

"It was his decision to make, not mine."

"He said you nagged him into it."

"I'd call it persuasion, not nagging. We talked. He came to the right conclusion."

"We don't care how you did it. Would you like to talk to him?" Flo took a deep, snotty breath as if she had been crying.

"No, what counts is that he is on the right track. Don't let him lie around the house. Get him into a program as soon as you can."

"Oh, we will. Don't be a stranger if you come to town. Promise me."

More promises. He wouldn't want to see her after he learned about the news article. "I'll try." She hoped Ty would as well.

Chapter Ten

So, this was rehab. Uncle T must have been well teed off when he picked the place because Tyson Ramsey did not expect to meet any spaced-out rockers or addicted movie stars between these plain and drab walls. Tough love, he guessed. The very atmosphere of the treatment facility made him crave a reefer for a little escape.

His mom had given him a tearful farewell in the lobby. Granny, solid as a boulder standing there next to a decorative plastic plant in a brass container, smashed him against the softness of her bosom. "You get well now, you hear?" He wanted to claim he wasn't sick, but that would get him nowhere.

As for Livy, they let her believe he was returning to campus. She begged to go along to see Mike the Tiger in his habitat complete with a waterfall and grab some of the rich ice cream made by the university students and sold at the AgCenter Dairy Store. She wanted a cup of Tiger Bite made with golden vanilla ice cream and blueberries.

His mother, adept at lying, fobbed her off by saying they had no time for that and were just dropping him off and coming right back, but she could stay the afternoon with her best friend to soften the blow. Blow, he wished he had some of that right now, too. Livy always cuddled up with Gran to watch the LSU away games. She'd notice his absence. What would they tell her then?

Checking in meant giving up his belongings, his phone—and his dignity in a strip search of every body cavity. Being naked wasn't a big deal for him. He'd been in plenty of locker rooms. But being probed came as a shock to his system and created a deep desire to tell the prober with his blue latex gloves that he had no criminal record, wasn't hiding anything, and didn't deserve this treatment. He sensed they'd heard all that before, gritted his teeth after the mouth check, and bore it. Once he got through the intake interview, he expected to be escorted to his room. Nope, escorted to the detox center for a five day stay and taking more drugs than he had on the street to help with any withdrawal symptoms.

Librium for anxiety, and he couldn't deny that he didn't suffer from that. Something to help him sleep, though he'd never had a problem sleeping. An antidepressant which he started to deny he needed, but considering how he'd felt that afternoon under the oak tree with Edie, lower than the beetles in the oak duff, maybe he did. Constant blood tests, monitoring of blood pressure day and night—and he did well, got off easy compared to the heroin addicts younger than himself and middle-aged alcoholics dealing with the DTs. Physically, his condition outshone them all since he'd only recently left training.

Some spent all their time sleeping, and he had to admit the drugs made him dozy. He fended that off by walking, learning the layout, meeting the staff and any patients willing to talk.

He dreaded the moment when someone would recognize him as a former sports star, but in the detox wing, those around him had more serious issues to deal with, making him feel almost safe from discovery among them. Those five days flew past.

Out in the general population, he acquired a roommate, no private suite for him. He had the feeling they were supposed to watch each other and report any breaking of the rules. He wanted out of this place as soon as possible and had no intention of doing so, but his assigned roommate, Lenny, a kid of nineteen from Lafayette who had already been in rehab twice for a meth problem that showed in his skinny body and bad teeth, proceeded to tell him how to beat the system, what to say in group sessions, and offered to hook him up with some good shit when he got out. Like a child he wanted to stuff his fingers in his ears and mouth la-la-la to drown him out. After all, he'd made a pinkie swear to be here and might as well give it an honest try whether he needed it or not.

Perhaps, he should have gone into the military strict as the rules and schedules were: up at six a.m., dressed and bed made by seven, breakfast from seven to eight, and small group session right after with a therapist, many more of these throughout the day. He couldn't gripe about the food, plain but plentiful, always eggs in some form, bacon and sausage, grits, cereal, juice and milk for breakfast, weak coffee if asked for, and seconds if you wanted. Pancakes on Sundays. Soup and sandwiches with fruit cups and pudding for lunch, sometimes large burgers with a choice of toppings. Dinner: usually something served over rice with a salad and vegetables, maybe an ice cream for dessert. The alcoholics who craved sweets during withdrawal griped about the lack of cake and pie. Ty ate what they put before him. He didn't want to lose his fighting weight and turn scrawny like the meth addicts.

He'd dreaded having to confess to a group. When asked who he blamed for his problem, he answered his mother and father, thought about Edie, and changed that to "And myself, I guess." He received a small round of applause for getting to that conclusion so fast. But when asked why he'd first blamed his parents, he couldn't explain honestly, only mumbled that they'd never married, carried on a long-term affair that he felt was wrong.

"Is that all?" responded a middle-aged woman, maybe younger than she looked with no makeup and bleached blonde hair in need of a touch up along the part. The lines of a heavy smoker marred her face. "My old man seldom had a sober day in his life and knocked my mother around just because he could. I thought that was how you dealt with the world—alcohol and violence. At least, your folks shared love. That's kind of romantic."

He had to admit he'd never seen Uncle T drunk or noticed a single mark on his mother's face or body. He supposed Livy was a testament to long-standing love and commitment.

Others had darker stories of being raised in meth labs or raiding their father's stash of cocaine at an early age. He considered his nice home, his loving Granny and beautiful mom, a little sister he adored, and shut his mouth.

Lunch and then lectures on topics like coping with anxiety without drugs, helpful but would take some practice. Others seemed pointless or irrelevant to him, but attending was not optional. Recreational therapy time consisted of volleyball games or long walks. Sometimes, he chose to run laps. At other times smashing a volleyball across the net helped with his anger at being in this place when he seemed to have fewer problems than most of those around him. More groups afterward.

Diner and mandatory Narcotics Anonymous or AA meetings. After that, an hour or two of free time before lights out, a little TV though channels were limited or a friendly card game. Anything that passed the time and didn't trigger yearnings for drugs or alcohol.

Staffing ran light on weekends, so fewer groups. Gatherings to watch the Sinners games or LSU play went high on the desirable list. Until that first Tigers game without him, he'd felt sheltered from the truth. Only his family and Uncle T knew where he lived. Edie didn't have his address. Yet when LSU's defense didn't hold up well in the first half, the commentators rehashed the whole story of his disgrace and wished him a speedy recovery in rehab. Where did they get that information?

He hunched down on his folding chair toward the back of the common room painted an institutional medium green, hoping no one would recognize the arrogant young man with the bleached-blond topknot as Ty in group session. He kept his head bowed as he passed the bowl of communal snacks purchased from the vending machines with coins from the accounts set up for small luxuries by loving families and shared with those who didn't have any. He'd paid for half of them and took none, not wanting so much as the crunch of a chip to turn heads his way. Still, some of the guys up front whispered and glanced over their shoulders. At least none of the old alkies shouted or pointed, "That's him, Tyson Ramsey, the kid who let down LSU." And himself.

Sunday and phone calls were allowed to specific numbers on a preapproved list. He spent his fifteen minutes on his Granny, Mama, and Livy. Uncle T never, and Edie, listed as his girlfriend, not yet. As his time passed and neared the end of a month, he wanted to call her, brag a little about how well he'd done, how he'd be out any day now, ready to start training and find an agent for his football career. He held off. Sometimes, he wanted to jump the fence and hitchhike back to New Orleans. Nothing wrong with him, oh, no. Other times, the hospital felt like a safe place he never wanted to leave to face the outside world awaiting his reappearance. Truth was since he'd been committed voluntarily, he could sign himself out at any time—but didn't do it.

The last week in the month, he'd had another breakthrough in his private session with the shrink assigned to him. No sofa to stretch out on in her small office, just a comfortable chair facing her desk and a pothos plant, its green leaves streaked with yellow, growing vigorously down its side. The bookshelves behind Dr. Octavia Diaz supported dozens of family pictures including her dogs and cats. In quiet moments when he didn't know what to say, he could trace the growth of her little brown children, two boys and a girl, and a parade of pets over the years. Now, his eyes on a calm black lab replaced by an eager, panting golden retriever, he pondered how to answer her question as she waited, peering at him over the top of her tortoise shell glasses with patient brown eyes. "Is your father proud of you?"

Finally, he answered. "You mean the man who pretends to be my uncle? Hell, no, not now. He was, I guess, from the time I showed talent in football when in middle school. Never missed one of my games even if he had to drive from Baton Rouge to see them. He paid for the best seats in Tiger Stadium and made sure my mom and granny and my sister had tickets, too—as far from him as possible. After a game when I performed well, he'd come by the locker room and give me a pat on the back. Once he said, 'Who wouldn't want a boy like this for a son?' That's the closest he ever came to acknowledging me."

"You don't think he is proud that you've sought help?" she prodded, her face so kind and motherly, her voice demanding an answer.

"He gave me the choice to come here or continue in college to get a degree without playing football. I tried the second and couldn't handle the humiliation. There's this girl…"

"A girlfriend?"

"Not hardly. She's kind of a pest, a cute, little pest, but she tells it like it is, no awe for me at all. She noticed I wasn't doing well and…and encouraged me to get help, not my dad, her." No way would he tell her about the pinky swear.

"Interesting. You really felt you had no other alternatives—like going out on your own, getting a job, or sliding down the slippery slope of using harder drugs?"

"No to that last, I won't do that. Look where a little coke and pot landed me."

"Good observation," Dr. Diaz doled out a compliment. "If you have that kind of control, why did you fail your drug test? You knew it was coming up. Why not hold off for a few days and test clean?"

Yeah, why? He'd gotten some especially good weed

and celebrated the purchase with friends, none of them on the team. When he'd come down, it was drug test day and skipping it would get him into trouble. Going had the same result. Then, they'd done a rapid retest, and he'd failed again. Goodbye career in football. Why had he thrown it away? The answer came to him. "Because I wanted to take that pride in me away from my father."

"You do realize you also punished yourself."

"I do now. And shamed my mother, granny, and sister who love me unconditionally."

"What about this girl? How does she feel?"

"That I'm not her problem. And she's right. When I'm done here, I'll find a trainer to stay in shape and enter the NFL draft in the spring. I guess that would be going out on my own."

"Good for you. Time's up. Go on, take a lollipop." Dr. Diaz pointed to a bowl on her desk that had to be made by a kid with no exceptional talent in making pottery, lopsided as it was.

Childish, silly, yet he selected a cherry one to go. Sunday, he'd call Edie.

Chapter Eleven

Slow as the line was to make a call, he maintained his patience, glad some people wanted to hear from him. Many in this place had none. The woman in charge of keeping time and dialing a number on his list reminded him of his granny, large and dark but not as flamboyantly dressed. "Calling your honey?" she remarked, though she probably shouldn't have said anything. Only the shrinks were allowed to pry into your private life.

"A friend." He took the receiver of the old-fashioned telephone and listened to the ring tone. Brrrg, brrrg, brrg. Edie failed to pick up. Right, she wouldn't recognize this number, probably thought it was one those random prison calls that sometimes popped up. By now, he could understand how even a con might want a friendly conversation. Brrrg, brrrg, brrrg.

He was about to tell Dorice, according to her name tag, to try his mother's number when he heard Edie's breathless voice on the line. "Hello?"

"Did I catch you at a bad time? It's Ty, Tyson Ramsey, calling from rehab heaven," he said as if she might need reminding.

"Ah, yes. I'm so sorry."

"About what? You're the one who convinced me to come here."

"About doing an article for *The Reveille* on your future plans. I guess you didn't see it. Every sports news outlet picked it up. If it helps, Coach said he hated to see such talent wasted and wished you a successful rehabilitation and career."

Ty took three deep belly breaths as one of his session instructors taught to control anger and anxiety. "I heard the word was out when I watched the LSU game. I can't deny it. It is what it is—but I should soon be out of here."

"That's great, wonderful!"

"I had a major breakthrough in my analysis. Hell, my shrink gave me a red lollipop, I did so good." There, he'd turned momentary anger into humor. Doing good, Ty.

"Really? You get lollipops as rewards?" She laughed, light and girly, so different from the tears and trials of group sessions.

"They're as good as cigarettes for currency here. Two guys offered me a dollar for it, but I ate it myself. Three, it takes three bites to get to the chocolate center. I'm getting so deep I'm solving universal questions now."

"Would you like me to send you a whole box of them?"

"Not allowed. Who knows what could be injected into the center? Forget about brownies and gummies, too. No outside foods at all."

"Sounds like prison." All the laughter had vanished from her voice.

"Pretty close to it."

"Again, I'm sorry." She did sound repentant. Just how much regret did she have?

"Nothing to be sorry about as I needed this, but it would be nice to have a reward waiting for me when I get out, like would you sleep with me?"

"What did you say?" She punctuated that with a small gasp.

"Sleep with me. I'm sure not getting any here. I did what you wanted me to do, and now you won't sleep with a guy who's been to drug rehab?"

"I don't sleep with anyone, and it was your decision, not mine." Outrage, and he'd provoked it.

"So, you're a virgin, little girl?" And went on to make it worse.

"I mean I'm no one's reward. Your reward is getting clean and moving on to the football career you wanted. This little girl is hanging up." If she hadn't been on a cell phone, she would have slammed the receiver. He'd turned away from Dorice, trying to get a little privacy, but Edie's voice had been loud enough to have the woman shaking her head and holding out her hand for the receiver.

He'd done it again, sabotaged his chance of getting something he really wanted, not Edie in bed, though he imagined it sometimes at night. Sure, she was small, but he figured she'd be lively. No, what he truly wanted was her respect, not easily earned. If he became successful again, the easy women would be back, hanging on his arm, offering to do whatever he wanted. Not Edie. If she'd been here in person, she'd probably sock him in the nuts, and he deserved it.

He'd messed up his career with drug use to get back at his father and hurt himself even more. Now, he'd erected a barrier between himself and the one woman who would always tell it like it is straight to his face, never loading on insincere compliments or lying. Why? Because he didn't deserve her, punishing himself again.

"Sorry you heard that, Miss Dorice," he said to the woman who looked so much like his granny. "I was way out of line."

"Uh-huh. I've heard worse, son. Only thing you hurt was your chance with this young lady. Too bad. You started out good."

"I'm signing up for another thirty days. I still have work to do."

"Good idea. See you next Sunday."

Chapter Twelve

To think, she'd gotten up early and spent her Sunday morning at St. Alban's, the Episcopal chapel on campus, to pray for that jerk, hadn't even stayed for the hospitality afterwards, which usually had superior baked goods, she was being so selfless. Heck, she'd left Ganesha another banana on his behalf. She'd answered an unknown caller number hoping to hear from him because Flo kept in touch and told her that was when he'd call—if ever. Run up the steps to her apartment while trying to extract her phone from a purse, so eager to hear from him, yet dreading her confession about the newspaper article.

That part had gone well. He'd shown some maturity, and she felt forgiven as they joked about lollipops. Then that lewd suggestion. He'd jumped pretty far and fast from teasing her in his interview about not dating black men. She blocked the number he'd used to get to her. They were done. But had they ever started? Sure, sure, at times she'd fantasized about what it might be like to have sex with him. Would her complete inexperience show? Could she make up for that with sheer enthusiasm? No use wondering now.

From the small open kitchen, the spicy aroma of chicken curry filled the apartment. Amoli took a moment to turn her head from Sunday dinner preparations toward Edie and ask who'd called. "Nobody, uh, it was Tyson Ramsey."

"Nobody now? He was the Big Man on Campus after your brother, Rex, not so long ago, but I have been away." She stirred her concoction, sniffed in the scent of the ten spices she'd added and took a small taste with another spoon. "Almost ready now. I need only to add the cream."

"My turn to cook next Sunday since I won't be going to church. I'll get fish or seafood."

"Sit down, stop pacing." Amoli set full bowls on the small dining table and laid down spoons. She poured two cups of masala chai tea and took her seat. "Now tell me what went wrong with Tyson Ramsey. Is he not still in rehab?"

Edie took a few comforting sips of the chai. A little heavy on the ginger, it opened her sinuses. Good because she wanted to cry. She dabbled her spoon in the curry and took a bite. Not too spicy for a girl raised on Cajun food. "The tea and the curry are both very good."

"Thank you. Tell me what you really want to say." Her friend, Molly, pushed a basket of naan bread forward but didn't take her deep brown eyes cloaked in wire-rimmed glasses off of her.

"I suppose he called to tell me he was getting out soon because he'd had a big breakthrough. I confessed right away that I'd written an article about him getting help for his drug problem." She tore off a piece of naan and dipped it in the curry, postponing the rest of the conversation.

"That is very good for your karma. I know you have been worried about it." Molly waited patiently, sipping her own tea. "What did he say?

"That I'd told the truth and it was okay. Best curry ever."

"You spoke about curry?"

"Ah, no. Lollipops, just joking around. Then, he said he deserved a reward for his progress and would I sleep with him when he got out."

Molly made a sucking sound with her teeth. "That is very bad. It shows no progress of the soul to ask for such a reward for doing right."

"I told him that more or less and hung up. I hope I never hear from him again. To think I've been going to church to pray from him for all the good it did." She applied herself to her curry with more appetite now, but Amoli did not let it go.

"You need not go to church to pray. I say mine in my room whenever I think they will not disturb you. Perhaps, he still needs those prayers whether he knows it or not."

"You aren't saying I should sleep with him when he gets out?"

"No, no. Being well and in balance is its own reward, but some extra spiritual help does not hurt."

"What I told him. Anyhow, I am done with Tyson Ramsey." She scraped her bowl. "Did you make anything for dessert, or should we go for ice cream, my treat?"

"We have kheer to sweeten your mood. I'll get it." Molly fetched a bowl of Indian rice pudding redolent with rosewater, cardamon, colored with saffron, and studded with nuts. Its flowery scent filled their nostrils, and Edie reached out with a spoon.

"Stop. First, I will take a portion to Ganesha. You know he likes his sweets." Molly put a dab into a dessert dish and left Edie to her own thoughts for a moment. When she returned, they split the rest between them.

"Are you by any chance praying for me, Amoli Bhat?" She savored a mouthful and swallowed.

"As I said, prayers are helpful to anyone."

"Do you think Tyson has any chance of

Lynn Shurr

straightening out in this lifetime?" She knew her roommate believed firmly in reincarnation.

"He has committed at least two of the great sins, lust and pride. He can overcome them. If he does not, he will pay for them in his next life."

Edie admitted to herself she liked the idea of having endless lives and experiences, not exactly part of her Episcopalian upbringing. "Do you think he will come back as a golden ram?"

"Hardly anything so magnificent and lustful. Perhaps, a dung beetle with a short life close to the ground forever rolling little balls of feces. That would teach humility, but we will never know."

"Oh, I love the thought. I wonder what I would be in my next life if I'm not forced into Protestant heaven." She though she saw a small mischievous smile gathering at the corners of Molly's lips.

"Why, I would guess a honeybee."

Edie tried not to show her dismay. "I must have done something dreadful to come back as an insect—unless I'm the queen bee."

"No, not the queen. The worker bees are very useful. They labor industriously to gather nectar and pollinate plants as they go along. Then, they fan the nectar in its cell until it evaporates into honey to feed the hive. They do not exhibit sloth or lust, pride or gluttony, greed, envy, or anger which gives each bee soul an excellent chance to move up in its next incarnation. You might return as a gorgeous bird—that eats dung beetles." Molly's laughter broke through, crinkling happy lines onto her brown skin.

Edie laughed along with her. "I think it is interesting that the Hindu and Christian deadly sins are almost the same. But I have experienced an angry bee or two. Run around barefoot in the clover enough and everyone does."

"Yes, however, you stepped on the bee first. They will swarm to protect the hive as well and give their lives which is very selfless."

"I think you will come back as a wise elephant."

"That is a great compliment." Molly began to gather the dishes, but Edie stood and stopped her. "I'll do the cleanup. Sit and have another cup of tea. You have cheered me up."

Her friend settled back at the table with a textbook that had to be six inches thick. Even the illustrations seemed heavy and esoteric. Science, never Edie's favorite subject. She preferred to study people.

The campus apartments ran more toward functionality, not luxury, so no dishwasher in the kitchen. Edie scraped the dishes and placed them in a sink full of soapy water. She warmed another cup of tea and started in on her task, humming happily as she washed, rinsed, and placed the dinnerware in the drainer to dry. How nice to believe all people had endless chances to improve.

As she wrung and hung the dishcloth, her phone rang again. Couldn't be Tyson as she'd blocked him, but she saw Flo's name appear on the screen. Her fine mood evaporated like the bubbles left in the bottom of the sink. How could she tell this wonderful woman that she'd given up on her grandson? She hesitated to answer, but doubted Flo would give up easily and call again.

She slid the phone icon to answer. "Hi, Flo. Is all well in the Big Easy?"

"As easy as it ever was and better with our business

booming. I tried you earlier, but you didn't pick up, honey lamb. You okay?"

"In church. I had my phone turned off. I said a few prayers for Ty." True enough, she would not lie.

"Same here. We lit a few candles, too. He didn't call yet today. Have you heard from him?"

"Yes, for the first time right after I got home. He said he'd had a breakthrough and will soon be home." True, all true.

"That's great. I wish he'd told us first, but he probably wanted to thank you for persuading him to get into rehab."

"Something like that. We didn't speak very long."

"No, they only give him fifteen minutes. I'll tell you what, honey, after we bring him home you come on down to New Orleans, and we'll have a big celebration dinner to welcome him home." Flo's big voice came across the air full of hope and joy.

She had to end the call soon or dash all the woman's belief in her grandson. "You should keep any celebrations to just family. I don't deserve any credit. Besides, I'm still working for the school newspaper and most of my assignments have to be done on the weekends. Maybe I can get down during semester break." She shouldn't make promises she couldn't keep, but she'd love to see Flo again sometime—when Ty wasn't around.

"I was hoping for sooner, my baby, but I understand. You be good now. Don't get yourself into anything you can't get out of, you hear."

"Yes, ma'am. We'll get together sometime. Gotta study. Bye now." She disconnected knowing she'd never forgive Ty if he broke his granny's heart.

Chapter Thirteen

The late October air was as crisp as it ever got in Louisiana. A blue sky formed a dome over the stadium known as Death Valley. Perfect football weather Edie judged, and she had two tickets won in the student lottery to the afternoon game, kickoff at three. Not being a fan, Molly had declined to go with her. She could easily give the coveted tickets away or squeeze in with her parents who always had a block of season tickets in a prime location better than hers which was close to heaven, but she preferred to sit with other students who cheered the team on as this would be her last semester to participate as one of them. Not that her father didn't shout his opinions out with gusto, especially when it came to any play involving Rex, which could be embarrassing.

Decked out in purple and gold, she'd walk over to the stadium in an hour, make her way around all the tailgate parties in the vast parking lot, maybe snag a burger or cup of jambalaya if offered as she passed, and begin her long climb up the decks to her place. Somewhere someone would be looking for a ticket. After the game as agreed, she'd meet her parents and Molly in front of the tiger habitat and go out to dinner with them, a long-established custom. Rex would join them once he completed the post-game interviews and got a shower.

At one time, the entire family had come out to watch Dean and Tom, the first of the boys to play for LSU, but, professionals now, they were on the road this weekend with the Sinners. Teddy worked out of town fulfilling his commentator duties, and wives with small children preferred to watch at home rather than drag their kids to a rowdy college game. Most likely, Stacy, Annie, and Xo would have their own little party at one of their houses and let their offspring romp while they watched the TV. As the tail end of the Billodeaux twelve, she realized times were changing fast. Who knew when she'd attend another LSU game once she left campus and yes, began the paid internship in January with *New Orleans Lifestyle*. She'd amassed so many credits trying to make up the Covid year, she qualified for a winter graduation, but decided her internship would be the icing on the graduation sheet cake, and she'd get her diploma in May with the rest of her class.

Antsy to get going, she considered leaving the apartment way too early and simply soak up the ambiance of the university on game day. Maybe she'd write a piece about it for the paper. Okay, she'd put on sunscreen, placed a twenty in her jeans pocket just in case she needed it right next to the tickets, and had subdued her curly hair with a golden headband ornamented with purple feathers which gave it a Mardi Gras vibe. Ready to go.

The doorbell rang. Of course, Molly had gone to the library. With a sigh, she went to the peephole and peered out, saw only someone wearing an LSU cap and holding up a garment bag that blocked the view.

Fairly sure he had the wrong apartment, she opened the door a crack and said, "Yes?" in an annoyed tone.

"Delivery for Edie Billodeaux," came a voice muffled by the plastic barrier.

"I'm not expecting anything."

"It's a gift."

Intrigued, she opened the door wider, and that fast, he slithered inside the gap. Tyson Ramsey always did have fine footwork and now blocked the exit very effectively. Not that she feared him, but his trick to gain entry pissed her off. She knew from Flo's last call that her grandson had gotten out of rehab last week after putting in an extra thirty days because he'd said he had more to work out. She'd turned down a chance to talk to him or come on down and have a home-cooked meal with them since he didn't want to go out. She should have been more careful opening doors now that Ty was on the loose again.

He must have interpreted her expression well because he lowered the bag and held up a hand in peace. "Really, it's a gift from my granny and mother for saving me from myself."

"I told you that you made the decision to shape up by yourself."

"Try to tell that to Flo. Got my mama to turn over her car keys to me and insisted I make the delivery since you hadn't come to visit. I drove all this way in game day traffic, so please take a look." He slid the zipper in the bag down seductively as if he were undressing a beautiful woman and kissing her nape with his full lips at the same time.

"I really can't accept...Oh, it's gorgeous."

She remembered well that silky blue fabric slashed with silver on the dress Stacy had tried on at Flo's Fabulous Fashions and ordered to be cut down to her size as the material had wrapped twice around her. This was no floor-length evening gown, though, but an outfit just her size, with a scooped neckline and cap sleeves, nipped in at the waist and swirling out at the knees. They'd taken her measurements, and she knew it would fit like the proverbial glove. Now, if she had an occasion to wear it…but no. She must not take the dress and steeled herself to say so.

He read her eyes as if she were an opponent on the football field. "I had nothing to do with this. I'm only the delivery man, so it isn't tainted by anything I've said or done. I'm supposed to tell you Miss Stacy paid for their time and no charge for the cloth as it came from remnants of hers. Try it on. If it doesn't suit you, I'll take it back."

"I don't have the time to do that. I have game tickets," she blurted out as the best excuse she could devise at the moment.

"The game doesn't start until three. Let me take a picture to show them since I realize you won't come around if I'm there." He offered the garment bag to her, a smile on his lips, temptation in his eyes.

"If this has anything to do with getting me undressed…" She warned him off.

"No, I'll stay right here, won't sit down, won't move a muscle. This is for my girls in New Orleans."

Longing to try the gown on, she held out an arm but moved no closer. He leaned forward to deliver the bag into her care. She jumped back, turned, and raced for her bedroom, slamming the door and turning the pathetic little lock into place. She thought she heard faint laughter following her, but no footsteps. He appeared thinner, but she wasn't sure if he'd lost weight or muscle mass after being out of training for so many months. Whichever, he could surely outrun her and knock down this flimsy door if he wanted.

She waited a moment for any approaching noise, and hearing none, stripped off her purple T-shirt and pushed down her jeans that now seemed snugger than when she'd put them on. Sneakers would disgrace this dress. She kicked them off and shoved her feet into a pair of black flats. That would have to do for now, but how lovely a pair of silver heels would look with this ensemble. She released the dress from its protective bag. It fluttered out like a butterfly parting from its cocoon and fairly floated over her head. She managed to raise the back zipper without snagging the delicate cloth, good, because she had no intention of asking for his help.

Too bad she had no full-length mirror, but what she could see in the one over the dresser took her breath away. Without even changing into special underwear, she'd turned into a princess, a role in the family usually filled by beautiful Stacy or glamorous Josee. With the help of a pushup bra, she could create a little cleavage with her small breasts if she wanted, but not today. She removed her feathered headband and ruffled her curls so they fell around her shoulders. The little silver fleur-de-lis earrings she'd put on this morning twinkled like stars in the dark mass of her hair. She didn't get much better than this, but maybe a little extra makeup, a bright lipstick would help. Oh, hell, no. She wasn't going on a date with the guy in the other room. Let's get this picture taken and shove him out of her life again. Taking a deep breath and noticing that the dress moved with her, not too tight or loose, she unlocked the door and moved back into the living area.

Tyson stood where she'd left him, hadn't made himself at home on their yellow vinyl sofa with one of Corazon's colorful afghans thrown over it or taken a seat on a straight-backed dining room chair. He had removed his cap which he twirled around a finger killing time. His hair, freed, burst out in a curly light brown corona as wild as her own locks but without a trace of gold in sight. However, when he glanced up at her and a beam of sun caught his eyes, the gold returned. She kept her distance.

"What do you think?" she said and spun around for full effect.

Jamming the cap backward on his head, he reached for his phone. "Do that one more time."

"I'd be happy to. This dress makes me want to twirl." She turned again, then paused and struck a pose she thought her supermodel sister-in-law, Josee, might assume on a photoshoot, one leg thrust forward, one arm in the air as if she might sway into a tango at any moment.

"Oh, baby, they are going to love these. Um, sorry, I shouldn't call you that. You deserve respect. And I apologize for coming on to you over the phone." He swallowed as if he'd conquered something he'd been chewing on for a long time.

She blinked. He hadn't used the term as if she were an infant nor in a particularly sexy way either, but somewhere in between. She'd hardly noticed. But the second statement nearly floored her.

"I think those extra days in rehab were worth it. Apology accepted. I guess you don't have an interest in LSU football anymore."

"Watched it every weekend I was gone. Rex is having another great year. Seems I was pretty easy to replace."

"Big university teams are always very deep. They have three players rotating at your old position, and all

110

of them are good, but none as good as you. I mean, that's what Rex says. If it isn't too painful, would you like to go to the game? I have an extra ticket." She waited, barely hopeful that he'd accept.

Ty removed his hat again, made an attempt to smooth his curls and stuff them all inside once more. "No haircuts in the hospital unless someone came in special to do them. Scissors not allowed. I haven't had the time since I got home to get a decent cut."

He took out a pair of dark glasses from a pocket and put them on. Beyond that, he wore a university T-shirt so new it still had creases in it, and she wondered if he'd bought it at the union on his way to her apartment in order to blend in even more. Same might be true of the cap. Wearing jeans and athletic shoes, he could be any of a thousand guys on campus today.

"Sure, I'd like to go if you aren't too embarrassed to be seen with me."

"No problem. I don't think people will recognize you, especially in the nose bleed section. Let's go." Did she sound too eager?

"Ah, I think you should change first, or we really will stand out in the crowd."

She looked down at the most lovely dress she'd ever owned and stopped herself from saying a girlish, "Silly me." Instead, she nodded. "Right. I'll only be a few minutes," and twirled herself back to the bedroom.

Maybe, she and Tyson Ramsey weren't done after all.

Chapter Fourteen

They waited near the tiger habitat where about a hundred people had arranged to meet but stood out from the others thanks to her father's height and Amoli's striking sari, appropriately purple and gold. In between them, her petite mother could barely be seen, but Edie knew that out of the three, Mom wielded the most power. Height didn't matter, and she hoped that applied to her in the years to come.

She'd tried to say goodbye to Ty after he escorted her down to the base of the coliseum, throwing a few light blocks to keep the crowd from trampling on her feet. She offered her hand and said, "Tell Flo and Portia I'm in love with the dress. I'll make time to visit with them once I start my job in New Orleans."

"When would that be?"

"Oh, January. I don't know where I'll be staying yet. I've got lots of family homes and condos to choose from short term. Meanwhile, keep in touch. I mean they should keep in touch."

She'd bungled this goodbye and had given him too much information. In the noise and excitement of the game, they'd had no chance to talk. Ty didn't mind being seated so high that the players seemed the size of chessmen on a big green board. He could predict the plays and how they should be run. Evidently, he'd retained a lot from his days on the team. Maybe, he hadn't played on drugs. His performances hadn't shown it. That meant his career did mean something to him, and he deserved another chance.

"Which way are you going?" he asked, a good question.

"That way to meet my parents, not back to the apartment."

"Great. My car is parked waaay down there. I'll walk along and keep you from getting crushed until you find them."

"Been here four years and haven't been crushed once."

"It could still happen. I'll lead the way. Holler when you see them."

Not waiting for more debate, he moved forward like an icebreaker in the Arctic Sea, the exception being that the temperature hovered around eighty. Given no choice, she followed in the vacuum of space he left behind. She imagined him reliving his days as a free safety pushing through the line to the open spaces in field, disposing of opponents one by one.

"There," she shouted. "You can see Molly in the sari and my dad right by her."

He swung right and soon had her united with her parents. "You'll be in good hands now."

Ty backed away, but was stayed by her father's outthrust hand. "Joe Billodeaux. Thanks for escorting my daughter. Lots of rough drunks in the crowd today. And you are…?"

Edie dove in to spare Ty, and maybe herself, an awkward moment. "A friend who needs to get back to New Orleans."

Molly, no help at all, said, "The Tyson Ramsey I

have heard so much about."

Edie registered the instant recognition on her dad's face, but her mother spoke up. "What a pity you are in a hurry. If you can make the time, would you like to join us at Anderson's for dinner? Best seafood place in town. We have reservations and won't have to wait."

Ty unleashed his perfect grin, one Edie hadn't seen all day. "To be honest, I'm in no hurry to fight post-game traffic and have no other plans for the evening. Thank you for inviting me."

"Ride with us. We'll bring you back to your car after we eat. Their lot is always so full after a game, no sense in using two spaces. Ours is nearby in the VIP parking. Let's get moving." Nell Billodeaux would have led the way if her husband hadn't grabbed her arm and cradled her next to his side to break through the mob.

Their group, slowed by fans telling her dad what a great game his son had played, reached their vehicle at last. He'd brought the double-cab truck from the ranch, a fairly new model considering he owned another with over a hundred-thousand miles on it which he wouldn't part with for sentimental reasons. He never made any secret about hating his wife's subcompact with no room for long legs, and these days, driving the unwieldy fourteen passenger van he'd toted his large family in had become unpractical.

"How about we put Molly up front since she's wearing such a pretty dress? Up you go, *cher.*" He didn't circle her waist, just gave her a hand, but when it came to his jean-clad wife, he bodily lifted her into the rear seat, then did the same for his daughter. "You're next, Ty, but I think you can manage by yourself."

"Yes, sir." He mounted, exposing his old athletic

grace.

Since both she and her mom were petite, the rear seat wasn't too crowded. Still, Edie felt the warmth of his body so near, the muscle of his thigh against hers. She stared straight ahead, sure that disaster lay just down the road.

****

Ty hadn't been angling for a dinner invitation, but he doubted Edie would believe that. He thought it might indicate that he'd been forgiven for his rank behavior at the Fourth of July gathering, lording it over a harem of admiring girls and causing chaos at the boat races. That guy didn't exist anymore, and if he did, had to be knocked down and run over with football cleats.

He'd had a near slip back at Edie's apartment when she went to try on the dress, tempted to creep after her and rap lightly on the door. In his fantasy, half-dressed she opened it wide and invited him into her feminine bed covered in extra pillows and stuffed toy unicorns. "You deserve a reward," she'd breathe, her voice low and husky and not at all Edie-like. Shocked back to reality when he realized he'd imagined his little sister's room, he kept his word to stay put and started spinning his hat to remain on track, another trick taught by the counselors. Idle hands are the devil's tools.

When she walked out, not a little girl at all, but a dancing queen with wild curls spilled across her shoulders, bright dark eyes, and cheeks red with joy, he recognized her as a real woman for the first time. Not a pesky kid, not someone he liked to tease and make suggestive comments to just to yank her chain, not even his unattainable fantasy lay because she'd always say no, but a flesh and blood grownup female. He'd share those photos with his Granny, but keep them stored in his phone.

Now as they sat at a table set for six amid walls decorated with sports memorabilia, some of it signed by the very man sitting across from him, he counted himself lucky that Joe Billodeaux did not read minds, though some of his football opponents might argue about that. The man had an early reputation as a womanizer who drank and brawled until he'd been given his big chance to move off the Sinners' bench and lead the team as their quarterback. Little Miss Nell had domesticated him, and they'd raised a large and diverse family together, children he loved more than football despite their occasional screwups. By the time Joe Billodeaux retired at the age of forty, he'd earned the nickname Daddy Joe. Uncle T would always be nothing but Uncle T, a giver of gifts and the lover of Ty's mother, not a true father.

He pushed bitterness aside and removed his dark glasses, unnecessary in the dimly lit restaurant. If he left that part of his disguise on, they would think he'd taken drugs. At a nod from Miss Nell, he also removed his hat and hung it on the post of his chair. He felt stripped naked on an ant hill, liable to be recognized as savory gossip at any moment. Running his fingers through his explosion of hair, he tried for humor, another great deflector. "Yeah, I know I need a haircut."

Miss Nell gave him a laugh. "I'm sure your mama thinks so."

A college-aged waiter, certain of lots of good tips after a game, filled their water glasses and took drink orders. Though Joe asked for a local beer, he stuck to water as did the women. Alcohol wasn't his problem, but no sense in giving anyone the idea that it was. When the waiter returned with a sweating bottle of brew and an iced mug plus a basket of garlic bread and took their orders, he tried to go cheap and settled for a large crawfish etouffee with a side salad. There had been a time when he'd opt for the highest priced item and someone else would pay for it. He'd offer to cover his meal since his granny had stuffed a wad of bills in his pocket and told him to take Edie out to dinner, which he hadn't intended to do because she'd refuse. His credit cards were still good, but hey, no income, and he wouldn't ask Uncle T to cover them as he usually did.

As expected, the women ordered salads, a large seafood for Miss Nell and spinach topped with shrimp for the roommate. Only Edie went rogue and got the high-cal crabmeat au gratin. She probably ran off those calories with her energy level, Ty guessed. Joe selected the large fried seafood platter, got a nudge in the side from his wife and changed that to broiled seafood with a side of slaw.

As crowded as the place was, they'd have a wait. The bread basket came around. He took his piece and passed it on to Joe across the table. The seating had fallen out with Molly, Edie, and himself on one side and Joe and Nell on the other by the empty chair. He'd helped the Indian woman with her seating, but Edie waved him away. "I can handle it." Why, because they might accidentally touch?

As good a time as any to bring up what was eating on his mind. "I was wondering if you could recommend a good trainer. I want to get in shape for the NFL combine, show what I can do before the spring draft."

Joe didn't laugh or scowl but gave the question some serious consideration. "I could say Mack's wife, Sarge.

She'd whip you into shape, but she mostly works with badly injured people and you'd need someone else who specialized in football skills. I guess I could help you with that."

Even in a crowded room full of the noise of cutlery on china and loud conversations about sports, he heard Edie's gasp. "I didn't mean you personally, sir. I plan to pay for a trainer. Well, I guess my granny will. Since Edie wrote that article about her shop and my mother's clothing designs, they have money pouring in. I'll pay them back and then some once I'm signed to a team—if you think anyone will have me."

"Talent like yours shouldn't be wasted. If you are willing to work hard and stay away from temptation, some team will take you, maybe not at the salary you'd like, but make a good start and that will change. We have a fine gym at the ranch. The rules are no drugs of course. You give your best every day, and you show respect and kindness to every person and small child, the elderly, and animals on the place. If you think you can live with those restrictions, I'll take you on."

Talk about large lumps in the throat. He hesitated.

"Oh, go on. With Rex launched in his career and none of the grandchildren old enough to follow in his footsteps, though some will, he's bored. Take the offer," Miss Nell urged.

"Okay, but I insist on paying you and your daughter-in-law if she's game."

"Paying for what?" the voice behind him said.

Miss Nell beckoned her football hero son to her side and accepted his kiss on the cheek. "Ty is coming to the ranch to train for the NFL combine. We're going to help him be the man he should be."

Rex replied with an ungracious, "No shit. Good luck with that," as he slid into his place next to her, a young version of her husband.

She covered his hand and gave it a squeeze. "At the ranch, we heal and don't tear people down."

Rex recoiled as if she'd broken his playing arm with that light gesture. "Right. Sorry."

"Tell him, not me." Nell nodded to Ty. Who did she remind him of? Oh yeah, a group counselor, the psychologist she in reality was.

"Sorry, Ty. I hope you can get your act together. It's just that this year would have been easier if you hadn't screwed up."

"Hey, you're having your best year yet. You don't need me."

Rex shrugged his broad quarterback shoulders. "Mediocre opponent with no defense this time. You were my defense."

"No one is the whole defense on a team. Those new guys, Eccles and Huddleston, are going to be awesome by the time the playoffs come around. I'm sorry I won't be there."

"Good, now shake hands," Nell prompted.

They both stood and grasped hands across the table. Ty kept his grip light, nothing to prove. Rex let his slide away.

Ty remained standing. "This is a family dinner. I shouldn't have butted in. Rex, if you like etouffee, you can have mine, and I'll be going."

"Am I Cajun? Sure, I like etouffee, but I had my heart set on the fried seafood platter." The waiter appeared at Rex's shoulder. "I'll get that order in for you right away, Rex. Beverage?"

"A draft beer."

"Hey, how come I can't have the fried seafood platter, and he can?" Joe groused.

"Because he played an afternoon of football and doesn't have a father who died of a heart attack—yet," Nell retorted.

Rex laughed at their bickering which changed the mood at the table. "My mom might be small, but she doesn't let a person get away with anything. Exactly like that one sitting next to you, so watch out."

Ty felt a tug on his hand, Edie looking up at him. "Sit down and eat what you ordered."

"Yes, ma'am." He sat and ate when the food arrived, marveling at the huge second chance he'd been served with the meal.

They kept the conversation light often asking Molly about her life in India and her studies, Edie's more interesting newspaper assignments, funny stories about the Billodeaux grandchildren. When the check came, Joe slammed down his credit card first, but Ty bargained to pay the substantial tip in cash. Rex took off in his own truck, back to the athletes' dorm while he hitched a ride with the Billodeauxs to his vehicle, a late model BMW sedan, one of the few cars left on the lot.

Joe eyed the vehicle, black and sleek on the outside with a gray leather interior. "Nice. I hope some eager agent didn't give you that and break the recruiting rules."

"There aren't any eager agents in my life anymore. No, it's my mother's car, sold to her by…a friend whose wife didn't like the color."

He noticed a deeper awareness in Edie's eyes. He'd be willing to bet she'd figured out the true identity of Uncle T by now, but they'd had no time for a private conversation. Maybe she'd take his phone calls again.

Holding out his hand, he shook Joe's before leaving the cab. "Thank you for taking me on, sir. I won't disappoint you. Let me know when you want to start training at the ranch."

He turned to Edie. "I guess we'll be seeing more of each other."

"Not really. I won't be home until Thanksgiving and Christmas after that. In January, I move to New Orleans, and you'll be in Chapelle."

Searching her face for the disappointment he felt and finding none, he replied, "Then, maybe not." He thanked Miss Nell for her hospitality, jumped down from the truck, and waved them out of sight, but not out of mind.

Chapter Fifteen

First day of college all over again, only now he wasn't a highly sought-after football recruit. Ty rode in the backseat of his mother's sedan with Livy buckled in next to him. Granny rode up front out of respect for her age and her size. They all had to tag along to see him settled safely at the ranch. Embarrassing. He'd lost the argument to fill a couple of saddle bags with gym clothes and ride his motorcycle to his destination. No, the motorcycle remained locked in the garage, leaving him at the mercy of the Billodeauxs for transport. He didn't doubt that Uncle T had something to do with the decision. The man gave when proud of his performance and took away when disappointed.

As they were buzzed into the compound through the wrought iron gates and meandered down a live oak alley to a mansion more antebellum than ranch house, his mother exclaimed, "Oh, this is so much nicer than…the last place we left you." She parked by the imposing front door surrounded by sidelights and a fan window over its top.

A large, black dog materialized from the deep shade of an oak where it had been lying by what appeared to be gravestones and began barking. "We'd best stay in the car till it settles down," his Granny suggested. "I know I can't outrun it."

"Ty could," Livy said with a great deal of faith.

That belief in him made Ty offer a slight smile. "This ole dog has gray on its muzzle so maybe I could. I'll get out and ring the bell."

"No, you won't. Don't need to start out with a dog bite on your leg. They opened the gate. They know we're here." Gran settled her arms over her broad bosom and prepared to wait, but not very long.

The wide door opened. They adjusted their expectation of a tall and regal butler down to petite Nell Billodeaux. "Hush, Lil. They come in peace."

She walked across a broad veranda and down two steps to rub the eager dog's head and greet her guests. "It's okay to get out. She doesn't bite but has a big bark, a good watch dog. I should have told you to drive to the back door where most of us go in and out."

"I can move the car if you want," Portia told her.

"No need. Come inside. You've had a long drive." Nell led the way to the open door and gestured to her left. "Powder room down the hall and coffee and cold drinks in the kitchen just beyond there. Help yourselves. I'll show Ty to his room."

He removed his duffel when his mom popped the trunk and followed them inside. He felt proud of her dressed with style in chocolate-colored tailored slacks and a bronze silk blouse she'd made from expensive remnants, a gold chain accenting her neck. She looked like she belonged here in the foyer of a mansion with a large chandelier overhead and a sweeping staircase with wide bannisters before them, though the carpet on the stairs showed the wear of many feet. His granny, dressed brightly enough to illuminate the entry, hustled away in her orthopedic shoes toward the restroom while Livy showed her awe, spinning around beneath the crystals dripping from the ceiling, making the cute Sunday dress her mother had insisted on bell out around her skinny legs.

Nell glanced over her shoulder as she mounted the first step. "Lil, outside," she ordered the dog who had slipped in with the crowd. "Livy, isn't it? Would you open the door for her?"

Now that the dog licked at her hand, Livy lost all fear. "Can she come with us? I'd like to get a dog, but Mama always says no."

"No use asking. She said no to me right up until I graduated from high school," Ty added.

"Dogs don't belong in the city," their mother stated firmly.

"Mrs. Freebourne who lives right next door has a dog."

"Yes, and her yapping is like having a second doorbell. No one can come and go in peace."

"I think Lil may stay inside and visit for a while. Whenever you come here, you can play frisbee with her. She loves that. Stacy brought her here right from a shelter in New Orleans. If you do decide to get one, check there first."

With all the debate about dogs, Flo managed to return and trail them huffing and puffing up the stairs, though Ty wasn't sure Miss Nell meant all of them to come along. She wore comfortable jeans and a red pullover sweater, probably cashmere, but casual. Instead of the heels his mother had on her feet, Rex's mom was shod in trainers, at home in her home. They passed bedroom after bedroom until Nell paused by a door.

"We'll put you in Mack's old room. Now that he and Sarge have built a house on the ranch, he doesn't stay here anymore. The bath adjoins with another room, but no one else is home at the moment so you'll have it to yourself. Plenty of towels in the cabinet under the sinks. Feel free to set up your laptop on the desk. We have wi-fi. Lots of hangers in the closet and room in the dresser."

"I only brought a duffle full of workout clothes." Ty deposited it in a corner out of the way. He eyed a number of empty shelves that most likely had held Mack's athletic trophies.

"Ty has a custom suit we made for him in the car in case he needs one to attend church or go somewhere fancy," his mother said.

"My husband goes to the Catholic church more often than he wants because of his mother. I admit I don't attend the Episcopal services much since my daughters are scattered, sometimes when Edie is home. Teddy and Jessie are members of the Methodist church. Ty can take his pick or sleep in on Sundays. Sarge usually gives the weekends off from training.

"Edie goes to church?" Why did that surprise him? She was such a good little girl.

"She's more spiritual than she seems, but she isn't likely to come home until Thanksgiving."

"Why, this is as nice as a high-priced hotel in the city," Flo said as she stroked the quilted spread covering the large bed as if judging the quality of the linens.

As children will, Livy spoke up. "But it doesn't have a big TV or a mini-fridge."

Nell took the criticism well despite Portia's frown at her child. "We didn't allow the children to have televisions in their rooms, and they knew where to find snacks downstairs if they wanted them. We do have a large screen in the den and an entire movie theater in the back of the house."

"Hey, lots better than the room I shared with Lenny at, uh, camp, kiddo. You won't hear any complaints from me, Miss Nell."

"Good. Why don't we go downstairs and have coffee?" Observing that Flo still sweated from her trek up the stairs, Nell added, "We do have an elevator. Wouldn't it be fun if we rode down in that? It's at the end of the hall. Why don't you and your granny go first, Livy."

"I'll press the button." Livy trotted off in her T-strapped shoes worn with while anklets as if she were the one going to church. Flo huffed after her.

"Kind of you not to mention my mother's size as we most likely wouldn't all fit in there with her." Portia shook her head. "I try to get her to diet, but no."

"Her size is her calling card, but just eating more healthfully might help. You wouldn't want to lose her, I'm sure."

"Sometimes…but she is what she is. I can't change her. She thinks I should gain weight."

"Well, she raised a beautiful daughter and has a pretty granddaughter as well. Why don't we join them?"

They moved down the hall and recalled the elevator, rode to the first floor where Lil greeted them as if she hadn't seen them ages. Evidently, the dog had squeezed in with Flo and Livy. Happily reunited, they went to the kitchen where Nell poured coffee for those who wanted it and made a quick hot chocolate in the microwave for Livy. She set a plate of oatmeal raisin cookies on the table for all to share. With Lil looking so hopeful, she got a dog biscuit for her.

"Now, if you have any questions to ask, feel free,"

Nell said.

Livy put up her hand as if she were in school and asked when Nell nodded at her. "May we come to visit Ty because we couldn't see him at all at that other camp he went to."

"Sure, but call ahead. He'll be in the gym a lot. I work at a local clinic parttime, and Joe is usually out and about on the ranch so people aren't always in the house to buzz you in. Ah, here he comes. He must have scented what he calls real coffee, not decaf."

Ty noticed how Joe Billodeaux could fill a room with his personality, all heads turning toward him in an instant. Dressed in ranch gear, he had the style of an actor playing the handsome cowboy hero. After washing his hands vigorously at the sink, he poured his own coffee and scooped up what remained of the cookies. "We don't get these often now that the kids are gone."

Ty stood up in the great man's presence and shook hands. "Again, thanks for having me here."

"You'll earn your keep. I can always use help mucking out the horse stalls and hauling feed to the cattle."

Ty wasn't sure if he joked or not and crafted a neutral answer. "Whatever you need me to do."

But Livy had picked up on the word horses. "You have horses? Can we see them?"

"As soon as I finish my break here, *cher* heart. Better than that, we have ponies, one just the right size for you if you have time for a ride."

"Joe and his ponies. We have five now to share among twelve grandchildren, though Beck and Wynn are riding big horses but Elena, Xochi's youngest, is only two," Nell explained.

"Elena loves a pony ride. She'll be a great rider someday." Joe downed his coffee and cookies and continued their tour out the kitchen door with Lil tagging along.

"I'll join you after I clean up the dishes. Our housekeeper and gatekeeper are having a day off visiting our mutual grandkids in town."

Ty's mother stopped. "Let me help with that."

"You aren't dressed for either the kitchen or the barn. Beautiful outfit, by the way. Stacy swears by your tailoring. Go on, it's just a few mugs and plates."

In the barn as Livy ran from stall to stall trying to choose a pony to ride, Ty remained silent. He recalled the last time he'd been in this building smelling of hay and horse, the bales he'd lounged against while getting high gone now. At the time, he'd thought no big deal in the face of Edie's anger. Now it was the desecration of a special place. Though the mess he'd made of the boat race trumpeted that he was using something, he felt a pang of gratefulness that Edie hadn't turned him in or he might not be so welcome now.

Livy of course decided on the white pony Joe called Princess. He had her saddled in no time at all and led Livy and her mount to the paddock for a few turns around the well-worn oval inside the fence. When she appeared comfortable, he swatted Princess on the haunch and let her go alone. The horse knew the drill. "Just pull back lightly on the reins when you want to stop."

"Anytime you want some riding lessons, Ty, let me know," Joe added with that great generosity he'd shown so far.

No way would he admit getting on a large horse might intimidate him. "That would be great. Does Edie ride? She isn't a whole lot bigger than Livy."

Joe gave him a side eye. "Size doesn't matter so much as confidence and command. A horse needs to know who is in charge. Besides, Edie hangs on like a tick on a dog's ear."

"Tenacious, then?"

"*Mais* yeah. She won't let go."

Portia called out to her daughter. "Okay, enough riding, Livy. Stop your horse by the gate. We need to go home now."

"Aw." But she obeyed.

Nell had joined them by the fence. "You're welcome to stay for dinner, but we're only going to order pizza and watch the LSU away game in the den."

"No, we've imposed enough. Ty, walk to the car with us and get your suit. We'll say goodbye there."

Nell left Joe to attend to the pony and escorted them. They loaded into the sedan, Livy's nice dress smelling quite horsey now. Flo, taking some time to adjust herself in the front seat with an extended belt, said, "You have some of your people buried here?" nodding at the small grave markers.

"Oh, no. Only our ranch dogs. I guess Lil will join them there in a few years. We're sentimental that way."

"This place has lots of heart, just what Ty needs. I'm grateful to you."

"So am I," Ty said as he stood there with the garment bag draped over a shoulder and watched his family leaving him again in a safe place, one he intended to make the most of.

Chapter Sixteen

Sunday after a pancake and bacon breakfast, Ty helped Joe in the barn. All the horses but one had been herded to pasture while they changed their bedding down to the clay flooring. Nothing like shoveling shit and straw to humble a person, he figured, yet Joe did it on a regular basis. Once that chore ended, his riding lessons began on the remaining mount, a big red quarter horse named Lazy Loser, which seemed fitting. After Joe showed him how to saddle his steed and get atop it, he led them to the paddock where Livy had gone round and round with such glee. Instructions followed.

Joe patiently explained neck reining to get the horse to go the direction it should and a kick to get him started. "Don't worry. Loser won't go beyond a walk unless encouraged. That's why he ended up a gelding, you know, snip, snip since he was no good for breeding. That's what happens to the ones who don't work out."

Ty wondered if that applied to himself as well, a loser not fit for breeding, but Joe's words didn't appear to be a threat of any kind.

"Okay, off you go. If Loser decides to head into the middle of the ring to graze, you pull his head up firmly without jerking. You've got the muscle to do it. He's not the boss."

"Does Edie ride this horse?" His last question before giving his mount the kickstart.

"*Mais*, no. She likes more spirit. Go on. Begin."

He circled the ring for what seemed like endless rotations, Joe giving him tips as they plodded by. "Relax your legs. Don't squeeze the horse. Straighten up in the saddle."

Relief came when Nell called them for lunch. He got off still feeling like he had a horse between his legs. "Good for the thigh muscles," Joe remarked. "Let's rub him down. Then you can go into lunch while I turn him out with the other horses." Despite his many derogatory comments about Loser, he scratched the horse between the ears and said what a good boy he'd been, no snacking on the job.

After learning how to brush a horse, Ty went into lunch feeling like he needed a grooming to get the horse hair off his clothes and the barn smell out of his own hair, which he'd had cut before coming to live on the ranch, shaved close up the sides and some taken off the bushy top, too. Other than being asked to wash his hands, Nell didn't seem to notice. She'd laid out a spread of cold cuts, cheeses, toppings, and rolls to make po-boy sandwiches along with a bowl of fruit. "We'll have popcorn later once the game starts."

Right. He'd forgotten this was Sunday and the Sinners had an away game. "Guess I missed church," he apologized.

"Not really. Joe took his mother to early Mass, a treat you do want to miss, and got back in time for breakfast. He said to let you sleep in as long as you wanted today because tomorrow Sarge will be back to start your training. She keeps military hours, so be ready to rise and shine at six, early breakfast, then off to the gym."

Warned, he made the most of lounging in Joe's vast den with its long, leather sofa and double recliners, so trophy-filled not a spot appeared to be left unadorned except for the coffee table where the popcorn and drinks sat. Even the large screen TV over the stone fireplace had been hoisted high enough to accommodate more awards on the mantel. Leftover pizza, salad, and ice cream for dinner, more football once the Sinners defeated the Falcons, and early to bed before meeting the dreaded Sarge.

****

He'd set his alarm for six, taken a quick shower but decided to shave to make a good impression. By six-twenty-five, he entered the kitchen to be told by the plump Mexican housekeeper in the bright apron that the coffee was over there if he wanted some, milk in the fridge, juice on the table. He fixed his coffee, got his milk, and sat down. Without another word, she plunked a plate of ham and scrambled eggs in front of him and set a plate of buttered whole wheat toast on the table.

At rehab, breakfast had been served strictly between seven and eight, often the best meal of the day, so few missed it. Was he too early at the table? Had he broken some unknown Billodeaux rule?

"This looks great. Thanks. I'm Tyson Ramsey. Sarge is going to help me get into shape again."

"*Si*, I know who you are." Brandishing a spatula, she turned. "Drugs, you ruin yourself with drugs, let LSU and Rex down. Now you come here for help. Sarge, she fly home last night on the red eye from Atlanta after the Sinners play to get ready for you. You better not disappoint her or your mama and granny." She shook the spatula so hard a fleck of egg flew through the air and landed on the toast.

"I'll eat this piece. More eggs for me." Humor hadn't bailed him out as the woman continued to frown deeply into the laugh lines of her broad, brown face. As she turned back to the stove, he added a little too late, "I won't disappoint anyone, ma'am."

"Damned right, you won't." A newcomer, entering the kitchen from outside, brought a blast of cold air with her. This must be Sarge, a compact woman of average height with light blonde hair cut short as a man's, except for a wave across her brow. Though her face might have been considered pretty, that thought vanished with one glance at her compressed lips and eyes gray and sharp as a bayonet, not a woman to be trifled with at any time.

Even if he hadn't been expecting her, he would have known Sarge from the numerous features in sports and celebrity magazines. The One-Footed Wonder, they'd called her, a name she detested just as he'd come to hate being the Golden Ram when he didn't live up to it. He'd seen Mack Billodeaux's cringeworthy proposal to this woman on his knees crammed between a coffee table and a sofa when it ran on *ET*. Her sister had sold it to numerous outlets, funded a lavish Catholic wedding, and put a down payment on a house with the profits. Not that he paid much attention to gossip media, but his granny sure did and discussed the latest at the dinner table with his mother.

He felt the need to stand in her presence at attention, but settled for rising from the table and extending his hand for a firm shake returned in the same manner. She poured her coffee, got her milk, but the cook offered to make her anything she wanted, an omelet, a breakfast burrito.

"Whatever you have ready, Corazon. Since Mr. Ramsey is up early, we can start training at seven. I've got the gym all set up." She ate without making small talk, a silence not broken until Nell walked in dressed in a robe and slippers.

"I see you've meet Corazon and Sarge," Nell said as she poured what was left of the coffee into a thermos and prepared another pot. "Sarge is Mack's wife and my newest daughter-in-law as well as a superb trainer. Corazon serves as our indispensable housekeeper and cook. She's also Junior Polk's mama and Xochi's mother-in-law. We'll deal with other family ties as they come up. It can get confusing."

The kitchen door rattled again, and Joe came in from the chilly morning to hang his denim barn jacket on a peg and report to the sink to wash his hands. He took a sniff of the coffee. "Missed the real stuff, eh. I need to get up earlier."

"In the thermos saved for you, though a switch to decaf wouldn't do you any harm," Nell prompted.

"If I wanted to drink dishwater I would. Thank you, Tink." He accompanied the endearment with a kiss to the top of his wife's curly head.

This is how families should work, Ty Ramsey thought as he watched Corazon divide the last of the eggs into a large and small portion with a side of ham and served both Joe and Nell. Placing the pan into the sink to soak, she filled two cups with the fresh decaf and joined them at the table, sliding one mug Nell's way, her work done for the moment. Here, he'd been priding himself at being up so early and the only one he'd beaten at that was Nell. Not a contest, he reminded himself, just something he needed to do every day from now on.

By now both he and Sarge had finished and put their dishes in the sink. "This way to the gym." She led him out the kitchen door and set a brisk pace down a path to a fenced-in pool covered for the colder months. By noon, they'd have a beautiful autumn day to enjoy, but at this moment, he was glad he wore a hoodie and sweat pants over his exercise clothes.

Sarge reached over the gate and raised a latch. Entering the pool area, she unlocked the door to the pool house and beckoned him inside. They passed through a large open area. "Space for summer camp activities," she noted as they went through another door that opened into a fully equipped gym. "Strip off your outerwear, and let me get your measurements."

Ty stood, arms out, as she ran a tape measure around nearly every part of his body. "I think you got everything but my head and cock." He threw in a smile which she did not return.

"The size of your neck matters, but the other two have no relevance to your training." She entered his stats in her laptop while he warmed up on the exercise bike, then launched into lunges, pushups, burpees, the usual stuff, thirty reps each, no sweat except he did. By noon, Sarge took a glance out the door and declared it too nice a day to run on the treadmill. They'd take the long way back to the house for lunch.

While he knew she'd lost a foot while serving in Afghanistan, he still gawped a little when she rolled up the leg of her khaki slacks, removed her prosthesis, and replaced it with a blade foot from her gym bag. Suggesting he stop staring at her and put his sweats back on, he answered with an embarrassed, "Yes, ma'am."

"This won't be a jog. It will be a run, but not a race.

Got it?"

"Yes, ma'am," he answered again.

They left the pool area and passed a sand volleyball court, entered a palm grove with winding pathways and exited onto a long driveway that passed two houses. "Teddy's house," she told him about the rambling ranch style with a patio overlooking the pastures and the bayou in the distance. "It's especially designed for two people in wheelchairs."

Spaced far enough away for some privacy, a two-story home with sweeping ramps up to a second-floor balcony and a row of French doors commanded the same view. The bottom floor appeared to house a garage, kitchen, and great room barely glimpsed as Sarge picked up the pace. "My house, the one Mack and I designed. We have an inside elevator, walk-in baths, and showers, plenty of bedrooms. We'd like to adopt some handicapped kids."

He noted the pride in her voice, but she fell silent soon after as they rounded the pastures and skirted a woods thick with live oaks and Southern magnolias. They pounded along a bayou side path, scaring off a great blue heron with a small snake in its mouth and upsetting a flock of cattle egrets from their cypress tree roost. The winter shaggy pony herd out to pasture raced with them along the fence line. Across the river, a huge machine cut ripened sugar cane and left a wake of dust behind it. They moved onto more winding pathways edged by small cottages and shaded by live oaks.

"The Camp Love Letter cabins," Sarge said as they emerged on a sidewalk. "The house is to the right. You can jog there to cool down and get cleaned up for lunch. I'm going back to the gym to change out my foot. We put in a good three miles. You handled it well."

"Thank you. The ranch is a big place. If I'd stayed in the city, I'd have to use a treadmill or go to a park for a run like this. In rehab, about all the exercise I got was running around the courtyard. I'm glad some of me is up to par." He wiped the sweat of his brow on the sleeve of his hoodie.

Sarge jogged in place. "You don't know the half of this place or what it can do for you. Beyond the woods and across the bayou are cane fields that Joe inherited a third of from his father. His uncles and cousins keep that part running, and he pays for new equipment, the crop insurance, things like that. He could sell out but won't because it keeps his family ties going. At least, that's what Mack says. I believe Joe likes driving the big cane tractors when he can get a chance. Okay, get going."

She'd thawed a little when he'd complimented the ranch as if it were her beloved. Turning toward the big house, he pondered what might make a friend of Corazon. He went in the kitchen door which everyone used in lieu of the formal entrance, and found that woman stirring a pot on the range. He inhaled the spicy fragrance of gumbo. "That smells great."

"Is chicken-sausage gumbo, not that okra kind you eat in New Orleans," she answered without turning around to face him.

"I love both. I know it's hard to make."

"Not so much when you know what you are doing— and use a rotisserie chicken from the store." Now, she did give him attention with a wrinkling of her nose. "You go shower before you eat at my table."

"Yes, ma'am." The way to Corazon's heart was through her cooking.

In half an hour, they were gathered around the table. Nell, still in the suit she wore to the clinic for her psychology work sat next to Joe in a dusty jumpsuit. "Did you see me driving the cane cutter?" Joe asked. "I noticed you running by at a pretty good pace."

"No, sir. I concentrated on keeping up with Sarge."

"And here's our girl."

Ty figured only Joe could get away with calling Sarge a girl. She'd never hear it from his lips, suspecting she'd make him get down and give her fifty pushups if he did.

Sarge entered, her hair dampened and her clothes changed, making him glad he'd done the same. Corazon dished out rice from a rice cooker on the counter and placed a bowl of gumbo in front of each of them, herself included. Potato salad and sliced tomatoes already sat on the table. Joe said the quickest grace Ty ever heard, and they dug in helping themselves to the sides. He couldn't complain about the food, not at all.

After lunch, they were back at it in the gym with Joe, having shed the jumpsuit, coming along to help with the bench presses. He knew he'd lost upper body strength, something a safety required a lot of, and he gave it his best—which wasn't good enough according to both his trainers.

"Don't worry, we'll work up to what you need to impress at the Combines," Joe promised.

"Yes, I expect you to reach that by the first of the new year," Sarge said. "Let's see what you got left of a vertical leap." She stacked the blue boxes and assessed, "Good, but not good enough. That will change."

No ifs, ands, or buts in Sarge's world. If being in rehab had given him a hint of what prison life might be like, Sarge's treatment of him mimicked the military experience. He guessed that might be another possibility if he failed in football, a decision Uncle T would have no power over—unless he used the enlistment for publicity. His scholarship boy making him proud again. No, this was about himself, not his father.

They wrapped it up as the November dusk began to close in over the ranch and walked back to the kitchen scented with Corazon's cheese enchiladas and Spanish rice. She'd left a salad full of avocado slices on the set table and gone home to her cottage to share the meal with her husband as usual according to Nell. They got their drinks and served themselves.

Conversation ran to the state of the cane crop to which he had nothing to add and an interesting nameless client Nell was trying to help. He guessed he was another one of those in her eyes. They dished up ice cream for dessert, cleared the dishes, and went into the large trophy bedecked den. He didn't last long watching a movie the women selected while Joe read *Sports Illustrated*. Excusing himself, he went to his room, showered again, thought he'd watch whatever on his laptop, but found himself dozing off, wishing he could tell Edie about his day.

Chapter Seventeen

One day was the same as the next differing only in increased reps and pressing higher weights. He hit the gym by 0700 as Sarge would say and got started, went until she said quit. Sometimes they ran side by side on the treadmills, but he came to prefer the three-mile run with changing scenery. Sometimes Teddy's little daughters appeared on their patio to wave as they went by or the Charolais bull, feeling feisty, charged them only to be stopped by the fence.

Corazon always set out good meals. He didn't have to lie to give her compliments. In the city surrounded by fine restaurants, his granny and mom seldom cooked if they were busy at the shop, excellent food but not homestyle. He put on some weight and hoped it to be mostly muscle.

Sarge left early on Fridays to be with her husband in their New Orleans flat if Mack had a Sunday home game, usually at noon. Or she flew out from Lafayette to catch his away games. Ty appreciated the upheaval he made in her life. After the first day rather than stay at her own home on the ranch, she slept in Lorena's former room to save time—and perhaps to keep an eye on his actions.

He wasn't up to anything but a little snooping. Easy to discover Edie's bedroom as soon as he opened that door. Her desk held a computer and printer with enough capacity to put out the Camp Love Letter news. A tidy pile of them rested on a corner. He took a few to read. Her walls still held pictures of Oprah Winfrey and Gayle King for inspiration along with lots of other admirable women. No frills or unicorns to be seen, just a small handmade afghan, pink edged in white, covering the bed as if Edie didn't have time for frivolous things without meaning, though a single penguin toy in a jacket did sit propped against a pillow. He picked it up as if he could divine its meaning to her simply by touch. No clue. Set it back on the bed.

If he wanted more reading material, he'd discovered a stack of old *Playboys* deep in Mack's closet and a few posters of a gorgeous blonde covered mostly by sand carefully rolled for preservation. These days, he could subscribe to the same on his laptop if he wanted or for that matter, watch hard core porn if he desired. Another good result of all the exercise was that he didn't.

He'd brought no drugs along and was so fatigued by evening he didn't crave them. As a change of pace, he helped Joe on the ranch, though mucking stalls would never make his favorite chore list. Sometimes, they hauled hay bales to the cow pasture and broke them up with pitchforks while the bull eyed them suspiciously. Once, he'd been invited to drive one of the cane cutters for a short while, definitely a cool experience. His riding lessons continued, and he'd been invited along to the Sinners home games to share Joe's fifty-yard line seats while the women and grandchildren tended to use the sky box. Once, he'd ventured up there hoping to see Edie with no luck. He remarked on it later to Joe who replied, "Too busy with her last semester, I guess. She'll be home for Thanksgiving."

Yes, she would, but he'd be in New Orleans with his

family if they came to get him. The days were doing a fast turkey trot toward that holiday. Usually, Nell prompted him to call home and one day overheard him trying to make plans for a visit to his mom and granny when they could find time to make the drive and pick him up.

"No reason they should do that trip twice in a few days. Just invite them to come here for Thanksgiving. We have plenty of food, football, and fun to go around. I'm sure Livy would love to play with all the grandkids, horses, and dogs," Miss Nell invited.

He made the offer, and they accepted, glad they'd only have to close the shop for one day as sales and special orders always ramped up going into Christmas and Mardi Gras. He would see Edie after all.

Chapter Eighteen

"You are not taking anything for the feast?" Molly inquired as she cradled a covered dish of Indian rice made with sweet peas, onion, garlic, and spices, against another magnificent sari in harvest colors.

"I'm taking myself. I haven't been home since school started," Edie replied as she held open the apartment door for her roommate.

"Why is that? Because you do not want to see Tyson Ramsey?"

"Not at all. I rarely go home except for holidays or between semesters. He apologized for his lewd behavior. I accepted. We're good. He hasn't called, so we're done." They made their way downstairs to Edie's small car.

"So, you are such a prize you need only to bring yourself?"

"Okay, okay, I'll stop for some loaves of French bread along the way. My family won't need it, but we can always make turkey po-boys with the leftovers."

"That's better." Molly carefully settled her rice dish on the floorboard of the backseat before getting in beside Edie.

They took off through the main gates of LSU, passed by the sketchy area gradually getting better as new student apartments rose up along the way, and hit the interstate. The sky shone so blue over the great

Atchafalaya swamp that even its brown waters reflected the color in open areas. Most of the trees stood naked of leaves, but here and there clumps of bald cypress still retained a fine rusty color, a day to be thankful for with hurricane season finally over and the temperatures dropping into the seventies.

Traffic stayed light into the small town of Chapelle, where she pulled into a local grocery and bought the promised loaves of bread. Then, on to the bumpy side road that took them to the ranch where the gates stood open in greeting like welcoming arms. Usually, the sight filled her with warmth, but she felt jittery for no reason at all. None at all. Ty would be traveling in the opposite direction toward New Orleans.

A car far fancier than hers turned in behind them. She saw Portia Ramsey behind the wheel in her rearview mirror and Flo right beside her dominating the front seat with her size. Livy must be in the backseat, and that meant Ty had not gone home for Thanksgiving. She parked next to Dean's massive SUV by the barn at the end of a long line of cars. The other vehicle turned in right beside her. Awkward, but her fault. She hadn't called them in a while or would have known the Ramseys were traveling here.

Doors opened and slammed again as the occupants got out. Molly reclaimed her rice dish, and Edie the French bread. Portia placed a pie carefully in Livy's hands and carried the other herself. That excused Edie from hugging anyone but Flo.

"Those pies look good. Pumpkin?"

"No, honey lamb, sweet potato from my own granny's recipe, it's that old. I'll give it to you one day."

"Oh, I'm not much of a baker. See, store bought

bread." She held up her loaves.

"But you might be one day. Never can tell about people."

They'd progressed far enough to be greeted by Lil and her sisters' little white dogs, Brody and Mati, all so old now they didn't jump and upset the pies, but simply gave out friendly woofs and tail wags. That meant Lori and Stacy plus their families had already arrived. She noticed Livy's eyes taking in the happy dogs and the pony rides going on in the paddock.

"Why don't you let me carry that pie and go join the other children?" she suggested.

"Oh, no, first we go make our manners to Miss Nell," Flo intervened.

"I'll carry the pie so the dogs don't get it." And there he was, Ty Ramsey, magnificent in a tailored blue suit with a fine pinstripe, nipped in a little at the waist to show off the broadness of his shoulders, not that he needed any help in the clothing department. Way overdressed for Thanksgiving at the ranch, but...

"You're looking good. I mean better than the last time I saw you," she fumbled.

"It's the country air and all that exercise, I guess, though I have learned that country air often comes with a whiff of manure in it." He cocked his handsome head and scanned her from head to toe, sneakers to jeans to a deep green top, and the small fall leaves earrings caught in her hair as if they had gotten stuck in a thick, dark forest. "You look about the same. I mean cute—but I hoped you'd wear the dress my mama made for you."

She realized between Molly's silken sari and all of Flo's family dressed in Sunday best, she won the award for shabby, but came to her own defense. "This is your first Thanksgiving at the ranch. It can get messy, very messy. Protect yourselves."

"I'll change after dinner. Maybe we can go for a horseback ride. Your dad is teaching me on Lazy Loser. He's just my speed."

Not only did he look gorgeous, but she sensed some of his confidence had returned. Very dangerous for anyone he chased on the football field and even more so for her. "Maybe if we have time. I promise I'll wear that lovely dress for Christmas Eve, Portia." She turned away from him to his mother and breathed a small sigh of relief when they reached the crowded kitchen and handed over their offerings which Nell exclaimed over and found a place for among the many dishes spread out on the dining room table with extra leaves added to hold all the food.

On her return, she spied her granddaughter, Lizzy, fingering the edge of the silken sari. "Lizzy, that's not polite."

"But it's so smooth and pretty."

"Still, no excuse."

"Do you remember Edie's roommate from college?"

The child shook her dark curls. Amoli knelt down. "My dress is a sari from India where I come from and made of silk for this special occasion. I do remember you. I am Amoli Bhat."

"I'd like to be a Molly Bat. Bats are good. They come out at night, swoop around, and eat bugs." Lizzy took flight around the crowded room and attracted Annie's boys in her wake.

Her sister, quiet blonde May, stayed put and confided, "I'd rather be a butterfly and sip honey."

"Perhaps, you will both get your wish one day." Amoli stood before the squadron of pretend bats tripped over her.

"Lizzy, boys, go get your pony rides." Nell pointed toward the kitchen door, and still gliding, they flew toward the corral. Nell shook her head. "Always chaotic here on holidays.

"We'll eat in about an hour, once everyone is here and everything is heated. Please, make yourselves at home anywhere you can find a space."

Seeing her chance, Edie said, "I'll take Livy out to the corral for a pony ride, too. The rest of you are too nicely dressed for all that dust and *merde*." She used her mother's preferred word for horse droppings and made a convenient escape from Ty. The two of them raced to get in line, Livy's patent leather shoes gathering a coating of dirt on their shiny surface.

Once it had been Rex and her job to give the pony rides, but the responsibility had been handed on to Dean's two oldest children, eleven-year-old Beck and ten-year-old Wynn who led her special white pony. Seeing Livy's eyes tracking Princess, she beckoned to her niece to bring the horse to them after off-loading little Elena.

Raising her voice, she announced, "Everyone, this is Livy who is our guest today so we are going to let her go first." A few groaned but none protested with Stacy as the stern adult supervisor eyeing the children. As usual, Stace appeared so casually chic that dust didn't cling to her nor *merde* to her shoes. Edie hiked Livy into the saddle and sent her off with an expression of euphoria forming on the girl's face.

Stacy shouted to her oblivious son, "DJ, don't race Pinto Bean. The other ponies will want to do it, and someone will get hurt. Here, boys, you can throw the frisbees for the dogs, but not very high, okay?" She doled out colored disks to Annie's children who had gotten pushed back in line. Lizzy grabbed Brownie's reins as soon as Beck lifted the husky KC down and rode off on her own.

Beck shook his head in disgust. "That kid has no breaks, but I guess I get a rest." He turned to a cooler full of water bottles and soft drinks, drew out a dripping cream soda, and chugged it down.

"How long have you been here?" Edie asked Stacy.

"Too long, but since my kids are doing the leading, it's my turn to oversee the pony rides. Beck is so responsible. He came back from the Covid seclusion in Germany with his grandparents after a year speaking fluent German and loving soccer. Dean did all he could to stay in touch, but would like to get sole custody from Ilsa before she whisks him away again without permission. That will only happen if Prince Dobbs gets his own son," she said of her stepson.

"Maybe we should pray for that. If you want a break, I'll take over."

"That is so nice of you. I am parched and my legs ache."

Not really nice, but a good way to avoid Ty. "Well, the only heels you should wear here are on cowboy boots. Go on. Get a drink and sit down." She pointed to the folding chair next to the cooler in the shade.

After the littlest ones, Pilar and the late arrival, May, had their turns and Lizzy reluctantly slid off Brownie, she suggested Annie's three boys be allowed to ride by themselves in the ring as they were all capable. Wynn balked at letting a guy have her princess pony, so Edie rephrased her idea. "Which of your boy cousins would you like to have Princess?"

Wynn looked them over, Daniel, the oldest, Gabe the roughest, and Drew the most quiet. With a big huffing sigh, she chose Drew. "He's the nicest."

"I call dibs on Pinto Bean," shouted Gabe before DJ dismounted.

"Will you take Brownie, Daniel?" Always good-natured, the boy agreed and accepted the reins from Lizzy.

"I'll take the small ones back to the house and get them cleaned up," Stacy offered.

"Livy, go with Miss Stacy. I'm going to help Wynn and Beck unsaddle the ponies and rub them down when the boys are finished riding."

Not a child to disobey her elders, Livy complied. Edie kept time, summoned the boys to bring their mounts into the barn, and sent them scooting to the big house. With three helping, the chore of brushing Princess, Pinto Bean, and Brownie went entirely too fast. She doled out carrots from the cooler as a reward and the two ponies remaining in the barn, Goldilocks and Black Star, nickered for theirs.

"Your turn after you do the afternoon shift," she told them.

"Oh," said the fastidious Wynn, brushing horsehair from her jeans. "I have to change."

"Me, too, I guess."

Beck had already taken off for the house and male company, but she and her ladylike niece strolled back and mounted the grand front stairs because most of the crowd would be in the den, kitchen, or dining room. Wynn did like to primp and slipped into the room designated for her parents use to freshen up, her long, blonde French braid still looking fine, but her clothes a bit grungy. Edie sought out her own room left just as it always was.

Only, had someone moved the toy penguin and helped themselves to copies of the Camp Love Letter newsletter? Not that it mattered, but the pile seemed shorter than she remembered. Well, she'd stalled enough.

After washing thoroughly, she rooted through clothes left behind in drawers and her closet for a change from her horsey garb, and discovered why she hadn't taken them to college. Finally, she settled on a cashmere sweater, light and yet warm for the day, but in a pleasing deep red color that flattered her dark hair and eyes and what curves she had. It went well with tailored black slacks. But then, her dusty sneakers seemed wrong, and she put on dark flats. The earrings were still good as they had one vermilion leaf in each cluster. Fluffing her always tangled curls, she checked herself in the mirror on the back of the door. Better than acceptable—but she wasn't dressing up for *him*. Yet a tiny dab of the very expensive French perfume Stacy had given her bridesmaids wouldn't hurt in case any barn odor lingered. Better not to offend with so many people packed together.

Taking the front steps again, she entered the Gulf Stream of humanity. It drew her toward the maelstrom of the dining room just as the triangle by the barbecue pavilion summoned everyone, no matter where they were on the ranch, to dinner, including the toothsome Ty.

Chapter Nineteen

Her dad stood poised to carve one large, crispy-skinned turkey while Brinsley the butler stropped his knife to take to another at the other end of the table. With only four bird legs to go around, Junior had brought a large tray of extras that he'd baked at his restaurant. Between and around them sat the sides: rice dressing made with ground beef, cornbread stuffing, mac and cheese with its top layer of melted American slices still unbroken, Edie's French bread now in pieces filling a basket, baked beans, whipped potatoes, and a vat of gravy, naturally. The Cajun starches all accounted for, other bowls held smothered green beans, slim stalks of asparagus, sweet peas with pearl onions, and yes, an enormous green salad. Desserts covered their own table: pies, sweet potato, pumpkin, pecan, and fresh apple; cakes, chocolate layer, snowy coconut, red velvet, and one made to resemble a turkey—and of course, Mawmaw's coveted bread pudding with a side of hard sauce.

Guest etiquette applied with Ty and his family going first along with Amoli who avoided any dish made with beef or ham, but had plenty to fill her plate. After that came the women with small children who needed help with their plates. When they cleared out to the kiddie table in the kitchen, the rest of the adults lined up. Still, there would be leftovers to take home or devour for supper while football games reigned on the TV and a kid's movie ran in the theater. This was a Billodeaux family Thanksgiving in all its glory.

Edie took in every sight and scent as she joined Jude and Rex among the uncoupled near the end of the line. A peek into the den assured her that Flo sat ensconced in one of the oversized recliners while Portia and Livy held dishes daintily on their laps on the sofa. Making use of the coffee table to hold his plate and drink, Ty sat cross-legged on the floor among them. Amoli, quite comfortable on a floor cushion, ate across from him.

Plate brimming, Edie peeled off into the kitchen, making an offer to help with the children to Xochi. "You always get stuck out here."

"I do have the most small children so it makes sense," her aura-seeing sister answered as she cut slices of turkey into bits to feed her three offspring.

Edie squeezed onto the end of one of the benches and tucked into her meal. She managed a few bites of turkey resting on a bed of rice and cornbread dressings covered in gravy before Daniel held up his cup. "More milk, please." That set off several similar demands. She made the round of the table with a pitcher placed there for just that purpose. Small amounts made for fewer spills. She'd piled the vegetables on the other side of her dish having vowed to eat more greens than starches but coveted the baked beans and mac and cheese most of the kids had chosen. The two-year Covid period seemed to have stemmed the flow of babies among the Billodeauxs with two-year-old Elena being the youngest. That all of them were able to feed themselves helped, too.

Jock Brown poked his head around the doorway and offered glasses of his Australian wine to the two grownups. Edie accepted, but Xo turned him down. "No thanks."

Suspicions aroused, she studied Xochi, noting the glow her sister always seemed to have when pregnant and the glass of milk she sipped. "Stacy was right. You've gotten pregnant again." A statement, not a question.

Xo fussed with the skirt of her dress that tied under her fuller breasts and not at the waist. "Hush, I'm not ready to do the big reveal yet. I thought I was hiding it fairly well."

"Pregnant means you're going to have a baby," Lizzy chipped in to be of help to the youngsters who might not know the word. "My mom is pregnant, too. It's going to be a girl—like I need another sister. I was hoping for a sixth pony next year."

May's lip quivered. "You're mean. I hope my new sister is nicer."

Before tears broke out, Gabe announced, "We're getting a sister in May. Angel Mama had that test on her belly last week, and they could tell.

"You weren't supposed to say," Daniel said, elbowing his brother.

Xochi forestalled a shoving match at the table. "That is all wonderful news. You will love your sisters. Clean those plates now, and you get to choose a dessert." Small faces began shoveling in Molly's rice, green beans, and cherry tomatoes plucked from the salad and left for last.

"You knew about the others, didn't you? You noticed changes in their auras," Edie guested.

"It's not my news to tell. Ty seems to be healing outwardly and inwardly. So, why are you avoiding him?"

Ah, clever of Xo to change the subject. "I'm not

exactly. Something about him makes me jittery."

Xo let loose with one of her warm laughs. "I'll let you figure that out by yourself."

"Done," Daniel declared. "I want choc'late cake."

"Me, too, me, too," sounded Gabe and Drew since they did all things together.

"Turkey cake for me," said the loyal Pilar. "Because Mamacita made it."

"Gimme a leg," KC demanded, having gnawed a real one to the bone.

Elena, flummoxed by turkey anatomy, whispered, "A wing?"

Lizzy and May spoke up for their mom's coconut cake. DJ, who had not yet graduated to adult company like his sister and Beck, announced gruesomely, "I want the head."

"You sit," Edie told Xo. "I'll fill the orders.

She delivered the three slices of chocolate first, then the coconut, but stood perplexed before Xo's beautiful turkey creation. Where to apply the knife since no one had made a cut yet?

"Just go for it," a voice behind her said. "Do it like a real turkey and cut off those legs first. Here, let me. I can see you are too squeamish." Ty seized her knife and severed those legs like a pro carver.

"I'm not squeamish. It's not a real turkey. I just hate destroying a work of art."

"One meant to be eaten. I'll bet some kid asked for the head."

"DJ of course. It has the most frosting but only yellow cake underneath all that. Don't forget a wing for Elena."

"Not a yellow cake fan? What can I give you then?"

He had a look on his face as if he might be teasing, but as usual she couldn't tell or come up with a quick response.

"A sliver of the red velvet, I guess."

"You'd better try Granny's sweet potato pie, or she'll never forgive you."

"Oh, I wouldn't want that."

He cut out a large wedge and topped it with a huge dollop of whipped cream from a nearby bowl. "Anything else your heart desires?"

"Ah—ah, we'd better get a spoonful of Mawmaw's bread pudding before it's all gone. She's doling it out at the end of the table, only a spoonful each to those she favors."

"You deliver the turkey parts. I'll get in line and run interference for the bread pudding."

She picked up her plates glad to get away from the heat of his body in the already stuffy room as a bead of sweat coursed down her cleavage. Did his golden eyes follow its path? In the kitchen, she served the cake and seized a napkin to blot her chest before returning.

Too late, Ty already stood before her grandmother who eyed him with suspicion. "You that boy here at the ranch that got himself in trouble, eh? I watch LSU games, you know."

Edie winced. She hadn't prepped him on how to handle Mawmaw Nadine.

"Yes, ma'am. I can't deny it. The bread pudding is for Edie, and I'd like to try it also,"

"You Cat'lic?"

"Yes, ma'am."

"You clean up your act and go to confession, you. Then, you might be good enough for our Edie." She dug out a large spoonful topped with meringue, put it on a separate plate, and drizzled on the hard sauce. She passed him the dessert as if it were the sacrament. "This is for you. Edie, at least you picked an honest one, *ma petite fille.*" She placed a smaller amount on Edie's nearly full dish.

"Thanks for the advice, Mrs. Billodeaux." He held in a smile with his perfect lips. Edie could tell by their slight quiver.

"Mawmaw to you. I met your people, fine folks. Raised you polite and in The Church. Be good. Edie, come, lean down." She whispered in her granddaughter's ear. "You have a Cat'lic wedding, and I tell you the secret to my bread pudding." Satisfied with her bribe, Mawmaw called out "Next!" in her cracked, old-age voice before Edie could deny any attachment to the former Golden Ram.

"I thought that went very well," he said as he made way for her back to the kitchen.

Explanations burst from her lips. "She's really old. She doesn't know what she's saying half the time. I mean she calls all young men boys and asks everyone if they are Catholic. It's an obsession with her because a lot of her great-grandkids are being raised Protestant."

"No offense taken. She sounded pretty sharp to me."

Reaching the kitchen, they found Xochi wiping faces free of frosting and releasing the children one by one into the outdoors again. Lots of room now at the table. He took a seat right beside her. As the last kid raced toward more pony rides and frisbee throwing, Xo rose. "Time I get my dessert." She stared at them as if making a study of their faces.

"Oh, I meant to do that for you." Edie got up.

156

"Sit, I'll be back. You know all the women will be in here soon for coffee, so don't waste your time with each other."

Was everyone pushing them together, even Mawmaw? Speechless, she tried the sweet potato pie. A full mouth prevented saying anything stupid or naïve. After scarfing up the pie, she managed, "Best I've ever tasted. Better than Corazon's pumpkin, but don't ever tell her I said that." She looked toward the kitchen door in case Corazon had returned from her cottage where she and her husband, Brinsley and Nurse Shammy had gone to eat in peace and quiet and get some rest.

"I won't. Have to say this bread pudding is outstanding. I could eat it for the rest of my life."

"Mawmaw might take the secret to her grave, though she did promise to leave the recipe to Junior in her will." This is what they were going to discuss—desserts?

"Your dad said he wanted to try some moves with me since a lot of the Sinners are here. Any idea what he has in mind?" His fork jittered in his hand.

"No idea. The flag football game can get rough sometimes. Nothing you can't handle."

"You think so?"

"Of course. Aren't you the Golden Ram?"

"Not anymore."

Xochi returned with a plate holding both sweet potato and pumpkin pie, a smidge of her turkey cake, and a portion of the bread pudding. "I couldn't play favorites," she said as she set her desserts on the table and went to the stove to put on the kettle for tea.

Jude clumped in with only bread pudding, no hard sauce on her plate. She sat down without greeting anyone.

"I guess I need to change my clothes if it's going to get rough. Ladies." Ty stood, nodded his goodbye to no one in particular, and went on his way.

"Want some tea, Jude?" Xochi offered.

"Yeah, I guess." More glum than usual on holidays, she picked at the bread pudding.

"I'll have tea, too," her newly arrived twin said.

Edie did a double-take with her head. Jude's choice usually ran toward dark roast coffee. No, couldn't be. Their mom strolled in and touted the decaf in the third urn on the counter. Stacy, following, took her up on the offer as did Josee.

Stacy sank onto the bench. "Let the men cope with the children for a while."

Jessie rolled in and parked her chair after getting decaf as well and lacing it with the milk on the table. Lori and Alix, the athletic pair, choose the dark roast as did Amoli who had joined them along with Flo and Portia. Sarge took hers black as sin. The group seemed to emit a collective sigh as they relaxed from cooking and kids.

Unusual for her, Edie thought as Sarge started the conversation. "I have some great news."

"Let me guess. You're pregnant. Jock and I have been trying for six months and *nada*." Lori stared into her cup as if wishing she needed to switch to decaf.

"No, but still something to be thankful for. Do any of you remember a little girl, a seven-year-old, who attended Camp Love Letter this summer with that group from a children's home. Her name is Shashana, a real firecracker like Lizzy but missing a leg from an auto accident when she was four. Her parents died, and her grandparents felt they were too old to take care of her.

The rest of her relatives didn't want a handicapped child. Mack and I are adopting her. The papers should go through in January." Sarge turned to Jessie. "I hope Lizzy will befriend her."

"Oh, they are two of a kind. She taught Lizzy to do real cartwheels. A new friend her age is coming at a great time. You know she and May are nothing alike and who knows what the new baby will be. Oops!" Jessie pressed her fingers against her lips. "We were going to wait a little longer to say, but yes, it's another girl. Teddy doesn't mind at all. He says he will still be king of the castle surrounded with lovely ladies."

"Okay, my turn." Annie allowed a joyous smile to emerge. "I'm having another one in May, a girl. The boys aren't too thrilled, but they'll come around. I only hope she's not too big after having to have Gabe by C-Section. I want a vaginal birth this time."

Jude groaned at the very idea of her twin having more kids.

All eyes turned toward Xochi. "Fine, I've been fooling no one. It's just that with Covid neutralized, I wanted to do something positive to restore the earth. Number four will be a boy."

"How wonderful! Three girls and a boy joining our family next year. I've been saying I missed having babies in the nursery. I can't wait to tell Joe. But he'll start looking for ponies again. I have to put an early stop to that." Nell beamed at her daughters and daughters-in-law.

Xo delivered a cup of tea to Jude and paused to massage her sister's tense shoulders. A wow escaped her lips.

"Dammit, you read me, didn't you? Yes, I'm

pregnant. See, Edie put ideas into Connor's head this summer, that we should get married and have a kid. He kept saying my biological clock was going tick, tick, tick, and we had no time to waste. I went off the pills early because I thought it was going to take a long time, but it didn't." Jude paused for a sip of tea. "I can't stand coffee right now."

Several heads nodded in sympathy. Lori sighed so deeply she could have cooled that tea with one breath. Their mother consoled, "Give it time, Lori. Do what your doctor said and let up on the heavy training. When football season is over, go to Bali or some other exotic island and relax. It will happen."

"Sure," Lori said as if she didn't believe it.

Stacy leaned in. "Connor didn't put a ring on it?" She waggled her sizeable diamond ring.

"He wanted to, but I wasn't interested in having a ring I'd just have to keep taking on and off at the hospital. Look, it's going down this way. No objections. We're letting the Rev marry us at the AME on the Friday between Christmas and New Year's Eve. Sorry, but I don't want a dozen bridesmaids, only Annie as my matron of honor. His brother, Li'l Joe, is going to be his best man. After we get it done, the church ladies are putting out a spread in the fellowship hall. It will taste wonderful and do awful things to our gastrointestinal tracts. Y'all can come, but I'm not sending out engraved invitations."

"Um-hmm, nobody cooks like black church ladies," said Flo, who had ensconced herself in the armchair at one end of the table and been served her coffee with milk and three lumps of sugar by Portia who stuck to unsweetened and unlightened decaf. "Don't throw me out if I show up. If you want a custom gown for your size and shape, Portia can whip something up for you. Stop by the shop on Monday."

"I might just do that," Jude acknowledged.

"Something high-waisted might be a good idea," Xochi suggested.

"Oh, come on. I know I'm getting a little pudgy, but I won't be that big by Christmas."

Almost whispering, Xochi said, "I think you might be carrying twins, but do get an ultrasound soon."

"No, no—no, no, no. I promised Connor only one."

It was Amoli rather than Xo who took Jude's hand. "Sometimes, there is a second soul waiting for a womb to return to earth. Perhaps, that is the case with you. You have been chosen by this soul."

Edie expected Jude to tell her roommate that she was full of crap and wondered when this did not happen.

Instead, Jude's eyes filled with tears. "Do you think that is possible?"

"I believe in reincarnation and second chances," Amoli assured her.

Jude mopped her eyes with a paper napkin. "Stupid pregnancy hormones."

"To think, we night raise daughters together, Jude. I've been hoping for years that you'd have this kind of happiness at last. Give me one of those napkins." She wiped her own tears away. More going on than met those eyes, Edie believed.

Mama Nell raised a hand. "That makes six new grandchildren for us. Those not pregnant, raise a hand before I lose count."

Edie shot her hand up high when Flo and Portia looked her way. How on earth would she have had the opportunity with Ty here and herself in Baton Rouge—though she supposed there were ways.

Stacy also raised hers as well. "You know Dean and I are done with all that."

Alix and Josee hugged Lori. "We've been trying, too, with no results yet. You have plenty of company. But watch out. We are the most competitive women in the family," Josee added to lighten the mood.

Joe appeared in the doorway. "Hey, ladies. Someone take control of the kids so we can put Ty through his paces. Y'all will want to see this."

"Oh, Joe. Next year we're expecting six more grandchildren," Mama Nell told him.

Edie watched her father's face for astonishment, but instead, he just grinned his most sexy smile and said, "We're going to need more ponies."

Chapter Twenty

Ty straightened his suit on the heavy wooden hanger, hung his tie around its shoulders, and put it away in the closet. He'd been taught respect for good clothes and never left anything he wore in a heap on the floor. He might not be Corazon's favorite guest, but she had no reason to complain about his tidiness with sweat-soaked workout gear put in the hamper and damp towels hung on the rack. Taking out a clean sweatshirt she'd washed and put away, he paired it with worn jeans and no name athletic shoes to prepare for whatever ordeal or embarrassment Joe Billodeaux might be planning for him.

Whatever the event, it grew in his mind, inflating in importance and growing warts of fear and failure. Yeah, he'd like to calm himself with a little harmless pot. No, in his case the drug wasn't harmless. It led to other cravings and would mean the end of his second chance, the end of any hope of a career in football. Still, he needed to quiet and steady himself. Some of the crowd ascended the stairs to use one of the many bathrooms or change their clothes as he had. Because it stood empty, he took the elevator and then the front door to escape without notice.

He headed toward the privacy of the barn.

The pony rides had resumed with Lizzy tearing up the sod in the paddock on a black animal with a white star and his own sister again astride the beautiful, small white mare called Princess being guided by Wynn. Beck led a petite palomino with one of the other young girls aboard, but he'd long since lost track of all the names. To his surprise, Rex, the shining star of LSU football, provided the adult supervision. Rex stood with his back turned talking to the slim, short-haired blonde he'd been told was the biological mother of one of Annie's boys, another complicated Billodeaux story he'd yet to get straight. Ty avoided them and slipped into the barn.

Ponies drowsing in their stalls after a lot of morning exercise paid him no mind, but Lazy Loser nickered in recognition. While he had no treats for the horse, he did pause to scratch behind his ears and smooth a hand down its long nose. He felt a kinship to the much-maligned mount. Just beyond, the bales of straw always ready for fresh bedding sat offering him a seat by the far wall. He lowered himself to a comfortable position, leaned his head against the barn wall, and put his hands together as if in prayer. The three deep cleansing breaths came next. He closed his eyes. Named three things he could hear: horses moving in the stalls, the happy shouts of children playing with the dogs, an annoying fly buzzing near his ear—and one more, lightly thudding feet racing in his direction.

He had no need to open his eyes to know Edie ran toward him as persistent as the fly. She stopped just short of stepping on his toes. Raising his eyelids, he saw she'd gotten right in his face. "You'd better not be out here getting high because this time I will tell my dad."

"Can you see it, smell it, hear the crackle of the paper?"

She took a step back, but continued to eye him with

suspicion, most likely checking the dilation of his pupils. Glancing down, she said, "Were you praying?"

He realized his hands still held their steepled position. "No, a meditation technique without the lotus position or a mantra. In rehab, we practiced it every day to live in the now and not dwell in our fears of the future. Name three things you hear, smell, see, and feel. I was just getting to the smells—hay, manure, and now you." Patting the bale, he beckoned her to sit beside him. To his surprise, she did.

"I certainly hope I smell better than the hay and horse droppings."

He sniffed her neck. "You should. That's some expensive perfume. My mother wears it for special occasions. You know where she got it."

"Uncle T, prominent politician, married to Charlotte Livaudais, a family with lots of political connections, two grown daughters—U.S. Senator Titus LeMaire. You are as your mother named you, Ty's son."

He shook his head. "I knew you'd figure it out."

"Not hard. I found the yearbook for the time your mother attended college at the library. I went through it page by page, and there he was, the aspiring political candidate pressing the flesh with students in a poli-sci class. The hand in question belonged to your mother. She looks so much the same. The attraction fairly jumps off the page. I satisfied my curiosity."

"Which is substantial."

"But I won't tell anyone. You know if you ever came out as his son, you could ruin him." She studied his face again as if seeking to measure the amount of hatred he had for his father.

"I've been tempted, but I won't hurt my mom, Livy,

Granny. No, it's up to him to acknowledge us or live with guilt if he is capable of that. Another thing I learned in rehab—that I might have killed my career to spite him. I won't do that again. Ah, why are you here anyhow? Shouldn't you be supervising pony rides and avoiding me again?"

"Oh, Dad sent me to find you. You weren't in your room, so I figured here."

"Yeah, here trying to cope with my fear of failing at whatever he has in mind for me."

"It won't be that bad. He put Jock Brown through his paces before you. In the end, Jock threw Lori over his shoulder and ran the length of the field to win our flag football game."

He gave her a considering look. "I can do that. You're a lot smaller and lighter than Lori."

"He called off the game this year. He only wants to teach you a few techniques that could help you since he has Junior, Jock, and Mack around for a demonstration. See, no need to meditate."

"I don't know. I could make a fool of myself. I don't want to fail him."

"No, you won't. Here." She cupped his face and leaned in until their lips touched.

He really, really needed to set her aside, but her lips stayed on his and his responded, adding heat, going deep. Edie, not the most experienced girl he'd ever kissed, but certainly the most enthusiastic as she was in all ways. Now, he lived in the moment, all fears forgotten, potential for the future bright and shining.

"Jesus God, get your hands off my sister." Rex stood silhouetted by the sun at his back as he led the black and golden ponies into the barn.

Ty dropped the hands that had automatically gone around Edie's back, pulling her closer, but she was the one to stand up and say, "I was giving him a kiss for luck. Dad wants him for some kind of demonstration."

"Then, he's getting more luck than he deserves." Rex shouted over his shoulder, "Beck, Wynn, let's put these ponies to bed. I gotta see whatever this is."

Edie squeezed his hand. "It's going to be fine. You go ahead. I'll be along in a minute." She sashayed down the length of the barn right behind him with a retort for her brother. "Stay out of my business, Rex."

Chapter Twenty-One

"My dad is looking for you," Mack Billodeaux said. Sarge stood in the shelter of his arms as if she'd melted against her man. Ty hadn't seen her in less than a military stance in the entire time they'd worked together. Her husband stayed at their place in New Orleans close to the Sinners training facility while Sarge sacrificed their time together to live at the ranch and rehab him. Fridays, she went off to wherever Mack played to cheer him on and came back late on Sunday always in a good mood. He hadn't spoken to Mack very much and didn't sense any resentment, but guilt over separating the couple washed over him.

"Yeah, I know."

"How's Mrs. Billodeaux treating you?" Mack's smile seemed genuine enough.

"Your mom is great. So is your dad."

"I meant this Mrs. Billodeaux." He gave his wife an intimate squeeze of affection, and judging by a coy smile, she appeared to enjoy it. An inside joke, maybe?

"Uh, she tells me what to do, and I do it."

"That's the way to get along with her."

"Right, like you always listened to me, Mack. We're delaying the game. I want to get a good spot to watch." Sarge elbowed herself free and went her own way while Mack walked along with him to the impromptu playing field. Edie drifted by as if they had no connection.

"There you are." Joe greeted him in his usual hearty manner with a slap on the back. "While we're all gathered, I want Jock to show you a move you can use if you go pro. It's going to up the number of fumbles you cause on your opponents, make you golden again. Junior is going to help us. Now watch this."

He tossed the massive Junior a football and gave him a go sign. From out of nowhere, Jock Brown raced to pursue him. As they drew near to clashing, Jock delivered a powerful blow to the ball held tight against Junior's side. It popped out and wobbled across the grass.

"Fumble," Joe cried, and Annie's three boys, already learning the game well, raced from the clump of watchers to cover it. As might be expected from his size, Gabe came up with it and held it aloft. Drew, the least aggressive, earned some bruises. His birth mother took him aside to comfort him. Nope, he'd never be a football player, Ty could tell, even at this early age.

"Now boys, if you caught the ball before it hit the ground, you could have run that back for a touchdown."

"Let me try, PawPaw," said Daniel, keen to take part.

"Maybe later. I want Ty to learn Jock's technique."

More spectators gathered, some carrying chairs from the stack in the barbecue pavilion, others settling the smallest children on blankets out of the way of being crushed. Edie sat with Xochi's kids, drawing the littlest onto her lap.

"Nothing to it," Jock said. "It's the reverse of my handpass committed on the ball carrier. See, I come up on him fast, nudge him in the side to get him off balance, then hit the football from the back hard. Give it go,

169

mate."

Junior started down the field again with the ball tightly tucked. Ty pursued him, had no trouble overtaking the larger man with his quickness, but the nudge he gave the big man appeared to have no effect. Junior trundled on toward an imaginary end zone. He came aside again and punched the ball which wobbled in Junior's grip but did not come out. Frustrated, he gave Junior a mighty shove that took him to the ground.

"Hey, hey, I'm not wearing my pads. This is supposed to be a demo." Junior rose up still holding the ball and brushing at the grass stains on his jeans with his other hand.

"Sorry, I got carried away." Had he failed a test? Shown too much anger or aggression?

Junior pounded him on the back. "Save that chip on your shoulder for a real game. I've seen you take down men my size. It's impressive."

"Come on, mates, a few more times until he gets it." Jock waved them into action.

The third time, he got just the right amount of shove, a perfect punch, and the applause of the varied audience. Off to the side, Edie clapped little Elena's hand together. He felt like giving her the game ball, but the demonstration wasn't over.

"Okay, you get the idea. We'll work on it some more. Mack, go downfield and get ready to catch a long pass. Ty, try to intercept," Joe ordered.

He raced into Mack's path with arms up, but only managed to tip the ball, not catch it. Mack adjusted to its skew and came down with it after all.

"Mack and I are both six-three, and Jock has three more inches on that. Here's where your vertical leap comes in. As the ball is completing its arc, you jump as if you have springs on your feet. That's the only way you'll defeat us since you lack height. Let's do it again," Joe requested.

And again, tipped, and again missed, and again caught. On a fifth try, the ball sailed over Mack's upraised arms—and Ty adjusted his path of interception to run behind the man, make a fine catch, and ape running it back for a touchdown. He spiked the ball in an imaginary end zone. The crowd went wild.

"Great, you knew where you should be rather than where I told you to go. That's a good Free Safety." Joe consulted his watch. "Game is on in the den and second desserts are available. Help yourselves." With a clap of his hands, he dispersed the fans.

Xo collected her yawning children due for a nap from Edie who lingered behind the rest.

Ty approached her with the football in his hands. "Your game ball, Madame." He presented it with a small bow.

"I don't think I brought you much luck. You did miss a few."

"If this had been a real pro game with other men on the field and chaos all around, I'd be lucky to catch so many or cause those fumbles. Junior and Mack are bigger and better than most of the college guys I trained with or played against. Your dad taught me an important lesson. I'm not going to win them all, but I can give it my best try on every play. I really do appreciate the time he takes with me.

"He's good that way. See, no need to worry." She cradled that old ball.

"Hey, Ramsey. That's our football, not yours to fool

around with." Rex strode up to them and snatched the ball from Edie's hands as if it were a real trophy, not a scuffed pigskin that needed a little air. "Doesn't Mom need you in the kitchen, baby sis?"

"I doubt it, but I will check, little bro. Remember, I'm older than you," Edie retorted.

"But not wiser when it comes to some things." Rex shifted his stare to Ty.

"I'm handy at kitchen work. Let's go." He intentionally took Edie's hand, felt her pulse jump as he led her away under the glare of Rex Billodeaux's eyes.

Chapter Twenty-Two

He released her hand as they entered the empty kitchen, everyone else either viewing football or dealing with tired children in the theater. He washed his hands and picked up a plate. "All that running made me hungry. I think there might be some pecan pie left. Will that go good with a beer?"

"You won't know until you try, I guess." Had he taken her hand simply to annoy Rex, or did it have another meaning?

"You going to watch the game?"

"I'll be there in a while." First, she wanted to steady her nerves. She poured some decaf and sat down at the table until Ty passed through again with his pie.

"I'll save you a seat," he offered as he snagged a beer from the fridge.

Second, she needed to seek out Trinity for some advice. She found her skinny nerd of a brother picking over the remnants on the sweets table. Totally unathletic, he appeared to have the metabolism of a hummingbird to burn up all the calories he took in—the envy of the women in the family. Most still wondered how a guy with glasses in heavy black frames and dark, curly hair always in his eyes had managed to attract and marry a supermodel like Josee Riley. Without being disloyal to Trin, she wondered, too. So unalike yet the pair appeared to have a solid marriage and business partnership creating video games, their affection for each other unmistakable. Josee always referred to him as her "dear man". Maybe the fact that he'd taken a bullet for her from an ex-boyfriend added into that.

To make her approach seem normal, she surveyed the wreck of the turkey cake and the remains in the pie tins. "No fresh apple left, huh?"

"Always the first of the pies to go, though I swear dad eats most of a whole one by himself." Trin helped himself to a slice of the only pecan pie remaining and moved on to the cakes.

She picked up a plate and followed. "Want to split the last slice of coconut?"

"Sure. Jessie does make a good one, pours that syrup between the layers to make it moist."

"So that's the secret. I'll have to ask for her recipe one of these days."

"Since when do you cook?"

"Not often or well. Say, do you have a minute to talk to me? The kitchen is quiet right now."

"As long as I can eat while we do it." He took a seat at one of the end chairs while Edie stoked up on more coffee, this time the real stuff for courage.

How to put what she wanted to ask? "Everyone wonders how you got Josee to marry you? Any secrets you'd care to share."

He put on a modest smile that spread into a grin. "Persistence, great sex, and saving her life."

"Skipping the first and last, what made your sex so great?"

"I'm not sure I should be divulging this to you, baby sis, but I studied the issue of what women like—orgasms of course—and I found her G Spot."

Edie schooled her eyebrows to keep them from raising. "There really is such a thing?"

"Oh, yes, but most men don't bother to search for it. I did." He shoved more cake into his mouth.

"Do men have a G Spot?"

"Oh, baby, men are just one big G Spot in every part of their body. Whatever a woman wants to give feels great from kissing to stroking, licking, and nipping, and then there is being inside of her body, all hot and wet." He squirmed in his chair, moved it closer to the table. "Ah, didn't you discuss any of this with Mom before you left for college?"

"She said to wait for the right man, make sure he uses protection, let nature take its course, and show some enthusiasm. But what does all that mean when you have no experience?"

"How about our sisters. Why don't you ask them?" She noticed his cheeks had flushed and probably not from a sugar rush.

"I did when I first got to the university. Annie and Jude said to stay away from frat parties. Stacy told me to avoid lecherous professors, and Rex chipped in by banning all athletes. Staying away from every temptation doesn't help much."

"Well, you're older now. Ask them again. Say, I'm missing the game. I'll lose my credentials as a manly man if I don't get in there and cheer and boo at the right times." Despite his words, he didn't stand up.

His wife glided in as if she still walked a runway and kissed the top of his head. "There you are, dear man."

"Am I missing a great game?"

"Not particularly."

"Good. There's something I want to show you in our

room."

"Oh really?" Josee's blue eyes widened in anticipation and added in some sparkle. "I don't think we'll be missed."

Trin appeared to have forgotten his little sister still sat at the table. "Come on, I bet we'll make a baby before Alix or Lori." They hustled from the room, heading for the elevator, almost ploughing over Annie on her way to refill her coffee cup. "Sorry!"

"You're forgiven." They didn't appear to hear her absolution. Annie turned toward Edie. "Where are they off to in such a hurry?"

"To make a baby, I think. Could I ask you something?" Edie patted the space next to her on the bench.

Annie sank down with a grateful sigh. "I do so miss caffeine, and it's a long way until May. Dre has the boys in the movie theater. I sometimes wonder what I'd do without her help, and to think she was such a pain when we first met, trying to get between me and Matt."

"I remember. She was into all that Goth stuff, but she has turned out well. It's not her I want to ask about. By any chance, did Jude lose a baby at some time, maybe when you two were in college? I mean, no one would have told me if she had and now, I'm curious. Amoli's words about reincarnation moved our cynical about everything sister."

"You've guessed, so I might as well tell you. She did lose a child in college. I begged her to keep it, tell mom and dad because they would understand. I even offered to pretend it was mine, but Jude wouldn't listen. I think it might have been the result of date rape, but she had been drinking heavily and took all the blame on herself. I'm the one who took her to the clinic in New Orleans and drove her back to campus. That's when she started building a shell around herself that grew harder and harder. Strangely, it made me want children more. I believed I couldn't have any. That proved to be untrue."

Annie glanced at her belly, not showing much at all yet. "Promise you won't tell our parents. They would be devastated. Or anyone else. Only you have figured it out. You're way too good at that."

"You have my word." She'd always felt left out of family secrets and now seemed to be a receptacle for them. "One more thing, what makes sex great?"

Annie laughed, her hand still on her belly. "The way it feels of course." She eyed her little sister. "The first time isn't the greatest, but it gets better and better as you discover what you like best."

"But what do men like?"

"As far as I can tell, everything. Women are more particular. The right man will be unselfish and make it good for you." Annie cocked her head as if waiting for more to come forth.

"Okay, thanks. I guess I'll watch some football," she added, trying to act nonchalant.

"Someone has been saving a place for you. That's considerate."

"I guess it is." Frankly, she'd found out more from Trinity. Kissing, stroking, licking, nipping, and as her mother said, enthusiasm.

Chapter Twenty-Three

He'd made a cozy nest for her on the floor near the foot of the recliner where his granny sat which should make her feel safe. He'd softened it with a throw pillow snatched from the crowded long, leather sofa and drawn a bowl of taco chips closer in case she wanted a snack. Now, if only she'd alight in it. Turning his head for the dozenth time toward the kitchen entry, Ty caught sight of her at last and waved a hand.

Seeming tentative, Edie moved into the groove between the recliner and divan and sank onto the pillow beside him. "Before you get too comfortable, can I get you something to drink?" he asked.

"Oh, no. I had two coffees in the kitchen. The only reason I'll be standing up before this game is over will be to go for a pee."

He laughed at her honesty and moved his arm around her shoulders, his hand dangling above her breast but going no farther. Across the den, Rex gave him the evil eye, very effective dark as his eyes were, and threatening. He ignored him. Sure, his arm would go numb after a while, but damn if he'd move it unless Edie told him to do so.

Although no blaze burned in the big stone fireplace on this mild November day, the room grew warm from the press of bodies. They didn't insult the game by talking. When halftime came, he found Edie snuggled against his chest asleep, one of the prettiest sights he'd ever seen with her dark lashes fanned beneath her eyes. Family shifting for a stretch or a restroom break woke her. She sat up straight.

"Oh, I'm so sorry. I drooled on your shirt." Edie made an attempt to erase the mark by rubbing her hand over one of his nipples. He removed it before the stimulation became a problem.

She looked at him in an odd way but stood. "Fortunately, this house has lots of bathrooms. I'm going to find one without a line."

He noticed that Josee and Trinity, flushed and happy, had shown up for the second half, but would she? Rubbing the feeling back into his arm, he stood, stretched, and held his ground until Edie returned with a cold Coke Zero in hand. She settled in without awakening his granny snoring into her chins. Joe, master of the remote, had turned up the sound with no one making a remark. Nice people, very nice like Edie.

The second half proved more rousing than the first, Cowboys-Raiders, trading touchdowns back and forth. He noticed Mack cheered for his former team, especially his friend Levon Young as the man made for the goal line for the final score of the game.

The shouting woke Flo who startled and checked her watch. "Lordy, six o'clock. We need to be heading back to New Orleans."

"You're welcome to stay over with us or in a guest cottage if you don't want to drive in the dark," Nell offered.

"Child, we gotta get the shop open for tomorrow. Big day for Christmas sales and special orders for the holidays. Thanks so much for having us. Tasty food and time with our boy can't be beat. Ty, get your mama and Livy out of the movie theater."

He'd started to obey until Edie spoke up. "I should collect Amoli, too. She has experiments she wants to keep an eye on at the university. We'll grab a sandwich, then get on the road."

He stopped in his tracks. "But I thought you were spending the weekend. We were going to go riding."

"It was a nice idea, but I'm Molly's ride."

"No problem, honey lamb, we can go back by way of Baton Rouge and drop her off. That skinny li'l Indian gal will fit in the backseat with Livy easy. Why don't you spend some time with your kin?"

For once, Ty appreciated his grandmother's interference, and Mama Nell added more weight to the suggestions. "Yes, stay over until Monday. We see you so rarely."

"I suppose I could if it's okay with Molly."

"I'll get her, too." He moved out fast to find her and his family before Edie changed her mind. He made a case for riding with the Ramseys on the way back to where most were in the dining room making up small plates of leftovers for supper.

Corazon had returned to work her magic with turkey, cheeses, and other cold cuts laid out on trays rimmed with sliced tomatoes, lettuce, and raw onion rings. Sides reheated sat on trivets. A huge basket of breads, both white and brown, the remnants of Edie's loaf, and Kaiser rolls sat next to the condiments. People slapped together sandwiches, added a scoop of baked beans or whatever else they wanted, and sought out places to eat.

"Sorry, the desserts are cleaned out, but we always

have ice cream," Nell announced. The hands of all her grandchildren shot up. "After supper of course."

Amoli took in the scene and graciously agreed to ride with the Ramseys after a quick bite. She gazed on Edie through her spectacles with a wisdom beyond her years, and spoke again to Jude before they left carrying brown shopping bags containing their washed pans and enough leftovers for yet another meal.

Back in their space in the den where Teddy's daughters waved at the screen and hollered a Happy Thanksgiving to their dad who was commentating about the day's games and the evening match, Ty leaned over his sandwich built of turkey, ham, Swiss cheese, tomato and lettuce on a Kaiser roll and watched Edie scarfing up the mac and cheese she'd denied herself at dinner by her own confession.

"We're on for riding tomorrow, then?"

She glanced up, unaware of a smear of cheese sauce on her chin and how endearing that was, and said, "Yes, we are."

He wiped away the sauce with his thumb and held it up. Instead of stammering with embarrassment, she licked it off and grinned.

Chapter Twenty-Four

A major exodus occurred early Friday morning with all family members connected to the Sinners up early partaking of coffee, orange juice, and squares cut from pans of breakfast frittata. After all, the team had a home game on Sunday and practice between now and then. Corazon doled out stacks of dollar-sized pancakes for the children as they arrived, sleepy-eyed, at the table. Ty joined them far from drowsy since anticipation of having time alone with Edie kept him awake most of the night. What to say? How far to go?

As big SUVs loaded with kids who would nap on the return trip roared to life, and Mack's Jaguar, holding only himself, Sarge, and a sack of leftovers, leapt from its parking space to hit the road, Ty found himself nearly alone in the kitchen. Corazon cleaned up and refused an offer to help. Evidently, Edie and Rex still slept in like college students.

Joe noticed him lingering at the table and asked for his help putting the pony herd out to pasture where they could stoke up on the still green grass before the first frost came and browned it down to the ground. Not that he needed his assistance. The ponies knew the routine well and would be eager for rest and fresh feed after hauling children around yesterday. Just in case one went rogue, not likely, they saddled Lazy Loser and Lazy Linda. Joe went ahead to open the gate while he brought up the rear hoping he didn't have to play cowboy. While he felt secure plodding along on Loser, chasing anything was out of the question. As they penned the ponies, the white bull in the adjoining pasture bellowed either in greeting or challenge. Stay outta the bull pen Lizzy told him often, and he planned to do so unless Joe stood by with a pitchfork.

As they ambled back side by side, Joe struck up a conversation, rare for him when doing ranch chores. "*Mais* yeah, we're going to need another pony for sure," he said almost to himself before turning to Ty. "How are those boots working out for you?"

He looked down at the toes of the boots, plain, no fancy stitching, that Joe had gifted him for helping out with the chores. "Great. Nice to know I won't be dragged to death if my foot gets caught in the stirrup. As a city boy, I didn't think I'd ever own cowboy boots."

Joe chuckled. "Not much chance of Loser running away with you, but you catch on quick to ranch life. I saddled up Linda today because I heard you and Edie are going riding this morning. You know when you have a skittish mare, you have to go slow with her, gain her trust, then you get to ride. And, um, don't forget a rubber raincoat and let the, ah, mare lead the way."

He'd wondered why Joe hadn't ridden out on his intimidating, huge red stud horse, Lazy Sonofabitch, whom he lovingly referred to as Sonny. The same advice applied to Sonny as it did to the bull, stay out of his stall. So, Joe had saddled Linda for Edie in order to drop a hint on how to handle her, Edie, not Linda who wasn't skittish at all.

"Thanks for the advice, sir, though I believe Edie would fit on one of the ponies."

"Don't you ever say that to her. She can ride rings around you on Linda. Like my wife, Edie is small but mighty. She might surprise you."

"Thanks, again." He'd have to stop teasing her about her size and calling her baby. Too bad because he enjoyed riling her. "I want to go forward doing the best I can in the best way possible." But it wouldn't be as much fun.

"I'm certain that you will."

Back at the barn, they found Edie waiting tricked out in boots, jeans, a western style shirt that appeared a little tight in the bust as if a few buttons might pop open at any minute, and a straw cowgirl hat with a red band suppressing her curls. Joe tossed Linda's reins to his daughter.

"I warmed her up for you. You can go for a gallop if you want."

Edie looked at Ty, a challenge in her glance. "You think you can handle a gallop?" She strapped something on behind her saddle and adjusted the stirrups for her shorter legs.

"I can, but Loser might have a heart attack if he goes too fast."

"That's why he lost his balls. You've still got yours, right? Let's go."

Joe frowned at her language, but Edie set her heels to her horse after a nimble leap into the saddle. Ty doubted she noticed as she left him in her dust. He patted Loser on the neck.

"Don't fail me now, pal. That's a mare ahead of us. Pretend you still have balls."

He pulled up his mount's drooping head and gave him an authoritative kick that got Loser to break into a trot and with more knee squeezing and urging up to a canter. They wouldn't catch Edie and Linda unless they chose to wait for him. Which they didn't.

He and his mount arrived at the end of fenced pastures where the path veered away from the bayou, but not so much as a puff of dust told him where Edie had gone. However, the white bull stared into the live oak and magnolia grove giving him a hint.

"Come on, Loser. Snack time is over." He forced his horse's head out of a savory clump of purple wild asters. "Give me some help, here."

Still chewing, Loser neighed. An answer sounded from the forest where no paths were evident. "Thanks." He edged the horse along the woods until he found an opening not blocked by a verge of spindly redbuds and dogwoods. Beneath the massive, low growing live oaks and tall evergreen magnolias a carpet thick with last year's leaves absorbed all sound. The heavy branches and broad leaves shut out the sun and discouraged weeds, but still he had to duck and weave through the maze like a prince in a fairy tale seeking his fair maiden. When he burst into a clearing, the stream of sunlight nearly blinded him.

There she sat on a plaid blanket surrounded by a wide bed of moss pocked with the tiny acorns of the live oaks and strewn with the red seeds and center cones of the magnolias trying to take root. With Edie's straw hat hooked over her saddle horn, Linda grazed on some grassy clumps at the edge of the moss circle. The mare gave her stablemate a nicker as if inviting him to join her. Loser moved in that direction without any encouragement.

Ty dismounted, knowing that Loser wouldn't go

anywhere as long as the eats held out. Edie patted a place beside her. When he arrived, she leaned back on the blanket. One of those straining buttons popped at the top of her shirt. She didn't appear to notice.

"Isn't it great in here? So quiet and private."

"A little spooky, too."

"City boy," she said as he sat next to her.

"What's beyond the woods—an enchanted castle with a moat full of alligators?"

"Sadly, no. Just more of my dad's cane fields behind a tall fence with a motion senser on top in case anyone tries to get in—or out as my brothers sometimes attempted in their teens. Once upon a time, Tom's kidnapper came in that way before all the security."

Seeking any cameras hidden in the foliage, Ty eyed the branches of the trees ringing the glade

"I know what you're thinking, but the grove isn't bugged, I believe because my parents liked to come here sometimes and, um, enjoy themselves. Probably still do. I suspect my brothers made use of this spot, too, with their high school girlfriends. Nothing to worry about. Lie down and enjoy it."

He tried, but Edie's hand reached out to stroke his arm and run over his bicep, giving it a squeeze. She unbuttoned the top of his shirt and fingertipped her way beneath the cloth to circle a nipple on the far side of his chest, putting her in perfect position for a kiss. He gave into the urge, gripping her with his arms, holding her in place for the descent of his lips on hers. She reacted immediately with a flick of her tongue and a nip of her teeth. Her hand came up and slid into his hair, sifting through the brown curls. The kiss grew hotter, deeper.

He took advantage of that wide open button hole and

maneuvered a hand inside to cup her breast and tease her nipple through her bra. The other worked the hooks to open it. At least, he hadn't lost his skill at that. Now, as he stroked her warm flesh and took her in his mouth, he reversed their positions and gained ascendency. Even with the heavy denim fabric between them, he knew she felt his arousal as she arched and pressed against it.

He went to his knees to snap open her jeans and pull the zipper down to the scrap of panties she wore. Finding the spot he sought, he began a gentle massage with his thumb, gradually increasing the pressure until she bucked beneath his hand and tore at his shoulders with her hands. He kept at it unrelenting until she cried out, startling the horses and sending a flight of crows into the air sounding their alarm.

Stopping himself, he began restoring her clothes with reluctance as she lay there limp and stunned by her own reaction. "Edie, was this supposed to be my reward for decent behavior?"

She shook her head against the blanket. "No, it's what I wanted to do, but we aren't finished yet."

"It's killing me, but yes, we are. I can't do more here on the ranch and betray your father's trust. I was raised to respect women, but lost my way in college with girls flinging themselves at me, giving me whatever I wanted. Besides, I didn't come prepared for seduction—because that is what you were trying to do, right?" He rolled to lie beside her.

Edie's nodded into his shoulder. "Did I do it right?"

"There is no right or wrong. It's all good."

"Yeah, that's what Trin said."

He bolted upright. "You told him what you were going to do?"

"No, no, just getting advice on what men like, kissing, licking, stroking, nipping, you know."

His turn to nod because he'd gone speechless.

"Then Josee arrived and hauled him to off to make a baby."

"That's another thing. I don't make babies, and you caught me without protection. I need some advance warning. Mack left a nice supply of condoms in his night table drawer, but I didn't think to bring any." He reached into her blouse and rehooked her bra since she seemed to be struggling with it, but got in and out fast.

With a sigh, she fastened her buttons. "You seemed like a guy who always had condoms in his pocket."

"That was the old me. I'm learning to resist temptation."

"Figures, when I'm ready, you aren't."

"Oh, I was ready."

Linda and Loser stared at them with rapt attention. The crows still flew above complaining with raucous calls. A sound like a bulldozer crashing through the trees upset them further.

Sonny burst into the glade with Rex astride. Edie's brother reined the stallion to a standstill at the foot of their blanket. The huge horse pawed, tearing the moss and flinging it behind him. Linda acknowledged this show of masculinity with an almost come-hither whinny. Loser bowed his head before such might. Ty scooted back on the blanket. Edie got up and went to Sonny's side.

She grasped his bridle and in no uncertain terms told him to settle down. "You, too, Rex. You're agitating him on purpose."

"Am not. I think Linda might be coming into

season."

"Then just get out of here."

"Not unless you come with me. Dad said you'd gone for a ride with Loser here." He made one word serve for both the horse and the man on the blanket. "I figured Sonny needed some exercise, and I'd catch up with you, but when I saw those crows circling, I knew…"

"That you'd find two people simply sitting here on a blanket enjoying the sun on a mild November day?"

"Hell, no. We didn't call it the make out place for nothing. Those crows are territorial and gave me away every time I came back here with Brandi."

"Another horse?" Ty ventured to jerk Rex around a little bit after being aggressed by his horse.

"His high school girlfriend. I spied on them once." Edie smirked at her brother.

"You did not!"

"I did. An advantage to being small is slipping through the woods quietly and hiding behind a bush. I sure hope your skills with women have improved since then."

Rex's face turned the color of Sonny's coat as he retaliated. "Your blouse is unbuttoned."

He made her look. The button that had popped when she lay down had failed again. She closed it, though it showed very little. "I didn't realize I'd be staying for the weekend. This is a blouse from high school. I've filled out some since then."

"Whatever you want to believe, Edie. I'm not leaving until…"

Ty stood, flapped the blanket, made Sonny shy to trouble Rex, and folded it neatly. He strapped it on Edie's saddle. 'There, we're all ready. Nothing else to pick up.

Not an empty wine bottle, crust of bread, or a condom wrapper. Satisfied?"

"No, but it will have to do. Don't try this again."

"Or what?" said Edie, not Ty. "Tell Dad and break our twin oath about never squealing on each other? I didn't betray you and Brandi."

"Ah, nothing much happened, Rex." Ty led their horses closer to Sonny.

He mounted because he knew Edie would refuse a leg up after what he'd just said. She didn't need his help anyhow. They moved out of the clearing with the stallion breaking the way, Linda pressing close behind him, and Loser bringing up the rear. No rush getting back to the barn until they came to a wide spot and Loser pushed forward to lope back to his stall and manger full of hay.

Having learned his responsibility to his horse, you ride, you rub, Ty put Loser in the crossties and removed his saddle, subbed the bridle for a halter, and set to work. The others did the same. No one talked until he announced he'd be spending the afternoon in the gym.

Brightening, Edie said, "I'll come along and keep count of your reps."

"I don't believe that would be a good idea." His mind filled with the soft mats on the floor, the massage table, even the shower where a couple could have sex. If he picked up a condom after lunch... No, no, no, no.

"If you want to do bench presses, I'll spot you," Rex offered. "I swear I won't let the weight drop on your windpipe or elsewhere."

"Sounds like a great deal." Ty led Loser back to his stall and the hay he had earned after the morning ride. He passed Edie glaring at him with eyes that he could barely see over Linda's back. No, he didn't prefer her brother's company. Accepting it seemed safer for both of them.

They dined on a lunch of turkey tacos with a choice of toppings laid out by Corazon. Joe and Nell had driven into town. Edie had gone to her room to change and not come back to eat with them. When he went to change into exercise clothes, he tapped on her closed door and received no answer. Better to let little girls sulk, he thought. That worked with Livy when she had a mad to work off. They'd have the rest of the weekend to talk things out.

He ended up walking with Rex to the gym. Both got on the treadmills to warm up, gradually increasing the speed higher and higher. He had no doubt he could outlast Rex who was more used to standing in the pocket than running the length of the field, but he stayed on only long enough to prove that was so. Speed and stamina and hitting hard had made the Golden Ram and would again.

When they got to the weights and he took his place on the bench press table, Rex had regained his breath. "See, it's like this. Edie is my twin and the baby of the family. She's almost innocent, believes in people she loves. We all want to keep her from being hurt."

"If she were here, she'd be telling you she's twenty-one, nearly twenty-two, and slightly older than you are."

"Yeah, we share a birthday in February, but guys protect themselves better. Some woman screws them around, they blow it off—or at least pretend to. Because Covid messed up her college social life, she doesn't have much experience."

"Agreed on that, but she does have enthusiasm for nearly everything she tries and has to grow up sometime."

"What's that supposed to mean?"

191

Ty's arms began to wobble under the weights Rex had piled on. "I mean if she wants me, I'd be good to her."

Rex helped him ease the barbell into its cradle with a loud clang. "You failed our team. How can I trust you with my sister?"

"I don't think that will be up to either of us to decide. She does have a stubborn streak."

"You don't need to tell me about that. I grew with her. Should I add some more weight?"

"Bring it on."

****

Hoping the kitchen would be empty by now, Edie entered, set her overnight bag by the door, and reached for her car keys. Corazon bustled in toting a laundry basket full of towels used by the house guests. She set it down immediately.

"You ate no lunch. What can I make for you? Cold turkey sandwich? Hot turkey sandwich? Toasted cheese?"

"Nothing, thanks. I'm leaving for Baton Rouge. I promised Ty I'd go riding with him, and I did. No reason to stay."

Corazon's heavy brows pinched together. "What did *he* do to you, *querida*?"

"Honestly, nothing that matters."

He'd said it. Nothing much had happened. She'd had her first orgasm, and it meant nothing to him. Of course, he couldn't know that. The women he was used to probably came three times during every encounter at the very least. Though, he had become aroused. She knew that much. Still, she'd learned men were easy to turn on according to Trin, even if the attempt at seduction

192

had been clumsy and unpracticed.

She'd worn that tight top on purpose to show off her small but perky assets, hoping they'd be enough to satisfy. No false advertising for Edie Billodeaux. If he'd found a padded bra, that would have been embarrassing for both of them. While the button had popped on its own, it led Ty where she wanted him to go. Turned out she liked being stroked and licked as much as any man, a new experience for her. Heck, she'd gone to her spring fling dance, aka the Day School's version of a prom, with a bunch of girls who hadn't been asked by any of the boys—and they'd had a great time. Who needed a guy to have fun?

Yet, Ty Ramsey checked all her mother's boxes. She cared for him. She'd shown enthusiasm, and nature had definitely taken its course. Plus, he'd stopped, he said, for lack of protection and out of respect for her dad, so call him considerate and concerned. Maybe bored because she didn't know what she should have done next. Delved into his jeans? Touched him? Now she thought of this! In the moment, she'd been so stunned by her own response, she hadn't given a thought to what he might like.

Just as well because if Rex had caught them doing more than sitting side by side on a blanket, bloodshed might have ensued. Instead, the men were in the gym working it out in a healthy, productive way. Goody for them. She sat at the table simply to gather her thoughts before she hit the highway.

"Toasted cheese. You are tired of turkey, I see," Corazon said decisively.

She grabbed a small frying pan and set it on a burner, buttered two thick slices of bread, put one into the pan and removed three kinds of cheese from the fridge to pile on before adding the lid. While the cheeses melted together, she poured a glass of milk for Edie, flipped the sandwich, and got out a plate to garnish with baby carrots. She placed two oatmeal cookies from the jar, forgotten with all the sweets yesterday, beside them. Deftly, she plated the meal, cutting the bread on the diagonal and then again into triangles. She placed her solution to a broken heart on the table and commanded, "Eat, you feel better."

Edie's lower lip trembled. This simple offering had been her comfort food as a child, and she did feel childish. But she'd pick up a wedge, eat, and enjoy it. In half an hour, she'd be gone. If he didn't want her, forget Ty. They were done.

Chapter Twenty-Five

"What do you mean Edie's gone?" Ty confronted Corazon in the kitchen. "She was going to spend the weekend."

Corazon, never intimidated by the young men in her household, shrugged. "She say you got your ride, now she return to school. I give her a nice lunch because she seem so sad." The housekeeper wrinkled her nose. "You boys go to the shower. Hot turkey sandwiches with green beans for dinner in one hour." She dismissed both Ty and Rex who stood there consuming a bottle of water from the fridge in several large gulps.

Rex tossed the empty into the recycle bin to rest among the beer bottles from the Thanksgiving football marathon, stretched, and said, "Guess I don't need to stay here either to watch out for Edie, but I won't leave until after the hot turkey sandwiches." He pecked Corazon on the cheek and trotted off to get his shower.

Ty followed. "I don't understand. I made Edie happy, not sad." Rex stopped so abruptly he crashed into his well-muscled back.

"Hey, roughing the passer." Rex turned, flaunting his five-inch superiority in height. "And how did you make my sister happy?

"Um, only make out stuff. She doesn't have much experience but catches on quick."

"I knew you two were doing more than sunbathing.

I'm glad she's out of here before you teach her more. Besides, I have a practice before our last game on Sunday and can't babysit anymore."

"You'll win. The team is on its way to another championship, and you know it."

"Coach says not to get too cocky. We still have plenty of playoff games before we get another trophy." Rex pushed the elevator button. "I think we exercised enough today. But honest to God, Ty, I do wish you were still playing for us. Then, we'd have a sure thing. So don't mess up again with football or my sister."

"I swear I won't."

Getting out on the second floor, they parted ways. After Rex closed the door to his room, Ty opened Edie's to find it as it always was, toy penguin on the neatly made bed and a stack of Camp Love Letter news notes on her desk. Not a single scrap of paper telling him goodbye or telling him off. Either would have been better than nothing.

He knew they watched him, Joe, Nell, and Corazon, but in a benign sort of way. If he talked on the phone, one of them might drift by to see if he talked to his mom or a drug dealer. The ranch sat too far from town for an easy walk, and he had no transportation without asking one of them for a lift. Maybe, they would loan him a car or truck. He hadn't asked. Nothing in Chapelle he wanted. What did the town have but a couple of good restaurants, a great bakery, plenty of churches, a library, a barber he should use soon, a few bars, and yeah, some street corners where drug dealers hung out. No town these days was immune to the last. He'd stay on the ranch. Safer here.

With Rex in the shower, Nell and Joe still away, he

had the best opportunity to call Edie if she'd only pick up. He went into his room and closed the door down to a sliver since he'd been requested to leave it open and unlocked during his stay, keeping his word but fudging it a little. The only way he'd find out what went wrong was to punch in her number and hope. It rang, one, two, three times and would soon go to voice mail. He could envision her seeing his name on the screen and debating whether to answer—and then, she did.

"What do you want?" Judging by her voice, her sadness had turned to anger.

"Why did you leave?"

"Because if nothing important to you happened between us, there was no sense in staying."

"I was covering for us. Did you expect me to tell Rex I'd gotten into his sister's panties and worked her up to an orgasm? Your scent was still on my hands. I thought that might be what made the stallion so edgy." He sniffed his fingers, but he'd washed his hands since then and all trace of Edie had drained away.

"Who knows what goes on in the male mind?"

"I thought you had me all figured out."

"Hardly. I don't know what you want except what every guy does."

"I'm not that guy anymore. I want more than a quickie in the woods. I want your respect for not taking advantage of you or betraying your dad."

She sighed so heavily he could imagine her warm breath on his cheek. "I understand, but sometimes I wish just a little of the bad boy remained, the one zipping around campus on a motorcycle, always with a girl glued to his leathers."

He had to laugh. "When I get my cycle back, that

can still be arranged."

"Promise."

"Absolutely. When will you be coming home again?"

"Finals start the first Saturday in December, end mid-month. Some of mine require papers or projects. I really need to get cracking. There's a graduation ceremony before Christmas if I want to go, but I think I'd rather get packed for my move to New Orleans. I start my internship at *New Orleans Lifestyle* on January second."

"Think you can work me in somewhere?"

"I will be home for Christmas and Jude's wedding, maybe stay until New Year's Day. I don't know right now, but the house will be crowded and add in that respect for my dad, I don't think we'll have much time to be together."

"You know, Edie, there are things we can do that don't include going all the way."

"Yeah, I didn't think of that at the time. I was too stunned by my first orgasm."

"If that was your first, men haven't been treating you right. I promised Rex I'd be good to you."

Her outrage burst over the speaker. "You involved my brother in this?"

"Before you hang up on me, we reached a sort of truce that if I got involved with his sister, I'd treat her right. That's all. No details shared."

"Are we involved? I thought we were done."

"Not by a long shot, baby girl." Oh shit, he couldn't believe he'd said that despite its fond tone. "I meant girl, just girl."

"I'm going to pretend I only heard the first part."

The kitchen door slammed. Corazon greeted Joe and Nell. Down the hall, the sound of running water stopped in Rex's shower.

"I have to go. But we will see each other at Christmas. That's not so far away."

"Not with all I have to do between now and then. See you soon."

"Yeah, see ya." In his haste to get into the shower, he couldn't come up with anything better than that bland send off. He'd make it up to her when they were together for the holidays.

Chapter Twenty-Six

Only they weren't. Oh, the days passed fast enough. Ty had seen a softer side of Sarge with her husband, but it didn't show now. She returned with new ways to strengthen him, one-legged squats and running through the cones both forward and backward. Joe spent hours throwing him high passes that required a leap and low ones nearly in the dirt, each one a possible interception on the playing field.

"Too bad you aren't taller. You would have made a fine wide receiver, yeah," Joe told him, a very nice compliment. "You got good hands, son."

How he wished that were true. He knew he had good hands, but if only he were Joe's son. Then, he wouldn't have been summoned to New Orleans before Christmas Eve because Uncle T wanted to see him. His mother declined to hear any arguments. Yes, she knew the Billodeauxs threw great get togethers, but it was time the Ramseys had a quiet family gathering at the house on Esplanade. She'd be coming to pick him up, taking a day off during their busy season. He'd better be ready.

He stood in the hall staring at his telephone screen when Nell drifted by, stopped, and said, "Bad news? You seem glum."

"My mother wants me home for Christmas. I'd rather stay here."

"That's a lovely thing to say, but family takes

precedence."

Sarge chose that moment to join them, overhearing all. She bopped him lightly on the shoulder. "Sometimes, we have to go home for Christmas and straighten out a few things."

"Are you going to Texas?" While Sarge didn't talk much and certainly not about herself, he did know she had lots of family near Lubbock.

"Oh, hell, no. I've settled my problems. I know what will take your mind off of this—increased weight on your bench presses. See you in the gym in ten." She went off, jogging as usual to her destination on her blade foot.

"Is it okay if I call Edie? I won't be on the phone long," he asked Nell.

"It's always okay for you to call Edie. You should do it more often." Nell took herself away, giving him some rare privacy.

Edie didn't pick up immediately, and when she did, he could hear the music blaring "All I Want for Christmas is You" in the background. Bottles clinked. People shouted, "Merry Christmas" across a large room.

"Sorry if I'm interrupting anything."

"We're putting the newspaper to bed until the New Year and having a Christmas party at the same time, my last time. I'm feeling a little nostalgic."

"On to bigger and better adventures. Finals went well?"

"Whoo-hoo, they did. I am an official college graduate. Since I declined the mid-year ceremony, I'll be bringing my diploma home to show you."

"I won't be here." He tried to keep disappointment out of his voice, but being Edie, she heard it anyhow.

All the giddiness in her voice vanished. "What

happened?"

He realized she feared he'd fallen off the wagon and been caught, booted through the wrought iron gates of the ranch never to return. He rushed to tell her. "Nothing terminal. I am summoned home for Christmas. Uncle T's orders."

"There go any plans we might have dreamed. But stand up to him, sort it out. Don't let him throw you off course."

"I'll try. It isn't easy to face down a senator."

"A man who has a secret family? The power is all in your hands."

"That's one way to look at it. I'm going to miss you more than I know how to say." He'd finally found the words he wanted to give her.

"Thank you for telling me that. Same goes for me."

Someone summoned her. "Come on, Edie, climb up on a desk so we can see you and give a farewell speech." A chorus of "Speech, Speech, Speech" sounded.

"Try to get your family to come to the wedding," she said just before someone must have lifted her up by a telling whoosh of her breath. "Bye for now."

She disconnected before he did. Sarge might be right. Heaving extra weights on the bench press could help take his mind off of someone else putting his arms around Edie's waist and raising her into the air. Maybe that same person would be celebrating her graduation with her tonight. Yeah, he needed to work off a bout of jealousy he had no right to.

****

Ty waited in the kitchen with his bespoke suit in its garment bag and a bag full of any other clothes he might need to spend a week in New Orleans with nothing to do but brood over not being where he wanted to be. The scent of gingerbread saturated the air as Corazon took tray after tray of cookies cut like stars, reindeer, and rocking horses out of the oven to cool. Nell stood by dropping food coloring into small bowls of white icing to decorate them.

Traveling through the den to await his mother's arrival, he'd sniffed the piney odor of the huge noble fir professionally decorated and then, as Nell said, wonderfully adulterated by all the many homemade decorations created by her children and grandchildren over the years. Poinsettias decked every nook and cranny obscuring the view of Joe's many trophies. Christmas on a grand scale, yet still homey and welcoming.

His mother pulled up at one sharp. She'd made it very clear she wanted to be back in the city by dinnertime, so he was surprised when she accepted a cup of coffee and a freshly iced gingerbread star from Nell who took a break to sit with her.

"Portia, it's been fine having Ty here for his training. He helps Joe with the ranch chores, keeps his room tidy, does all Sarge asks of him. I can't speak more highly of him."

"That is so good to hear. We did worry."

Ty rather felt he'd brought home a report card featuring nothing but A pluses. He reached for a cookie to stuff in his mouth before he said something rude about always being watched. Corazon whapped him on the hand with her spatula. "But sometime he steal cookies before they are ready." She smeared a cut out Christmas tree with green frosting and shoved it at him.

"Thanks. You're a great baker, Corazon."

"And these are for your family, my special pumpkin

bread made with chocolate chips, not raisins."

She offered two loaves wrapped in foil to his mother who answered, "Thank you. I am sure we will enjoy them. Come along, Ty. Livy is waiting for you to set up the tree so we can decorate. We only have an artificial one, pre-lit, but it has been his job to put it together each year since he turned thirteen."

His mom rose and cradling the pumpkin bread headed for the door. He stayed behind a moment. "Wish Edie a Merry Christmas for me. Sorry I missed her."

"Just missed her. She's been moving into her apartment in New Orleans all week, but should be home tonight. You'll be back here for more training before you know it. Enjoy your time off. Call and let us know you arrived safely in all this holiday traffic," Nell said in lieu of goodbye. She stood in the doorway waving them off.

His mom's Beamer purred its way to the open gate, took the potholes in stride, and soon carried them to the highway where Ty ticked off the towns they passed through, Franklin, Morgan City, Thibodaux, Hahnville, and Des Alleman, before turning off toward New Orleans. All the while, Edie traveled in the other direction crossing the Atchafalaya causeway. How would they ever get together if they were always apart?

"You're very quiet," his mother said.

"Nothing to talk to you about."

She made an attempt. "How is your training going?"

"Good. You're taking me away from it."

"As Nell said, you'll be back soon enough, but you have to think beyond that. What's next?" She wasn't about to let him off having a "what if" conversation.

"I compete in the Combines and enter the draft, hope a team makes me an offer."

"If they don't, what then?"

"I go free agent and wait."

"How long?"

"I can't answer that."

"There are other opportunities you could take advantage of." She spared him a quick glance from the road and back again.

"Like what?" He knew what her next words would be.

"Your Uncle T says he might be able to place you in government."

"I'll teach gym before I accept that."

"You're better than that, smarter than that. You could go back to college, get a degree in computer science, law, or business. It's no shame to accept a hand up."

"Or a handout. Mama, playing in the NFL is my dream now, not his, all mine. If fail, it's on me alone, but I won't fail. Stop pushing me into being obligated to my own father. I think we can drop the Uncle T shit now unless Livy is around."

He noticed his mother flinch in profile as if he'd slapped her. He had no desire to cause her pain, simply wanted her to face facts for a change. Catching sight of his own face reflected in the window glass, he admitted to not handsome, not kind, but hard and sullen.

Wordless again, they passed over the swampy area before getting into the Metairie traffic and eventually making their way to the house on Esplanade. As usual being careful not to hit his tarp-wrapped motorcycle, his mom secreted her car in the garage using the automatic opener and closed the door again. They exited directly into the yard through a side door.

Before they reached the screened porch, Livy exploded from the house and ran to meet them. She hugged her brother around the waist, and he returned the affection. His sister was all he missed about this place. Inside, tempting aromas rose from the oven and his granny beckoned without getting up from an already set dining table. "Come here and give me some sugar, honey bear."

Obedient to her wish, Ty placed a kiss on her cheek and accepted another waist-height hug. "You all muscle now, my boy, no fat on you, but better than being just bones."

"We had your favorite delivered, lasagna from Mona Lisa, garlic bread, and if they kept their promise, a nice big salad made by Livy and your granny." His mother set the pumpkin bread on a counter, put her purse and car keys away.

"We did, we did!" Livy jumped up and down. "Can I put it on the table now?"

"Let's wait a little longer. I could use some wine after that drive." His mom helped herself from a bottle of red uncorked and resting on the table. She poured two more for himself and Gran into fine crystal glasses, the kind most people got when they married. He leaned against the sideboard and sipped his. Nothing much changed here—except for the table set for five with the good china. He stood up straight, stiffened.

"Are we having company?"

"Uncle T is taking time from his busy schedule to spend tonight with us and to see you."

Before he could utter something he'd regret in front of Livy, his sister reminded him of her presence by saying, "I bet he'll have presents for us. He always does.

After dinner, I get to stay over at Granny's. Can you come, too?"

"Sure. I'll sleep on the couch. In the morning, we'll walk to Café Du Monde and get beignets for breakfast."

He vowed he'd never sleep under the same roof as his father again. Though his bedroom sat the farthest from his mother's, he'd spent enough nights hearing the sounds of their fornicating or imagining it. Though the ranch had proved to be as special as Edie said, he did miss being in the heart of the French Quarter where great food was served steps away in any direction and a guy and his bros could troll Bourbon Street reveling in music and booze plus all sorts of carnal entertainment and walk back to wherever they planned to spend the night. Those days might be over for him now, but he still missed the lively vibe of the city.

"You won't go anywhere until you've talked to your—uncle." His mother had almost blown it, not him, but Livy latched onto the tone and looked back and forth between them.

All of them heard the approach of a vehicle, the upward slide of the garage door opening, the boom as it closed. Livy raced to the screened porch again to give her Uncle T the same kind of greeting she'd lavished on her brother.

"I'm so glad to see you. You don't come to see me enough."

Now that his sister had gotten older, she'd been prompted not to ask about presents, but he did appear bearing a shopping bag from Schifferman's, the expensive jewelry store on Canal Street, and a box of pricey Godiva chocolates which he immediately deposited in front of Flo. She opened the two-level gold box at once. "Why, thank you, Uncle T. You never forget me."

"Because you and your daughter are unforgettable."

He hadn't changed much from that picture Edie had discovered in the yearbook—taller than Ty and always would be at six feet, thicker in the middle but not out of shape, blond hair thinning and barbered to disguise the fact, always covering things up, and those hazel eyes that turned to gold and could not be changed. He'd passed the last on to Ty and Livy and probably wished they'd agree to wear contacts of another color. Otherwise, Ty remained grateful that he had his mother's full lips and prominent cheek bones to separate him from this white patrician more distinguished now than handsome.

"For lovely Livy." Titus offered her a small jewelry box that contained a golden heart on necklace chain. If it came from Schifferman's both would be eighteen karat gold, not cheap junk that might turn green with age. He put it around her neck, and Livy beamed up at him. Doesn't mean he loves you, Liv, Tyson wanted to tell her.

"For my precious Portia." A set of diamond stud earrings of a tasteful size winked up at her. Ty had seen bigger worn by football players. She immediately took out her small, gold hoops and inserted them in her lobes. His mom had a box stuffed with expensive jewelry she had no place to wear, but he supposed the cache served as a rainy-day fund that could be sold or hocked.

"And this is for Ty to celebrate his progress in overcoming his problems." Uncle T flashed open a box containing a Garmin fenix sports watch. It had dozens of functions beyond telling time from a stop watch to tracking heart and oxygen rates. Ty had seen plenty of them on the wrists of Sinner players who visited the ranch. Joe had several but took them off when doing ranch work.

"I haven't overcome them yet. Hold that until I do. And when I do, when I prove myself which I will as an NFL player, it's my achievement, not yours. Then, I'm paying you back for my rehab, my tuition, the motorcycle in the garage, and whatever else I owe you including this damned watch. Make a list."

Livy's eyes went wide. His mother pressed her fingers to her lips. Granny nearly choked on a dark chocolate salted caramel. No one spoke to Uncle T that way in this house or on the Senate floor. Always be grateful. Always be polite, or he might go away and not return.

"I have no doubt you will. I can see you are coming into your manhood," said the senator who regularly debated other men of power. "Would you consider it as an early Christmas gift?"

"Yes, he would." His mother took the box and thrust it at her son. He breathed deeply, suppressed the urge to knock it to the floor.

He accepted the watch from her hands, set it on the sideboard. He didn't need to put it on or wear it.

Uncle T gave him a practiced politician's smile. "That's settled. I smell a delicious meal in the making. Are we ready to eat?"

Livy, so anxious for a return to normal, rushed to the refrigerator to display her salad. Uncle T carried it to the table all the while lauding it for having olives and red onions in the mix which he loved or claimed to. Granny Flo closed the candy box and set it aside for later while his mom brought the lasagna from the oven and set it on trivets as the centerpiece for dinner.

"Ty, please bring the bread." He helped out as he always had.

Once they were seated, the wine made the rounds again. Ty passed the bottle without topping off his glass. He remained largely silent, tried to concentrate on enjoying the fantastic lasagna in the moment, as Uncle T told amusing tales about his fellow senators and the president. Livy did not need to be coaxed to relate school girl triumphs. Granny Flo boasted about her booming business and bragged about her daughter's growing success as a designer for the rich and famous. That's when the chatter hit a large pothole in the conversational road.

"Do you think it's wise to pursue that kind of a career, Portia? We promised to be discrete and quiet." Uncle T poured the last of the wine into his glass.

"No one knows about this family except the people who sit at this table, and it will remain that way."

Except that Edie knew and had found it easy to discover. No, she wouldn't tell. "You don't have to worry about my saying anything. I'm as ashamed of you as you are of us. Joe raised his illegitimate son with pride," Ty let himself say.

"You can't compare a senator to a famous football player. Our lives are far too different. It's not a matter of shame. If my second family is discovered, all of you will be hurt as well as Charlotte and the girls."

"And your career," Ty snapped. "You weren't a senator when I was born, and Joe had just begun a career to be proud of when Dean came into his life. Do your own comparison."

Livy, seated next to Ty and across from their father,

took his hand under the table and whispered, "What girls?"

"Titus, I think the time has come for me to have a life of my own, and I am seizing it with both hands," Portia said as if she meant it and was not just trying to erase her son's harsh words.

You go, Mom. Tell him off. Kick his ass out of here. She didn't.

"No one needs to know of our relationship. We will continue as before if you still want it." It, of course, was sex. Or so Ty assumed.

"I believe we should discuss this later after the children leave." He emphasized the word children, putting Ty in his place in the hierarchy.

"Yep, time to go," Granny Flo said. She blotted her big lips of red sauce and heaved out of her chair. "You have your overnight bag packed, Livy?"

"Yes, ma'am, but don't we have dessert?" she asked with childish innocence.

"Run along and I'll share my chocolates with you, and you know it's a rare thing for me to do. You, too, Ty. You can drive us in your mama's car. We'll return it in the morning."

Though he'd hung his suit in the closet, his bag still sat by the back door as if he'd anticipated leaving the same day. "I'm ready."

He found his mother's keys in their usual place. She said not a word as they left. Maybe it ended here tonight.

Chapter Twenty-Seven

He eased the expensive car down a narrow alley and parked it in the small, unused yard of the building next to his Granny's store after Livy hopped out and opened a wide gate. Flo padlocked it, and they entered her domain through the warehouse bursting with new gowns, out through the sewing area strewn with half-made dresses, and up those narrow stairs with his Granny huffing and puffing like an aged and overweight dragon climbing to its lair. He worried about her as he and Livy followed to the apartment that would always be more of a home to him than that other place.

She flopped into a comfy chair that bore the deep imprint of her behind and sighed. "I'll make us coffee in a bit."

"I can make the coffee. You rest." Ty went to kitchen and performed a task he'd done for years when the women were too busy to take a break.

He heard Livy homing in on the candy box. "May I have my dessert now, Granny?"

"Pick out two you want, but leave the square ones alone. Those are caramels, and I like them best."

"Um, I'll take the seahorse, and this round one."

Granny must have taken the second caramel because silence reigned as they chewed. By the time he brought the mugs to the worn coffee table marked with the rings of many cups, both had swallowed, and Livy got down to what she had on her mind.

"If Uncle T is my uncle, then he must be the brother of the daddy who left us because mama has no brothers or sisters. So his girls are my cousins. How come he never brings them along to play with me?"

His granny gave him the eye. "You made this bed, now you lie in it, Tyson Ramsey. Explain to this child."

"His girls are all grown up and married. They don't live around here." No need to lie.

"What are their names?"

"Emily and Madison."

"I thought one was Charlotte. I'd like to be named Madison."

"Charlotte is another relative. Madison is his favorite president. That's how she got her name."

He'd read an interview with the great man which is why he knew this detail. At one time, he'd used the internet to learn all he could about his father. There were things to admire, his support of civil rights, his dogged determination to bring more government money to Louisiana, always wheeling and dealing to do so, leaving little time for one family let alone two.

"I guess our Uncle T must feel really bad about his brother running out on us because he is so good to us."

Much as he wanted to say guilty, not good, he didn't. He left the myth of a father who had abandoned them in place. Let her have a few more years of belief in the Santa Claus that was Uncle T. "Maybe. How about a Christmas movie? You want some cocoa to wash that candy down?"

"Yes and yes."

"Pick something. I'll make the cocoa."

Thankfully, Livy fell sound asleep watching the

perpetually running *It's a Wonderful Life* in black and white on Flo's big screen. She liked the angel but didn't get to see him earn his wings. With Livy settled in her own room, once his, they switched to a football game neither paid much attention to. He knew his granny and that he'd earned a tongue lashing.

"Boy, you done upset the apple cart, and we got the fruit rolling every which way under our feet. Can't put those bruised apples back in the barrel. What are you going to do about it?"

Time for another deep breath. "Exactly what I said. Make my own way, pay him back, and never be under his thumb again."

"Fine for you. What about your mother and Livy?"

"What about yourself," he shot back.

Flo absorbed the blow, simply placing a hand on her big bosom. "I don't need his help, never did, but I played the game. That house you despise so much, your mama's name is on the deed. I pointed out if he kept it in his name, someday someone would find out what went on there. I made sure y'all got your due. Tuition at St. Aug's ain't cheap. But you can be proud you got that scholarship to LSU on your own talent. Too bad you smoked it away. A good lesson is we all make mistakes that change our lives. You gotta make the best of it."

"I'm trying."

"Don't you ever believe he didn't love your mother or you and Livy. If he didn't, he'd have stayed away, sent a check now and then. But he came to your games, got you that fancy motorcycle for your deliveries, treats Livy like the little lady she is. Remember that and try to keep yo' mouth shut."

"I don't plan to claim him. I am in a bind though,

and hate myself for asking this. My allowance was cut off when I went to rehab, and they took the motorcycle away. I need some wheels and spending money, not a lot. Just enough for small stuff so I won't have to ask the Billodeauxs for rides and can pay my own way if we go anywhere. I'll reimburse you with interest when I get my signing bonus." He couldn't meet her wise brown eyes.

"A man needs some manly things. I'll talk to your mother about the motorcycle and set you up with some cash. The shop is doing real well. Consider it my Christmas gift to you, but don't misuse either, understand?"

"Yes, ma'am. One other thing, I want to go back to Chapelle for Edie's sister's wedding and stay there until I sign a contract. That way I can be sure not to open my mouth again at the wrong time."

"It's going to be a long time without you, honey, but yeah, maybe for the best. Anything else?"

"No, Granny. I could use a haircut before the wedding, and I'd like to pick out some Christmas gifts for Miss Nell, Corazon, and Edie from the shop. Add it to my tab."

She ruffled that overgrown hair as if he were still five and had to get it cut for the first day of school. "Sure, honey bear. You be certain to tell those fine ladies you got it all from Flo's Fabulous Fashions."

Chapter Twenty-Eight

He hadn't expected his family to invite themselves to the wedding, but Granny insisted they go. "Those AME women know how to cook. Besides, we made Jude's wedding gown and one for Annie, too. I want to see the faces of the people when they walk down the aisle."

That meant his mother had to drive towing a flashy black motorcycle with gold detailing behind her elegant ride. Livy couldn't be left behind, so here they sat in a back row awaiting the wedding march with a sea of Billodeauxs and their closest friends spread before them.

Still adorned for Christmas, the interior of the old red brick church held as many poinsettias as the Billodeaux household and perhaps some had come from there. Candles flickered in each arched window and on the altar, their light seeming to grow more brilliant as the December night descended. Ty recognized X-avier Hopkins, the Sinners' running back known for his speed and his musical talent, at the organ. Caressa, his frequent partner and French Quarter singer, stood nearby dressed in a gold choir robe, filling the air with her rich voice so awesome the crowd remained respectfully quiet.

This interlude gave Ty some thinking time. He'd kept his promise to Livy, sleeping in late but taking her to Café du Monde for beignets hot from the fryer and mounded with powdered sugar. They carried a greasy bag full of the square donuts back to the apartment for Granny. He'd dawdled there, putting off going home, but Livy insisted they needed to set up the tree and get it decorated.

Uncle T had gone. For a while, it seemed like old times. He set up the artificial tree, checked the lights, and stood back to let Livy and his mother decorate. Beside the bright, shiny balls and tinsel garlands, she did hang ornaments he'd made in childhood as well as Livy's newer creations that were often embellished with scraps from the shop. When small, he'd doubled whatever he made at school, one for mom, one for Uncle T—that probably went into the trash.

Gifts appeared under the tree soon to be opened it was so close to Christmas. He'd relied on his granny again for something for his mother, an alligator handbag she'd admired but not set aside for herself. As for Livy, he'd gone out on Christmas Eve to find the juvenile version of the video game, *Josee's World* that didn't contain the romantic liaisons but did retain the glitz and glamour of high fashion modeling. She'd be able to dress the models from a huge selection of finery or design her own creations. He'd bought an extra-extra-large Sinners T-shirt for Gran to wear on game days at a tourist shop. For Miss Nell and Corazon, he picked out cashmere shawls, a deep red for Nell and a vibrant green for Corazon from the stock at the shop, but froze over what to get for Edie. Nothing sexy but not girlish either.

"You know that dress we made for her and you delivered?" his gran asked.

Yes, the one that had gotten him back into Edie's good graces, led to an introduction to Joe, and placed him right here, right now, at a wedding for her sister. As he'd shopped for the video game at stores open late for last minute buyers, his thoughts were on Edie wearing that dress on Christmas Eve as she'd promised.

"Here. This is what you need." Granny took a necklace from the jewelry case, silver stars hung on thin wire, earrings to match. "Perfect to go with that gown we made for our honey lamb." She'd wrapped them all in Flo's Fabulous signature paper, wild swirls of red and green punctuated with gold stars and topped with faux velvet bows. That and a fine turkey dinner with her sweet potato pie for dessert made for a happy Christmas day like the ones from his childhood even if Uncle T had left his mark in the form of a gold bracelet with a little heart charm for Livy and a modest diamond solitaire necklace his mother could wear in public without being questioned. The sports watch still sat abandoned on the sideboard.

Only finding a last gift on his pillow that night changed things: a slim, black Spanish leather wallet filled with large bills and a note saying, "Your back allowance. You earned this. From your proud father." This, the first acknowledgement he'd ever had of their true relationship. Grown men didn't cry into their pillows, but he went to sleep with a large knot in his throat. The next morning, he paid his granny back for his purchases, and while the women worked in the shop accepting returns, doing alternations to gift gowns, preparing for the winter sale, he rode his motorcycle across the causeway to the north shore for miles and miles, tasting freedom in the wind.

The chords of the Wedding March brought him back to the now where he sat in another custom suit made by his mother and gran, their Christmas gift, black with a pale gold lining, a shirt and pocket square of the same color, a stark black silk tie crossed with golden tie clip. He'd gotten that haircut he needed, shaved close on the sides, full but not wild on the top, and lightly streaked with blond, not bleached. The Golden Ram hadn't returned, but he was on his way.

****

She knew when he entered the church despite the oceans of relatives and close friends between them. A slight stir occurred in the rear. Flo's always exuberant voice asked someone to scrunch over a little bit more to make room for her family. Up until that second, Edie thought he couldn't make it, but she'd worn the blue and silver dress just as she had on Christmas Eve.

He didn't call her until after Christmas Day. Having experienced a Billodeaux Thanksgiving, he possibly believed they wouldn't be able to talk long in all the noise and happy chaos. The next day, he rang and spilled out the story of losing his temper when confronting his father, his family standing right there, especially Livy.

"You know, smoking pot kept me mellow, helped me suppress what I felt. On the football field, I could channel that anger. Right now, I have to do it myself and failed big time. I did go to an NA meeting to let it all out. That helped. Otherwise, I stayed home afraid to run into old friends who'd offer me weed, and others who wouldn't want to be seen with me since I let the team down. It's been a long week, Edie."

"But you'll come to the wedding?"

And he had, not that she could see him over the heads of taller people sitting between them, especially when all stood for the very short procession led by Annie clad in muted high-waisted silver so cleverly draped that her four-month pregnant belly barely showed. A scooped neckline with rows of argent bugle beads drew the eyes up farther to her glowing face and black curls held back by a beaded headband. She carried a hand tied bouquet of white calla lilies from the local florist, Beau's Blooms, Edie figured, just as the cake would come from Pommier's Bakery in Chapelle. No extra fuss as Jude had decreed.

Jude appeared on their handsome father's arm, he in his custom tux that all the men in the family owned and she in pale gold with the same matching bugle bead collar. The color became her sister's black hair and slightly terrified dark eyes. Even though she wasn't as far along as Annie, the Ramsey women hadn't been quite able to hide the larger baby bump. A fuller bouquet of yellow callas with more greenery helped to disguise her figure. Somehow, Flo and Portia had convinced Jude to wear a small, golden tiara in very good taste since she'd refused a veil.

As confident as always and quite handsome out of his doctor clothes, Connor Bullock stood at the altar hemmed in by his massive brother Li'l Joe, named for Edie's dad, and his preacher father about the same size but gone to fat. Connor definitely had his mother's looks, the light skin, the green eyes, the slender build.

The Rev, a broad grin on his dark face, waited as Joe gave his daughter away and stepped to one side to join Annie now holding both bouquets. He spoke about the joy of uniting two people in matrimony, made even more special by the fact that their families had been close friends even before their births. He'd been requested to keep it short, and soon launched into the traditional wedding vows to love, honor, and cherish in sickness and in health. They had declined to write their own vows.

The groom bent to kiss his much shorter bride, brief but with feeling, before X pounded out a resounding recessional and got everyone moving toward the reception hall behind the church. Connor and Stevie Riley, godparents to the groom, lingered behind as Stevie always served as the family photographer. The wedding party was recalled to pose in front of the altar along with the parents of the newly wed.

The rest escaped, waiting with patience to dig into dishes set out by the church ladies on many tables covered in white linens. Despite the tempting aromas filling the room, Edie desired only one thing—to find Ty in the crowd. She spotted Flo already lined up by the first table and ready to go, Portia and Livy with her, but no Ty. The hands placed on her shoulders made her jump. Ty whispered in her ear, "Could we step outside for a minute?"

She nodded and led the way out a side door and into a prayer garden with a bench for meditation and red Christmas camellias in bloom since the frost hadn't pinched the buds yet in this sheltered area surrounded by a holly hedge. He led her to a bench, and she shivered against him as they sat, the air too chilly for her dress but the sky above clear and full of stars to make up for that. He removed his jacket, warm from his body, and placed it over her shoulders.

"Your shirt is the same color as Jude's gown," she remarked, then wished she could take it back, a supremely romantic moment ruined by her curiosity.

He nodded. "The Ramsey women do not waste a shred of cloth. I think it was left over from the wedding dress. That's what I got for Christmas, a new suit, shirt, and tie. But here, I picked this out for you with a little help from Granny." He pulled a slim jewelry box from his coat pocket.

"Oh, silver stars. I love it. Help me put it on." She turned her back while he fumbled a little with the catch and finally got the necklace on. Removing her fleur-de-lis earrings, she replaced them with stars.

"I have nothing for you."

"Except this." Ty leaned in to initiate a kiss, but her lips were already there, parted, and ready to lick and nip and take his tongue inside as if she knew they'd have little time for preliminaries. Her fingers combed his hair. "So soft," she murmured when they took a breath. "I like the gold highlights. Never cared for the bleached look."

"That's not coming back."

They tangled again, heating the air around them. His coat slipped off her shoulders, and she felt no cold, only the mingling of tongues and lips, the excitement he aroused in her.

"Hey, who let the door to the prayer garden open? We're losing the heat," said a voice that could only be the Rev's basso voice. He drew the slightly cracked door closed with a thud.

They paused a minute before getting up, not having lost any of theirs. A test of the door proved that it had locked behind them.

"It's okay. There's a gate over here where we can leave and then come in the front door." Edie led the way, not dropping his hand for a second.

"I'm glad one of us knows where we're going."

"I've been to plenty of services here. When I got bored during hospitality hour, I'd come out here to play. In the summer, it's beautiful with lots of flowers blooming. I'd swing on the gate."

"Thank heaven for that gate."

They made their way around to the front and entered the hall warm with bodies closely packed. The buffet line had begun to move. Flo already had a full plate and a table secured. The bride and groom were seated, accepting congratulations, not eating much on their plates. Xo, coming out of the church kitchen, nearly bumped into them, sloshing hot tea from a cup.

"Ginger tea for Jude. I brought some just in case. She's feeling nauseous, but that should pass in a few weeks. Ahem, Ty seems to be wearing most of your lipstick, Edie. Don't worry, Dad and Mom are down front with the Rev and Arminta Bullock congratulating each other on finally uniting our families with the bonus of twins on the way. That will be the third set for the Rev, first his own, Connor and Riley, then Riley's two girls, now Connor and Jude's—but I suspect you had more to do with it than they did, little sister, with your suggestive ideas."

With Ty hastily putting his pocket square to good use, Edie answered. "It was supposed to be you and Connor, right? After all, he went along to bring you back when you were kidnapped."

Xo shook her long dark locks, always in gentle waves, never snarled curls. "Would not have worked. Connor is suspicious of all things *traiteur*, even ginger tea. I wouldn't give up my gift for him. Jude and he, so much alike in attitude and beliefs."

"Stubborn and grouchy?" Edie said.

"I suspect parenthood will change that. Got to deliver this tea before it cools. Oh, Ty, she's got some smeared below her lower lip."

He promptly wiped it off. "We better get in line." He reclaimed his jacket and let her go first.

Plenty remained on the spiral cut ham surrounded by potato rolls and condiments. A fresh tray of triangle cut chicken salad sandwiches reached the table just as the last were gone, but the mound of fried chicken drumettes diminished quickly. Plenty of potato salad and slaw available. Deviled eggs, some topped with paprika, some with an olive slice, sat in what might be heirloom plates made to hold them. Barbecued meatballs filled a hot pot. They accepted petite cups of gumbo for a starter and filled plates with a dozen selections. Just a spoonful of each could have made up two meals. Toasts were being made with sparkling cider according to church rules—and in deference to Jude's condition, though not everyone knew that.

Tables had not been assigned. Flo waved them over to saved seats. "What a nice spread. Glad you're driving home, Portia, because this heavy feed is going to put me right to sleep. Nice necklace and earrings you got there, honey lamb."

"Thank you. They're from the best boutique in New Orleans, and they are perfect. Ty isn't driving tonight?"

"No, I didn't have time to tell you. I'll be staying here from now until the Combines."

"Oh, I have to be in New Orleans by the second to start my job." Her disappointment must have shown as she stopped eating.

"I brought my motorcycle back with me. We'll get a ride in before you leave," he offered in consolation.

"I'd like that." He had transportation again, but three hours to New Orleans was far to go on a motorcycle.

Her parents had freed themselves from the Rev and

stopped by the table say hello. Her mother, who rarely missed anything, complimented the new necklace.

"Ty got it at Flo's place."

"I suspected as much."

"We stopped by the ranch to drop off my motorcycle before coming here. I left gifts for you and Corazon there. Sorry, Joe. I didn't get anything for you. They were clean out of ponies in New Orleans."

Joe flashed that smile of his. "As Jock would say, no worries. I got a nice dapple to replace one who passed on. My present is being able to aid in honing a talent like yours."

"Not worth much now, sir."

"But it will be."

"Joe, we are supposed to be mingling. But so happy you came. Be careful on the way home. Jude and Connor are driving back to New Orleans tonight, then off to Bali in the morning for two weeks. We almost invited ourselves along."

"Mom, that would be dreadful."

"I guess your dad and I should go alone one of these days."

"That sounds better." Her parents went off to do their mingling.

Caressa and X came to visit. Flo exclaimed, "What they done to you, Carie? You look half-starved."

She was much thinner than Edie had seen her last, but it hadn't affected her terrific voice.

"New agent. He claims if I drop the weight, he can get me out of New Orleans and booked on the road, maybe open for some big names."

X put an arm around the waist he once couldn't span. "She was fine the way she was, but won't believe me. I'm not liking this guy and the way he runs her life."

"Come on, X, all good things come to skinny people, especially tall blondes, and I can't do much about my color or my height except wear heels that kill my feet."

Edie had to agree with her as she noticed Josee and Stacy, like living advertisements of that fact, talking to very tall and much darker Riley, Connor's twin sister and pro basketball player. Why did she have to be short and brunette and for that matter, unathletic?

"Don't you dare mess with this hair." X gave Caressa's beaded braids a flick.

"Well, honey, me and Portia will be happy to fit you whatever size you be. Just don't waste away. Portia is opening her own design studio soon right next store to our shop."

"I'll bet she could make you a gorgeous wedding gown no matter what size you are," Edie found herself saying as she glanced at X's arm holding the singer close. He dropped his hold on Caressa. "I mean, they did wonders for my sister in a very short time."

"I'll remember that if the time ever comes. We'd better get going or all the celery sticks will be gone." The couple, or perhaps not a couple, moved to the very end of the buffet line.

With no room for dancing but plenty of room for wedding cake no one left until they had a piece. With the understanding that the bride and groom would leave shortly, a box of Konriko rice passed from hand to hand. Edie and Ty stood close enough to hear Jude remark as the grains rained down on them, "Just what we need, a fertility charm," as the couple got into Connor's Mercedes and went to start a life together.

Chapter Twenty-Nine

Ty walked his family to their ride in the parking lot with Edie tagging along. Once stowed and belted into the backseat with the windows up to prevent a chill from getting inside, Livy fell asleep almost immediately. Still, he spoke quietly to his mother.

"You decided to set up your design studio. That's great. Does that mean your relationship with my father is over?"

"Yes, I am going ahead with my plans and no, our relationship is not over. Ty, we have our own way of doing things and worked it out. You're grown now and beyond that, it is none of your business." His mom jingled the keys to the car Titus had given her and prepared to leave.

"But…"

"No buts."

Edie placed a hand on his arm. "Take a deep breath and let this go."

The warm air exhaled from his lungs clouded the windshield for a moment as his granny got into the front passenger seat causing the suspension to emit a slight groan. Edie helped Flo find her seat belt and clicked it shut. She'd followed him outside without a coat, typical Edie not wanting to miss anything. They waved goodbye.

He put his arm around her shoulders and brought her

inside again where they found Joe stacking chairs and Nell wiping dishes too big or too delicate to go in the washer, though he suspected they'd made a generous contribution to the church other than their manual labor.

"Why don't you help your mom in the kitchen?" he suggested, but she didn't go. He'd have to say what he wanted to say to her father with her standing there.

"Ah, Joe, sorry to interrupt and I'll help with that in a minute, but I wondered if I could take Edie clubbing in Lafayette on New Year's Eve. She leaves for New Orleans right after, and I'd like to spend some time with her since I'm not going back to the city."

Joe threw him a puzzled look and ran a hand through his thick iron gray hair pushing back that ever errant curl women found so attractive. "I don't recall any guy ever asking permission to take out one of my daughters."

"Well, considering that I don't have the best reputation…"

Joe flicked his hand in the air. "Neither did I at one time or my son Mack. I guess it's fine, but have her home by midnight."

"Dad, this isn't a prom date," Edie interjected.

"As I recall you didn't have a prom date. I drove you and your friends afterward from party to party and slept in the van in between because I wanted to make sure you all got home safe and sound. I still want to keep you safe, *cher* heart."

Ty watched her plant her feet, stiffen her shoulders, and stare up into her dad's eyes. "I'll be twenty-two in February. We're going clubbing on New Year's Eve and will be home when the bars close." He thought she might add a "so there", but Edie stopped short of that.

Joe swung his head in Ty's direction. "Knox Polk

tells me you brought a fancy motorcycle back with you. You aren't planning to take her out on that on the most drunken night of the year, I hope."

"No, sir. I can rent a car." He had, but saw the sense of backing off the idea.

"Now that would be a waste of money when we have several sitting around at the ranch. But say, we have our usual reservations at the Hilton for dinner and dancing until midnight. We're sharing a table with the Rev and his wife, Li'l Joe since he's staying over, no game until Tuesday, and Riley and her husband. That leaves us an extra seat. We could squeeze the two of you in, I'm certain. We have limousine service, too."

"That's very generous of you, sir, but…"

Edie rose up on her toes and tugged on her father's sleeve to regain his attention. "No, no, and no again. We'll take my car and won't drink."

Joe shrugged his shoulders, a defeated man. "Ask your mother."

"Come on, Ty." With a grip he could only call possessive, she led him to the kitchen where Nell scrubbed the big gumbo pot. "Mom, Ty and I want to go to some of the Lafayette clubs together on New Year's Eve. We'll use my car, not drink, and be home by two, okay?"

"You're twenty-one and have shown good sense usually. No need to ask me, but Ty, take care of her. She can be impulsive at times."

"Y'all be sure you bring protection," an elderly mother of the church cackled as she patted a precious deviled egg plate dry. Her sisters joined in for a good laugh at the young people. "Well, I was young once and know how it go."

Not a blusher, still he felt his skin heat. "Yes, ma'am."

Nell, suppressing a smile, added, "I already have six grandchildren expected next year. Let's save some for another time."

"Do tell," the ladies clamored. The eldest again added her two cents. "Told you our little bride was in the family way." Nell ignored that as obvious and began to count them off.

They made their escape. "I should stay to help your dad with the tables, but let's get you home. You want to rest for tomorrow night."

"Oh, for heaven's sake, I am tired of being treated like a child by you and everyone else." Edie followed that with a stamp of her foot.

Stacy walked up, her car keys in hand. "Sounds like someone needs a nap. Ride with me. We're leaving early tomorrow morning to get back to New Orleans, and I want to relieve Nurse Shammy and Brinsley as babysitters. Nearly nine, they'll be as tuckered out as the kids."

"Fine, I'll go, but I am as unhappy about it as Wynn and DJ when you sent them back to the ranch right after they had something to eat."

Ty brought her coat because she'd probably go without it and catch cold, the very last thing he wanted to have happen to his plans. He followed to Stacy's SUV, managed a quick kiss to her on the back of her neck when Stace moved around to the other side of the car.

"It's going to be great," he whispered. "You'll see."

Much as Edie wanted to wear the blue and silver gown again, even she knew it was too fine and fragile for a rowdy night club, not that she'd been to one. Just didn't have the interest. She supposed women wore sexy outfits with high heels, especially on New Year's Eve. Again, she'd been caught by surprise and only brought a few garments with her for a short stay.

This time, she unearthed a black turtleneck from her poetic period in high school. A plus that it fit tighter now across chest. She'd brought snug black jeans with her and added her silver heels from the wedding ensemble. Draping the star necklace around her neck and inserting the earrings to twinkle in the dark of her hair, she thought, okay, enough, with the addition of more makeup than usual and crimson lipstick. She concluded that she'd look great on a motorcycle tonight, but only so-so riding in a hybrid compact.

Her parents were gone. Ty awaited clad in his pale gold shirt, open at the neck, sleeves rolled up, dark slacks, and what her dad would call dancing shoes of supple black leather, possibly Italian. The slim gold chain at his neck seemed stylish, not gangsta. And his hair—she loved the new highlights. His eyes glinted golden when she appeared.

"Will this outfit do?" she asked.

"Anything you wear is fine with me," he answered, but she believed she caught a tiny bit of disappointment in his voice.

"Sorry, I have no sexy clothes here." Or anywhere else.

"I am proud to be seen with you anytime. Should I drive or you?"

"I'll drive on the way out since I know Lafayette better. Parking is always terrible, but I know a few places."

She took them to the old downtown area far from the

celebration at the Hilton. Music throbbed into the chill night air each time a door opened at one of the clubs that lined the street. During the short walk from a pay lot, he kept his arm around her, warding off the cold. Some of the clumps of cypress trees used as streetscaping bore Christmas lights making the narrow area more festive and less spooky. They entered the nearest night spot not far from the museum where she'd gone to see dinosaur skeletons as a child. This street, a different place at night.

While Ty paid the cover charge, she observed the scene, the people gyrating to loud music, tables tight packed to get more customers inside, and a busy bar dispensing both beer and hard liquor drinks. She noticed her mistake immediately. While her jeans and heels were in tune with the crowd, her turtleneck was not. Tops on the women ran from overtly sexy to downright transparent. Too late to change now. Her mom probably had more suggestive tops in her closet. She wished she'd asked.

"Quick," Ty said. "Over in the corner, a table for two. Go claim it. I'll bring whatever you want."

"What I want is to rescind my promise not to drink, but I guess Coke Zero with a twist of lime to make it look alcoholic."

"You got it."

She wormed her way to the table, actually a four-top robbed of two chairs and still bearing the empty bottles and dirty glasses of the last occupants. She moved them aside and soaked up some spills with a wad of paper napkins. Ty appeared with the drinks, his something clear with a lemon slice in it.

"Club soda. I won't let you suffer alone."

"Not suffering. Not a big drinker." She took a

swallow or two.

Hot in here, very close. Sweat trickled down between her breasts encased in a skimpy black bra. Skimpy was all she needed. She hoped the perspiration would be absorbed by the lace, but not likely. So dark in here, nobody would notice armpit rings anyhow. Colored lights strobed over the stage where the band rocked out, more loud than talented.

"Let's dance," she suggested, but she should have known better. Ty had grace and footwork. He drew the eyes of other dancers. She was his short, dark shadow, invisible and soon parted from him in the crush, dancing alone while other women gyrated in his golden orbit. Escaping from the mob, she made her way back to the table and the consolation of a soft drink. A guy, younger than herself though he might not realize it, thin, acne-riddled, seized the opposite chair.

"Hey, baby, you look uptight. Need something for a little relaxation?"

"No, thank you. That seat is taken."

"*Occupado* by a buddy of mine. He'll want my wares." He smiled in a slimy sort of way, bad teeth, very bad teeth.

The musical blast stopped abruptly. The band announced they were taking five. Ty separated from the other dancers except for a few girls who followed him back to the table.

"Sorry, I brought a date," he told them.

"Aw, can't we all be besties and share?" a fake redhead said, looking Edie over as if she couldn't believe her eyes.

"I don't think so."

She left with the other disappointed women.

"Ramsey, my man, need a lift?" Her table companion stood.

"Lenny, who let you out of rehab?"

"Signed myself out. This the girl you did an extra thirty days for? Sure she's legal?"

"Entirely, older than you and lots wiser. You know they'll throw your ass out of here or call the cops if they catch you selling."

"Naw, too busy on New Year's Eve to keep an eye on the dark corners. The bouncers are mostly here to break up fights. How can I set you up? Got some prime weed so strong it'll blow your mind. Have to try it to believe me."

"No, thanks."

"You kiddin' me. You were the king of weed."

"Was, past tense."

Not sure how long he could resist, Edie stood. "Ty, I feel sick. Sorry to ruin the evening, but can we leave?"

"Lenny, take your shit somewhere else. I need to take care of Edie."

"All right, man, sure. Don't want baby girl to barf all over me." Lenny took himself off to a group who appeared to be high already where he might have better luck.

Ty tucked her under his arm and cleared a path for them to the door. "If you feel you have to hurl, go ahead and do it. Don't try to keep it down."

"I think I just needed fresh air." She inhaled deeply even though beer fumes and exhaust from a parade of close-packed cars filled the atmosphere.

He paused under a street light bearing an angel effigy outlined in white bulbs. "You were saving me again, weren't you?"

"No. Yes. Maybe, but you were holding your own. He just wouldn't go away."

"We can go another place."

"I don't think I like clubbing."

His full lips twisted. "It's definitely more fun if you're high on something. Let's go somewhere quiet and private."

"What did you have in mind?"

"Give me the keys, I'll drive."

Chapter Thirty

He pulled under the portico of the Courtyard Marriott that served the airport from a distance to avoid the noise of takeoffs and landings. "Stay here. I'll get the key."

It all became clear. "One question. Did you take all your dates to nice hotels?"

"No. Their room or mine, lots of other places on a campus."

"On the back of your motorcycle?"

"Maybe once or twice. You aren't that kind of girl."

"I could be." Edie could tell her arch smile confused him.

"Look, I reserved a room in advance, but I can cancel it. I figured room service, champagne, and then whatever you wanted to do—with no acorns digging in your back or horses watching or possible cameras in the trees. Hell, we could just sit on the bed and watch a movie."

"Porn?"

"No, not porn."

"Because I've never seen any. It might be interesting."

"Only for a short period of time. I didn't plan to take you to the clubs, but you were so insistent with your folks I thought you really wanted to go. Then, you promised no drinking, too. I just wanted to be with you alone somewhere without Rex riding in on a stallion or my disrespecting your dad."

She measured the frustration in his voice and the way his hands fiddled with something in his pocket. Command to self. Don't mess this up, Edie. "Get the key."

"Um, here, if this would make you feel more comfortable."

He offered her a ring, a wedding band intricately engraved. She thought she could make out the initials P and T entwined in the design. "Your mother's?"

"Yeah. He gave it to her to wear when she was expecting me. Supposedly from the father who ran off, whose brother, Uncle T, stepped in to help us. What a fiction that was. Nothing legal about it. Got it out of her jewelry box, my chain, too. I'll give both back as soon as I can, but I don't think she'll notice."

"It's beautiful, but Ty, I honestly think no one cares about a ring anymore, especially on New Year's Eve. If this is like all the hotels I've stayed in when the family traveled, we can park around back and go in a side door with the key card."

His frustration changed to embarrassment, his eyes failing to meet hers. "We didn't travel when I was a kid. I mean, I stayed in hotels with the team, but we had to be in our rooms by midnight before a game. Not so suave, huh?' He pocketed the ring.

She took his face in her hands, raised it. "I don't need suave, and I'm glad one of us has experience. Are you still the man who carries condoms in his pocket?"

"I am tonight."

"Then, get the key." She punctuated that with a kiss, throwing all she'd learned into it. The windows began to steam over, but a tap on the glass ended that. They jumped apart and stared at the face pressed up against it. Not her dad, not anyone they knew, but a merry, drunken middle-aged man who shouted, "Get a room, why don't cha," and laughed

His disapproving wife, yes, she had a ring, yanked his arm. "Let them alone. Why should you ruin everyone's romantic evening?" She stalked inside the lobby.

"Aww, honey, lighten up a little. Lots of time until midnight." He staggered behind her, didn't catch up before she closed the elevator door and ascended without him.

"Why don't I park around back while you check in?

"Good idea. Keep your doors locked."

"Yes, Dad."

"Lots of drunks out tonight, but you can handle it of course."

She watched Ty go inside, be accosted again by the drunk who slung an arm around him, squeezed his shoulders. He removed the guy to a safe distance, shook his hand, and escaped to the desk to get the key cards. She switched seats and drove around the side of the hotel, parked in a pool of light from a streetlamp, and stayed vigilant.

He met her there quickly enough, smiling, waving the cards in their little paper folder. As he opened the door and helped her from the car, he said, "Lucky night. My father hasn't cut off my credit card. I haven't used it since I went into rehab, but I have to say the old man always paid my bills. I wonder what he'll make of this one."

"What if he had?"

"Asked to use yours, I guess, but I'd pay you back when I got my contract signed, same as I will do for him. Let's forget about him and bring in a New Year, a better year than the one before this."

They took the stairs to the third floor and opened the nearby door into the room, pretty standard, a high king bed opposite a good-sized TV over the dresser, a desk, a comfortable chair near a reading lamp, a sparkling clean bathroom with a walk-in shower. A small, round table bore a bottle of champagne on ice, two flutes, and a dish of strawberries sitting on a card declaring "Compliments of the hotel."

Edie helped herself to a berry while Ty wrestled with the champagne, coping with the seal, the wire, and finally the cork which flew into the air from too much pressure and released a spray of foam down his front. Edie laughed. "Suave."

"You know it. I think we can safely have a glass each and not drive back drunk. Do you mind if I take off my shirt?" He had it half unbuttoned, no undershirt, simply an expanse of muscular chest, lightly furred in golden brown, that chain hanging around his neck like the snake in Eden.

"Not at all. You can take mine off while you're at it." Women could be suave, too, right? Somehow, she'd thought her first time would be in a dorm room or the back of a car, or a cheap motel after a prom from listening to friends talk, all except Amoli who kept a strict chastity but did not judge others. This was grand, like a honeymoon night. He'd planned, thought of what she might like. She'd take all he had to give.

He put down his drink in a hurry, unlatched her starry necklace with tenderness, setting it aside. He freed the bottom of her turtleneck, ran his hands upward, leaving a path of frissons in their wake, and struggled with the long, tight sleeves and high neck until he'd turned it inside out to toss aside. The grin on his face said best gift ever. "That was like opening a plain brown wrapper and finding a centerfold inside."

Nice to hear and glad she'd worn her only sexy bra that pushed what she had up and together, but she knew exaggeration when she heard it. Trying to be casual, yes, I do this all the time, Edie sat in the overstuffed chair and picked up her champagne again. Ty wheeled the desk chair over, sat, and finished his portion in two gulps, but he waited with patience as she sipped hers and ate another strawberry as lasciviously as she could. She'd had plenty of champagne at charity events attended with her family and this wasn't a cheap bottle, but she'd never sucked and licked and bit into a piece of fruit with so much seductive concentration. He took a berry, ate it in one bite, but still he held back, giving her time.

When she stood, so did he. As she began to slide down the zipper of her jeans, his hands moved to help her. Since they were tight like the top, she finally lay down on the bed and let him do the rest all the way to sparkling high heels easily cast aside. He left those matching black lace panties on for the time being. She knew what came next as he arched over her for one of those prolonged kisses she'd gotten good at and missed when his lips strayed down her neck to her breasts and beyond, tickling and arousing all the way.

His hands delved into her panties, the same she'd worn in the glade but he hadn't had the time to appreciate. The fingers and thumbs began stroking. She closed her eyes and waited for what came first. So ready, so prepared, the storm within built and built and broke faster than she expected, but this time, she refused to lie there limp from the experience. Half sitting, she reached for his belt buckle, his zipper that opened wider under the pressure it had been holding in much like that bottle of champagne. He took it from there, too urgent to wait any longer. Clothes off, condom on, he disposed of those panties and surged inside with one virile push.

She tensed, gasped. He froze. "Edie, haven't you done this before now?"

Keeping her eyes closed in order not to see his disappointment, she shook her head against the pillow.

"I mean the girls I went with, none of them were…"

"Virgins."

"Yeah. I should have done this differently, taken more time. I'm so sorry."

"Well, I'm not." She pushed her pelvis up and moved against his shaft, amazed that the bit of pain she'd experienced vanished and the lightning began to strike again. She dug her nails into his buttocks and demanded, "Move, and don't stop until I tell you."

"Yes, ma'am." He started out slow and moved on faster and faster, spurred by her hands on his hips. He cried out, "Oh, baby, oh baby" over and over. When she screamed loud enough to hurt his ears, he let himself go with her, collapsed against her body, and rolled aside, careful with the condom, making sure it did not spill.

"Considerate," she thought, still in a sexual haze. He'd said "Oh, baby" more than once, for the first time telling her she was a woman, not a child in any way anymore. Sex *had* come naturally to her, perhaps abetted by some of the romance novels she read and hadn't believed. If so, there was more to be experienced, but could anything else be this good?

Now under covers, he held her close. She closed her eyes, enjoying his warmth, and slept.

The noise of bells ringing, cars on the not-too-distant highway honking horns, and rowdy guests shouting, "Happy New Year" in the hotel corridors woke them.

She ran her hands through his hair. "So soft" and initiated their midnight kiss.

"Not the rest of me," he said when they paused.

"I think we have time to do it once more and still make our two A.M. curfew."

"You'll be sore."

"Are you sore after a good workout?"

"Sometimes.'

"Is it worth the pain?"

"Yes, if it makes me a better player.

"Then, I think I need more practice." She got her way.

Chapter Thirty-One

Ty learned that New Year's Day at the ranch differed in every way from Thanksgiving, Christmas, and the Fourth of July. They'd gotten home around one-thirty to find Mama Nell still up but wearing a modest nightdress, knitted red slippers, and the cashmere shawl he'd given her over her shoulders as she made hot chocolate on the stove.

She offered a beaming smile. "Happy New Year. I couldn't sleep until I knew you were home. Hot chocolate, anyone?"

They'd been so careful, driving in slowly, trying not to make noise on the pathway that lit as they passed, carefully turning the key in the lock of the kitchen door, and assuming the light had been left on for them to find their way. Trapped.

Edie found her feet first. "Where's Dad?"

"Snoring. He said you were adults, and he trusted you.

"And you don't?" Ty forced himself to say, dreading any questions she might ask because he couldn't lie to her.

"Of course, I do. I never could sleep when my children were out, always had to wait up." She filled three mugs from the pot and turned off the range. "Sit a while, unwind. Did you enjoy the clubs, Edie? You weren't very into them in the past."

"I don't think she did. At one point she felt sick, and we left, just walked around, enjoyed the Christmas lights." Ty spoke for her as he noticed Edie touching her turtleneck, a look of panic on her face.

Nell sniffed the air. "They must have made most of those places non-smoking since the last time your dad and I went into one years ago. The odor gets into your hair and on your clothes."

He continued the conversation, wondering if the scent of sex also did that. They should have showered. "Most of them are, but really crowded, people spilling drinks on you. I got soaked." His shirt wasn't entirely dry. "Somebody getting drunk on champagne."

"We finished off two bottles at the Hilton, but spread out over a lot of people. I don't think it will stain and smells better than beer or whiskey." Nell took a closer sniff. "We'll wash it today." Ty leaned away from her.

"Thanks." He finished the contents of his mug. "We should all get some rest."

"Yes, the rule around here on New Year's Day is we sleep as long as we want and have brunch whenever on leftovers. The church ladies packed some wonderful foods for us. After that, it's football games, whatever else you want to do, and more leftovers."

He knew what he wanted to do but doubted they'd have the chance on Edie's last day at home. She'd barely touched her hot chocolate and was unusually quiet. Guilt? Regret? He hoped not.

"Go ahead. I'll clean up." Nell waved them away.

Before they got to the elevator, Edie choked out what was bothering her. "My necklace, we left it on the nightstand. What if the hotel calls here to say someone found it?"

That was all? "They won't. I gave them my cell phone as a contact number. Regardless, if you are up for a motorcycle ride, we'll go there tomorrow and see if they have it. If they don't, I'll ask Granny to order another."

"Do you think my mom noticed it was gone?"

"No, we left after them. You were still upstairs putting on the most difficult top possible. Edie, do you regret what we did?" They stood outside her bedroom door. How easy it would be to slip inside, but no, couldn't do that here.

"Not for a minute, and I am ready for that motorcycle ride." She gave him a light kiss that might have gone deeper if they hadn't heard Nell on the stairs before they parted.

****

Ty got up first, maybe anticipating something that most likely wouldn't happen. Edie straggled into the kitchen not much later, flipped the switch on the coffeemaker, and sat down with a huge glass of orange juice to admire his chosen breakfast of cocktail meatballs on a French roll with a side of slaw and a glass of milk. They both wore jeans and nothing special T-shirts, though his fit snug and so did hers. After a while, she selected a bowl of mac and cheese to go with her beverage.

Joe entered, unshaven but dressed. "Someone has to tend the stock." He fueled himself with caffeinated brew to get started. Observing Ty's meal, he said, "I know you weren't drinking last night if you can eat that for breakfast. Any left?"

"Enough for another po-boy. I'll fix one for you and

help with the animals when you're finished." As he prepared the sandwich, he dropped what was on his mind into the conversation. "I was thinking of taking Edie for a ride on my motorcycle today if that is okay. I have two helmets, and there won't be much traffic until people start going home in the evening." He strove to make it seem as safe as possible.

Edie took a gulp of her juice, cleared her throat, and said, "What he means is we're going out on his motorcycle today. Maybe we'll take a lunch and cruise around all day. People who are almost twenty-two don't have to ask permission."

"Point taken. But you won't want to miss all the bowl games, Ty. Got to keep an eye on the competition."

"We'll be back in time to watch some of them together."

Nell entered dressed as she'd been late last night but looking more tousled and content. She must have been listening before joining them. "Did I hear the word motorcycle? Don't you need special clothes for riding them, leathers and such?"

"I'll give Edie my jacket. I have another one that will do. Jeans are fine. Boots are a good idea. I won't let anything bad happen to her."

"Mom, Dad, cut it out. Go take care of the horses. I'll pack the lunch."

"How about I get dressed, and we have an unveiling of that machine in the barn as soon as I have something to eat and get my clothes on." Nell poured her coffee and rummaged in the fridge for food. She appeared to settle for quick and easy, popping two pieces of whole wheat bread into the toaster

"Sounds like a good idea." Joe finished the last

meatball, rose, and gestured to Ty to come along.

They worked mostly in silence for a while side by side feeding, watering, cleaning the stalls with only the horses making a commentary of snorts and neighs until their turn came. Joe put Sonny into the paddock where the stallion raced round and round the oval filling the air with the thud of his hooves. He put Lazy Linda into the crossties and assigned her stall to Ty.

"I think Rex was right. Linda is coming into season. It's a little early, but the weather has been hotter and sunnier than usual. Mares get feisty around that time and are harder to handle. They want what they want. You need to be careful around them."

Ty leaned on his pitchfork for a minute. He sensed another of Joe's lessons coming on. "How many times do mares come into season?"

"Oh, about once a month."

"Like women and their periods?"

"You could say that, but they don't breed in winter. We've barely had any cold weather this year. I might take her up to Bodey Landrum's ranch and have her covered. Wouldn't do for her half-brother, Sonny, to get at her, and he is sure aware of what's going on. Can't hardly miss when a mare is in heat. So, be careful around her, real careful. We're about done here. Wash up if you're taking that cycle out on the road."

Ty glanced at his motorcycle sitting veiled like a bride under the tarp that had protected it on the drive from New Orleans, thoughts he shouldn't have rolling through his mind, as he scrubbed his hands under the faucet that filled the trough. The women joined them. Edie, now wearing her riding boots and carrying a packet of sandwiches and relish tray leftovers, water bottles, and a couple of pralines, went directly to the object on all their minds. She handed her mom the picnic lunch.

"May I take the cover off now?"

"Go ahead," Ty said.

She struggled a little with the cords keeping the tarp in place, but at last whisked it away.

Joe emitted a low whistle. "Sweet machine."

Ty put a possessive hand on it. "A Ducati Scrambler I got in my teens to do deliveries for Granny. I had to wear a chain across my body to lock it up whenever I got down to keep it from being stolen. I thought it made me look tough." A bit of hay settled on the black and gold body. He flicked it away.

"I-talian like a Maserati," Joe said.

"I wouldn't mind taking a ride of the back of that myself," Nell speculated.

"If I can get his permission, we'll do it." Joe tucked his wife close.

Ty realized he'd just done the same when Edie leaned toward him. Maybe not a good idea. He rushed to say, "Let me get the jackets. We'll be on our way and home in time for football."

They were still admiring the bike when he returned wearing a beat-up bomber jacket that looked like it had been through a war, a find from a thrift shop his mother frequented, and carrying another for Edie, all black leather and zippers. He held it out for her slip her arms inside, then rolled the cuffs up twice and zipped her up to her chin. A really poor fit, way too big, but if they should spill, she'd have some protection. He settled the helmet on her head, made sure the strap was tight enough.

"I look ridiculous, don't I?" Edie asked.

"You look safe," her mother answered. "Go on. Have a nice ride."

"Games start at noon," her dad reminded them.

Her parents walked back to the kitchen to open the gates for their escape. The wrought iron bars parted as the motorcycle approached with more of a lascivious purr than a Harley rumble. Edie clung tight to his waist, her head so near his shoulder he could feel her warm breath in the space between his helmet and sheepskin collar. Once off the old, rutted roads, he opened it up on the highway, keeping to the less bumpy left lane. As he'd predicted, traffic was light, good Christians in church praying for a better year and New Year's revelers sleeping late or nursing hangovers.

They had this bright blue morning with just enough chill reddening their cheeks mostly to themselves, though they sped by fields plowed for next year's cane crop or being harvested of their seven-foot stalks even on a holiday. Next, the industrial corridor followed by the airport where they stopped for a red light before making the turn toward the hotel. He asked if she was all right back there and felt her nod against his back.

Not far, and they'd returned to the place where they'd been last night. Before going inside, he made the suggestion on his mind half the night. "Do you want to get a room again for a few hours? We won't have another chance before you leave."

"No, I want to ride some more. It's exhilarating. I can feel the thrum in my heart. Finally, I'm the girl on the motorcycle!"

Okay, let her lead the way. Maybe it hadn't been as great as she claimed, but he had no complaints. They went to the desk. He asked if a silver necklace with stars on it had been left in 301. The clerk, so fresh-faced he must have only recently come on duty, fished it from a locked drawer filled with forgotten cell phones, chargers, watches, single earrings and other adornments, possibly a bejeweled nose ring and an ankle bracelet with a palm tree charm dangling.

"Here you go. The maid turned it in."

Ty gave him a twenty. "Make sure she gets this. Tell her thanks. It's not expensive but has sentimental meaning."

"Sure will. Y'all have a happy New Year."

"Same to you."

Outside again, he zipped the necklace into one of Edie's pockets and straddled the machine. She climbed aboard with greater confidence now. "I guess you want to go home."

"Did I say that? No, go back to the light and turn left. Head straight through town, then turn it loose when we get into the country again."

He obeyed her orders. Once beyond suburban sprawl and the trailer courts, where the houses small and large sat on huge fenced acreage with horses, cattle, and goats grazing, he let the Ducati come into its own. He felt Edie grip his shoulder and shout in his ear, "Slow down. Small bridge coming up. Turn right on the first dirt road."

He dialed down the speed and took the slight hump of the concrete span across a muddy coulee with care. Access to the lane meant driving across a large drainage pipe in the ditch lining the road. Easing along the path, they passed through a broken gate and under an arched wooden sign proclaiming Sunset Beach in letters so faded Edie had to tell him what it said. Down a slight slope, he stopped by a small lake entirely hidden from the highway. A slim crescent of sand, all that remained of the beach, led to a cluster of decrepit buildings and a diving pier on its last legs. As for the lake, the wild had taken it back. Cattails clumped around its edges. A great egret stalked minnows in the shallows. The frogs in the lily pads, who had ceased courting at the approach of the motorcycle, took up their song again.

"Isn't this great?" said Edie. "Once Mawmaw Nadine wanted Dad to bring her here for a Sunday drive. Some of us kids tagged along. The boys ran off trying to catch bullfrogs, but I stayed and listened. When she was young before community pools, people paid a quarter to get in here. They had booths that sold frozen custard, cold drinks, and hot dogs. Families could stay all day and into the night. Sometimes, they set off fireworks. Louisiana doesn't have great beaches and most couldn't afford to go to the Florida panhandle back then. She and her husband did their courting here. I researched Sunset Beach when I was a teen, interviewed people who'd come here, and the local newspaper printed it as a feature on a Sunday."

"I'll bet they didn't pay you a cent."

"A few cents, but not much more, my first professional piece."

"Looks pretty depressing now."

"I guess so, but you know what else it is? Private. Long forgotten. I'm ready after that motorcycle buzz."

"For what? Lunch?'"

"Motorcycle sex of course."

"Edie, you aren't that kind of girl."

"I told you I could be. Only hoping you're still the guy with condoms in his pocket."

He nodded. "Two left over from last night. But here?'

"Just tell me how to go about it."

"You have to be sore from last night and all this riding."

"Nope. Xochi was my Secret Santa this year. She gave me some of her aloe gel with a note that said, 'Enjoy'. She says she can't read minds, but I do wonder. Anyhow, I put it on last night and this morning. Works great. Been thinking of this since we left the ranch. Believe me, I don't need much foreplay to turn me on. Let's do it."

A dream coming true and he was trying to talk her out of it? "Okay. No need to get naked. Um, lean back on the seat and let me straddle you." He unzipped her jeans, pulled them down over her hips along with cotton bikini pants already damp, and tested her with a finger.

She shivered. "I told you I'm ready." Edie tore at his belt and zipper, nearly unbalancing the Ducati.

"No, let me take care of it." He did, but wanted to do more than simply plunge inside and enjoy himself tempting as that idea was. He teased her for a while with his unsheathed penis, rubbing against her cleft until her breath came quick, and she wanted to arch.

"No, no. Stay still or we'll upset." He leaned back and covered himself with a condom before taking her deep and steady. Her legs went around his waist, her hands to his shoulders. He pumped as long as he could before reflexes took over, made him speed up, and come in one giant spasm. He leaned his forehead against hers and bid her to stay still again until he got his equilibrium back.

"Did it happen for you, Edie?'

"Oh yes, but you were too far gone to notice. What's next?"

His legs felt wobbly as he dismounted carefully, removed the condom and wrapped it in a tissue he found in his jacket pocket. Then, he put his and her jeans back in place. "Lunch. I really need some lunch."

Edie seemed unsteady, too, as she took the packet from the saddlebag. "Wedding ham on rye, carrot sticks, celery, and green olives, two pralines that didn't travel well, but the crumbs will be good, and two bottles of water. I didn't think to bring a blanket this time, but I do have wet wipes."

He nodded to a concrete picnic table and benches that had braved the elements and perhaps had been used recently since they seemed somewhat clean. He used a wet wipe on his hands and the table top, drank half a bottle of water, and sucked up brown sugar crumbs and pecans for immediate energy. Then olives for some restorative salt and the two ham sandwiches she'd made for him while Edie nibbled on her own, and a few vegetables as a concession to good health. Now, he thought he could get them back to the ranch without crashing, but Edie kept staring at the picnic table.

"This seems very sturdy, and we do have one condom left."

"Unlike the Ducati, I am not a machine. I need some time to recover from the best sex of my life."

"You're just saying that."

"Nope, most of the time I was high or drunk, don't remember a whole lot about it. Sober sex when you feel everything and know what you are doing with a special person has a lot going for it, not to mention your enthusiasm."

"I know I have that. So, it's home we go." But she didn't make any move to leave.

"I think we should. I told your dad I'd watch the games with him."

"With all his sons playing football or commentating, or in Trin's case immersed in computer games about football, I think he's a little lonely on days like this. He'd probably like to adopt you."

"I'd be good with that." He meant it. To have a father there for him like Joe who taught him and set an example of what a man should be would be a gift.

Edie shook her head. "Nope, don't need another brother, only a lover, and you fill the bill beyond my best dreams. Feeling recuperated?"

"Flattery won't make it happen either. Time to saddle up and get you home."

Back at the ranch, he dropped Edie at the kitchen door and turned the cycle toward the barn, but Joe caught him before he drove off. "It's halftime. Mind if I take Nell for a spin around the ranch before you put that sweet baby to bed?

Though guilty flashes of himself and Edie at the Marriott flew into his mind, Ty said, "Sure. Take it easy on the rough patches."

Nell appeared right behind them already garbed in boots, jeans, and a rather stylish leather jacket that probably would have fit Edie just fine but hadn't been offered. "Are we going to do this?"

"Right now." Joe wasted no time in getting them seated before he sped down the paved entry road leaning into the curves.

Ty and Edie wandered into the den where four football games played in boxes on the large TV. One showed a marching band and another a bunch of commentators analyzing the first half while the Outback and Citrus Bowls played on. They snuggled on the couch, making out a little, and heard the Ducati go past the house once, then twice, and after a longer interval, a third time when the sound of its engine died by the door. Ty went to return the cycle to the barn and give it a wipe down just like one of the horses when heavily ridden.

Joe and Nell had returned rejuvenated, it seemed. "I got to get me one of those," Joe said, giving the Ducati a pat.

His wife countered with, "I think we are getting a little too old for...tearing around on a motorcycle."

"Never too old for *that*, Tink."

Edie, who had followed him out, knew her parents well. "Next time it might fall over on you. You have to be careful what you do on it. Mom, you can use some of the aloe gel Xo gave me if you're sore."

Ty choked on a sip of the beer in his hand. "Um, I'll put the bike away."

Before he escaped, he caught one last sentence from Nell, "Not sore, only unused to...unusual activities, but thanks. I've got some gel of my own."

Edie tagged after him as he walked the Ducati back to the barn and wiped off the dust with a soft rag before dropping the tarp over it again.

"I told you the grove wasn't bugged. I bet if we go there soon, we'll find motorcycle tire treads about this wide dug into the moss." She bracketed a wheel of his motorcycle.

"You shouldn't tease them like that. It will give them ideas about what we were up to."

"Oh, I am sure they already know. Good thing my

dad loves you like a son or things could go badly. He attacked Matt Keaton when he found out Annie was pregnant before they got married. They get along great now, though."

"I won't be getting you pregnant. I promise that, but we're wasting time. You have to leave in a few hours for New Orleans. We won't see each other again for a long time. By then, I'll know if I have a career, something to offer you."

"If one career doesn't work out, we'll find you another. Are you recuperated now?

"Yes, but we aren't going to do that. I could show you some other things—up in the hay loft. Isn't that what country boys do?"

"My brothers certainly did."

Neither noticed the time passing. Joe and Nell didn't come seeking them. At dinner time, they rang the triangle calling them inside for more leftovers. Edie packed her bag, only remembering at the last second to retrieve her necklace from the motorcycle jacket. She left in the dark for New Orleans to start her career with the city magazine. Her parents said their goodbyes and gave them time alone for theirs.

After an evening of watching the Rose Bowl and analyzing every play with Joe, Ty returned to his room full of resolve to claim his place in football and Edie Billodeaux. Hanging up the bomber jacket, he remembered what he'd put in the pocket and flushed it away as he'd almost done with his life. The only regret he had at this moment—that they hadn't used the last condom.

Chapter Thirty-Two

Sarge returned on Monday and inflicted her strict routine on Ty again. She increased their runs for endurance and timed him on wind sprints for speed. Placing him on a balance board, she had Joe sling pass after pass at him, high ones, low ones, some that skewed off to the side, an exercise she'd picked up while rehabbing Mack. She nagged him about increasing his vertical leap and increasing the number of reps on his bench presses. Still, she seemed somewhat distracted.

He tried to mention it in a kind sort of way. "Something on your mind?"

She snapped at him. "I know you're used to being the center of attention, but I have a child arriving as soon as Mack finishes his season. Of course, the Sinners are in the playoffs again. They always are. Is it wrong to hope they don't make it to the Super Bowl? Then, we won't be able to pick up Shashana until February. I wanted to get her settled in her new school and set up a daily routine. She wants a purple room, but I think lavender like Lori's old room. It's the most beautiful bedroom I've ever seen." Sarge stopped to take a breath.

"Hey, it isn't all about me. We could take an afternoon off to paint the room, move furniture, whatever you need. Sorry, but I can't stop the Sinners from winning. To be on a team like that is every player's hope." He'd gone to the playoff games with Joe and other family members. Usually, Edie came, too, but with the roar of the crowd and so many people around, they barely had time to talk, let alone do anything else. All he'd gotten out of it was a yen to join the Sinners and an even deeper yearning to be intimate with Edie. Both appeared impossible right now.

"Joe and I have honed you into a weapon few teams should be able to resist. Twenty more reps," Sarge said without losing count during their conversation.

"If they can forget about my past."

"Mack had to swallow his pride and take what was offered after his cut from Dallas, but once you prove yourself, they'll up the ante. And hey, I'm taking you up on that offer to paint and haul. There's the most adorable little white bed with a canopy to be put together, too. I have a wallpaper frieze of purple and yellow pansies so it will be different from Lori's wisteria, brighter and more colorful, with a bedspread to match. What do you think?"

He could put what he knew about interior design on a postage stamp. "Sounds great. My sister would love it, and they are around the same age. Sign me up for paperhanging, too."

"That would be wonderful. It's hard for Mack to get away right now."

Sarge had shown him a softer side of herself, but that didn't mean she let up on his training. When the Sinners lost their last playoff game to a savvy old quarterback from Green Bay, Mack came home and was immediately pressed into racing him in the wind sprints. Joe pried Junior away from his prized restaurant to provide more competition.

Most of the family took a day off to go to the

adoption court and welcome Shashana Cherry Billodeaux into the family, Cherry being her former last name. He'd gotten to see Edie at the celebratory dinner but not much else as Joe herded everyone back to the ranch before dark so the child could sleep in the bedroom they'd prepared for her.

He went to bed exhausted most nights, a good thing since otherwise he fretted about Edie alone in the city. Okay, not alone. She had brothers and sisters galore in the Big Easy and visited his mother and granny regularly. She occupied Jude's former apartment since Jude had moved into Connor's luxury three-bedroom condo nearer the hospital. When he mentioned her safety to Joe, the man laughed. "I have enough security on that place to ward off the most determined attacker. Knox gave her a pistol, too, but I'm not sure she'd use it. Most likely, she'd talk the guy out of anything intended. Lots of cameras in that alley, too."

"Good, good, I feel better now." More cameras. If he ever got to visit her there, he'd have to remember that.

What really kept him awake was the knowledge that the kitten he liked to play with had turned into a tiger of a woman in bed. What about if she invited men to scratch that itch, men that weren't him. He'd hinted at it during their weekly phone call. Was she meeting a lot of interesting people?"

"Oh, yes. My job isn't all being sent out to get coffee and beignets or picking up lunch. They encourage me to look for small businesses like your granny's to feature. I've already discovered a hat maker down a side street who molds custom made felt hats, each one unique, and interviewed him. I also proposed a series called Day in the Life of... I'm going to spend a day with a Jackson

Square artist first, maybe some of the street performers. The staff is teaching me layouts, too. I'm learning so much."

She had the same enthusiasm for her job as for sex evidently. "Going out much at night?" he asked.

"A few times with my co-workers. Sometimes to Mariah's Place where I get to visit with Mariah herself who is like a grandmother to me. I've visited here often enough in the past that there isn't much they have to show me. What do you think of Day in the Life of a Drag Queen?"

"Should be interesting."

She chattered on. He halfway listened enough to put in a word now and then. The only thing he wanted to say shouldn't be said over the phone, but what other chance would he have? If he hesitated, she might find someone else she preferred, someone with a certain future. Preoccupied, he failed to notice her silence. "Ah, what did you say, Edie?"

"I asked if you were ready for the Combines. Dad is taking you, right?"

"Yes, we're going to Indianapolis together. February is coming up fast, but I think I'm ready to do my best."

"I'll be there."

That meant so much more to him than he could put into words and so he didn't. "You won't lose your job by taking off too soon?"

"I'm trying to sell them on a human-interest story."

"Not on me alone, I hope."

"No, on any guys from New Orleans or LSU. I think they'll buy it, especially if it doesn't cost them any travel money."

"That would be great, to have you there." Then, he'd tell her, once he showed the world of football what he had to offer.

****

The NFL Combines—the most prestigious meat market in the world as far as Ty was concerned—where they weighed and measured the prize bulls and one former golden ram, their arm and hand length, their body fat percentage. Joe had gotten him the invitation.

Rex received one without pulling any strings and politely declined to attend. At press conferences where reporters asked him if this was arrogance on his part, he'd replied calmly that he'd shown his worth by leading his team to two national championships and while he respected the rigors of the Combines, he also had no wish to be injured in the process. If this affected his position in the draft, then so be it. Rex, Joe, and he knew it wouldn't. If only he hadn't screwed up and could rest on the laurels of three stellar university seasons.

But no, he had to undergo it all, the interviews where the number one question always dealt with his drug use. He gave the same reply to all. He'd gone through rehab and was four months clean. He attended meetings for former drug users and worked out his problems by training hard. In fact, he felt he had more to offer now in maturity than when he'd left the team, a nicer term than being kicked out. He dropped Joe and Sarge's names without shame which always impressed.

Some of the interviewers tried to shake him with off the mark questions. Did he have any homosexual tendencies? Thinking of Edie bubbling and fizzing with pride over her press pass and sleeping in an adjoining room while he shared with Joe, so close and so far away, he answered with a positive no, but wanted to add, "Why should that matter?" He knew a few gay guys who played good ball, but held back this reply lest they ask him about his friendships—which they did anyhow. He listed Rex, Junior Polk, and Mack. Honestly, he had no others right now and no desire to play for the ones who questioned his sexuality just to get a rise out of him. Some queried about his family. Easy to speak warmly about being raised by a single parent and his granny who had both worked their way to success.

Others simply showed some of his old tapes and asked him to comment. That included the Sinners' scouts. "Great play, brilliant," they remarked now and then. "Are you still this good after missing a season?", a legitimate question. He answered, "Better, Joe Billodeaux and Sarge have been training me." Heads nodded. Notes were taken.

He endured the Cybex test that involved a machine measuring his joint and ligament strength and flexibility. Talk said this test might be dropped in the future due to possibility of injuries, but for now it stood in place, and he'd done well, probably better than some who had suffered injuries in the past. As for the Wonderlic Test, he'd aced that. Answering fifty multiple choice questions in twelve minutes seemed easy to him though he hadn't finished the last few. When he learned the average score was twenty and he'd gone way beyond that, he gave himself a pat on the back for his cognitive ability. Or as Joe would say his ability to read the field and be where it counted.

Then came the physical feats. Sarge had cautioned him that he wouldn't excel in all of them being shorter and not as heavy as others. He'd managed to bench press

225 pounds fifteen times thanks to Sarge's insistent training to reach that goal, respectable but puny next to the record set by a big lineman of fifty-one. He followed her instructions to explode from his crouch and extend his arm to tilt the flag in the vertical jump at twenty-four inches, very good but not as far as some of the taller men. Again, his height hindered him in the broad jump. Using all his leg power, he managed seven feet, eleven inches, good but not great.

Finally, he took the tests that mattered most to a safety. He ran the cone drill in 6.45 seconds, the shuttle run in fifteen, getting faster with each lap, and his forty-yard dash made him proud at 4.3 seconds. That's what he truly had to offer: speed, agility, and intelligence. There were times when he swore he heard Edie cheering for him when most of the audience remained passive and mute, hard to impress. Maybe her enthusiasm was inappropriate. Screw the critics, it spurred him on. In the end, he scored an 8.1 overall, on the cusp of being a great player given the chance. Exhausted mentally and physically, he couldn't have responded if Edie crawled right into bed with him, but he did get her exuberant hug and a hearty handshake from Joe who said, "Great work, son."

Now on to the next problem. What to do with himself between the Combines and the NFL Draft?

Chapter Thirty-Three

"Mais, yeah, you'll stay with us," Joe declared. "We're having a draft party for Rex and why not you? We know how it will go with Rex, chosen number one by the worst team in the league. I tried, tried hard to get him a better deal behind the scenes, but they wouldn't budge. He didn't want to have their jersey and hat thrown on him and have to pretend he's happy about it. Chances are you won't go as high but might score a better team. I know the Sinners could use you."

His dream team, playing with the Sinners in the city he loved close to the woman he had unrevealed feelings for. Maybe he'd wait until after the draft to tell her. The only trouble with this plan was that they would be apart for another month, and who knew what could happen in that span of time? Meanwhile, he'd earn his keep helping out on the ranch and working on his skills in the gym with Sarge's occasional pointers.

Her training fee was no longer being paid, and besides that, she found herself preoccupied with motherhood. Shashana rode the regular school bus with Lizzy and May, shunning the handicab that picked up disabled students. She had no problem showing classmates her artificial leg and doing a summersault with it or announcing that the Billodeauxs had adopted her because she was special. He wished he had half the confidence of that kid who sometimes stopped by the gym after classes and counted reps for him, saying she could go beyond one-hundred if necessary. It wouldn't be long before she'd ride better than he did on Teddy's old horse, Rascal. Every time he failed to meet a personal goal, he kept Shashana in mind. She would never give up trying.

****

On Draft Day, the Billodeaux house attracted as many people as their other celebrations. Crammed on the long leather sofa, the two huge recliners and all over the floor, the audience passed bowls of snacks ranging from parmesan popcorn to Corazon's famous crispy baked chicken taquitos. Vats of Junior's chili, both hot and mild commanded the top of the stove, and the kitchen table held baskets of corn chips and bowls of grated cheese and sour cream for anyone who wanted an addition to the meal. Cold drinks and beer were serve-yourself from the fridge and several coolers.

Of course, his mom, granny, and Livy had been invited, bringing with them four giant muffuletta sandwiches cut into small wedges from the famous Central Grocery. Once again, Nell and Joe enthroned Flo in one of the recliners with Livy tucked in beside her. His mom sat gracefully on a folding chair slightly behind them. He took a seat on the floor with Edie nestled close, sure that everyone noticed. Rex possessed the other recliner all by his lonesome.

The folderal and hype finally ended. All eyes stayed on the big screen as the first selection was announced, "Rex Billodeaux, quarterback, LSU" to play for, yes, the worst team in the league. Though the family cheered, and Edie waded through the grandchildren to place a paper crown bearing a large number one on the dark head of her brother, Rex failed to rejoice. He said to Edie, "What if I hadn't gone first?"

"Oh, I made nine others and another with a fill in the blank for Ty. Cheer up. It won't be so bad."

"Jesus God, it's damn cold there. They don't even celebrate Mardi Gras."

"Language," Nell murmured. She stood by her son's side with a consoling hand on his shoulder. "I'm sure you'll find something to like up there."

Joe stood. "Raise those bottom dwellers up as far as you can. When your three-year contract is over, and I am sure it's going to be a good one with my agent working for you, you'll be able to take your pick of great offers."

Mack placed a cold beer in his hand. "Drink up, Rex. You'll get over the bad stuff just like I did."

Before chugging his beverage, he raised it to Ty. "Hope you get a better placement."

Considering that Rex wasn't his best bud and not fond of seeing him with Edie, the gesture was gracious and surprising.

The family waited patiently for Tyson Ramsey to be called through the next ninety-nine names and five and a half hours of television time. Younger children went to bed. After all, this was a school night. Some had a second bowl of chili to go with pieces of Rex's celebratory cake which proclaimed "You ARE Number One!" in purple icing on a yellow background with tiny footballs adorning the edges. By ten-thirty, the group began to disband, some going back to New Orleans, others toting sleeping children to their nearby homes. It seemed each and every one took the time to shake his hand, squeeze a shoulder, give a peck on the cheek. "Tomorrow for sure," many said.

His granny asked him to go home with his family, but he said he wanted to wait out the next two days with Joe. He'd send most of his belongings with them and ride the Ducati home when the draft ended in two days, sooner if his name was called. Edie had to head back to the city. She left his crown behind and told him fill in the blank no matter what the number and be proud of it, to stop by her apartment as soon as he got to town. Considering that her body was pressed against him in the deep shadow cast by the barn over her car, he nodded into her curls. He would not, could not disappoint this woman.

Joe let the all-day second and third round events run on the gym's TV and the big screen in the den. On the second day, Huddleston and Eccles, the two safeties who had replaced him at LSU, went to the Sinners in the low three-hundreds. Pretending that he didn't care, Ty continued with his exercises, but Joe got on the phone.

Not bothering to lower his voice, he reamed out whoever was on the receiving end. "I tell you Tyson Ramsey is golden compared to those two slugs you just took. Yeah, what of it. The kid is clean now, and he'll have the support of Dean and Junior, Mack and Matt Keaton. Did you see the scores he put up in the Combine, or are you blind like half the refs in the league? Okay, okay, make something happen, or you will be sorry when he plays against the Sinners on an opposing team." Joe took a deep breath much as Ty had done when he didn't go in the first round. "That ought to do it."

Still, they waited. His number came in on Saturday at four-hundred-fifty-one, selected by the Sinners. Joe's agent would handle the rest, but he'd have to be a miracle worker to turn that number into big bucks.

Chapter Thirty-Four

Ty straddled his motorcycle, its saddlebag stuffed with the last of his clothes, not long after the announcement. Mama Nell drew him in for a warm hug before asking that he drive safely and call when he arrived in New Orleans. He promised. Joe did the manly back pat and handshake. "Good times ahead," he assured his protege.

Sarge offered an atypical embrace and a "Go get 'em. If it doesn't work out, the Army would be overjoyed to have you. You'd be a shoo-in for officer's training."

At her side, Shasha, as they'd come to call her, added, "Come back soon, and we can go riding. I'll beat you in a race to the woods."

"I believe you, Sha." He gently tugged on one of the braids on her head and thought of his sister.

Before he'd released the Ducati from its tarp, he took the time to phone Edie, making sure she was in and not busy with her job—or someone else. "I'll be in the Big Easy around one," he told her. "We'll go out to lunch."

"Then you were chosen by some team? At what number?" Her voice held far more excitement about his prospects than his own, but then it always did.

"Tell you when I get there. It's bad news, good news."

"I'll have lunch ready for you. We aren't going out."

Her voice held a promise he hoped he interpreted right.

He wanted to be on his way, but had to make one more call. Fabulous Flo's must be busy today with the tourists out enjoying a fine and flowery March day, parting with their money, glad to be away from the gloomy north, because she didn't pick up. He left a voice mail. "Hi, Granny, tell Mama I'll be home tonight. Don't know exactly with traffic and everything." Edie being the everything.

Making good time, he went the back way, avoiding the gridlock of Baton Rouge, but having to watch his mph in the small-town speed traps along the way. Once he made his left turn toward New Orleans and rode up the ramp to the four-lane, he paid no attention to the greening cypress trees, large birds wading in clumps of lilac water hyacinths, or the occasional eagle overhead. He had only Edie on his mind as he caught up with city traffic on the other end of the swamp and maneuvered around any slow pokes along the way, maybe a little recklessly. Off on the Canal Street exit and a left made on the green arrow took him into Edie's side street. He killed the engine and walked his bike into the quiet cul-de-sac where she waited in her fortified dwelling.

He chained the Ducati under the fire escape and withdrew the paper crown with 451 written in black marker. Placing it on his head, he rang the bell for the second-floor apartment. Her steps seemed to fly down the staircase as if she had wings on her heels. When the door burst free of all its security devices, Edie jumped into his arms, her legs wrapped around his waist, her lips on his. He enjoyed that for a minute or two before setting her down.

"That's quite a greeting for a humble number 451."

"Which team?"

"Thanks to your dad, the Sinners who still aren't too sure about me."

"They will be. Best of all, you won't be going off to some faraway place full of gorgeous women to tempt you."

"Only you tempt me—and maybe lunch."

"We have Italian roast beef sandwiches from Johnny's Po-Boys. I hope they haven't gotten too soggy."

"Great either way. What's for dessert?"

"Oh, I didn't think about that. There might be some Klondike Bars if I haven't eaten them all."

He loved the way she often failed at flirting. "You were supposed to say 'me', baby girl."

"I'll show you who's a baby. Those sandwiches are about to get a lot soggier." She darted up the stairs faster than she'd come down. "Lock the door, would you?" she shouted over her shoulder. That slowed him a little, but he ran on her heels by the time they got to the third-level bedroom and slammed that door, though no need with only the two of them headed for the covers.

She was ready for him, more than ready. In the haste, he'd barely noticed that she wore only an extra-large black Sinners T-shirt, apparently with nothing on underneath, that hung to her knees. Even her feet were bare as she climbed onto the bed and stood up to whisk off her only piece of clothing. Falling to her knees, she lunged for his belt buckle and the zipper to his jeans which left her in no doubt as to his readiness. "Hurry," she commanded.

No coyness or sexy sophistication for Edie, just exuberant joy. "Hey, hey, slow down. Hold something for me. No, not that!" He removed a condom from a pocket and handed it to her to keep in readiness while he got out of his clothes, the boots and the leather jacket, the paper crown.

By then, Edie had ripped open the packet and held up the lubricated ring. "May I put it on you?"

"It would be my pleasure, but get it on nice and tight all the way to the bottom. That's good." He gave an involuntary shudder as she finished. Gently, he laid her back on the covers, massaged her breasts, small and perky like she was, and toyed with her black curls.

"Please," she said and guided his hand where she wanted it to be. Oh, she was ready. As he glided into her it felt like a true homecoming, a place he wanted to be always and often. He tried to make it last, but their urgency prevented that. Too soon she arched, and he followed to his release.

Under the covers now instead of over, he held her tight in his arms. "I wanted to ask you this before we did anything else, but too late for that now."

"Ask," she murmured against light brown hair on his chest.

"Edie, I'd like us to be exclusive. I mean not see or be with anyone else. I wish I had a class ring to give you, but I don't."

"I don't need a ring. Sure you won't get bored with me?"

"I've been with enough women to be certain. But what about you? Has there been anyone else, well, since we did it on the motorcycle?"

Her amazement showed itself in a puff of warm air against his nipple which reacted in reply. "No! You are all I want, now and forever. You'll play for the Sinners.

I'll move up at *New Orleans Lifestyle*. We can see each other whenever we want now."

"I'd like it to be that way, and I'll work hard in training camp to get a permanent spot on the team. I know my contract won't be much to start even with your dad's agent working on it, but it will grow. I'll make sure of it."

Edie nuzzled against him. "Even if you don't, we'll have a future together."

"And lunch. I could really use lunch right now."

"So much for romance."

They ate at the small kitchen table off of plates with an olive leaf pattern that Stacy had purchased when she and Xo lived in the apartment after college and set up their translation service. It still retained its plum-colored décor as the twins who'd followed them had no desire to redecorate while they worked hard as nurses. The roast beef sandwiches were past their prime but delicious none the less. They scarfed them up along with chips and soft drinks with Klondike Bars for dessert, and then revived, had second dessert in the bedroom.

****

Darkness descended as Ty made his way to his mother's house. He should have been here earlier, but, well, Edie in bed. He went around back to the garage and walked his bike through the backyard entry where he found an unpleasant surprise, his father's sedate but expensive sedan parked closely to his mother's car. Shit.

Livy heard his approach and did her usual burst from the backdoor to welcome him. His granny appeared behind her to crush him to her big bosom. His parents held back in the dining room where a slightly cold pizza party appeared to be in progress. "I got hungry because you were late, but we didn't cut the cake," Livy admitted.

A sheet cake very similar to the one presented to Rex sat amidst the boxes of cheese and pepperoni and everything-on-it pies, only it had been iced in chocolate, not LSU colors, but bore the same edging of small, plastic footballs. "Congratulations to our Sinner" it read in white frosting. "How did you find out?" he asked.

"Oh, we've been watchin', honey bear," his granny said. "As soon as I had your message, we got right online and googled you. Up popped your number and who claimed the best safety in the crowd whether they know it or not. I'm getting seats in the Dome so we can see you play in person. We're so proud of you."

"Yes, we are." His mother stepped forward and gave him a kiss on the cheek. She wore the expensive scent that Titus LeMaire often gifted to her. He must be planning to spend the night.

The man who was his father hung back a little and made no physical moves on his son, perhaps dreading a rejection he wasn't used to suffering. "You've come a long way since summer. I believe you have a great career ahead once you get your chance."

The words reminded Ty of things his father had said after his high school and college games. He held in his anger at never have been acknowledged as this man's son and answered with a simple, "Thank you." He wouldn't say he wanted to make this guy proud. That pride belonged to himself—and Edie.

Livy broke into the conversation. "Please eat, Ty. We can't have cake until you do."

So, he took a seat and filled a plate with two pieces of everything pizza, had some of the salad his mother had made, and followed that up with a big chunk of chocolate cake, his favorite. No expensive gifts appeared, not a thousand-dollar sports watch or the keys to a luxury car, and that suited him just fine. He'd done the work for himself, not for presents that had often seemed more like bribes. The adults split a bottle of champagne, and Livy raised her toast with ginger ale, simply, "To Ty."

"All right now, Livy girl, time to go home with granny if you want to stay overnight," Flo said.

Livy ran for her overnight bag. How many times had he been shunted off out of the way when Uncle T planned to stay for the evening? One day, she'd notice they had the same striking hazel eyes that burned gold in a slant of sun, but for now, she presented her cheek to the man who'd sired her and said, "Night, Uncle T."

"I'll drive them over to the shop. Tomorrow, you'll have to come see my place," his mother said.

He saw the trap now. He'd be left alone with his father for whatever reason. "No, let me take them."

"Not this time." His mom herded Livy and Flo out the door.

"That leaves us," Titus LeMaire said. "I wanted time to say some things you didn't want to hear earlier. Portia is the love of my life, but I discovered her too late."

"Ever hear of divorce?" Ty couldn't help but answer.

"I had a responsibility to my wife and daughters, to my constituents. Neither Charlotte nor I believe in divorce. Marriage is a responsibility not to be shaken off lightly. I can't tell you how often I wanted to claim you as my own. Once I broached the idea to Charlotte, that perhaps we could adopt the boy I was sponsoring at St. Aug's. He has a mother, does he not, she said. You have daughters. You will have to be content with that." With a small laugh, Titus said, "Your mother wasn't keen on the idea either. In fact, she wanted another child and along came Livy because I always tried to give her all that I could."

"Does your wife know about us then?" His hands tightened into fists, but at least Livy had been planned and not been merely an accident between a college student and a married man.

"She must suspect, but has never said a word. If you don't bring something to light, it doesn't exist in her eyes. It hasn't been easy on any of us, but I did try to give you all you needed in life to succeed. I'm asking for your understanding."

Ty stood. "It's a lot to understand, but for tonight I'm not going to stay here while you bang my mother." He forced his hands to unclench, breathing hard, keeping his temper under control.

"Son…"

Ty strode from the house and took his bike from the garage. He went to where Edie waited.

Chapter Thirty-Five

She'd showered and washed her hair, letting the cream rinse soak in before attempting to comb her curls. When the doorbell rang after dark, Edie threw on another oversized T-shirt, her usual sleep garment, and tiptoed soundlessly to the entrance of her apartment. She used low tech, the peephole, to see who lurked outside spotlighted by a bright lamp that came on automatically when night fell. Ty, back for some more, and she didn't mind a bit.

His first words once she disarmed the alarms killed that hope. "Can I stay here tonight?"

"Sure, but what happened? I thought you'd want some time with your family."

"That was the plan, but *he* was there and going to stay the night with my mother once Granny got Livy out of the way."

They made their way to the kitchen, not the bedroom. "Coffee, or maybe chamomile tea?" she asked studying his face, gold eyes glinting from the overhead light and anger coming off him like steam on the roads after a New Orleans downpour.

"You got to be kidding. I could use a slug of bourbon if I can't have pot."

"Sorry, I'm clean out of both. Chamomile it is. Xo grows it. Tell me." She moved away to prepare the tea, but he caught her, drew her tight, and simply held her like a much-loved security blanket before letting go. By the time they had their hands wrapped around mugs of a hot and soothing beverage, he'd spilled a great deal of what bothered him.

"At least, he didn't try to buy your love this time. I think he is trying, but it's a difficult situation to explain away. He did declare his love for your mother. He isn't simply using her like you always thought. You should leave your mind open. One day he might claim you."

"I'm not sure I want that anymore. He should stay out of my life. I almost clocked him tonight."

Edie took his clenched hand, spread it open, and kissed the palm. "But you didn't. That's progress."

"I need to stay out of his way. Could I…could I live with you here until I can afford a place of my own. I wish I could help with rent. I'll be getting a signing bonus soon, but it won't be great."

"Well, I do have a second bedroom to spare—and my dad owns the building now, so no rent to pay."

"Just my luck you have two beds. I'll try to stay in it, but I can't promise."

"Who asked you to? Come on, let's get some sleep. See how you feel in the morning."

Her T-shirt didn't remain on very long, nor did his clothes, but they spooned together, drawing warmth and strength from each other until the church bells woke them Sunday morning. Edie decided sex before breakfast would never be a bad idea. She suspected her parents felt the same.

While Ty showered, she applied her limited cooking skills to scrambled eggs augmented with grated cheese, diced green peppers, and onion, Corazon style. Brown bread popped from the toaster. Milk and orange juice plus the dark roast coffee favored in the city and at the ranch were always on hand. She had it ready when he appeared clothed in clean, wrinkled garments from his saddlebags, but with a slight scruff on his cheeks because he hadn't shaved. She loved the slight rasp of his breakfast kiss.

As they ate, he laid out plans for their Sunday. Flo's Fabulous Fashions and his mom's adjacent store now named Portia's Place—Custom Designs opened at noon. He'd promised to visit and see all the changes they'd made in his absence, begging Edie to go along.

"Ha, I often have coffee with them when I am out on the town covering everyone's social events which no one else wants to do. You know, both the senator's daughters had big society weddings covered by *Lifestyle*. I looked them up."

"Always nosy. You can bet Livy won't have one."

"I wouldn't place money on that. Your mother is doing well and Flo's is thriving, too. I'll bet her wedding gown will be out of this world gorgeous and Flo will see to the food. I'd love to go along with you."

"After, maybe we could take the Ducati over the causeway and explore some of the small towns. Lots of good restaurants there and riddled with B&B's if we should feel tired."

"I like your thinking. Let me fix myself up a little. I can't go into Portia's Place looking shabby."

"There's nothing shabby about you, Edie. You shine, you always shine." He peered at her over the rim of his coffee cup, making the best use of his eyes to get what he wanted.

"Flattery will get you nowhere. It takes time to bring me up to par. You stay down here."

"Not flattery," he called after her, but she steeled her will and kept moving.

As usual, it took three tries to decide what to wear—a sweet floral dress made from some of Flo's remnants and earrings dangling small clusters of cherry blossoms that she'd found at the Museum of Art. White sandals, why not, since the day promised to be warm.

"You look like spring," he said when she entered the living room where he'd spread out on the very feminine purple couch and watched the start of an east coast ball game. She felt like spring, blossoming, growing up, as he gazed at her.

They took her car as she hadn't dressed for motorcycle riding and parked it in the space behind Portia's shop, now paved over to keep down the mud and weeds, and possessing a narrow metal balcony with a flight of stairs from the second floor in place of the old fire escape. While the view wouldn't be much but the backs of other buildings, a small table and two chairs sat outside with some pots of red geraniums brightening the area.

They entered through the backdoor which had a buzzer on it to warn of arrivals. Because of this, Portia waited for them in the arched doorway leading into the shop. She enfolded both of them in one hug preventing her son from pulling away.

"I'm so glad you both came. Can I make you some coffee? That fancy machine does espresso, too, and I've almost learned to create a cappuccino. The champagne is for clients, but you are welcome to it."

Ty peered around the elegant, modern space where a tray of flutes sat near the state-of-the-art coffeemaker and a set of graceful white ceramic cups. Rather than a shabby table with a couple of well-used chairs, his mother took her breaks at a marble-topped bistro table with a wrought iron pedestal and two high-backed stools having wooden seats and black frames that could have been stolen from a French café. Part of the small refrigerator served as a wine cooler.

"I guess Granny doesn't come here on her breaks," he said grudgingly. Edie elbowed him in the ribs for being a jerk.

"When we have time for coffee together, we meet at her place where she has her favorite chair and a lot more room since we moved the sewing machines upstairs into this building. We have four seamstresses now and an area for pressing the gowns. I offered her the space to expand her apartment, but she said she was happy with her place where she can relax and not worry about spilling anything. There's a pass through between the two places and a staircase that can serve as fire escape. Want to see?" Portia gestured to the interior stairs much like the one in her mother's building.

"Yeah, why not? Edie, you coming?"

"No, I've been before. I'll just stay here and paw through the gorgeous gowns too long for me to wear." She figured they needed time to clear the air after last night, and she didn't need to be in the middle.

"Anytime you want one cut down, tell me. We owe you our success, and thank Stacy for her referrals next time you see her."

"I will. It's about time I pitched an article on your place, too."

"Oh, I might be overwhelmed then. Let's wait a while."

"Yes, we wouldn't want our pictures in the paper,

would we?" Ty said.

Edie gave him a scowl he'd never seen before. "Behave and respect your mother."

"Now I'm in trouble," he said lightly as his mom took the stairs.

She wandered out into the short hallway edged by four generous fitting rooms containing pedestals for the measuring of wedding and ball gowns and a chair for guests of the clients. In the shop proper, the clothes hung from wall units, uncluttered and easy to remove, leaving room for white spindly chairs with upholstered gold-brocaded seats and an ornate coffee table where the patrons might rest their champagne flutes and snack from a bowl of unsalted almonds while being shown dresses. It sure wasn't Flo's.

She nodded to Portia's assistant, a young Asian-American woman studying design and thrilled to have the job. Taking a moment to be jealous of Ming's lovely face, delicate petite form, and waterfall of straight black hair hanging to her waist, she sighed before saying, "If Portia is looking for me, I'll be next door. Thanks, Ming." She dreaded the moment when Portia introduced her to Ty. She didn't need competition, sure he'd soon be famous again and a target for other women.

Stepping outside, she studied the slim mannequins poised as if ready to step into a limo to go to the ball in Portia's gowns in one window and in the other, a billowing wedding gown like a confection made of whipped cream, too much for her taste. She'd disappear in it. Passing over to Flo's full of bright outfits for summer hung on her oversized models for display, she snagged a giant chocolate chip cookie from the plate and thanked heaven she seemed to have her mother and

Trinity's hummingbird metabolism. She said hi to the part-time Sunday clerk who knew her well and asked for Flo's whereabouts.

"Upstairs with Livy. It's quiet right now, but we'll have more business once people get done with Sunday dinner and the tourists out strolling come across us." Like all of Flo's employees, Almay whose name had contracted from Alma May, possessed a comfortable girth and a welcoming smile on her dark face. "Oh, would you look at that. She ain't headin' for our shop."

A chauffeured Mercedes had stopped at the curb. The uniformed driver hopped out and opened the passenger-side door for a woman so thin she'd gone beyond fashionable with sunken cheeks and a protruding collar bone noticeable under a chic, cream-colored silk blouse worn with narrow black slacks, low heels, and a scarf, probably Hermes, throwing some much-needed color onto her pale face. Still, her blonde hair, though very short, had a fashionable cut that Edie could envy but never wear. Gold glinted on her ear lobes and off the impressive diamond wedding set on her ring finger. Closing the door, her driver lent her an arm into Portia's Place.

"No, ma'am, she's sure not coming here," Almay repeated.

Edie, who had just bitten into her cookie, swallowed hard, choked a little on the crumbs. "That's Senator LeMaire's wife. I know her from the society pages."

"Looks like a big sale for Portia, then," Almay assessed.

"I don't think so."

Two hefty women strolled into Flo's as Edie squeezed out. She hoped and prayed that Portia wasn't in the process of showing Ty the front of her shop. Nearly bumping into the chauffer leaving to move the Mercedes, Edie found Charlotte LeMaire ensconced on one of the spindly chairs listening to Ming offer her coffee or champagne or water and assuring her that the owner would be out to see her very shortly.

"Water, sparkling if you have it."

Edie, waving her forgotten cookie in the air, rushed past them. "I'll get it, Ming. You keep Mrs. LeMaire company. She charged through the fitting room area and into the backroom to find only Portia charging the coffeemaker. Turning from her task, Portia said, 'Want an espresso to go with that cookie, Edie?"

"No, no. Charlotte LeMaire is outside. She wants a sparkling water. Do we have some? Jeez, I mean where is Ty? He'll recognize her."

"Perrier is in the cooler. Ty is upstairs playing a video game with Livy. She felt shorted of his attention last night. He'll be a while. Thank God." Her dark eyes rolled. "This is what Titus feared if I gained any notoriety. I took a chance with the shop."

"You deserved a chance." Edie set down her cookie, opened the bottle of Perrier, and poured it into a flute with trembling hands that allowed it to overflow. She wiped it off with a dish towel. "Do you want me to tell her you've gone home sick and that Ming will help her?"

With a shake of her smooth, black waves, Portia said, "No, maybe she simply wants a new gown from the hottest new designer in town. If it is something more, time to face the music. I'll take the water to her."

Edie nodded and handed it over. She had to admire Portia's calm and steady hands as she walked away. Following a few steps behind, but not entering the shop, she listened in as Ty's mom said, "Hello, I'm Portia Ramsey. How may we help you today? Anything special you'd like that we don't have we can custom make and keep your measurements for any further gowns."

Edie had heard Portia's usual greeting may times and it rolled off her tongue with practiced ease as if she weren't talking to her lover's wife.

"I have no need of new clothes though they are quite lovely. Many of my friends are wearing them. No, I'd like to talk to you privately."

"Certainly."

They were coming her way. Edie ducked into the last fitting room and pulled the curtain across the opening. She heard the sound of Portia closing off the fitting room door from the shop. The women passed as she stood on a chair, afraid they would see her feet. Once they were in the kitchen, she sank onto the seat. She supposed they felt secure with the other door closed.

"You do know who I am?" Charlotte said in her assured patrician voice.

"Of course, our senator's wife. I'm honored you've chosen my shop," Portia answered with admirable aplomb.

"And I know who you are and not just because you've gone public with your designs. I've known for years. Titus lost interest in me when our daughters were six and eight. My friends said that was normal. We'd been married ten years, had children. The bloom was off the rose. I accepted that for a while until he began to 'go golfing' right after Christmas dinner and supposedly doing all night political planning or going weekend duck hunting with no ducks to show for it. I hired a detective. I have photos of the two of you together, oh, not in bed.

You've been terribly discrete. But playing in the backyard of that house he bought for you with a golden child who has his eyes." Charlotte paused as if she needed to sip her Perrier. "Once you were content to work in your mother's backroom. Now, you've gone public."

"Are you planning to expose us, get a divorce, ruin his political career and my new business?" Portia challenged. "I know you have the influence to do that."

"Once I might have considered it, but Titus always swore we would never divorce. Naturally, he wanted my family's support in climbing the political ladder, but I do have to say he did not ignore our daughters entirely, always treated me well, never a birthday forgotten or an anniversary. In the end, I realized I could live with the situation as so many women do, but that has come to an end."

"I suppose I get no say in this?" Portia dared her.

"No, you don't. You see, I have pancreatic cancer and at the most six months to live. I've done the treatments to no avail." With a brief laugh, she added. "I've never worn my hair so short, but the style does become me. Titus said so. Anyhow, I haven't much time left."

"You want me to step aside for the duration."

"Yes, it won't be very long. Then, when I am gone, please take care of Titus as I have done. Make sure he takes care of his health and his career. After a suitable time for mourning, you might begin to see each other in public, perhaps even marry. I feel you owe me this much consideration." Again, a pause as if the woman needed to wet a dry throat.

"At one point he wanted to adopt your boy. As a

mother, I knew that would hurt you, but that you wouldn't let go. It might have broken the two of you apart if I hadn't played the heartless villain and refused. Earlier, I had offered to give him another child, but he claimed I was too fragile for more. Then, he gave you one instead. Your Livy is young. He might adopt her if you marry and give her a wonderful wider life. I don't begrudge that. My daughters had all the advantages."

"We will discuss it." That was all Portia seemed able to say.

"Good, then we are through here. I wish you success with your shop and your son. I've often thought he might not have gotten into trouble if Titus had been more present in his life. Ah, but then, more than one of my friends have a child who has gone to rehab."

"He's on the right track now and has a girl he loves. That can make a big difference."

"Yes, love. It doesn't always last. I must be going. Jarvis should be outside by now to take me away."

Edie stayed hidden as the women went by her hiding place again. As Portia returned, she ripped aside the curtain. "You can come out now, Edie. We'll have coffee, and you can finish that cookie you left on the counter. Did you hear all that we said?"

No use denying it. "Yes, I didn't exactly mean to, but I did."

"Good. I don't have to repeat it to you. I'd like you to convince Ty to go along with this plan and mend fences with his father. It would mean the world to me."

"I'll try," she promised. But what stuck in her mind was one simple phrase. He has a girl he loves and Charlotte's answer, "It doesn't always last."

Chapter Thirty-Six

When Ty returned to the shop, having allowed Livy to beat him at a few games, he found them having coffee and sharing the oversized cookie. He'd come through the dress shop and pronounced it classy. "I'm glad you are coming into your own, Mama."

He made a grab for part of the cookie, but Edie batted his hand away. "Go next door and get your own."

"Yeah, that was one of the advantages of hanging around Flo's, always cookies after school. Be right back." He ducked out past the changing rooms.

"Did you want to tell him now?" Edie asked.

"No, I'd like you to do that when the two of you are alone. I admit I'm cowardly, but what he just said about my shop and coming into my own is the nicest he's been to me in a long time. I want to hug that to myself for a while. Besides, right now you do have more influence over him than me."

"Okay. I hope you're right."

Ty returned with his own cookie. His mom practiced her cappuccino skills on him. The moment, the day, was as sunny inside as out. He kissed Portia's cheek before urging Edie up and out to go for their motorcycle ride.

She needed to change her clothes and predicted how that would go. Nooners were fun, too, but at last, she got into jeans and boots and a leather jacket she'd bought for herself. She had lots to think about as they crossed the twenty-four mile causeway over Lake Pontchartrain to Mandeville, awfully close to the water on both sides. She clung tight to Ty's back for the half hour it took to get to land again. It provided thinking time about how to approach the delicate subject of Portia, Titus, and Charlotte, plus took her mind off the seemingly never-ending bridge.

Once back on land, they wended their way past colorful restaurants—the Rusted Rooster, Crazy Pig, Hambone, and Liz's Where Y'at Diner—finally settling on overstuffed shrimp po-boys with fries, a whole for him and a half for her. By late afternoon, they settled on one of quaint B&Bs, all with welcoming hosts and wide verandas. They dined at a great place across the street from the one they'd chosen and shared a bottle of wine they'd picked up along the way on the porch as the sun went down over the lake. Their genial hostess provided a small cheese platter, declaring them a "darling young couple", and they still hadn't tried out the mattress in their room. An idyllic day raced to its end.

Not long ago, she'd asked her mother the best time to approach a man when you had something to say he needed to hear. "After sex?" she'd asked with hesitance.

"Good heavens, no!" her unflappable mother answered. "Never attach conditions to your sex life. You'll ruin it. I'd say when you've both had a good day, a good meal, a little liquor, a mellow time."

This moment was as mellow as it would get. She considered this her first grownup date, no raucous college party fueled with alcohol or sneaking off to a hotel room when supposed to be clubbing. No, they'd turned their phones off and wandered in and out of little shops, buying only the wine, but commenting on items they liked or didn't as if planning to furnish a new home. Good a time as any to start the conversation.

"Ty, today Charlotte LeMaire approached your mother at the dress shop. I overheard their conversation."

He sat up straighter as if someone had pierced his back with an arrow. "Why didn't she tell me?"

"You aren't on the best of terms right now, but need to hear what Mrs. LeMaire said."

"Probably called Mama a whore." He tossed back half a glass of wine.

"Nothing of the kind. Said she'd known the situation for a long time, and now it was coming to an end."

"She threatened my mother, her new business?" Those clenched fists that indicated his anger appeared.

"That's what I thought at first, but no. Ty, the woman is dying. She asked that your mom not see Titus for the next few months, but after she is gone, wants her to take care of him."

"With luck, they'll break up over this."

"I don't think they will. Twenty-three years and two children say their ties are strong. Charlotte suggested they might marry after a suitable time and give Livy all the advantages. That's very generous of her." Edie straightened his fingers one by one, poured more wine, and waited.

He took his deep breaths, folded his hands together. "That's between the three of them. I have nothing to do with their decision and must live my own best life. Edie, I want you to be part of that. I love you and am beginning to understand how powerful a bond that can be."

So did she.

****

The B&B's mattress proved outstanding. They left

it with reluctance early in the morning as they'd told their hostess they would. Still, she supplied them with warm blueberry muffins, cups of vanilla yogurt, and a container of early Louisiana strawberries, small and sweet, to take with them as they tried to beat the commuter traffic and the possibility of a tourist panicking in the middle of the causeway span and having to be rescued in order to get Edie to her job on time. He hated offering the credit card his father paid, but that would not last much longer now. Even the lowliest NFL rookie got a base pay of around $800,000.

They stopped by the apartment to enjoy the quick and easy breakfast, giving Edie time to change her clothes and tame her hair for business. When they turned on their phones, both mobiles lit up as if a major hurricane might be coming their way from all the messages. No, too early for a named storm, only both families trying to get in touch.

Ty's mother wanted to know when he'd be home. He messaged immediately that he'd be staying with Edie and would be around. He was good with Charlotte's plan for Livy's sake but left it up to her. His agent wanted to make an appointment to discuss his contract with the Sinners. Several Sinners, mostly Edie's kin, sent him congratulations. Dean asked if he wanted to work out with him. For sure.

Meanwhile Edie worked through her messages, nothing important from work, but half a dozen from family asking if she knew where Ty had gone. With me, she answered over and over. All is well. Just took an afternoon off together. Stacy got back to her first. Would she have time for a girls' luncheon at her place tomorrow? She showed the message to Ty and asked if he minded being left adrift for a while.

"No, go on. Have a good time. I'm going to work out with Dean, catch some lunch, and then go meet with my agent, or rather your dad's. Joe couldn't have helped me more. With the base pay raised to $800,000, I'll be okay, and he's seeing what he can get me as signing bonus."

Edie shook her head over what he did not know. "If you are training with Dean, better set your alarm for five a.m. He gets there early. As for salaries and signing bonuses, you won't believe all the deductions."

"If I get enough to start paying my father back and buy the groceries here, I'll be happy."

"You shouldn't be because you deserve more. Also, I suspect the Billodeaux grapevine has been at work. I get along with Stacy, but she is so much older and elegant that I don't hang out with her much. Josee is her best friend because they are two of a kind. Mostly, they make me feel small and messy by comparison though they never say that. So, I suspect some kind of trap."

"Why would you think that? You have a great family. Besides, I like you small and messy. What you see is what you get with Edie Billodeaux, nothing fake, all genuine."

"Thanks, but just shows you don't know them well yet. They will intervene if they think it's for your own good."

"Well, so did mine carting me off to rehab."

"After you agreed to go."

"After you pointed out it was my best path to the career I wanted."

"See, we do intervene. I have to get to work. We'll see what tomorrow brings." After receiving the best goodbye kiss of her life and anticipating the same at bedtime, she walked out into the world a very happy young woman.

Chapter Thirty-Seven

Driving his big SUV, Dean arrived at five-forty-five to add Ty to those he'd already collected: Rex who was staying with him, Matt, Tom, and the Aussie, Jock Brown. Ty gave Edie another delicious kiss as she stood dressed in a robe to see him off. Noticing Tom and knowing that as a kicker he didn't do heavy training other than keeping his legs in great shape, she realized something was up.

Dean had rallied all of the guys in the family still in New Orleans. Mack had rushed to the ranch as soon as their season ended to practice fatherhood, and Junior hit the highway at the same time to return to his beloved Xochi, his three kids and one on the way, and his equally beloved restaurant. Too bad because Junior had the softest heart despite his great size, and Mack knew all about making up for bad behavior. Teddy, who had married Jessie against her parents' wishes, had an understanding and sympathetic nature, but he rarely came to the city unless he had an announcing gig.

Edie got through her morning by staying in the office and rewriting press releases to fit on the upcoming events pages. Her mind constantly turned to Ty when she wasn't fretting about what Stacy might be cooking up. When noon came, she told her editor she might be late getting back from lunch, but hoped not.

Outside Stacy's home in the garden district, familiar

vehicles lined the street, one of the twins' subcompacts, Alix's small SUV, a Tesla Josee must have borrowed from Trinity, and Jock's Toyota Predator. Annie had most likely walked from her nearby house. Oh, how she wished Xo, ever the mediator, were there, and Sarge who could call any group to order. She squeezed her vehicle into a tiny space and went up the walk to face whatever awaited.

With the door unlocked, she let herself inside and homed in on the chatter of women in the kitchen at the rear of the house. Pausing by the formal dining room, she noted Stace had taken out the good china and set the mahogany table with silver and a fresh flower arrangement. Plates holding generous portions of seafood salad, which in New Orleans meant shrimp, crawfish, and crab loosely bound by mayo nested in abundant greens, already sat at each place with baskets of savory crackers nearby. The sideboard held two open bottles of chilled white wine and the same number of fresh strawberry pies topped with mounds of whipped cream no doubt contributed by Annie. At least, she'd get a good meal out of this.

Her appearance in the sunny kitchen with its view of the courtyard and burbling fountain where the poufy white dogs, Mati and Brody, played, brought the conversation to an abrupt halt until Stacy piped up, "Here's the guest of honor at last."

She wasn't late. They'd all come early to conspire. She should have waited just outside the kitchen entry to get a clue as to what was going on, but she could guess. "Looks like we aren't eating in the kitchen today."

"No, we're celebrating your success at *New Orleans Lifestyle*. I understand they want to keep you on as permanent staff. Don't do anything to mess that up, Edie."

She played dumb, put on her most innocent face, and said, "Like what?"

Josee kept the situation from going too far. "Let's eat. She doesn't have a long lunch hour, I am sure."

The group trailed Josee into the dining room where Stacy sat at the head of the table. They insisted Edie take the seat at the other end and arrayed themselves around her. Rather than feeling like queen for a day, the large chair dwarfed her and made her wish for the cushion Annie placed on Jude's seat along with raising her swollen feet and ankles onto a footstool. Six months into her twin pregnancy, Jude appeared as wide as she stood tall and highly uncomfortable while Annie's belly, starting her seventh month, seemed smaller than it had when she carried Gabe. This time she carried a baby girl.

Lorena poured wine into each glass until she got to Josee who covered hers. "I'm sticking to water." She already nibbled a cracker.

With a heavy sigh, Lori said, "You're pregnant, too."

"We were trying and not getting anywhere, but at Christmas Trin was talking to Edie in the kitchen and suddenly he spirited me up to a bedroom while everyone else was watching the game, and that's when it must have happened. He might not be a football player, but he is competitive and wanted to beat Tom and Jock to fatherhood. So, a late August or early September baby girl on the way. I'm nearly over the morning sickness and can enjoy this lovely meal. Shall we?" To make her point, she picked up her fork and speared a crawfish tail.

"Ah, what did you say to Trinity to get that result?"

Lori asked. "I might try it."

Edie knew her face turned the same shade of red as the cherry tomatoes ornamenting the salad greens. "Nothing special. I just asked him what men liked sexually. He said everything, and I told him to be more specific."

Laughter sprinted around the table like a winning athlete. "Oh, my poor husband. I think you turned him on. But do give him credit, any other man in the family would have run away before they answered that question. Was his advice helpful?" Josee asked.

"Very." Edie stuffed the largest shrimp she could find into her mouth to keep any more words from coming out.

"Don't worry, Lori. Tom and I aren't having any luck either. We female jocks have to stick together. I'm here for you," Alix vowed.

"Besides, pregnancy isn't all the joy it's cracked up to be. No wine or coffee, but all the nausea you can stand. Now the obstetrician wants me on bedrest for the duration until June but says the babes will likely come early. I blame you, Edie, for even suggesting Connor and I get married at the Fourth of July celebration."

"Sorry," she said, studying the cracker in her hand very hard as if counting its sesame seeds.

"Let's stop picking on Edie and get to the point," Stacy said. "With all your sexual inquiries, we're worried about you. The last thing you need right now is a baby out of wedlock."

"I'm on the pill now," she muttered into her wine glass, following that with a big swig.

"You should double up with condoms," Jude insisted. "You never know where it's been, especially if the guy has been very popular with the ladies in the past. Annie and I learned the hard way."

"We do."

"Aha, you and Tyson Ramsey are doing it. Is it wise to be shacking up so soon? You're very young and only starting your career." Alix pointed out the obvious.

"I do have two bedrooms at the apartment," she said to take some of the heat off.

"But does he stay in his?" Alix asked.

"He's only been there one night. Say, didn't I hear you lived at Tom's condo when you joined the Sinners, and you weren't much older than me at the time." Now that the attack was on, she planned to defend herself with all the knowledge of the family she'd gleaned even when they didn't want their baby sister to know.

Alix, chagrin showing all over her pale Nordic face, answered, "I paid rent for my own wing."

"Did you stay there?" That silenced her sister-in-law. She turned on Annie, who really didn't deserve to be skewered as she'd said little. "And you, living with Matt and getting pregnant."

"I was his baby's nurse until we got careless. There are worse things that can happen, I know. It all turned out so beautifully."

"Sure, after Dad aimed a punch at Matt and dislocated your shoulder instead. I was right there when it happened."

"They get along great now. Look, we're just concerned for you. We all know Ty's history with drugs. What if he starts toking again and gets you hooked?"

"I won't let either happen, and I won't get pregnant. He's extra careful because of his mother's history. You do know I turned twenty-two in February. I can make my own decisions, so butt out." She pushed her chair back and stood as tall as she could.

"No, no, don't go. I have a craving for strawberries and will eat both pies if I take them home," Annie implored.

That lightened the mood. They ate dessert. As she prepared to leave, each and every one of her sisters by birth or marriage promised to be there for her, no matter what. She hoped she wouldn't have to call on them. As she started her car, her biggest concern was how Ty's lunch with the men went.

Chapter Thirty-Eight

What a great morning, working out with Dean and Matt, Sinners he'd idolized in high school. They introduced him to others who didn't let up on their training during the offseason. Mostly weight training and the treadmill, but he practiced his vertical leaps and agility moves. Showered and more than ready for lunch, the men elected soul food over burgers and chose the Catty Car Corner on their way back from the training center.

Ty ordered the bone-in fried pork chop with collard greens and mac and cheese as did half the others. The rest went for red beans, rice, and sausage. They squeezed themselves around two tables and drew lots of glances from tourists who'd come for the mild spring weather and gorgeous azaleas and got a peek at a pack of Sinners. Some approached shyly asking for autographs, not his in particular, but if passed a sheet of paper, he did sign it, too. So, this is what it was like to be a Sinner out in public.

But not exactly. Dean, always the team leader, started it off. "We heard you and Edie have moved in together."

"I did ask if I could stay with her. She said yes. I offered to pay rent, buy groceries as soon as I get my first check."

"Yeah, I know how that goes," Tom said with a

wink sent his way.

"Word travels really fast in your family." Like a lightning strike, he might have said.

"It does. Stacy called Flo last night to find out what was going on with you two. She said you'd messaged to say you'd be living with Edie. While your mom is a little hurt, they both are okay with it. They think Edie is a good influence and will keep you clean."

Fast losing interest in his fried pork chop, he played with the mac and cheese before saying, "It's my responsibility to stay clean no matter where I live, but yes, she is good for me."

Rex, impetuous rookie that he was, broke in, "Just what are your intentions toward my twin sister?"

Not hard to answer as he'd thought about it many times. "If I make the Sinners team and have some kind of future to offer her, I'll ask her to marry me in a New Orleans minute."

"Those can be very long and drawn out, I learned," said Jock as he sat devouring the red beans and rice.

"I'll get there as soon as I can. She knows I love her."

"But have you said the words?" Tom asked.

"Yes."

"Well, he works faster than most of us. We can tell you where to get a big honking engagement ring with your signing bonus," Matt said.

"You'd better move as fast as you can or there will be consequences," Rex glowered.

"I'll help you with that, mate. Edie is a sweetheart," Jock offered.

He tried a little humor. "I ran the forty-yard dash in 4.3 seconds. If you break my legs, I won't be of much help to the team."

"Calm down, Rex. There will be no violence. If he stays clean, minds his temper, works hard, and treats Edie right, we're all good with giving him some time. If not, we will see you are transferred to the worst team in the league." Dean stated this with his usual cool in the pocket demeanor.

"Oh, no you don't! That's my team," Rex objected.

"The second worst team, then," Tom offered.

"Okay, we've said what we had to say. Eat hearty. Practice again tomorrow. Pick you up at five-forty-five." Dean went back to his meal.

Ty checked the time. His agent resided in one of the tall office buildings of the central business district. He could walk there easily and have time to spare, but at the moment wanted to be anywhere else than hemmed in by belligerent Sinners. "Ah, I'm going to take mine to go. I have to meet my agent in fifteen minutes. I'll walk back to Edie's from there."

He paid with his credit card and left with a carryout box in hand grateful to be outside with the noise of traffic and the clanging of streetcars filling the air. He debated leaving his meal for a group of enterprising gulls fighting over a spilled bunch of fries they'd probably scared a child into dropping, but it seemed wasteful, so he continued on to the correct address and, consulting the guide outside the elevator, made his way to the eleventh floor to the offices of Super Sports Management. Only he and a receptionist polished from her sleek, short blonde hair to her toenails showing pink in her peep toe pumps sat in the waiting room.

"I'm here to see Mr. Stein. Tyson Ramsey, appointment at 1:30 p.m."

"Mr. Stein isn't back from lunch as yet. You're quite early." Despite her formal words, she added a slight smile, also painted pink. She eyed his takeout box exuding the aroma of pork chop. "If you'd like to eat that, I could show you to our lounge."

"I think I'm too nervous for lunch right now. Maybe I should just throw this away."

She reached out a hand with perfect manicured nails. "Here, I'll keep it for you. Why don't you read a magazine?"

He picked up a *Sports Illustrated* from a stack on the end table and tried his best to immerse himself in the issue. Rex Billodeaux graced the cover as the number one pick in the NFL draft and rated a feature article on his high school and college career and his future prospects. He could have done so much better than 451 if he hadn't messed up. Someday, he wanted to be on the cover, curse or not.

Time ticked by. There had to be another entrance since he remained alone with the receptionist until her phone rang, and she replied, "Yes, he's here. I'll send him in. Mr. Stein will see you now." As she disconnected, she added, "Don't worry, Sam is a really good guy—once you get to know him. Go all the way down the hall to the last office."

"Thanks." He passed through the portal straight to the back past other, lesser offices. He knocked, not too loud or too soft, he hoped.

"Come," said the man on the other side who did not sit at his desk but perched on the edge of it like predatory bird. He had the nose and black eyes to fill the role. His gray hair feathered around his crown, an expensive haircut covering a bald spot. Wearing a sports coat with a shirt open at the neck, no tie, his fairly in shape body was framed by the many photos of his most famous clients. Joe Billodeaux's visage held the central place of honor.

Ty stepped forward and took the man's hand in a firm shake, but not too long.

"Sit," Sam Stein commanded. "Now, I'm not going to lie to you. I had one of my boys work out your contract because you aren't worth my time yet, but I've read it over. It's solid for a rookie who had low placement in the draft. You'll get the usual $814,377 base pay and a 1.4 million dollar signing bonus that you get to keep regardless if you make the team. Your contract runs for the usual four years, but we can renegotiate at the three-year mark. I know it doesn't sound like much, but you will have opportunities for more bonuses if your team goes to the playoffs—and the Sinners always do—or if you make all pro. Sound good to you?"

"Yes, sir." What else could he say when a top agent like this had taken him on at Joe's urging.

"Our cut is the usual three percent. Expect to pay forty percent in taxes. Don't forget your union dues and insurance. Talk to Joe about investing in a 401K and other stocks since he's the reason you're here. I have to say he has never steered me wrong. Go on, look it over, then sign here and here."

He tried to concentrate on the pages before him, but Mr. Stein continued to talk. "You know, representing Joe Billodeaux made my fortune, better known for his French Quarter antics than his great arm, but he grew up when he got off the bench and into the game. I expect you to do the same like his son, Mack. Got ditched by his original agent and had to pick himself up and start over.

The first year was rough, but now he's earning big money. So is the Aussie Joe recommended. I made my fortune on long shots. Got a good feeling about you, kid."

Ty took a glance at the wall behind Stein. The men he'd eaten lunch with were all there—and Rex's cover shot had already been framed to join them. Alix stood out among the few women represented. He signed there and there.

"I'm only going to say this once. I don't represent guys who think they are God's gift to football. We strive to make the best deal for you, but try that shit, and I'll let you go. Understood?"

"Yes, sir." His palms were sweating now, and he prayed that wasn't noticeable when they executed a final handshake. He scooped up his copy of the document and started out of the office with a side window view of the mighty Mississippi churning to the sea, about the same way his stomach felt.

"Oh, Mr. Ramsey, your bonus should be in your bank account by the end of week."

With another thank you, he escaped to the hallway where some of the doors now stood open exposing men toiling over sheaves of paper like the one in his hand. He wished he knew which one had spent time on his, but that could come later. He wondered how much money would be left to pay back his father and get Edie a decent ring.

The receptionist called to him as he walked in a daze through the waiting area where several chairs were occupied by people with honed athletic builds. "Don't forget your lunch, Mr. Ramsey."

"Oh, thanks."

"Was he hard on you? Don't worry, it will get

better," she said, her smile a little wider now.

Honest to God, he didn't remember his walk back to Edie's place. She found him asleep on the purple sofa, his knees drawn up near his chin. Her gentle shaking woke him.

"Hard day?" she asked.

"First the workout, then the workover. If I don't treat you right, they'll see I'm traded to the second worst team in the league, though Rex and Jock seemed to favor bone breaking. I made a lot of promises I hope I can keep. As for the agent, I didn't impress him, but he got me a decent but not great contract and warned me he drops male divas as clients."

"Uncle Sammy? He's usually such a dear. He always has peppermints in his pockets, maybe for an ulcer, but I got my share as a kid when he visited."

"Not today. No peppermints for me. Was your luncheon with the girls really a trap?"

"Oh, my, yes. I'm too young to be living with a man. You might draw me into your bad habits, and so on."

"What did you tell them?" Was he going to lose her to pressure from her family? The clammy hands were back.

"I told them to mind their own business. Brought you a piece of strawberry pie for dessert."

"For first or second dessert?"

"Any way you want it." Oh, she did catch on quick. Amazing what could be done with strawberry pie.

Chapter Thirty-Nine

Trouble started when the OTAs, Organized Team Activities, began. Up until then if he'd majored in poetry instead of football, Ty might have called his life idyllic with Edie curled at his side in bed every night, practice with the pros, Sunday dinner with his family since his mom observed her hiatus with Titus, and sometimes being invited to one of Dean's pizza parties where the Billodeauxs appeared to accept him as Edie's man. Invited to use Matt's pool anytime, he was learning to swim coached by the three boys who also enjoyed a good water battle with lots of splashing.

When the first of three OTAs came around, Dean had taken his family to Alaska to escape the heat for a couple of weeks. He'd rented a luxury chalet near a great fishing stream with plenty of hiking and wildlife seeking opportunities. Matt stayed close to home with Annie's due date nearing. Tom and Alix had gone off to help at Camp Love Letter. Jock and Lorena flew to Australia to spend some time at their home in the vineyard, riding their horses, playing with the dogs, drinking a fair amount of wine, and searching for platypuses in the creek behind their house. He was left on his own at this voluntary training session meant to build team unity and keep the men in shape during the long offseason.

He could wear what he wanted, only a helmet required for drills, stay two hours or four, attend or not, but he determined to be at every one along with most of the rookies including Huddleston and Eccles who vied for the same position. They'd shunned him at the Combines, not so much as a nod of recognition, not that he'd cared as he outscored them in most events. Now, they were here, unable to ignore his presence packed in classrooms where coaches reviewed film or went over the many plays they needed to memorize. He always took a place in the rear, not wanting to drawn their attention. One day, he'd collided with the bigger, beefier Huddleston accidently, or maybe not because his former college teammate answered his "excuse me" with a whispered, "The Sinners only got room for one or two of us, and it won't be you."

He shrugged it off. "May the best man win." Nothing he could do about always being ready to intercept kicked or thrown balls, being the fastest, or running rings around both of them in agility training. Though the coach for the defense always attended and timed them, he did not remark on the results, only pointed out areas they needed to improve. Meant to be low key sessions with no body contact on the field or groups set up in opposition, he still suffered more accidental bumps than others, usually initiated by Huddleston and Eccles, but sometimes those who appeared to be taking their side. Every time he took a slight hit, he breathed in deep and moved away.

Otherwise, he kept his promises to Edie's family. He went to his NA meetings, worked hard on his skills, and while he hadn't yet purchased a ring, he'd celebrated her being made part of the permanent staff of *New Orleans Lifestyle* in June by taking her to Baja to watch for whales and enjoy the beach, something that hadn't been part of his life growing up but wasn't unusual for her. He'd also picked up a huge dinner tab when the whole family came to celebrate her promotion using a new credit card that didn't send the bill to his father. Still, his expenditures were modest compared to some rookies who bought luxury homes and expensive cars for their mamas. His mother already had both, and his granny didn't want them.

Mostly, he strove to pay off the debt to his father. He'd sent a large check to the senator for the Ducati and the sports watch which he now felt he could wear. He no longer had any desire to be acknowledged by the man or to bear his name and so made the note as business-like as possible in case an aide should open it.

Dear Sir,

I enclose a check for one Ducati motorcycle and a sports watch, repayment for your personal loans to me. I will strive to pay down my tuition for St. Augustine's preparatory school within the year.

Yours truly,

Tyson Ramsey

Within a week, he received a reply, not from his father, but from his high school thanking him for the large donation in his name to their scholarship fund. Next time, he might just as well send it direct and inform his father. Though this had taken a chunk out of his signing bonus, he felt more like his own man now, and as Sarge had said when she congratulated him, most people could live on a million dollars well-invested for the rest of their lives. He'd set up his 401K with Joe's help.

When the OTAs were over and the pros returned for mini-camps, perhaps Dean noticed his increasing isolation from the younger members of the team though he hadn't mentioned it, trying to be a man who could handle it himself. The quarterback had taken the time for an address on what it meant to be a Sinner.

"There is no jealousy here. We work together toward victory. None of you will fail to support your teammates on or off the field. We need all of your skills. Huddleston, from looking at you, I'll bet you throw a mean block. Ramsey, I've never seen anyone faster to grab an interception—and when that happens, I expect all of you to clear the way for him."

Eccles seemed irked not to be mentioned by name and some of the others went shame-faced, staring at the floor until Dean clapped his hands and led them out to practice. After that, a few of the guys who'd ignored him began speaking to him, inviting him out for a beer at Mariah's Place, the hangout with good bar food and music, making him one of the team.

The grueling summer training camp, held at the Ochsner Sports Performance Center in Metairie, arrived with the two-a-days in the heat, toughening the Sinners for the playing season. The center offered both grass and AstroTurf fields, a cafeteria, and a gym inside a 75,000 square foot indoor facility where the New Orleans basketball team practiced. No need to go out of state anymore. On a day open to ticketed reporters, observers, and fans, he spotted Joe and Edie in the bleachers right down front. Edie wore her press pass proudly. Joe signed some autographs. He went to say a few words to them during a water break.

"You look great out there," Edie said, kissing him on his sweaty cheek.

"That's a reward you'll never get from a coach," Joe joked.

When he trotted back to the field, he ran into a literal wall composed of Huddleston and Eccles. "You are so whipped by that little Billodeaux pussy—but I suppose Joe being her father doesn't hurt your chances any," Eccles said very close to his face. They were near in size and weight, but Ivor Eccles had a skin of medium brown and mean dark eyes. He had brains if he chose to use them.

"Yeah," Huddleston, the big white boy who followed, not led, added.

Ty felt his hands clench into fists. He could take any insult to himself but not to Edie or Joe. Faintly, far away, he thought he heard Edie's voice cry, "No!" If he gave these two what they deserved, he'd be the one most likely to be cut. Taking a huge inhale, he forced his fingers open one by one, formed his hands into a praying position and exhaled with gusto into Huddleston's face.

"You should be so lucky to have the love of a woman like Edie. I'm sorry for you, Hubert. Good afternoon, Ivor." He'd gotten in one dig because Huddleston hated his first name and wanted to be called Hud. Eccles craved to be known at Ice, but so far hadn't earned the name. Before either took a swing at him, he walked around them, sauntering back to work.

He hadn't gotten too far when Huddleston roared like a gored bull, "Coach, coach, Ramsey blew air in my face and called me Hubert."

Ty slowed his pace but didn't turn around. Hud had picked the wrong man, the old and very cranky Head Coach Marty Buck with skin like wrinkled boot leather and nothing more than a Sinners' cap covering his bald spot. "That's your name, ain't it, and what? Did he have garlic for lunch. No fouls committed. If you can't handle this, what are you going to do when you hear trash talk about your mommies or get poked in the eye after a play? Go running to your kindergarten teacher? Get back to practice."

In the past after an insult about his mother or a low blow, Ty would have settled it by starting a fight that got him benched and cost his team yardage. No more. He'd used his mind, not his temper. Maybe this would be the end of trouble with those two. Training camp had only a day to go. Soon the powers that be would make their cuts and assign starting positions, men to the special and practice teams. Others would be on their way home. He could hold steady until then.

Or so he thought. He made a habit of always leaving the cafeteria early and starting his stretches before most were on the field. Leaving last, usually at the same time as Dean, became a habit, too. In the showers, he's had the chance to see the quarterback's legendary tattoos, one on each hind cheek, hearts with devil's tails made famous by Joe who'd encircled his autographs with those in his early career. Inside one, "Sinners" was written in script, and on the other, "Stacy" in the same lettering. Though they were eyed by rookies, no one mentioned them or dared imply that Dean was "whipped". To Ty, they represented devotion to the team and to his wife. He rolled that around in his mind as the warm water pelted down on him.

Dean had gone by the time he went to his locker to dress. On its floor lay a crumpled, wet towel not there when he'd gone in. He stooped to pick it up, and his nostrils flared to the sweet scent of fresh marijuana. Inside its folds lay a tightly rolled reefer—a present for a job well done in training camp? He doubted that. Was he tempted to reward himself, yes. Would he, no. He moved to dump it into a waste receptable, but then considered if found, all suspicions of bringing it to the training center would fall on him. So, he lumped it, towel and all, into his gym bag and tore out of the center on his Ducati.

Once locked safely in Edie's apartment, he sat on the purple sofa resisting temptation until she got home. She noticed his troubled look at first glance. "What happened?"

He revealed the contents of the towel. "Someone is trying to set me up for failure."

Edie, enraged on his behalf, said, "Those two thugs who stopped you the day Dad and I were watching the training. I'm calling Dean right now."

"No, no. I have to handle this myself, or maybe with your help. Been sitting here thinking about it. Here, take my phone and follow me to the bathroom. I want you to take a recording of me getting rid of this." He'd thought of the words he wanted to say in advance.

With the shot all lined up, he revealed the towel-wrapped doobie. "Someone left this gift in my locker." He gave an appreciative sniff. "It's good shit, probably cost you, but there is only one place for shit like this to go." He broke off pieces, shredded them in his hands, and flushed them away. Turning, he washed his hands thoroughly at the sink and then, holding them up, faced the camera again. "All clean."

"Brilliant, my hero," Edie said, wrapping her arms around him.

"Don't think I wasn't tempted. I could have ridden out into the country and smoked it in peace."

"All the more heroic that you didn't."

He ran his hands through her curls. "You would have smelled it on my clothes and given me hell. I thought of that, too. But I do have an appetite. What are we having for dinner?"

"Me, of course. Later, we'll go out."

****

Before the team hit the playing field on the last day of summer training, Ty asked to meet in private with Coach Buck, the defense coach, and Dean. He showed them the recording without much prelude. "Someone is trying to sabotage me."

They all agreed on that and waited for Coach Buck to say the names. "Those boys who complained about Ramsey here calling them by their first names. Now, who are they?"

"Eccles and Huddleston," the defense coach supplied. "They're all trying out for the safety position."

Dean nodded. "I noticed they've been harassing Ty and getting others to do the same. Did my lecture do any good?"

"Some. Thanks for that."

"Well, get them in here. I haven't got all day," Coach Buck barked. Dean went out smiling to summon them.

With the two sitting on the edge of their chairs, Coach Buck started in on them. "Someone is trying to get Ramsey kicked off the team by offering him marijuana. Would that be either of you rookies?"

Huddleston blurted, "I didn't put the pot in his locker. It was Eccles' idea. He bought it and everything."

"Idiot," Eccles snarled.

"Yeah, no one mentioned where the pot was found. Show them the tape and what Ramsey did with it," Dean said as he stood with folded arms behind Coach Buck.

The defense coach put it perfectly. "You're off the team, Eccles. Collect your things, turn in your playbook, and go. Huddleston, we'll see about you later."

After the chill in that room, the already steaming playing field felt good beneath Ty's feet. He'd taken one more step toward making the team and getting Edie that ring, but in the meantime could do something else to show her how he felt. He went deep into the city to the best tattoo artist he knew, handed him a crude drawing, and bared a buttock.

"Right here in red."

The inker studied the design. "These devil's tail hearts have been real popular since old Joe's days with the Sinners. Sure you don't want something more modern or maybe just Sinners on the inside? It's a hassle to remove them later."

"I'm certain."

When Edie arrived home that evening, he told her he had something to show her in the bedroom.

"I think I've already seen it, but I'm willing to take another close look."

He let her take off the protective covering. Her hand went to her heart.

"Oh, Edie's Sinner. Better than a ring because you can't take it off, at least not easily."

"Bear with me for a few days. I'll have to be on top."

"I can wait for my turn considering this is a best gift I've ever been given. I'll be gentle." And she was.

Chapter Forty

He'd made the first cut. Next came the preseason games, basically showing what the players could do against real opponents, two at home, two away. Some talk went around about Eccles' sudden departure with murmurs that he might have been taking drugs, but the truth remained among the men in that small room. Ty didn't worry much about Eccles. He'd go free agent and had enough talent to get on somewhere, which had been his own backup plan. As for Huddleston, the guy let him alone.

Edie and Joe came to each and every game and saw him intercept three balls and cause two fumbles using the plan he'd worked out and practiced with Junior, but Junior only played a quarter or two, and the same with Dean. Deciding to mend fences, he approached Hud about completing the same bump and punch maneuver in the last of the preseason games.

"Look, Hud, Junior isn't playing the second half, but I've noticed their favorite rookie receiver is a sloppy ball handler. I'm going to try the bump and punch on him. You be there a few feet in front of us and ready to catch the fumble and run it back to our goal. If it doesn't work, we'll both take the guy down, okay?"

"After what me and Eccles did to you, you're gonna let me catch one of your fumbles and run it in?"

"Yep. Let's give it a try."

Ty did his thing and Hud got ahold of the fumble. He wasn't quick enough on his feet, but gained a few yards for the team and hung on to that ball for his dear life and possibly his career when the opposition piled on and tried to squeeze it out. That single play might have earned him his place on the return team and as a backup for Ty who went on as a starter for the defense. Now, they were teammates.

What he called the Billodeaux Baby Blitz came to an end the first week in September when Josee gave birth to a six-pound, two-ounce baby girl with a head of dark curls. As they made the obligatory visit with a gift in hand to Josee and Trinity's north shore home not far from their expanded video game headquarters, Edie held out her arms to hold the tiny bundle named Elle.

"She's a beauty, but cursed with the Billodeaux curls like Annie, Jude, and me."

"No curse at all. You're cute and adorable, and so is my daughter," Josee declared.

"Really? I always thought you considered me short and messy."

Josee, so nicely dressed and made up that she might have been doing a photo shoot, answered. "You can't help being short and there is no telling yet if Elle will be, but if you ever want help with your hair, let me know."

Standing by with the gift, a silver rattle and teething ring engraved with the baby's name, the sixth one they'd purchased, Ty kissed the top of Edie's head. "Thanks, but I love her just the way she is."

"Good answer," said Trin hovering nearby.

Ty thought he was getting the knack of this big family business through lots of practice. In less than a year, he held and admired more babies than in his entire life. The baby blitz began in late April when Jessie with what she called her permanent epidural gave birth to the expected girl. Had she been a boy they would have used Teddy's middle name, Wilkes, for the child but feminized that to Willa. With a bald head and big blue eyes, Willa smiled early and often, so much like Teddy they said, especially when her fuzz turned to cornsilk blonde hair.

Annie went into labor the second week in May and had the vaginal delivery she'd hoped for in bearing her six-pound, nine-ounce girl, small, dark-haired and eyed, a true Billodeaux baby named Jennifer Jude, that quickly devolved to Jenny, then JJ because that was what the boys called her.

As if a psychic message had been sent to Annie's twin sister, Jude began having contractions that night. Six weeks from her due date, her long bed confinement ended, thank heaven for that. All the women in the family had spent considerable time visiting and trying to cheer her. The only one really good at breaking through her mopes was Amoli Baht who drove from LSU where she'd retained the apartment and now had an Indian roommate who was not offended by the smell of curry or the statue of Ganesha. She'd brought Jude two baby quilts made from worn cotton saris, soft and bright, and already treasured, as were the babies despite Jude's best attempts not to be enthralled by tiny fingers and toes.

She'd picked the name for the four-pound, two-ounce girl, Molly Ann, showing whom she cherished the most. Connor, who had scrubbed in for the C-section and lifted his son from the womb, had naming rights for the slightly bigger, four-pound, five-ounce boy. Much as they loved the Rev, neither wanted to stick the kid with the name of Revelation Jeremiah, first grandson or not. Connor Riley had already used Arjay to honor the man. With a sigh of capitulation, they decided on Jeremiah which could always be shortened to Jerry or Jer. Both babes went to the NICU until they gained more weight where they were visited, rocked, and fed frequently by their mother and Annie.

He now knew far too much about epidurals, vaginal births, and C-sections than any man should, but the Billodeaux women were all outspoken on the subjects and expected their mates to be in the delivery room to participate. On a ranch visit, he asked Edie with caution what she thought about having children while watching her play peep-eye with Willa, who always laughed.

"Oh, someday, but not soon. I think I'd like the regular epidural for pain control. No way am I going to have a natural birth with a midwife at home like Xochi did this last time."

That relieved his mind. He'd sat in the crowded waiting room for the outcome of Jude's surgery with other family members and endured Connor's detailed description of the delivery, calling his wife a trooper who had opted to watch rather than being put under with anesthetic, just using an epidural. They'd been given a quick glance at the newborn twins behind the glass in the nursery before they were whisked off to the NICU. Both had dark curls and were so very tiny was all he'd observed. Twins, kind of frightening.

But all that had been better than sitting in the living room of Xo's big Victorian house listening to her scream out baby number four, the expected boy named Raphael soon reduced to Rafe. Radiant after her ordeal, Xo said only how grateful she felt that the child hadn't been as huge as KC.

While dreading the Fourth of July celebration at the ranch because of his poor behavior last year, he managed to have some fun, offering his strength to Rex's boat again and promising not to fail him this time. In fact, Rex outdid his father and older brothers for the first time and gave out pats on the back to his crew. "I'll give my all on the football field, too," Ty told Dean, winning back the respect he'd lost.

Lorena and Jock had returned from Australia to celebrate their anniversary, married at the ranch on the Fourth a few years ago. They'd brought along enough Brownlowe Valley sparkling wine for everyone to participate in a toast to the couple which Joe offered from the bandstand, later to be occupied by the Cajun Stompers once the sun began to sink. "To many more years of happiness."

When sharp-eyed Edie noticed Lorena, standing on one side of her dad, had taken only a few sips, she shouted, "You're pregnant, right?"

"Due in January. We took a side trip to Bali." A private joke, but everyone laughed and applauded.

Alix, looking a bit less like an athlete, her tall frame more soft and rounded, added, "Me, too! I didn't want to say anything because…you know, didn't want to hurt your feelings. Due in January, too."

"Right in the middle of playoffs," Tom groaned, but kept his arm protectively around his wife's slightly thickened waist.

"More ponies," Joe whispered, though his whispers were as loud as most people's speaking voices from dealing with the roar of stadium crowds. Besides, he'd forgotten to turn off the mic.

"No more ponies. Six is enough," Mama Nell countered immediately.

"But we have two more grandchildren on the way next year. Granted, Shasha is already riding Rascal just fine, but we don't want to leave a child without a starter pony. Two more ought do it. Maybe three."

"We'll see."

"He'll win," Edie confided to Ty from where they stood at the base of the stage.

Someone in the crowd banged a spoon against a champagne flute. Brinsley the butler, still passing out glasses, winced at the crassness.

"Another announcement." Prince Dobbs, his dreadlocks down to his waist, the Jesus tattoos showing on his brown skin exposed by a wife beater T-shirt, mounted the stage and wrested the mic from Joe. "Come on up, babe. Show 'em what we got started," he beckoned.

Ty, seeing how the scene might unfold, got to the steps which lacked a handrail, and offered his arm to a very pregnant, tall blonde woman who seemed drained by the heat and her condition. He didn't know her name or her story but the danger of a fall seemed imminent. Once he delivered her, he stepped back. The obnoxious man cupped the woman's big belly. Ty, being around so many expectant women this year, feared she might go into labor right here and now.

"Y'all know me, Prince Dobbs, once the Sinners' best wide receiver, but now a humble preacher of the word of the Lord. This is my lady, Ilsa. Now I made a promise some years ago that when she gave me a son, we'd get married. The Good Lord sent me a message saying I'd have a son of my own when I gave up being a

Sinner and applied myself to spreading the Good Word. No offense, Beck, you're a great kid, but not my very own flesh and blood. When I turned my job over to Mack Billodeaux, the Lord kept his word, as he always does. Here he is, King David Dobbs, soon to be born. Once Ilsa gets her figure back, we are gonna have a blowout wedding at my Church of the Dreadlocked Jesus, and a fantastico reception in its mega-sized meeting hall. All y'all are invited. Back to you, Joe." At least, he helped "his lady" back down the steps to firmer ground.

Ty followed. He'd never known Joe to be anything but laid back, but now noticed a clenched jaw and narrow eyes displayed on his face. "Your dad seems pissed."

"On Beck's behalf, I'd guess, and maybe over Ilsa's four daughters who didn't get a mention. He hates to see children hurt. This family has a long history with Prince Dobbs. Once he attacked Stacy, but Dean prevented anything from happening. I'm not supposed to know about that, but the tabloids got a whiff of it, so I found out later. The internet is a wonderful and terrible thing for research. Nothing ever goes away. Still the Sinners kept him on because he was great. Frankly, his career was waning when he 'gave' Mack his spot. He'd been asked to take a cut in salary. More good may come of this, if Ilsa finally lets Dean have full custody of Beck. Going into his teens, he needs a better role model than Prince Dobbs."

He digested her comment about the internet. Would he always be known as a pot head who'd ruined his career? "Were they here last year—or was I too stoned to notice?"

"You didn't notice much except all the girls hanging on you, but no, they weren't here. They don't come unless they can make a big splash of some kind or other. Let's get another glass of that chilled champagne to wash the taste from our mouths."

"Sounds good. Edie, will I always be known as a druggie?"

"No, Ty, because I am going to write a whole new story for you."

If Edie said it, then it could be done. He worked hard the rest of the summer, won his place on the team, and now had to prove himself at the first game of the year.

Chapter Forty-One

He had to live in the moment. Forget about nature balancing the birth of Josee's baby with the passing of Charlotte LeMaire the next day or of Edie's face when she told him that *Lifestyles* had assigned the obituary tribute to her. "She was a long-suffering woman. Give her due," he'd said.

With a vibrant picture of Charlotte dressed in a red suit, long blonde hair in a chignon, pre-cancer, heading the article, Edie told of her devotion to her husband's political career and her family. Beyond that, she showcased the many good causes that Charlotte had raised funds for or served on their boards, always without pay. Edie interviewed her two daughters who had each given their mother a grandchild, both girls, before her death which she had faced bravely. They supplied warm anecdotes about always getting a phone call and a special delivery cake on their birthdays when they were at boarding school, a custom that continued into their college years. Because of their father's political business, they'd had few family vacations, but sometimes, their mother whisked them away for a girls' only trip that might end up in Hawaii or New York City.

That Emily and Madison had no idea of their father's other family or Edie's connection to his illegitimate son by a black woman was obvious. Charlotte had taken that secret to her grave as promised.

Yet, the family must have been pleased by her piece since the senator sent flowers to the magazine's office with a thank you note.

He wasn't here today to see his son's first pro game, still seeing to the details of the funeral and inheritance, but this event marked the beginning of his supposed time in mourning before he could reconnect with Portia. Since the man had been staying away, Ty no longer feared being ambushed at his mother's home. Things had gone better there. He'd confided a few pieces of his life to her, especially his love for Edie that made him better understand her long-term relationship with Titus. He'd joked about asking Edie if she wanted children and her answer.

"Edie has good sense, but it is wise to discuss this before marriage," his mama said.

The words escaped his lips before he could stop them. "Yeah, like you did."

As hurt washed over her lovely face, growing older now, at least a decade younger than Charlotte LeMaire but vulnerable to disease and scandal just the same, he took them back. "I'm sorry I said that, Mama. You could have chosen not to have me, and I wouldn't be here today."

"You were worth the sacrifice. Your granny so wanted me to finish college, but I'd agreed to live quietly in order to have time with your father, to have us be taken care of by him. That time is past. I hope you can accept that we will be together in the future.

"I'll try—because I do understand more about love now, how you might want to be with someone forever."

"You'll make a better father than he did. He wasn't very involved with his daughters either, but wants another chance with Livy and his grandchildren. Maybe, he's learned a lot, too."

She, Granny, and Livy now sat up there in the Billodeaux's sky box along with a multitude of babies, older children, and their mothers. Edie sat with Joe in his fifty-yard-line seats along with Lorena and Alix, both showing off their slight baby bumps, and Sarge because Shasha wanted to play with Lizzy up in the box. Since most of the male members of the family were out stretching with him on the field, only Trinity represented the guys. Soon, Teddy's mellow voice would fill the air announcing the game, providing the color.

He'd sat with Trinity while Josee labored and her mom had taken over for a while. They'd gotten coffee and a burger in the cafeteria away from the women filling the waiting room. He'd confided that he wanted to give Edie a ring if he could prove himself in this first game. Trin wrote down a name on a napkin—Leslie at Schifferman's. "He'll get what you want, but be prepared to pay big bucks. Of course, you can always ask for the Sinners discount."

He knew the place where the rich shopped for jewelry on Canal Street and approached the fabled Leslie, a smallish man with an elegantly trimmed silver mustache and beautifully barbered hair, in his native habitat at the end of rows and rows of cases filled with colored gems and place settings chosen by society debs. He stood behind an imposing counter and waited for Ty to come to him, no effusive greeting or hint of eagerness. "How my I help you?"

"I need an engagement ring, something with a lot of sparkle like her but not too big because she has small hands."

Lynn Shurr

"I see." Leslie studied him as if assessing his net worth.

"Ah, Trinity Billodeaux told me to ask for the Sinners discount.

"If you are a Sinner, you don't need a discount, just a very good credit card. Let me see what I have in the back." A wry little smile followed.

He wasn't gone all that long, yet sweat began to run down Ty's back. Could he afford this? Was the time right?

Leslie returned with three rings displayed on a black velvet cloth. "Which catches your eye?"

"This one." He had no doubt he'd chosen the perfect ring.

Leslie gave him the rundown. "Here we have a 2.8 carat cushion cut diamond with a split band and a diamond halo all set in platinum."

"Um, how much?"

"Thirty-thousand, one-hundred and eighty dollars."

"No discount, huh?"

"I do believe Mr. Trinity was jesting, but perhaps I could deduct the one-hundred-eighty dollars from my commission. You *are* the new safety for the team. Am I correct?"

"Yes, the one who messed up with drugs but is entirely clean now." He might just spill it out as he removed his shiny new platinum credit card and laid it on the counter.

"Then, the best of luck to you and Miss Edie."

"You know all about us?"

"The Billodeauxs have brought me much business over the years, but in this case, Mr. Trinity called ahead and described his sister."

"I guess that saved a lot of time."

"Indeed. I'll put this in a box."

Now, the ring resided not in a velvet box but on a chain around his neck like a good luck charm. If he played well today, he'd give it to her after the game. If not, he'd wait. The ring helped him center himself, erase the past, dwell in the present. What three things did he scent?—Gatorade, hot dogs, beer. What three things did he see?—bright stadium lights, his teammates, the tips of his cleats. What three things did he hear?—the roar of the crowd, Teddy's voice announcing the coin toss results, Edie shouting words of encouragement. What three things did he feel?—the bench beneath his butt, the sweat running down his back, the ring pressed against his chest. He folded his hands and closed his eyes for a moment.

"Hey, you praying?" Hud said.

"No, just preparing for the game." The interruption hadn't bothered him at all. He was ready.

Dean chose to receive which meant he'd have to wait for the defense to get out on the field, but not as long as he thought. Dean got a man into the end zone in four plays with three passes and one handoff to Matt Keaton who bulled it across the goal line. After the PAT kicked easily by Tom, he got into position to shoot down the field to wherever the ball carrier appeared.

The opposing quarterback threw a pass that should have been longer to reach its goal. He gauged exactly where it would come down, put on some speed, and snatched the ball out of the air with a short leap. He hit the ground running back toward the Sinners' goal. Behind him, Junior, who had been nearby took a pursuer to the ground. Ty stiff-armed another, found a hole and ran through it. Hud at his side created a gap for him. He jigged and jagged and just kept running, now along the sideline, keeping his feet inside of it. The goal line came up fast, and he crossed it. The crowd chanted a name he hadn't been called in a long time, "Golden Ram, Golden Ram."

Better than that, his teammates boffed him on the helmet, slapped his back, and he swore he got a brief hug from Hud. Dean came over to deliver a handshake. "You're all Dad said and more. Why don't you take that ball over to Edie?"

He did. Tears in her eyes, she hugged it to her breasts. Today was the right day, but not the right time yet. He made his way back to the bench, downed some Gatorade, and waited for his next chance. Aware of him now, the other team set two guards on him to make sure he couldn't do that again. Still, he managed to outrun them more than once and caused a fumble that Junior picked up and another with Hud. He did his fair share of blocking as well. Final score 35-14, Sinners. They'd had the home field advantage here in the Dome with its always noisy, supportive, and crazy-dressed crowd, and their opponent had a low ranking, but this was one high he'd never forget.

While the sports reporters mobbed Dean for comments, he slipped through the crowd and found Edie and her family cheering, still in the box. He stretched up, took her hand, and dropped the ring, chain and all, into it. "Will you marry me, Edie Billodeaux?"

He didn't mean to make her cry again, but since she bounced up and down and screamed, "Yes, yes, yes!" he figured all was well. She leaned down to kiss him, the chain threaded in her fingers, the diamonds flashing in the stadium lights. Attracted by the commotion, cameras began recording their moment. Their image appeared on the large screens of the Dome as Edie cupped his face and mingled her tears with his sweat.

A reporter broke from the pack around Dean and Coach Buck. Leading with his mic, he shouted, "I see congratulations are in order, Tyson Ramsey, and for more than your brilliant play today."

"Yes, thank you. It was the right place, the right time, the right woman."

"And you, Miss Edie? When will you tie the knot?"

"At the right time, in the right place. I've already got the right man."

Chapter Forty-Two

The right time was Louisiana at its best in mid-March after football season and in full flower from huge purple azaleas to pink banana blossoms. The right place was New Orleans where a good part of both families lived. The debate began over which church with Flo, Portia, and Mawmaw Nadine pushing hard for a Catholic service. Edie would have held out for civil ceremony in a small venue until Ty spoke up.

He favored St. Augustine Church, where he'd worshipped at a child, built on land once the Tremé Plantation and the oldest Black Catholic parish in the United States. Dedicated in 1842 and without pews, free people of color began buying seats for their families and slaves. Whites did the same, creating an unexpected integrated congregation. The original pews remained, along with a pink Italian marble altar, and many original stained-glass windows of male and female saints. The building stood huge and white behind a welcoming arch with a bell tower off to one side. A tilted cross made of frozen chains and dangling manacles marked the Tomb of the Unknown Slave. One entered through a pair of red doors.

By the time Ty left off giving her a history lecture much as he'd done when they first met, she could see herself walking through those doors as a bride even though she grumbled about having to take instruction in

Catholicism and counseling about marriage. They'd use the parish hall for a catered reception with a live jazz band. Both church and hall were big enough to hold a swarm of Billodeauxs, the Sinners team, and dear friends. Unlike Price Dobbs' ceremony, not everyone was invited.

He had offered his own reception hall, so lavishly decorated it might have belonged to a hotel, at a price. His German mother-in-law had described it with a few words, "*Mein Gott, so Baroque*." It could be rented for nearly any occasion barring bachelor and bachelorette parties, all fees going to support his Church of the Dreadlocked Jesus. Ilsa had walked down the long aisle of the sanctuary under a ceiling painting of Jesus holding out a hand to a man who looked remarkably like Prince, in a tight mermaid gown, her neck bearing so many diamonds that it looked like a small chandelier had fallen on her. Her four daughters, all in white, preceded her with the eldest, Princess, pushing King David Dobbs in a decorated pram. Prince did have enough feeling for the boy to name Beck as his best man, thus assuring all the Billodeauxs would attend.

When asked what Edie wanted for her wedding, she replied, "Not this!" What did please her was writing a feature article on St. Augustine Church for Black History Month and being given permission to cover her own wedding where she got to plug Portia as the designer of her gown and extol their own unique plans.

The florist asked her for her theme to which she replied, "Ah, I don't know, maybe Spring." The woman took off with that designing bouquets of hand-tied white tulips and bedecking the sanctuary and hall with pots of seasonal flowers: daffodils, hyacinths, tulips of many colors, and small, bright azaleas. Good because the guests could take them home and plant them in their yards, a point Edie made in her wedding article.

In lieu of the surf and turf, five-foot high champagne and chocolate fountains favored by Prince, she wanted hand-carved beef, ham, turkey with a variety of breads, condiments, and toppings and plenty of side dishes like a festive occasion at the ranch. As for a cake, it was non-traditionally chocolate, and decorated with dipped Louisiana strawberries because that's what they both liked. The topper consisted of a small spring bouquet. All leftovers were to go to a soup kitchen for the poor. But not the alcohol, wines again supplied by Jock along with local beers. Mariah Coy, honorary godmother to all the Billodeaux kids, did send champagne. She'd gotten over her snit about not being invited to Jude's hasty wedding, and came in all her glory of huge white wig, gold lame dress, and heels far too high for her age.

The matter of her attendants had presented a unique problem. Nearly all of her sisters and sisters-in-law were nursing and had small babies. In early January on a Monday, Lorena gave birth to an eight-pound, six-ounce baby boy named Michael Nicholas for his Australian uncles. Jock proclaimed him a right good little ripper who would be known as Mike, not Mick. On the fourth week of the same month, a Sunday, Alix labored to bring a little girl into the world. Tom muffed a crucial field goal that most likely caused the Sinners to lose the Divisional Title and another chance at a Super Bowl. None of this took the shine off of Tyson Ramsey being named All-Pro in his rookie year.

Tom took the blame and hurried off to the hospital in time to see the birth of Mia, a strawberry blonde with

Billodeaux brown eyes, seven-pounds, five ounces. In the end, they rented the church nursery as well as the hall. She chose Stacy, Sarge, and Amoli as the only ones who would not have to race to the nursery for one reason or another.

Ty had no trouble picking his three from the Sinners he'd grown closest to: Dean as best man, and Junior and strangely, Hud. His father, the senator, an honored guest, sat discretely in the audience staring at the back of Portia's head in the first pew with Flo. They'd begun their fictionalized meeting at a Christmas party where "friends" introduced them and started dating with the coming of the New Year. They'd decided on a quiet wedding in October. Titus announced he would not run for the Senate again in order to spend time with his family. By the end of his term, he hoped to adopt Livy. She was thrilled by the idea of having Uncle T as her dad. Ty was at peace with all of that, but he wouldn't be changing his name to LeMaire. He'd be his own man, forever Tyson Ramsey, passing that name to his children, he told Edie.

As Stacy walked down the aisle on the day of the wedding, tall and regal in the blue and silver gown designed by Portia, followed by Sarge who got another use out of her silver-fringed flapper gown she thought she'd never wear more than once, and lastly, Amoli in a gold and silver sari, Edie felt equal to them all. Portia had dressed her in a white, ankle-length gown with a full tulle skirt and ragged hem showing off her small feet in silver slippers. A tight satin bodice with puffed sleeves accented her youth, nothing sexy about it, more a princess than she'd ever been. Rhinestones sparkled in the netting of her skirt and the short veil nestled in her curls with a clip of stars to match the earrings and necklace Ty had given her.

Everyone would see a young woman beginning married life with a man she loved. But inside, she knew she was that girl on the motorcycle, pressed tight against her Sinner's body, ready to take on the world.

A word about the author...

Once a librarian, now a writer of romance, Lynn Shurr grew up in Pennsylvania Dutch country. She attended a state college and earned a very impractical B.A. in English Literature. Her first job out of school really was working as a cashier in a burger joint. Moving from one humble job to another, she traveled to North Carolina, then Germany, then California where she buckled down and studied for an M.A. in Librarianship. New degree in hand, she found her first reference job in the Heart of Cajun Country, Lafayette, Louisiana. For her, the old saying, "Once you've tasted bayou water, you will always stay here" came true. She raised three children not far from the Bayou Teche and lives there still with her astronomer husband. When not writing, Lynn likes to paint, cheer for the New Orleans Saints and LSU Tigers, and take long road trips nearly anywhere. Her love of the bayou country, its history and customs, often shows in the background for her books. You may contact Lynn at www.lynnshurr.com or visit her blog— lynnshurr.blogspot.com.